Dear Readers,   P9-CQI-704

I hope everyone is having a wonderful summer! This past year has been very good to me, and it's been in large part due to your enthusiasm for my work. I've written books that I love and now get to share them with you. Thank you for coming along on this journey with me. Thank you for recommending me to fellow readers. Thank you for the wonderful e-mails.

Sometimes authors take poetic license with our fiction and *Kiss Me Deadly* is one of those times. I hope you'll agree that creating a Powerball lottery with rules and regulations (which the state of Florida doesn't have) makes the story better. However, I tried to remain true to the other references to the Sunshine State, including the fact that Davis Islands is only one island—and sorry, I don't know why the correct spelling includes an "s."

My writing schedule for the upcoming year is a busy one. Next up after *Kiss Me Deadly* is another futuristic romance titled *Solar Heat*. You can read a sneak peek in the back of this book. Then, sometime in spring or summer of 2008, Tor will release another romantic suspense. If you'd like to keep up with me and my work you can find me at www.susankearny.com.

Best,
Susan Kearney

TOR ROMANCE BOOKS BY SUSAN KEARNEY

Kiss Me Deadly

SUSAN KEARNEY

tor romance

A TOM DOHERTY ASSOCIATES BOOK
NEW YORK

KISS ME DEADLY

Copyright © 2007 by Hair Express, Inc.

A Tor Book
Published by Tom Doherty Associates, LLC
175 Fifth Avenue
New York, NY 10010

www.tor.com

Tor® is a registered trademark of Tom Doherty Associates, LLC.

ISBN-13: 978-0-7653-5667-3
ISBN-10: 0-7653-5667-8

First Edition: July 2007

Printed in the United States of America

0 9 8 7 6 5 4 3 2 1

This is for the book wholesalers who work behind the scenes to bring books into the stores. A big thank you to Kent Haverman, Brad Wagoner, and Dave Van Overbeke at Anderson News, LLC, who went out of their way to make me feel welcome. And to all my new friends at Levy Home Entertainment, LLC: Pamela Nelson, Emily Hixon, Laura Pennock, Justine Willis, Abby Karlovitz, Jennifer Markowski, and Kathleen Koelbl—touring on the LOVE Bus was a fantastic experience.

Acknowledgments

First and foremost I'd like to thank my awesome editor, Anna Genoese, for allowing me to write a romantic suspense for Tor. Her encouragement and support mean everything to me. Leslie Henkle did a great job on publicity, as did the entire sales and marketing team at Tor. And to Seth Lerner for his fabulous cover, thank you, thank you, thank you.

I also want to thank my critique partners, Charlotte Douglas, Suzanne Forester, Julie Leto, and Jeanie London—without them, this book wouldn't have come together as well as it did.

There are so many other people who contributed: Clifton Curry and Chet Tharpe, who patiently answered my questions about the law and Alesia Holliday, who checked my research. Thank you all—any errors are strictly my own.

In addition, I want to thank Patricia Smith for her support, as well as Stella Cameron and Karen Rose for taking the time to read and give an advance quote. To Shannon Avilles for the publicity advice.

And to my readers—thanks for following me to a new genre.

Chapter One

MANDY NEWMAN GLANCED in her rearview mirror at the pickup truck that had swung around the corner to hug her rear bumper. What was up with him? This same pickup truck had been following her since she'd left her parking garage. Now he was close. Too close.

There was no telling if the tailgater was a drunk or simply a lousy driver, but a rear-end collision wasn't on her to-do list today. Neither was coping with the rain that made the oil-slick street treacherous. But considering that the Sunshine State's daily afternoon showers were a fact of life during the summer rainy season, the other driver ought to know better than to follow so close.

Another glance revealed the pickup was still sticking to her rear bumper like a sandspur, the driver revving his motor as if bent on making her sweat. Why wasn't he hitting his brake, backing off, giving her maneuvering room? Perspiration trickled down her neck and Mandy flicked up the AC. Fog cleared from her windows. But he was still there.

Damn him for crowding her. For worrying her.

Come on. Keep it together. Surely he was harmless? Not a sicko spoiling for a fender bender.

Keeping a wary eye on her mirror, Mandy tried to shake off the tension in her neck and shoulders. All she had to do was ignore the jerk. Not let her nerves and fatigue from another long day of court set her on edge. Reminding herself that giving in to paranoia was all too easy, especially after these past months of working a mind-numbing number of back-to-back divorce cases, she took several deep breaths. After all, just because her clients often feared their abusive, greedy, and hostile spouses, she didn't need to let her imagination run amok.

The truck's driver, a white man with dirty blond hair sticking out from a baseball cap pulled low on his forehead, probably had nothing to do with her or her work. He could simply have poor eyesight . . . or have forgotten his glasses. *Yeah, right.* More likely he was a whacked-out junkie or a pervert who got off on scaring women.

Mandy stopped at a red light on South Franklin Street and he just barely tapped her rear fender. Son of a bitch. Even as she told herself the bump had to be an accident, Mandy checked her door locks, uncaring if she was overreacting.

Sweat beaded on her scalp, and the air conditioning had nothing to do with the shiver of apprehension that had her heart beating triple-time. She needed to get away from him, but changing lanes in the Tampa rush hour traffic that now resembled a parking lot wouldn't be easy. Not with rumbling delivery trucks and commuters hemming her in. Besides, she only had to drive another five blocks to safety, to her island community, where security guards would stop the moron from following her through the gate. Deciding her best option was to keep going, Mandy inched forward, a wary eye on the rearview mirror. Another four blocks and she'd be safe. Five minutes and she'd be home free.

After she turned at Channelside Drive onto the Harbour Island Bridge, the traffic gushed as if from an unclogged drain, and she relaxed, tension streaming away from her. The rain seemed to be letting up, the sky lightening and the two-laned bridge pavement shimmered with broken rainbows in the early evening heat. Below Mandy, the Hillsborough River flowed out to Tampa Bay between Harbour and Davis Islands, where a cornucopia of condos, custom homes, and high-end apartments knotted together along the waterfront and sprawled over every spare inch of dirt. As she traversed the bridge, she picked up speed. So did the silver pickup.

One moment she was driving in total control—the next, her car bucked. Good God, the pickup had bumped her. Again.

Bastard. Why was he gunning for her? Who the hell was he? A drunk? Someone trying to rob her? An angry ex-husband of a client? She should have called the cops when she'd noticed him following her. She should have listened to her gut. She should have—

Her car spun sideways. Out of control. Toward the guardrail.

Mandy slammed on the brakes. *Bad move.* Her tires squealed and skidded on the slick pavement. Clenching the wheel, she fought the spin. But her car careened sideways, smashed into the guardrail. Concrete crumbled. Horns blared.

Her airbag exploded in her face.

She slapped it down, choking on the powder in the air, and opened her eyes. And gasped.

Pitched downward, her car dangled about twenty feet over the water below. Through her front windshield she had a bird's-eye view of rippling river, of rain drops plunking into the water and muttering a warning. She could be next.

Oh . . . my . . . God. She screamed. Started to claw at her seat belt to escape the car before she plummeted.

Somewhere above and behind her, an engine roared. Craning her neck, she glanced over her shoulder, praying that help was coming.

Wrong again.

The silver pickup rammed her car a second time. Fear slicked across her skin. He didn't want to rob her. He didn't want to kidnap her. He wanted to kill her.

So she had to stop him. But how? It wasn't like she had a weapon in her front seat and could pull out a gun and shoot him. Or had a rope handy. So what could she do?

Behind her, the guardrail cracked and metal pieces rained into the river. Her car slid, teetered. The truck crashed into her again, shoving her vehicle all the way over the lip.

No. Please . . . no.

She had no time to release her seat belt. No time to escape. No time to pray.

Her car plunged toward the water, flipping, somersaulting through the air. Mandy fought blackness. Nausea. Dizziness. The terror of not knowing up from down.

Bracing her hands on the wheel, holding her breath, closing her eyes, she froze. But even as Mandy's ears roared and the water rushed up to smack her, she gulped air. She was *so* not ready to die. She had to survive. For Gabrielle. It was bad enough that her precious baby girl didn't have a father. She couldn't lose her mother.

Whatever it took to make it back home to her daughter, she would do. If that meant turning herself into Lara Croft, so be it. If it meant coming up with a plan, she'd be brilliant. If it meant gritting her teeth to avoid biting her tongue, she wouldn't so much as utter one yelp.

But inside, she howled. *She was not going to die. She was not going to die. She was not—*

Her car punched through the water, slamming the air from her lungs and bruising her, wrenching her. But even in pain, surely she still could swim.

If only the car would float long enough for her to leap into the water. But it didn't float. She sank with a giant sucking noise, as if the river were taking her to hell.

Cold water cascaded over her, hissing like a deadly sea creature. Blinded in the dark, panic rose up to choke her and she pounded her palms on the window.

Wait a minute. What was she doing? Dizzy, confused, she finally figured out her car was upside down and sinking toward the river bottom. And she didn't have the strength to break the glass with her bare hands.

Still, she had options: *Get out or drown.*

Fighting her seat belt, she fumbled and finally released the buckle, placed her hands above her head to break her fall. She toppled sideways and ended up sitting on the ceiling in a deepening pool of water.

Unable to see, dazed, Mandy groped for the door. She touched smooth leather. *Idiot.* The handle was upside down from this angle.

Everything's backwards.

Her fingers finally closed on the handle and with desperate strength, she yanked, then shoved the door with her shoulder. But it wouldn't budge. Too much water pressure from outside.

Damn it to hell. She had to get out.

Trapped like a crab in a trap, she clawed the door, hammered the window with her fists. But she was going nowhere.

Water poured in. Her air bubbled out. The car kept plunging. Inexorably, with a moan of tortured metal, it settled on the bottom, the roof denting beneath her. Water hissed past her feet, her waist, her neck.

She would not shut down. Or break. She would not quit. Gabby needed her. Besides, she hadn't scheduled dying into her day planner. And no way in hell was she letting that SOB get away with murder.

Think.

Could she escape after the pressure equalized? After the car's interior totally filled with water? At the idea, terror crawled into her veins and cramped her muscles.

But if her only chance at life was to wait for the water to rise over her head, she would take it. Immediately she felt better for devising a strategy.

Yeah, right. As if the best planning in the world would stop her from becoming fish food.

Water rose past her chin, and she lunged upward and banged her head. *Easy.* Ignoring the pain, she tilted her head back, clamped her mouth shut and breathed through her nostrils. She didn't care if every cell in her body urged her to flee, if she wanted to open the door, she had to remain still, and wait for the water to close over her head.

For Gabby, thankfully safe in her grandmother's care, Mandy would keep it together. For Gabby, she allowed the water to swallow her alive. For Gabby, she waited for the water to rise, with her nose pressed against the floorboards, gasping in the very last pocket of air.

Water closed over her mouth, nose, and eyes, filled the entire car, draping her in wet blackness.

Now. Make your move now.

Mandy dived down to the handle. Shoved. The door wouldn't move.

Oxygen dwindling, mind whirring like a propeller, Mandy refused to cry. Every good lawyer had a plan B. And she was a damn good attorney.

Come on. What did she need?

Leverage?

Yes.

Grabbing the wheel with one hand, the handle with the other, she planted her feet against the door. Licks of pain shooting through her, straining every muscle, she thrust with her back and calves and thighs.

The door gave with a pop.

About damn time.

Rushing out, she banged her shoulder on the doorjamb. Lungs already on fire, head pounding as if she'd drunk too many margaritas, she kicked hard for the surface.

I'm coming, Gabby. Mommy's coming.

Mandy's chest ached, but she fought against the urge to open her mouth for air.

Keep kicking.

Overhead, rays of light beckoned with tempting promise. So close. But, so far . . .

Chapter Two

A HALF-HOUR LATER, Mandy had gone from swimming with the fish to being a Florida tourist attraction. Jackson's Bistro perched over the harbor like a tiered wedding cake, and the diners had abandoned their duck breast, pistachio-encrusted red snapper, oak-grilled steaks, and sushi to stare at her from expansive outdoor decks on every level.

She didn't like being the focus of hundreds of eyes and tried to ignore her soaked clothes, running mascara, and lack of shoes. Sitting on the bench wrapped in a tablecloth, still shaking, she reminded herself she was lucky to be alive.

Traffic cops had closed off one lane of South Franklin Street and the Coast Guard patrolled the river, directing passing boats away from the area where bridge debris still fell in intermittent whooshes. No police officer had arrived to interview her.

A paramedic had offered a blanket to replace the soggy tablecloth a bystander had given her, then bandaged the cut on her head. She'd waited so long to give her statement, that some of the singles crowd had actually returned to their dinners. Shivering, trying to throw off the vestiges of shock, she sipped hot coffee and waited for a uniformed officer to question her.

Mandy didn't deal well with unexpected delays. She liked her meetings punctual, her files in order, information at her fingertips. She didn't like anyone messing with her routine—never mind waiting on bureaucracy. So despite the fact that she was shivering more from shock than a wet chill, she made a to-do list. Notify insurance company. Download her schedule from the computer onto a new day planner. Order a new cell phone, credit card, driver's license, purse, briefcase. Damn. Her life was in her purse. She sighed. At least she had all the information she needed to replace the missing documents on a flash drive and could call it up on her computer. Where the hell was the cop? She was ready to have them pursue and capture the bad guy so she could put this behind her.

Weary, she fought for patience. She yearned to go home, take a hot bath, and hold her daughter. But after a cop had checked with her to make certain no one else had been in her vehicle, he'd instructed her to remain on one of Jackson's dockside benches. Now, he seemed in no hurry to return.

Mandy tried to calm her trembling and wondered about the man who'd tried to kill her. Why her? Did she know him through her work? Could he be married to one of her clients? When he found out his efforts had failed, would he return?

Don't go there. The police would identify his vehicle and lock him up. Right now—she had to believe that.

Finally an officer shouldered his way through the gawking diners and approached. "Show's over, people. Go back to your two-for-one shooters." Dark-haired, dark-eyed, and thirty pounds overweight, he offered her an irritated look. "Ma'am. I'm Officer Delgado."

Automatically, she reached for her purse to find a business card, but her purse, checkbook, and briefcase with the once-a-week office pool's Powerball ticket in it, swam with the fish at the bottom of the Hillsborough River, along with her cell phone. She was damned lucky not to still be there, too.

"Amanda Newman." To her own ears, her voice sounded raw, as if she'd worn out her vocal cords screaming.

"I know who you are, ma'am." Officer Delgado's tone soured, drawing her attention to his expression. Intelligent eyes underscored with dark circles, a boy-next-door round face, and a professional demeanor didn't quite manage to hide his hostility. "You're the reason I work two jobs. You're the reason I only see my kids every other weekend."

Delgado. The name clicked. She hadn't recognized her client's ex-husband in his uniform. Besides, it had been a year since his divorce was final. Mandy had represented his wife, and they'd both been pleased by obtaining a fair resolution that allowed her to avoid working until the youngest child reached kindergarten. As divorces went, theirs hadn't been particularly ugly. Yet from the hurt in his tone, Officer Delgado clearly resented Mandy's part in the settlement.

"It wasn't personal, officer." Mandy cupped the mug and sipped, the caffeine replacing the adrenaline that had kept her going until now. "I represent clients to the best of my ability."

"You certainly do." His tone carried disdain. Not enough for her to complain to his superiors, but enough to let her know he wasn't sympathetic that she'd almost died.

He glanced up at the bridge and frowned. "I'll be filling out paperwork for hours."

Muscles she didn't know she had ached. Her hair dripped down her cheeks and she tugged the blanket tighter around her, even as her tone grew fiercer with every word. "Officer Delgado, do you think I ran my car off the bridge to spoil your day? Because if so, I assure you—"

"You lost control of your car in the rain and skidded off the bridge. You're alive. Ma'am, there's no need for hysterics."

Hysterics? She stood, the shock from the accident wearing off as coal-hot anger inflamed her. He had no right to patronize her just because his marriage had failed and she'd represented his wife and had looked out for his children. Some cops genuinely wanted to help people, but this one was on a power trip. "You want to see hysterics? I'll

call Judge Herschell. She's tight with the mayor and we'll
see how she likes one of her police officers browbeating a
citizen—"

"Sorry, Ms. Newman." Delgado combed his fingers
through his thinning hair. "It's been a rough day."

"You've had a rough day?" She rolled her eyes. Her evening was shot to hell, the work she'd taken home with her
was now grouper reading material. "Some whacko just tried
to kill me."

"Kill you?" Delgado's glance sharpened. "This wasn't an
accident?"

"Du-uh." She gestured to the Harbour Island Bridge and
the crowd kept back from the edges with yellow police tape.
"Someone must have witnessed a guy in a silver truck running me off the bridge."

He raised an eyebrow. "You're claiming attempted murder. That's a serious charge. Right now it looks more like an
accident."

So now he was psychic and knew what had happened?
She doubted he had the brains to read skid marks. She spoke
through gritted teeth. "I . . . did . . . not . . . drive off the
bridge. This was no *accident*. A truck rammed me *three*
times."

"You're certain?"

She gestured to the diners at the restaurant and joggers
and dog walkers alongside the bridge. "Someone had to
have seen something."

Like a hostile defendant on the stand, as if every word
cost him, Delgado spoke into his shoulder radio. "Anybody
talk to any witnesses?"

A voice crackled back. "A cab driver reported a late
model silver pickup with a dent—"

"That's him."

"—fled the scene."

He'd gotten away? And now she might never know who
he was or why he'd rammed her through the guardrail.
Maybe he was some psycho like that kid who'd shot a
woman through her front windshield as she drove under the

interstate overpass. Or maybe he'd mistaken her for someone else.

Or maybe he disliked her like Delgado did, because she'd
represented his wife in court. But she was still here. Battered, cold, and bruised, but she was going home to Gabrielle
tonight. As hard as Mandy tried to hold on to that pleasant
thought, the idea that her attacker had fled—and might try
again—made her stomach knot. Thankfully, nowhere in
Tampa was safer than on Harbour Island, where security at the
guard shack checked visitor IDs and didn't allow strangers
onto the island.

"Another witness got the license plate number," an officer
on the bridge joined the radio conversation.

After hearing her charge verified, Delgado regarded her
with a tad more respect. Her spirits lifted, latching onto the
hope that the law might actually catch her attacker—what a
concept. But then the same officer added, "But the truck was
reported stolen last week."

Damn. The up side was that at least she now had Delgado's attention. "The truck followed me from my parking
garage. Don't those buildings have security cameras?"

"If he followed you, why didn't you report him?"

She refrained from rolling her eyes. "I didn't know he was
dangerous until he rammed my car off the bridge." Out of
every cop in the city, why did she have to have represented
this one's wife in divorce court?

"But he followed you from the parking garage."

She fisted one hand on her hip and wished she hadn't lost
her heels in the swim. She would have enjoyed towering
over Delgado but would have to settle for looking him
straight in the eye. "Officer, as far as I know, there's no law
against following another car. Besides, it was only for a few
blocks.

He could have lived on the island and it could have been
coincidence he was going my way. I don't appreciate you in-
sinuating—"

Delgado held up his hand. "Ma'am. Clearly, more happened here than I previously believed. I shouldn't have given

you any attitude. Your profession won't stop me from doing my job. Let's start over."

She swallowed her ire. Lawyers were pretty much hated by the general population—until they needed one, of course. No one ever seemed to think lawyers wanted justice, that they fought for mothers and children.

"Thank you." She didn't know whether he was feeding her a line to prevent her reporting him to his superiors, but he sounded sincere enough for her to force a deep breath and calm down.

Delgado flipped to the next page of his notepad. In addition to noting the parking garage's location, he wrote down her name, home and work addresses, and phone numbers.

"Can you describe the man you saw driving the truck?"

Mandy closed her eyes and tried to recall details. Memories of hissing black water and the claustrophobic feeling of the river closing over her head caused new tremors to rip through her. With determination, she shut down the images and focused on the guy responsible. "White. Long, stringy blond hair, medium build. He wore a baseball cap. Sorry, that's not much help. I didn't get a good look."

"But you're certain he wasn't anyone you know?"

She sighed, wondering how anyone past the age of ten could think in absolutes. "I'm *not* certain of anything. You're aware I practice family law and I meet numerous people through my work. Many hate my guts," she admitted, cutting off another apology from the officer with a shrug. "It comes with the job. For all I know, you could have hired the guy to kill me."

Delgado laughed.

Up on the bridge, Mandy winced at the sight of more flashing blue and red lights as additional police officers headed their way, along with Department of Transportation workers and a tow truck, yellow light whirring, that blocked one side of the road. Car horns blared as residents turned back into the city, forced to use a different route. Meanwhile, not only had the cops shut down the bridge, the Coast Guard was redirecting river traffic. She wondered if the fine print in her insurance policy covered the likely expense of fishing out her vehicle.

Delgado's tone warmed a few degrees. "What about your personal life? Any ex-boyfriends after you? Lovers' spats? Angry husband?"

"None of the above." Between Gabrielle and work, her every hour was full and she could prove it with her day planner—if it hadn't been stashed in her briefcase at the river's mucky bottom. But anyone who knew her, friends and coworkers, could verify that she didn't have time for a social life.

"Can you think of any specific cases where opposing counsel's clients might want you in a watery grave?" Delgado asked.

Often her job turned ugly. When love turned to hate, blame and acrimony flared and any bystander could be caught in the resulting conflagration. It had happened to her—more than once. "Two years ago I put a man reputed to have mob connections in jail. Before the divorce he'd forged his wife's name, mortgaged all their assets, and placed their joint funds in his name in a Bahamian bank, leaving her bankrupt. When I proved his actions in court, the judge came down hard on him."

"You think he decided to retaliate . . . from his jail cell?"

As a gust of chilly wind blew off Tampa Bay, she shrugged and drew the blanket more tightly around her. "He's not the only ex-spouse who might be gunning for me."

"Anything specific come to mind?"

"Only yesterday I arranged for a former client to hide from an abusive ex-husband in a local women's shelter."

"Did the spouse fit the description of the guy in the garage?"

"I've never met her husband. I'd have no way of knowing for certain which of my clients' spouses might hold a personal grudge." At the doubt on his face, she explained, "Look, my firm handles hundreds of cases. Two years ago I received death threats. Last year, in court, an irate husband attacked me, but the bailiff intervened before I was hurt.

Since then my clients' spouses have been better behaved, but several have violent pasts—a stockbroker who battered his wife and a pediatrician accused of child abuse. Even if I gave you a list, it would be so long it wouldn't do any good."

"No one in particular sticks out, no one at all?" In his now respectful tone, Delgado pushed for an answer, but she'd been an attorney too long to divulge information without thinking carefully first.

If she gave the names of the pediatrician and stockbroker, he'd ask for motive and she couldn't reveal details without violating attorney–client privilege. Yet it wasn't the women she represented who might want her dead, but their soon-to-be exes.

Yikes. This might get sticky.

"No," she spoke resolutely, staring at Tampa's impressive skyline, where lights had begun to wink on as the sun's last rays disappeared to the west. "No one in particular sticks out."

Delgado closed his notepad. "I'll give you a lift home."

"I'd appreciate it. Thanks." She wasn't about to turn down a ride just because of his previous bad manners. In her line of work she accepted that allegiances shifted, and the cop who might be an eye witness for a battered spouse might the following week testify against a wife who violated a restraining order. She tried not to hold grudges. Besides, Mandy couldn't wait to shuck her wet clothes, take a hot shower, and hold her baby.

But as much as she longed to go home, thoughts kept circling like the sea gulls overhead. If Gabby had been in the car with her . . . oh God. That thought made her suck in a deep breath and close her eyes.

"Ma'am," Delgado said. "You okay?"

Mandy forced herself to meet the man's concerned gaze. She couldn't think about Gabby in that car or she'd fall apart. She nodded.

But she wasn't okay. Every muscle ached, and she couldn't stop the tremors that shook her. Meanwhile, she couldn't stop worrying. Had the attack on the bridge been random or something more sinister? She prayed that she had been in the wrong place at the wrong time.

Maybe, just maybe, her brush with death was simply the result of really bad luck.

Chapter Three

MANDY OPENED HER condo's front door with her key-coded lock and slipped inside her dream home. Despite her clothes, reeking of river water, sticking to her skin and every muscle protesting, she felt lucky to here. The high ceilings and spacious tile foyer with the stained glass chandelier welcomed her. Tension slid off her shoulders. After taking a deep breath, Mandy called out to her mother, hoping she could delay telling her how close her only child had come to dying until after she'd cleaned up.

"Hi, Mom. I'm home."

"You're late." Her mother's voice carried over the sound of banging pans accompanied by the squeak of dishwasher trays. The delicious scent of fried chicken from dinner lingered and made Mandy's stomach rumble. Since her mother hadn't come barreling out of the kitchen in hysterical tears, she clearly had no clue about the wreck. That would buy some time.

"Where's Gabrielle?" Mandy called out.

"Asleep in her room."

Of course she was. Between leaving court late, the accident, and giving her statement to the cops, Mandy had come home way past the baby's bed time. By now, Gabby would be asleep, tucked between her stuffed lime-green alligator and her favorite book, *Swim, Baby, Swim*.

It was unrealistic to hope Gabby would be awake, standing in her crib, arms held out to her and demanding, "Up. Up. Up." That Mandy had failed to realize it was past her daughter's bedtime showed how rattled she still was. But even with Gabby asleep, she had to see her daughter.

"I'll check her and then hit the shower, okay?" she called to her mother, who was still busy in the kitchen.

"I'll warm your chicken."

"Thanks." One of her mother's many part-time jobs had been as a short-order cook, and her deep-fried chicken, even reheated, sounded really good right now—cholesterol be damned.

Mandy padded across the hall to Gabrielle's room. She'd always wanted the best for her daughter and last year she'd gotten a steal on this condo. Living in a gated community was a long-time dream Mandy had finally achieved and she was pleased she could provide her daughter with an extra measure of security. The place had been a mess, but nothing that soap, water, and hard work couldn't fix. For the nursery, her mother had sewn the bright pink and yellow curtains, and Mandy had sponge painted the walls. She'd purchased an antique dresser in a shop downtown, sanded and varnished the old wood, and stenciled it with huge daisies. A lamp shade her mother bagged at a craft show received the same treatment, and Mandy had been so excited to find crib sheets in a pale gold that matched the walls. They'd created a beautiful room for Gabrielle and together they were raising a happy child. Gabby had a two-parent household, even though she didn't have a father.

Mandy made a beeline for her daughter, a heavy sleeper. Next to her stuffed green and gold alligator, she lay on her side in her crib, sucking her thumb, and Mandy ached to pick her up. Still damp and grimy from her dunk in the river, Mandy grabbed a baby wipe and cleaned her hands. If she couldn't hold her baby, at least she could touch her. Lightly, she smoothed the short curly blond hair that framed Gabrielle's chubby cheeks, pulled the blanket to her chin and tucked it around her tiny body, which was clad in her favorite yellow pajamas with the panda bear embroidered on the front.

A lump of love and pride rose in Mandy's throat. She ached to give her baby all the things she'd never had— financial security, a safe and happy home, and all the comforts that implied. Her daughter would never be evicted. She would never go to bed hungry, or so hot from lack of air conditioning she feared she might melt.

Mandy couldn't have loved Gabrielle more if she'd been planned. Or if Mandy had been married or in any kind of relationship with Zachary Taylor, her baby's father.

Yet, at the thought of him, her heart ached. A little less than two years ago, after she'd received a death threat during a nasty divorce case, the firm's senior partner, Catherine, had hired her son Zack as Mandy's bodyguard. Although Mandy had known Zack for several years, having met him through his sister and her best friend, Dana Hansen, in law school, she'd never spent any time alone with him. But during their two weeks together, their attraction to one another had ignited during one night—then burned out the next day after Zack had returned to his job in California. Still, Mandy had amazing memories of Gabrielle's conception and, as a single mother, she'd never regretted that incredible night.

"Dinner's on the table," her mother called from the other room.

After a light kiss on Gabrielle's forehead, Mandy closed the baby's door and hurried across the hall to her own bathroom. If her mom caught one look at her shoeless daughter in damp clothes and runny mascara, she would have freaked out. So Mandy needed to clean up fast.

"Give me five more minutes."

Mandy shucked her wet clothes, hit the shower, washed her hair twice, careful not to dislodge the bandage on her forehead. She was about to slap on conditioner, when her mother pounded the bathroom door.

"Amanda. Come out of there, right now."

Mandy shut off the water and shrugged into a robe mere seconds before her mother barged into the spacious strawberry and cream master bathroom.

Five inches shorter and fifty pounds heavier than Mandy, her mother appeared wan, as if she, not Mandy, had almost died a few hours ago. Her worried eyes, the exact same shade of green as Mandy's, were wide with fright. The last time her mother had looked this upset was when Gabrielle had fallen while learning to walk and required three stitches in her knee.

Had her daughter awakened and hurt herself trying to climb out of her crib? Fearful, Mandy knotted the belt of her robe. "Gabrielle? Is she okay?"

At the mention of her granddaughter, her face softened. "*She's* safe and asleep in her crib." But then her lips tightened. "And luckily she's too young to understand what *I* just saw on the ten o'clock news."

Mandy stared at her mother, surprised and concerned, until she realized the accident must have been on TV.

"How could you fail to tell me before I heard about you on the news?" Her mother demanded, confirming Mandy's suspicion.

"I didn't—"

"When I saw the crane pull your car from the water . . ." Her mother's eyes welled with tears. "You could have died."

"I'm sorry." Hearing her mother sniffling, Mandy reached for a tissue and handed it to her. "I didn't want to scare you. I wanted to clean up first . . ."

Her mother dabbed her eyes with the tissue and frowned at the bandage on her forehead. "Are you all right?"

"A few cuts and bruises. I'm sore and banged up, but otherwise okay or the paramedics would have taken me to Tampa General."

"You and Gabby are all I have." Tears rolled down her mother's cheeks. "The newscaster said you were attacked because of your work."

"Mom, that was sheer speculation."

"But even if your career *might* be putting you in danger, you should stop taking clients with violent spouses."

"That's like buying an alarm system after the robbery. Besides, I can't cut my case load and income too much."

"But you have job security," her mother argued.

"True. But I have to pull my weight. And now that Catherine has already semi-retired, she could bring in a new senior partner—one who doesn't consider me part of their family."

Being a single parent and the family's sole support wasn't easy, but Mandy wouldn't change her life if it meant not having Gabby now. Mandy's life wasn't two point five kids and a picket fence. That had never been an option with Zack, who'd been up front when he'd told her he wasn't and never would be altar material.

She sometimes fantasized about what might have happened if she and Zack had spent more time together, but with reality slapping her in the face on a daily basis, she kept this daydream short. Zack was DEA, through and through. His brother had died of a drug overdose and Zack's work was not what he did, but who he was.

So she'd coped as best she could. "Thanks to my career, we have medical insurance, a safe place to live, and Gabby has a loving caregiver. That's you, Mom." She smiled and forced a soothing calm she didn't feel into her tone. "Let's not argue. Gabrielle wants for nothing."

"Except more time with her mother." Her tone was pleading for her understanding. "I worry that someday she'll resent you for working so much."

After Mandy's father had died when she was twelve, her mother had worked two shifts, often leaving Mandy on her own. And her mother still felt guilty, but Mandy, even as a child, had understood the need to work to pay bills. Thanks to the public library, Mandy had survived those years, and hadn't ended up on drugs like so many others from the neighborhood. "Mom, she'll understand, just like I understand that you had no choice about working double shifts to feed me."

Her mother was great with her granddaughter, and Mandy

was grateful. But even if Catherine okayed it, cutting back was not an option. She had too many bills. Too many plans for Gabby's future. If accomplishing her goals meant splitting her every waking hour between work and family, then that's what she'd do. "I want Gabrielle to grow up in a safe home, go to a good school, have regular dental care. There's nothing wrong in my wanting her to have what I didn't have."

"I did the best I could." Her mother's eyes teared again. "You still blame me because I couldn't provide better?"

"Mom, I've never blamed you." Mandy unwrapped the towel and rubbed her head vigorously to dry her hair. No matter how many times she'd told her mother that she didn't blame her for their poverty, her mother didn't listen.

Far too often Mandy still saw women in similar situations. Helping women get through their divorce was one of the reasons, the primary reason, Mandy had become an attorney. She considered herself fortunate that she had a career she loved, a career that, at the same time, provided a secure future for her daughter.

The phone rang, cutting off any reply her mother might have made. Mandy tried not to sound relieved when she said, "I'll get it," then strode into her bedroom for the phone.

The familiarity of her surroundings reassured her in a way her mother hadn't. She wasn't at the bottom of the river. She was home. Safe in her room that she'd decorated with the same care she'd done Gabby's. Plush cream carpeting matched the sleek Italian furniture and the lounge chair by the windows where she often read briefs late into the night under an arching chrome reading light. Lots of silk plants in ceramic pots; one of them, a giant palm tree, brought the tropical outside into her personal space. At the moment creamy floor-to-ceiling curtains covered her waterfront view of the Hillsborough River, and she appreciated them being closed. She'd seen quite enough of the river today. The sleigh bed was festive and cheerful with its strawberry duvet and an assortment of embroidered pillows. She picked up the phone, which rested in its cradle on her nightstand beside a picture of her little family, Mom, Gabby, and her, dressed in pirate costumes they'd worn during the Gasparilla Parade last February.

Mandy checked caller ID. It was Dana. "Hi. I'm okay."

"You could have . . . died." Over the telephone, her friend's voice broke and Mandy braced herself. Another of her nearest and dearest had just gotten the news. "I'm a wreck. I got off the plane from Chicago and I heard . . . I called your cell phone first—"

"It's at the bottom of the river along with my purse, credit cards, and our Powerball lottery ticket." Every week the women in the office bought one ticket, playing the same numbers. This week it had been Mandy's turn to make the purchase.

"Well, it's certainly not your lucky day. You can buy another ticket tomorrow." Dana hesitated as if reluctant to say more. Mandy envisioned her friend's worried eyes and wished she could give her a hug. Finally, Dana spit out her words in a rush. "I'm not sure that I'll be able to sleep until I see you with my own eyes and make sure you're really in one piece."

Mandy's throat tightened with thanks that she had such a good friend. Dana's husband, Sam, was no doubt waiting on nearby Davis Islands for his wife to come home. But even after working a twelve-hour day, then flying home from O'Hare, Dana would land on Mandy's doorstep within the hour, toting a gallon of her favorite rum raisin ice cream if Mandy said she needed company or a shoulder to cry on.

"I'm exhausted," Mandy admitted, pulling back the duvet, sitting and sinking against her pillows, doubting if she'd sleep a wink tonight. When she closed her eyes, would she envision the water pouring into her car, the door jamming, her lungs burning?

"I'll come straight over," Dana offered.

"No need. I just want to rest."

Considerate as always, Dana didn't push and changed the subject. "The newscaster said your attacker might have been the spouse of one of our clients."

"They were speculating," Mandy sighed. "The cops have no idea who he was." But spouses of clients had threatened her several times before. Had one tried to follow through? Or had the attack been random?

"We need to go through your cases. See if anyone matches the description you gave. I do wish the newscaster had kept the details private. We don't need a lunatic on the loose, knowing you can identify him."

"Maybe that will give him a reason to stay away."

Dana released a long sigh. "I don't want you to take chances, especially when we don't know who was after you or why. Let's hire someone to protect you."

A bodyguard? After what happened last time?

"No way." Mandy's refusal burst with too much force for Dana not to realize she'd struck a nerve. But discussing the subject was like pouring acid on a nerve. Mandy had only known one bodyguard. Zachary Taylor.

"Someone tried to kill you, Mandy."

"I know." Mandy couldn't tell Dana her real reason for refusing a bodyguard—she didn't need any reminders of her last experience with personal protection. Memories of meals with Zack, the constant presence of him sharing her days and nights—the time he'd ended up in her bed. She didn't want any reminders, at least not without some inkling that the attack had been personal rather than random. Mandy made up the first excuse that came to mind. "I don't want to give up my privacy. It will confuse Gabby and stress out my mother."

"Sweetie, you should be worried about your safety and not everyone else. Look, we'll get someone you know. Maybe I can contact Zack—"

"No!" This conversation was going from bad to worse. She'd never really understood why she'd let Zack get close or why she'd responded to him like she had. She wasn't the impulsive type. She'd finished college and law school by adhering to a strict set of rules and was proud of her self-discipline. When other girls had partied, Mandy had studied. When other girls at the firm hit the clubs, she'd worked overtime on her cases. However, the night Gabby was conceived—Zack had been ready for sex and she'd been ready to have him. Somehow, the man had brought out a physical and emotional side of her that she hadn't known existed. Even now the tantalizing memories seemed almost as if she'd been another person . . . and while she wanted to put the incident down to hormones—she couldn't. Since a tiny part of her still longed for the extraordinary, to free that part of herself again, seeing him again was not a good idea. She took a deep breath. "The guy who hit me probably picked me at random."

"You sound frazzled. At least take a few days off."

"I do have work to do." Rearranging all her appointments for even a few days wouldn't be easy. . . . It would throw off her schedule for a month.

"Mom won't mind. Spend some time with Gabby before we head to California."

Mandy restrained a groan. She'd almost forgotten about the depositions in California. Now wasn't the best time to leave, but she had to work and the appointments had been made months ago. "Okay. I'll stay home for a few days. I should be safe enough between the island's security and my alarm system. And I'll think about protection, okay? If I need it, I'll arrange it myself." And she'd hire a female bodyguard.

"Take as much time off as you need." Dana hesitated as if reluctant to speak, then suggested, "I don't want you worrying about your family's safety while we're in California. So why don't you send Gabby and your mom to our beach house while we're out of town?"

"I don't want to impose."

"It's not imposing. You're family," Dana insisted and Mandy winced. Dana believed she was speaking metaphorically, not literally. After Mandy had discovered she was pregnant, she'd considered what to tell Zack, what to tell his family—never forgetting their one-night stand had been just that, a one-night stand.

While she might have fallen for Zack, she couldn't say the same about his career. Zack himself had blamed his undercover work for his failed marriage. Before offering him the job, the DEA had warned his wife in an interview. At the time, she'd said she wouldn't mind if Zack was gone for months on end. At the time, she's said she wouldn't object if he disappeared in the middle of the night without explanation. She'd stated she could live with a husband who couldn't talk about his work. But his soon-to-be ex had been wrong. She couldn't deal with Zack's mysterious silences, his sudden and unexplained absences. And Mandy didn't know if she could, either.

If Zack had married Mandy, he would have been gone most of the time in his DEA job and she didn't want that. If he'd left the DEA, she would have destroyed his dream. Knowledge of Gabby could only make him feel guilty and distract him, and distractions could place a DEA agent's life in danger. Besides, telling him about his daughter would certainly make Zack unhappy and she didn't want to torment him.

So her pregnancy had trapped her between a rock and a hard place. Early on, she'd realized little good would come from telling Zack about Gabby. Her daughter didn't need a grudging father and Mandy didn't want a grudging man in her life. So Mandy had finally and reluctantly decided to keep Gabby's father's identity a secret—for as long as Zack remained undercover. Maybe longer, depending on his career choices.

But if Dana had known Gabby was really her niece, she'd be even more insistent on sending the baby to safety. Dana doted on Gabby, often accompanying them on their outings, early morning walks along the island's bike paths, where the two friends took turns pushing the stroller while they chatted. Family or not, with Mandy's mother and daughter's safety uppermost in her mind, she couldn't refuse. "Thanks, Dana. I'm sure they'll love the beach and I will feel better knowing they're safe."

"Good. I thought we might try to meet my dad and Zack for dinner while we're in L.A."

Mandy tensed, her thoughts racing. She'd never intended to keep Gabby a secret from him forever, wanting to tell him in person—when the time was right. Since she couldn't spill the secret to his family before she'd told him, the secret weighed on her, but she was doing the best she could in a bad situation.

During the last two years, she'd seen no reason to alter her initial decision to keep her secret. Zack's contact with his own family had been sporadic and infrequent, and he hadn't called Mandy—not once.

But if he could free himself from his undercover work, he'd return Dana's phone calls. Visit with her. Mandy dreaded what might happen if Dana mentioned to her brother that Mandy had a child. Would he count backwards? Would he care?

She clutched the phone, careful to keep her tone casual. "I don't want to be in the way. You don't get to see your brother and dad that often."

"That's why I originally agreed to do the deposition. But Dad's in Vegas for an equipment convention and Zack . . . Zack and I are playing phone tag."

"Anything wrong?" Mandy had to ease her grip on the phone.

"It's probably nothing." Dana kept her tone light, but she wouldn't have brought up being concerned about Zack for no reason. "He's under deep cover on a drug case. He might not come up for air for months."

Mandy glanced at the nightstand and the framed picture of her and Gabrielle holding hands. Gabrielle had the same ridged nails as Zack. Vividly, Mandy still recalled his strong fingers running through her hair, candlelight glowing off his powerful chest.

"Zack can take care of himself," Mandy said. She'd learned in their short time together that although he didn't keep a schedule, he rarely let a few days go by before he made time to work out. A crack shot and a natural athlete, he possessed split-second reflexes that could mean the difference between life and death.

She wondered if he ever thought about their brief encounter, and if so, where she ranked in his memories. For her, their one night together was a highlight of her life.

At the time, she'd thought she might be in love—now she dismissed the feeling as chemistry. Surely, he wouldn't think of her as often as she thought of him. Because every time she looked into Gabrielle's sapphire irises rimmed with a circle of sky blue, she saw Zack's eyes. When Gabby smiled, Mandy saw his smile. She was grateful that if Dana had ever noted the similarities, she'd never once mentioned them.

"L.A. will be work," Dana insisted, "and you need a change of scenery. And for fun, we're putting your choices at the top of the to-do list," Dana teased.

Mandy didn't want to risk running into Zack but couldn't say so. Nor could she back out of the trip. They'd only be out there for three days. "I was hoping you'd take me to that California restaurant, the one where you and Sam met," she admitted.

"Deal. And I'll drop by and give you the keys to the beach house in the morning," Dana offered.

"Great. See you tomorrow."

Mandy hung up and her mother breezed in, dinner plate and a large glass of ice tea in hand. "You should eat."

"Thanks." At the mention of food, Mandy's stomach rumbled again. She'd exerted a lot of energy swimming from the car and then shivering. Her aching muscles demanded nourishment to heal. She accepted the plate of fried chicken, mashed potatoes, and greens. "I appreciate you looking out for me."

Her mother offered a rare smile. "I am your mother, after all."

Her good mood made Mandy's request easier. "Mom, while Dana is taking me with her to L.A. this weekend, can you take Gabrielle to Catherine's beach house?"

"You're still going?"

"I'm taking off the next few days to spend with you and Gabby. The trip with Dana is work, and it's just a precaution for you to go to the beach. But I'll feel better if I know you are safe."

Her mother's tone filled with worry. "Do you think now is a good time to leave?"

"What do you mean?"

Her mother bit her lower lip. "The police haven't arrested the man who knocked your car off the bridge. Suppose he goes after you again?"

"The trip isn't for a few days. If we have any problems at all, if I think you and Gabby are in any danger, I won't leave."

Her mother sighed, rolled her eyes, leaned over and kissed her cheek. "I don't know why I say anything. You never listen. I'm worried about him going after *you* in California."

Mandy always listened, but she had to use her own good judgment. "Mom, the chance of him following me to another state is minimal. Try not to worry so much. Just have fun with Gabby."

"I will. Besides, you know I can't resist spending as much time with my granddaughter as I can."

"Thanks, Mom."

Chapter Four

One month earlier

SOME DEA AGENTS dealt with grief by swilling beer. Some shot China White or Mexican Mud. Others chased away nightmares with mindless sex. A few turned to God. For once, Zack had his own method—he fought pain with pain.

Zack absorbed a punch to his chin, his chest, his stomach, needles of agony stabbing his body. Hands lowered, he shifted slightly, his feet refusing to obey his command to remain a target and hold still. Instead, he danced around the ring, bracing for the next blow.

Sweat ran in rivulets down his battered face. Since his nose was too bloody to breathe through, his breath had turned ragged. Usually when he boxed, wrestled, or used a combination of karate, judo, and jujitsu in the gym, a crowd gathered to watch, but apparently, tonight, the other fighters had no stomach for the beating he was taking.

"I quit." Zack's opponent, Steven, raised his arms over his head as if he were under arrest.

"Afraid?" Zack taunted.

"Yeah, I'm afraid you'll suffer brain damage for refusing to defend yourself. I'm out of here."

"You can't quit when you're winning," Zack protested past a bloody split lip.

"Damn it, Zack. If you want to be a human punching bag, find someone else to knock you out."

Infuriated that Steven was refusing to deliver more pain, Zack struck the man in the shoulder, hopefully with enough force to make him reconsider. "Fight."

"No more. I fell for that trick two minutes ago. It won't work again."

"Come on."

"You've got more balls than sense. I'm done. So are you."

"Coward," Zack ground out, but Steven walked away, shaking his head. "All right then—" Zack spun, bouncing from foot to foot with catlike grace, like Mohammed Ali in his prime. Well, maybe a few years past his prime. He issued a challenge to the men jumping rope, pressing weights, and running on treadmills. "Which one of you ladies will take me on?"

No one met his gaze.

One of the gym's most respected trainers entered the ring, placed a hand on his shoulder. "Zack, go hit the shower. See the doc." He referred to the physical therapist who patched up the guys after they got dinged up.

Zack shrugged the hand off his shoulder. He didn't want pity or sympathy. "I need a workout."

"No, you don't. You want punishment. You could have beaten that guy with your eyes closed. You've thrown exactly three punches, one every five minutes."

Zack cursed.

"You're a mess," the trainer said. "I don't know what happened on your last assignment and I don't care. I haven't seen you this whacked out since your divorce five years ago."

"But—"

"Just don't come back until you straighten out your sorry ass."

"Fine." Zack held up his hands so the trainer could remove the tape that secured the gloves to his wrists. "I was just leaving."

Zack tossed the gloves into his locker but didn't change from his sweaty T-shirt. Like a bar-hopping drunk who knew where to go for his next drink after his favorite watering hole closed for the night, he walked two blocks down Santa Monica Boulevard and entered another gym. This operation wasn't full of ex-cops, DEA, and FBI. The home of brawlers, bikers, and street fighters, this seedy joint didn't offer a juice bar or bottled water. The mats reeked of vicious sweat. Dust smudged the windows around faded posters of Hoyce Gracie, Ken Shamrock, and Tito Ortiz.

Here, padded gloves were for rookies. Bare-knuckle fights were the norm. Zack tossed his gym bag onto a bench, avoided the reflection of his swelling shiner in the cracked mirror, and eyed the biggest, fittest, meanest dude he could find. "Want to go a few rounds?"

A six-foot four-inch, bald-headed fighter with "Bryan" tattooed on one cheek eyed him and shook his head. "Mate," he spoke with a British accent, "you look like you've already fought one too many blokes."

Zack forced a lopsided grin through his split lip. "That was my warm-up."

"Come back when you're healthy."

"Don't be a wuss."

Zack had graduated from the DEA's special training school with off-the-chart test results in discerning relative size, balance, bodily awareness, and perception of timing and motion as well as scoring extraordinarily high in muscular reflex tests—plus a host of other tests with names that sounded like scientific gibberish—which all meant he was one tough, highly trained fighting machine—even when injured. His superiors considered him an unqualified success.

But the trainer at the last gym had known better when he called him a mess. Yeah, the last op had gone down real smooth. Smooth as death.

Despite all Zack's expertise, two months ago he hadn't moved fast enough, hadn't sensed the danger, had trusted

when he shouldn't have . . . and for his mistake . . . an innocent bystander had died. Zack had held Todd as the boy's
life blood drained out.

Zack had no answer then. He had none now. Hands sticky
with blood, he'd held the kid as he'd died, felt his last shud-
der. Zack had paid for the best damn funeral money could
buy. But nothing eased the guilt or the painful memory of
those eyes staring into his, eyes that still trusted, eyes that
didn't comprehend that his death was Zack's fault. The kid's
confused question still rang in his dreams. Two months later,
blood still colored his sleep, seeping into every second of
every ticking hour.

Ignoring calls from friends, family, coworkers, Zack ran
day-long marathons, but he couldn't run fast enough to escape
his guilt. So finding peace had come down to this moment.

Bryan raised his brows in skepticism. "What kind of
happy juice are you on?"

"The kind that will whip your ass," Zack growled. "I'm
betting I can take you in three rounds." With a sneer of disdain calculated to prick the man's pride, Zack tossed a C-note
at Bryan's feet, then climbed through the ropes into the ring.

"You want me. You got me." The man removed his bling,
a thick gold necklace studded with diamonds, a gold pinky
ring and a watch. He peeled off his shirt, exposing more
body tats—a cross on his back, a dragon on his chest, a chain
around his biceps. He handed his wallet to a friend, telling
him to hold the bets, then cracked his neck, closed his massive hands into fists, displaying more ink on his knuckles.

Zack hoped the guy lived up to his fire-breathing dragon
tattoo. He yearned for a cleansing burn that would supplant
guilt, shame, and grief. Whatever it took. He needed to forget the bullets spraying an innocent, the stench of death, the
sad little grave.

And so he faced the dragon and hoped Bryan could do the
job. The two men stood eye to eye, touched fists. The dragon
breathed fire with a fury of pummeling blows. Zack rocked
back on his heels, spat blood, and countered with a punch so
low, Bryan easily blocked and jabbed his chin.

Finally, Zack had found a worthy opponent. One with the brawn to make a dent, one with no scruples, one who wouldn't hesitate to knock his head off. Zack danced on the balls of his toes, blocking a punch here, his defensive reaction more out of habit than any real desire to protect himself.

Bryan came in fast, hard, with the confidence of a predator. Although they were the same height, Bryan, thick-armed and muscular, outweighed Zack by fifty pounds.

Already bruised, Zack's flesh absorbed more blows. Searing pain radiated through his gut. His legs weakened, buckled. Staggering, he held himself up on the ropes. Bryan's fists rained in a vicious downpour of jabs. For a few priceless seconds the pain of the body supplanted the pain in his soul. Zack's vision narrowed, a sign of the beginning of unconsciousness. Sheer determination kept him on his feet, bracing for the next blow.

Then he saw Kevin's face, the brother he'd adored, as unexpected and vivid as if he were still alive. Once he'd thought Kevin walked on water, that he was one step higher than Spider-Man. But he'd learned Kevin was as human as everyone else, that his brother's seemingly bottomless energy came through a needle. It had started so innocently, just a push, a little more energy, to do a little more, to be a little better. Before Kevin knew he was in danger, he was lost. He'd fought his addiction, so hard, but the lure had proven too strong and Kevin had given in. He'd given up. Kevin shook his head at Zack. *"Don't give up like I did."*

Instinctively, Zack blocked, counterpunched, and snapped a roundhouse kick to his opponent's jaw. Bryan staggered. His eyes narrowed in surprise and he grinned. "Where did that come from?"

Zack stared into Bryan's face, recognized the surprise that mirrored his own and took his first step away from the darkness and toward the light. Kevin's voice rang out in Zack's head again, *"Don't give up."*

And Zack realized what he'd been doing—trying to kill his guilt at whatever cost.

Turning his back, Zack walked out of the ring.

Chapter Five

AFTER SPENDING THREE days with Gabby, Mandy had hugged her daughter goodbye. She'd miss her daughter during her trip to California, but Gabby was in good hands with her grandmother, especially since they'd gone off to the beach. While the last three days had been peaceful, if Mandy didn't count rearranging her schedule, drying out the contents of her purse that had come up with her car, and dealing with her insurance company, she felt better that her family wasn't where a stranger could find them. Thankfully, the guy who'd struck her vehicle hadn't shown up again—not even when she'd ventured off the island to grocery shop.

Earlier this morning, Dana had picked Mandy up at her condo but insisted on stopping at the office to say goodbye to her mother, Catherine, before heading for the airport. Mandy didn't mind. She wanted to pick up her mail and a few files to read during the six-hour plane ride to the other coast.

Dana parked her Jaguar behind the office building of Catherine Taylor and Associates, in a space marked by a sign with her name on it. Mandy exited the car to see three girls and Lisa Slocum, their paralegal, sitting at a picnic table under hundred-year-old oak trees draped with Spanish moss that towered over the office building. Lisa gestured for Mandy and Dana to join them, her dark brown eyes bright, her hands busy with the collage they were all making.

Dana shooed Mandy toward the girls and Lisa. "Go say hello. I'll pick up your stuff and meet you back here."

"Thanks." Mandy placed her sunglasses on and headed over to join the group. Lisa used her free time to work with foster kids. Apparently she'd grown up in the system and she enjoyed encouraging other girls to get a college education.

"Girls, say hello to Ms. Mandy," Lisa suggested. Dressed in a soft gray skirt and white shirt, Lisa looked young enough to be the girls' big sister. Except Lisa appeared well dressed and confident, her nails manicured, her perfect makeup setting off her flawless skin while the three girls wore clean but ill-fitting clothes, clearly hand-me-downs.

One girl sucked her thumb, but the other two offered shy hellos. Mandy knew children from broken homes often lacked social skills and understood that Lisa played a critical part in their lives. She admired her for taking the time to give back.

"Hey, Mandy." Lisa held up a picture of a pink computer she'd just cut out of a magazine. "Think this qualifies as a design essential?"

"Only if I could pair it with a matching phone," Mandy said.

A girl with blond pigtails glanced between them. Then she took her thumb out of her mouth and pointed to a magazine page of sleek cell phone covers, one with bright pink stars. "How about this?"

"Sweetie, I think that's perfect." Lisa patted the girl on the back, and Mandy watched the child flinch, as if unaccustomed to affection.

"That's just what I had in mind," Mandy added.

The girl smiled shyly. Mandy smiled back.

"You all keep working while I talk to Ms. Mandy, okay?" Lisa told them.

The two women walked to the parking lot, far enough away so the kids couldn't overhear. No longer shaded by the oaks, Lisa squinted in the bright sunlight. She frowned at the traffic flowing by, glanced at the kids and cleared her throat. Mandy expected Lisa to ask her about a case, or for advice with one of the children's legal problems. Maybe even an adoption. Lisa was always trying to find a real family for her kids and Mandy's hopes rose. If Lisa needed her help, she'd make time in her schedule, even if she had to cut back on sleep.

Although a paralegal, Lisa intended to go to law school if her scholarship came through. Meanwhile, when they could, Dana and Mandy helped when legal issues cropped up with Lisa's foster children.

"Have the police found the guy who knocked you off the bridge?" Lisa asked, surprising Mandy at the subject of conversation.

Mandy shook her head. "The vehicle was stolen and wiped clean of prints. I don't think they even have any leads to follow."

"Have you gone through your cases? Maybe a picture in the file will jog your memory."

"I tried. Nothing rang a bell."

Lisa shivered in the hot sunlight. She took Mandy's hands in both of hers and stared hard into her eyes. "You be careful. I have a bad feeling about this."

Dana walked out of the back of the office building, holding Mandy's mail and files. "We need to get going. There's no telling how long it'll take us to get through airport security."

Mandy gave Lisa a quick hug. "I'll be fine. Don't worry about me. You go take care of your girls, okay?"

Lisa nodded, her voice low and serious. "Watch your back."

FROM MANDY AND Dana's table on the flowery terrace of the Ocean View Café, Mandy gazed at the hot pinks and oranges of the Pacific sunset. While she eagerly anticipated

dinner and the exotic Mediterranean cuisine that Dana had
said she'd enjoyed in this restaurant during college, Mandy
put off making a decision between tabouli or herb pizza. As
far as Mandy was concerned, no food could compete with
the spectacular display Mother Nature provided as the glowing sun sizzled down into the sea. Mandy had always had an
affinity for the water. Manhattan Beach, with the deep sapphire of the serene ocean, the salt tang of the gentle California breeze, and the swooping gulls, fed her inner peace and
soothed the ragged edges of her unnerving week.

"I'm glad I came out here," Mandy admitted to Dana.
While she'd spent quality time with Gabby over the past few
days, she hadn't been able to relax. She'd been jumpy and
suspicious of strangers. Yet, no one had bothered her. Now
the trip was giving her a chance to put her harrowing week
behind her.

"This is where Sam took me on our first date," Dana's
tone was mellow, full of good memories. In the soft glow of
the sunset, she appeared younger than her thirty years and
wistful. "I knew the night Sam and I met that we'd be happy
together."

"You were right."

Dana had what Mandy wanted. A best friend, a lover, a
husband all wrapped in one. She had a man who came home
every night, who understood her work, who supported her
dreams. Dana and Sam's relationship reminded Mandy that
marriage could work, that it was possible to find the right
man.

"I wish we could have a baby." Dana sipped her wine.

"You will." The irony that Mandy's one night with failed
protection had resulted in Gabrielle while Dana and Sam
couldn't get pregnant after two years of trying saddened
Mandy. And made her feel guilty for keeping Gabby's father
a secret. A niece wasn't a child of her own and Mandy
couldn't imagine Dana loving Gabby any more, but it was a
secret between them, one that grew heavier as Dana fulfilled
her longings for her own child by buying Gabrielle expen-
sive baby toys and clothing.

"I'm considering adoption."

"If that's what you want, go for it. You and Sam can afford to adopt as many children as you like."

"Sam says we should give it more time. In truth, he's spending so much energy on business that I'm not sure how good a father he'll be." Dana sipped her wine. "But my biological clock is running out."

"You're only thirty, and maybe once Sam has a child, he'll make room in his life."

Dana rolled her eyes. "He's consumed with not just his law practice but his real estate ventures. It's hard to make time for everything and I want four kids." Dana's tone revealed a hunger she usually repressed. Her five-bedroom home must seem empty—even with a husband and their pets.

Apparently, not even Sam was perfect. Still, Dana was lucky to have him and Mandy tried to keep the conversation upbeat. "With adoption, maybe you can find siblings."

"Yes. That's why I don't understand why Sam is so reluctant to—"

Dana's cell phone rang. So did Mandy's. They exchanged a long look of alarm. Back east, it was just after 11 P.M. Too late for business.

Gabrielle.

Fingers shaking, Mandy dug into her purse for her phone. Dana did the same.

Dana retrieved her phone first and checked caller ID. "It's Catherine." She flicked it open and answered, "Hi, Mom."

Mandy's phone revealed that Sylvia Jacobson, the firm's senior secretary, was on the line. She couldn't recall Sylvia ever calling during the evening and her anxiety heightened. Had her attacker found out where she'd sent her family? At the thought, her throat tightened. Sylvia was down-to-earth and sensible. She would never have called at this time unless there was some kind of emergency.

Mandy's pulse kicked in—even as she fought back her fears. "Hello."

"Have you heard?" Sylvia's voice practically hummed with excitement, not disaster.

"What happened? Tell me."

"Are you sitting down?"

Across the table, Dana's eyebrows rose and she broke into a wide smile and laughed, her tone bubbly. "You're certain?"

Mandy answered Sylvia's question. "I'm sitting beside the ocean and drinking wine with Dana."

"Perfect." Sylvia had lived in Florida for thirty years but the rare times when she got excited, her New York accent returned. Tonight she spoke in a Bronx dialect as thick as if she'd never left the Big Apple. "This is the best news ever. We won the Powerball jackpot."

They'd won?

Mandy had never won anything in her life. She'd never been lucky—except with Gabrielle.

They'd *really* won?

For a moment she could only stare, trying to reconcile Sylvia's news with her own shock. Dana's laughter bubbled out in the evening air, driving home the news and Mandy sank back in the chair, clutching the phone.

Sylvia could have told her that a UFO had landed in downtown Tampa and she might have believed it more easily. The odds of winning the lottery were . . . astronomical. She'd never have bought a ticket except the other girls talked her into it. She was far too practical. Yet, someone had to win. Why not them?

"You're sure?" she asked, still hesitant.

"You bought the usual numbers, right?"

"Yes." Every week one of the women at the law firm was responsible for buying a ticket. They always played the same numbers. "This week was my turn."

"Where's the ticket?" Sylvia asked.

"I have it right here." Mandy dug into her purse, opened her wallet, and extracted the new ticket. Giddy with excitement, she fought not to stammer. "I've got it. 3-5-15-16-38-42. With the Powerball slot of 65."

"You hang onto that ticket, girl. We're rich." Sylvia spoke as if she was still in shock. "We're *all* megarich."

They'd won the Powerball jackpot.

It was unbelievable. Incredible. Shocked, stunned, Mandy wasn't sure what to do. Jump up and down? Pump her fist over her head? She knew she needed to tell her mom, hold Gabrielle and swing her in circles until her sweet face lit up with laughter. Then perhaps winning a boatload of money might feel real. What a week. Fate certainly had her scrambling. On Tuesday, she'd almost died and on Friday, she'd won . . . what? What exactly had they won?

"How much?" Mandy's heart thudded. She had no idea what the ten-state Powerball jackpot was up to. She wasn't much of a gambler; she'd just joined the office pool to share the fun with the other six women—Catherine, the senior partner and founding officer; Mandy, Dana, and Maria, the younger partners; Sylvia, their secretary; and Lisa, the paralegal.

And oh, wow. Together, they'd all won the Powerball jackpot.

"It's amazing. We won 180 million dollars."

"Oh . . . my . . . Lord. "With six ticket holders that leaves us 30 . . . million . . . each." Not in her wildest dream of achieving financial security had she ever thought to have this kind of wealth. She was rich. Megarich.

"We have one of only two winning tickets."

Mandy frowned, trying to concentrate. "What did you say?"

"There are only two tickets and we have one—"

"What happens if the other ticket isn't claimed?"

"Then we get it all. But that's not—"

Nerves had Mandy smiling, laughing and talking at the same time. "I bought two tickets with the same numbers. The first one was destroyed during my accident."

"You're sure?"

"When my purse was retrieved, I checked and the ink was gone on the ticket. I ripped it to shreds, flushed it down the toilet, and bought a second one."

"Oh, God." Sylvia's voice dropped to a whisper. "That means we've won 360 million dollars. Sixty million each."

Even after taxes . . . they'd be set. More than set. It was a good thing Mandy was sitting because her knees had turned liquid and her insides to jelly. Never again would she have to worry about her family's financial future. She could afford to send Gabrielle to Harvard and her mother to Paris and . . . sheesh, she could buy herself any new car she wanted, take a vacation, work less and spend more time at home. The possibilities made her giddy. If her knees weren't so weak, she would have stood and danced. Instead, she leaned over and hugged Dana, who hugged her back, her smile wide, her eyes lit with laughter.

Sylvia squealed in delight through the phone. "I wish I could kiss you. This means Ben and I can buy a house for each of our kids and set aside money for the grandkids. Just last week, I was reading up on a new experimental surgery our health insurance refuses to cover that might improve Ben's quality of life. Can you imagine?"

Ben, an ex-cop and paraplegic, had taken a bullet to the spine one week before he'd retired. Yet, the man amazed everyone who knew him. Every day, he packed Sylvia a homemade lunch. He sent her flowers on each one of their seven children's birthdays, and on Sylvia's, he'd bought front-row seats to the ballet and even accompanied her without complaining. They'd been married forty-five years and still adored one another.

Sylvia giggled like a young woman. "Tell Dana I'm giving my two-week's notice."

"Just like that?" Mandy checked her watch. The winning numbers had been announced less than thirty minutes ago. "You didn't have to think about quitting for very long."

"I'm sixty-five. I have luxuries to buy. Exotic places to go. People to spoil."

All smiles, Dana tapped Mandy on the arm. "My mother said she'd prefer that we keep our win out of the press for now. Please tell Sylvia."

"Tell her yourself." Mandy handed Dana her phone.

For Dana and Catherine, the win wouldn't change their lives so very much. They were already wealthy. But for the

rest of them, winning meant . . . more security than she'd
dared ever dream of.

They'd won the lottery. Sixty million dollars. The amount
kept looping in her head. Six, zero, zero, zero, zero, zero,
zero, zero. She stared at the ticket, barely able to comprehend how much her life would change. Her future suddenly
seemed as wide as the Pacific and just as limitless.

"We all should speak to our lawyers and accountants immediately." As she talked to Sylvia, Dana sounded as though
she'd been planning to win this kind of money for years.
"Once word gets out that we won, people and charities will
line up at our doors with their hands out. While I plan to donate some of this windfall, there'll be lots of cons seeking to
pull one over on us. We also have an obligation to our clients
to keep their cases on track. The less distractions from the
press, the better." Then she hung up the phone and grinned at
Mandy. "Lisa and Maria aren't answering their cell phones.
They still don't know."

"You sound so calm." Mandy held out her hand to see her
fingers shaking. Eagerness to tell her mother bubbled
through her, but Dana motioned for the waitress and ordered a bottle of champagne. "Money doesn't solve every
problem."

Mandy thought of the babies Dana wanted so badly, and
thought she understood. But right now was a time for cele-
bration. She picked up the ticket. Lisa could now pay for law
school. Sylvia would retire and travel. Mandy didn't have a
clue what she'd do. Winning didn't seem real. Not yet. "Can
you believe this is worth three hundred and sixty million
dollars?"

"Keep your voice down," Dana shushed her, but a smile
brightened her eyes.

"I'm not sure I can control myself. I want to scream at the
top of my lungs. *We won. We won. We won.*" Mandy held out
her glass for the bubbly. "I still can hardly believe it."

"Believe it. You deserve the money as much as anyone.
Go ahead and daydream. Dream big." Dana poured them
both champagne and shot her a fond grin.

Mandy's cell phone rang and she checked caller ID. "It's Lisa."

"While you talk to her, I'll call Sam."

As Dana speed-dialed her husband, Mandy answered Lisa's call with a broad smile. "Hi. You've heard?"

Lisa's excitement hummed through her voice. "*Everyone's* heard."

"Who is everyone?"

"The press are camped outside my apartment . . . as if I'm some kind of celebrity. I suppose I am. We all are. I'm going to law school. Now, I don't have to wait on the scholarship."

"You'll make a great lawyer. I'm so happy for you. For us." Mandy laughed and heard Lisa's doorbell ringing. "Did you say the press is outside your apartment?"

"All three television stations sent vans, both the *Tribune* and the *Times* are asking for interviews. My roommates can't even get out of our driveway. My phone just keeps ringing. I can barely make an outgoing call."

"How did the press find out so fast?"

"I have no idea."

Knowing Dana needed to do damage control, Mandy quickly ended the conversation and interrupted Dana's call to her husband. "Word's out. The press is camped on Lisa's doorstep."

Dana groaned, her lips tightened in annoyance. "Sam, I have to go. Love you." She turned to Mandy, her brows knitted. "I'll make security arrangements."

"What for?"

"We'll all need professional help to control the media frenzy."

"We should be fine—at least until we go home."

"A secret this big won't keep." Dana flipped open her phone. "I want to try Zack one more time."

Mandy didn't protest. Zack hadn't answered the phone in weeks. Maybe her luck would hold. Dana speed-dialed and picked up her glass. "Let's make a toast."

"To luck?"

They clinked glasses. "To luck."

With her phone still to her ear, Dana brought her glass toward her lips, then halted and broke into a delighted grin. "Zack? Is that really you?"

Mandy's stomach dropped. She had always known she couldn't avoid Zack forever, but just like winning the lottery, knowing Zack was on the other end and the moment of truth might be at hand didn't seem real. Life suddenly seemed out of whack, turned upside down from normal. Her luck seemed to be swinging on a pendulum—from very, very bad to very, very good to very, very uncertain.

Chapter Six

OVER THE PHONE, Zack pretended a lightness he hadn't felt in a long time. He loved his work but he missed his family and the unexpected call from Dana was a welcome distraction. He spun on his barstool to gain a little privacy, snagged a bottle of whiskey from the bartender, and poured another shot. "So how's my favorite sister?"

"I'm your *only* sister."

Dana's slight southern drawl reminded Zack of Florida—brilliant sunlight, violent thunderstorms, summer lightning, hot nights, and . . . Mandy Newman. One reason he hadn't returned Dana's phone calls was because he couldn't seem to talk to his sister without images of her best friend showing up in his dreams—which was odd because Dana had never brought up Mandy's name during one of their rare calls.

As time passed, he should have forgotten Mandy. But it didn't happen. During the day he could put her out of his mind. But at night, images of Mandy's body moving over him, her long legs wrapped around his hips, seeped through the mental barriers he erected during the day. He wished he could forget how good they'd been together that long-ago night. But he hadn't.

So he sipped his whiskey and pretended to his sister and himself that the amazing night with Mandy had never happened—pretended that he and Mandy hadn't connected beyond a good time in the sack, or against the wall, or in the shower. Pretended they hadn't been . . . insatiable.

Pretended that he hadn't suppressed his sexual urges and that he had a normal sex life. He had only himself to blame. When he went undercover, he was in full survival mode. Even casual hookups could lead to deadly complications.

Zack downed his shot of whiskey and cleared his throat. "So you're in L.A.?"

"When I left you those messages, I thought we'd get together, see what you look like."

Zack winced and checked his reflection in the mirror behind the bar. He looked a hell of a lot better than four weeks ago, but the fading yellow bruises could still be seen, as could the scar on his forehead that had required ten stitches. He didn't relish the idea of his sister telling their mom what her son looked like.

When he didn't respond, Dana changed the subject. "So can you break from the case?"

"We wrapped up last month. I'm waiting for . . . reassignment." That wasn't exactly a lie, but not quite the truth, either. He needed to be cleared first.

"That's perfect," Dana continued, "I could use your help."

"Uh-huh."

Dana's tone changed from sister mode to confidential and businesslike. "I need you, Zack."

Dana needed him? "What's wrong?" Zack stood up from his bar stool so fast a bit of dizziness overtook him, a lingering side effect of his fight.

"Apparently, I've won the Powerball jackpot."

Zack whistled and moved slowly until he leaned against the bar. "Good looks, brains, and fabulous luck, too. Now you can afford to do all the pro bono work you've always—"

"Listen, Zack. I need you to run interference with the press until we go home on Sunday."

We? He stared into the bottom of his empty shot glass, thinking hard. "Who is *we* and why do you need protection from the press?"

She ignored his questions. "When they find us, they're going to descend like locusts."

"No kidding." The press could be annoying but surely his sister could handle them.

"And we're practically in your backyard. We're leaving the day after tomorrow so you could use your magnificent agent skills to keep the press away."

"I don't work between assignments anymore." Besides, he was far from normal, never mind *magnificent*. These days he'd recovered enough to walk mostly without pain, but he still barely felt fit for work. He also knew his sister well enough to realize that she hadn't told him *who* she was with because she realized if she did, he'd say no. That meant she'd brought along either her husband Sam, or Mandy. He'd never liked Sam but had tried to hide his dislike from Dana. Contrarily, Zack had liked Mandy too much. But since an undercover agent's work could put him out of touch for months, even years, there was no point in renewing their . . . acquaintance.

"I don't know anyone else out here I trust." Dana knew exactly which of his buttons to press.

He shifted from foot to foot, torn between staying down for another drink or doing as Dana asked. He would like to see her.

"Come on, Zack. What's the big deal? Mandy and I need you."

Damn it. It *was* Mandy.

"Someone did try to kill her last week."

"What?" Someone was trying to kill sweet Mandy? In spite of himself he tossed bills on the bar and headed toward the exit. "What are you talking about?"

"Meet us at the Park Hyatt at ten and we'll tell you all about it."

Leave it to his sister to make him forget his depression for the first time in weeks. When she hung up on him, Zack swore again. Then he laughed. He was going to see Mandy and he was actually looking forward to it.

ZACK ARRIVED AT their hotel before Mandy and Dana and had staked out a quiet corner in the bar with his back to the wall and a view of the entrance. He ordered whiskey but didn't touch his glass, preferring to contemplate . . . possibilities. Since he and Mandy had hooked up, he'd avoided asking Dana questions about Mandy during his infrequent phone calls to his sister, and she'd volunteered no details. None. In fact, he couldn't recall Dana ever once mentioning Mandy's name. Now that he thought about her omission, it was strange. The two women were best friends. They'd met in law school and worked in the same law firm. They'd won the lottery together, had come out to L.A. together. They obviously were still tight.

Zack concluded that either Mandy had married or that she'd specifically asked Dana not to mention her. But that would mean Mandy had told Dana about their night together. Yet the morning he'd left, Mandy said she had no intention of telling Dana what had happened. So unless Dana had guessed the truth, either Mandy had changed her mind and spoken to Dana about them . . . or she was married.

He'd bet on married and he checked his anticipation in order to lessen his disappointment. What man wouldn't be attracted to Mandy? Especially if they knew what kind of passion lurked behind her lawyer facade?

The first time Zack had met Mandy, during the Christmas holidays while she and Dana were in law school, she'd seemed sensible, practical, down to earth. She worked hard, her discipline impressive. Her attention to detail, her schedules had tempted him into teasing her, but his impression of her didn't change until that magical night when Mandy had thrown aside her day planner and he'd learned that she really knew how to let loose.

He recalled the last time he'd seen her, naked and tangled in the sheets, her hair tousled, her lips swollen from his kisses, and his groin tingled. Damn. If just the memory of her could get to him, what would seeing her again, protecting her again, do to him?

It's only for the weekend. He'd only come because Dana had said someone had tried to kill her.

And since when had he started lying to himself?

He wanted to see Mandy. To him she represented sexy goodness. Life. Happiness. Of course he'd probably put her on a pedestal in his thoughts because during his darkest hours, he needed to remember that the entire world wasn't full of greed, betrayal, and death.

Mandy was one of the good people and he'd treated her badly. He hadn't even called to say goodbye . . . but the DEA had immediately sent him undercover. Six months later when he'd finally been free to sneak a few discreet personal phone calls, he'd figured it was too late to repair the damage. He'd only stir up lingering feelings that should be left to die a natural death.

Zack heard the click of heels on the marble floor of the hotel foyer. His gaze took in Dana, but he concentrated on Mandy. Eyes sparkling, laughing at something Dana had just said, she walked with a confident feminine sway that made his mouth water. His gaze automatically targeted her left hand. No wedding band. The constriction around his chest eased slightly.

Some women didn't wear their wedding rings.

For all he knew Mandy might be allergic to precious metals, but nevertheless his anticipation rose. Zack stood and hugged Dana. He turned to Mandy to find that the smile had left her eyes. She regarded him with a vibrant expression he couldn't read but that nevertheless rippled under his skin and piqued his interest.

"Hi, Zack." Mandy offered him an impersonal hand shake, stunning him with such a cool reception. But that didn't stop his zing at seeing her again.

"Hi, yourself." Amazed at his thrill at being near her, he

took her hand, leaned forward and inhaled her spicy scent.
And planted a kiss on her mouth.

She stared at him, her pupils dilated. She snatched back
her hand quickly—too quickly for him to believe she remained as unaffected by his presence as she appeared. Was
she irritated that he seemed to have forgotten about her for
two years and then blasted back into her life as if no time
had passed, all the old sexual dynamite ready to explode?

Dana's eyes narrowed and she punched Zack in the arm.
"Behave." His sister filled the silence with chitchat about his
damaged face, giving him a moment to assess Mandy's reaction. He'd rocked her with his little peck on the lips, but
she'd quickly recovered, her face once again a neutral mask.

Good move, dude.

Dana reached up to touch his face. "Look at you."

Her lips tightened, telling him that she knew something
was wrong. She might not know what, but with that special
sense between siblings, she knew he'd been struggling.

"What happened?" Dana asked.

He brushed her hand away. "Nothing."

Zack could see Mandy shift her gaze between them and
the look in her eye softened, reminded him of when she'd
gazed up at him in the dark.

He pulled out the chair next to him for Dana. Mandy took
the seat opposite, as far away from him as she could get. But
now, he could see her watching him, taking his measure. She
was curious about him. She couldn't have missed his sister's
concern, but there was something more, too. Something he
couldn't put his finger on. If possible she was even lovelier
than in his memory. She still had the same smooth skin that
he could skim his fingers over for hours, the same exotic
cheekbones in a face both strong and feminine, the same
nose, straight, short and charming. Two years hadn't
changed her much. Except for that look in her eyes . . . wariness maybe?

He tossed back his drink, appreciating the burn. "So
who's trying to kill you?"

"Dana's exaggerating." Mandy's slight southern drawl

came out smoky and careful, like someone who'd drunk a bit too much and was now overly conscientious about enunciating clearly.

Dana had no such difficulty, but kept her voice down low, so the other customers couldn't hear. "Someone followed her from her parking garage, rammed her car, not once, not twice, but three times, until she went over the lip of the Harbour Island Bridge." Dana motioned over a waitress. "Mandy ended up in the river and it's a miracle she survived. The cops found her attacker's truck later. It had been stolen and wiped clean of prints. The police are clueless. There were no cameras at the parking garage."

Shocked, Zack stared at Mandy, feeling a wave of emotion, a lot more potent than he should have felt. She could have died. He could only imagine that she must have been terrified, and hearing Dana retell the incident couldn't have been pleasant. Yet, she had her emotions reined in tight. He wished he could do the same. At the idea of someone sending her car off a bridge, he clenched his teeth so hard, his jaw ached.

They ordered drinks. Mandy picked up a napkin and began to fold the edges. Keeping her eyes on the napkin as if it was the most fascinating object in the world, she avoided Zack's gaze.

"Did you get a look at the driver?" Zack asked.

"Yes." Unlike his sister, Mandy didn't elaborate.

"You recognize him?"

"No."

Zack frowned. "Do you think the attack had anything to do with winning the lottery?"

"No." Mandy sounded certain, looked up and met his eyes. Zack, the so-called expert on reading people, hadn't a clue what she was thinking. But he clearly recalled looking straight into those eyes as he'd entered her body—and all the blood in his veins went south.

Dana kept the conversation on track. "The winning numbers were announced tonight. Her attack happened on Tuesday."

"It was probably just a random thing." Mandy shrugged, the movement rippling down her blouse, and despite his best efforts not to look, drawing his glance to the swell of her breasts, causing his jeans to suddenly seem too tight. Mandy had noted the direction of his gaze and sucked in her breath, flushing, but managed to speak in a calm tone. "You know how Dana is . . . she worries about everyone."

Dana sipped her drink, seemingly oblivious to the undercurrent between Mandy and him. "You know, I'm sitting right here. I heard what you said about me."

"Has the guy who attacked you shown up again . . . since the accident?" Zack asked, suspecting not even an icy shower was going to cure his hard-on.

Mandy shook her head. "He was very likely just some nutcase who won't come back."

Dana clearly disagreed. "Most likely he's connected to work. I wanted to hire a bodyguard, but Mandy didn't. And now that we've won—"

"You're using the press that hasn't shown up as an excuse to get what you want," Mandy accused, but the twitch of a smile took the sting from her words.

Dana narrowed her gaze. "It makes you a target all over again."

"You're just as much a target as I am."

"But I'm not the one walking around with the ticket in my purse."

Zack frowned, glaring at two businessmen who approached the table beside them. They got his message, choosing a spot farther away. "You have the ticket *with* you?"

Automatically, he assessed the suits at the bar, the couple making out in a booth and the single lady eyeing the suits, perhaps a high-class hooker, and dismissed them as potential threats. Always careful, he reminded himself to remain on guard. He'd seen a man's throat slit for less than a C-note. Lost a partner in the space of a breath. For big bucks, even a solid citizen might turn violent. At least with his mind on danger, the bulge in his crotch had lessened.

"I just found out tonight that we won." Mandy looked at Dana. "Should we put it in the hotel safe?"

Zack didn't wait for Dana to answer. "You trust a hotel manager not to steal it?"

Mandy smiled, whipped the ticket out of her purse and shoved it over to him, clearly pleased with herself. "Here, you keep it for us. Then we can go back to enjoying ourselves."

With a cynical chuckle, Zack pushed the ticket back across the table. "Giving it to me won't keep you safe. If a thief targets you, they might shoot first and search for the ticket after you're hit."

"Oops." She plucked the ticket from the table and placed it carefully inside her wallet. "I guess the bubbly we had to celebrate has gone to my head."

Dana's phone rang and they heard her side of the conversation. "Lisa, keep trying to call Maria, okay?"

Zack listened to his sister as Mandy ripped pieces off her cocktail napkin and rolled them into tiny paper balls, once more refusing to look at him. Dana continued, "All right, try to reach her again in the morning."

Dana hung up. "Maria still hasn't answered her phone. Lisa says she's on a hot date."

"Lucky girl." Zack looked directly at Mandy, willing her to raise her eyes, hoping she'd pick up the edge in his voice that said she too could get lucky if she so desired.

Mandy speared Zack with a look, surprising him with her sudden ferocity. Her tone held an edge. "So you going to stick around for more than a few hours?"

Zack kept his gaze locked on her, unwilling to let her go so easily, not when their attraction brought his senses to life. "Why not? I haven't been in such beautiful company in at least two years."

"Zack, take a look in the mirror. No woman in her right mind would want you right now." Dana rolled her eyes at the ceiling. "Mandy and I are sharing a suite. You get the sofa bed."

"Ouch." Zack frowned. And hoped that Mandy wasn't in her right mind.

"EXCUSE ME A minute." Dana pulled back from their table at the hotel bar and headed for the ladies' room, leaving Mandy alone with Zack. For a moment, she wanted to bolt and follow Dana, but she refused to take the coward's way out.

She assessed Zack instead. The father of her child. A privilege he hadn't wanted or earned. He was a charming flirt, but was he capable of being a decent father? Mandy honestly didn't know. But she didn't have many choices. She would have to tell him about their daughter. Her only choice was to pick the right time.

That's what she'd told herself ever since she'd learned she was pregnant. But now that the moment of truth was at hand, how did she determine if this was the right moment? Zack was flirting with her, for goodness' sake. He'd left town without so much as a goodbye and never looked back. Now here he was trying to charm her, as if he had every right to walk back into her life and make the most of their two days together.

What about his life? One look at his once-handsome face told her he was entrenched in his undercover work as deeply as ever. And what was Dana so worried about? Mandy knew her friend well enough to know that something was up with Zack, something that had Dana worried, something she hadn't shared.

Could Mandy really drop a bomb into his lap that would change his whole life in the few minutes they had alone while Dana was in the restroom? *No*. Not while she wasn't sure what was going on with Zack, or what was happening with the attack on her, or in the uproar of the lottery win. No, she needed time to learn what was up with Zack, to decide when would be the right time to change his life forever.

"Miss me?" Zack asked, then tossed down his drink as if he required reinforcement to hear her reply.

Yes. "No." Talk about loaded questions.

"I've missed you," he admitted, the yearning in his voice

plain to hear. But Zack had a reputation as a ladies' man. He flirted as easily as he breathed. He only let her see what he wanted her to see. She had no idea if he intended to pick up where they left off or was killing time while they waited for Dana, or felt obligated to try and make up for the callous way he'd dumped her when he'd left two years ago.

"So what exactly did you miss, Zack?" She donned her best courtroom expression, wishing he wasn't so easy on the eyes. He wasn't knock-your-socks-off handsome. Zack was too hard around the edges for that. The bruises, cuts, and scars only added to the effect. His cheekbones were too sharp, his jaw too jaunty for a pretty-boy look. Still, the five o'clock shadow and the mussed hair gave him that bedroom aura that reminded her of his sultry kisses and slow hands.

Mmm. Zack was good at everything, but he was especially fantastic at kissing. Some guys applied so much pressure that their mouths felt like an invasion. Some were so tentative that she'd wondered why they'd bothered. But Zack had a knack for kissing her just the way she liked. Best of all, he took his time.

And when he finally got to lovemaking, he'd made it the most incredibly sensual experience of her life. Sometimes she thought that she was remembering incorrectly—that it couldn't possibly have been so awesome. But then the details would flood back. The way he caressed her earlobe had driven her wild. The man had sensuous moves that should have been banned. While their night together couldn't have possibly been so perfect and her memory must have exaggerated the details, she couldn't deny her attraction to him.

Because the sexiest thing about Zack was when he focused all his intensity on her—just like he was doing right now.

One corner of his mouth turned up in a crooked grin. "I missed the way you manage to sound skeptical, yet interested."

She snorted. "I was interested once, but I don't repeat my mistakes."

"Why was I a mistake?"

Duh? Because he'd walked out and hadn't called in two

years? She refused to say the words out loud and let him know that she'd even cared.

She shrugged a shoulder to try and cover her slip. She needed to assess this man, figure out the best approach to take, not rehash the past. Not when her child's future happiness hung in the balance. "You weren't what I was looking for."

He folded his arms across his chest. "In what sense?"

"It just didn't work for me." She hoped he'd let the subject drop.

He cocked his head and his eyes sparkled. "I didn't satisfy you?"

Of course he had. She'd be damned if she would give him compliments—especially when she wanted to smack him upside the head just for asking that question. He was talking about sex, albeit incredible sex, but she had more important things on her mind.

Luckily for her, she didn't have to reply because Dana returned and slipped into her seat. She looked from Zack to Mandy, her tone light. "Did I miss anything?"

Chapter Seven

MARIA GARCIA HADN'T wanted any interruptions tonight, especially after the package Ray Starker had sent. The dude liked to dress his woman for their dates; and that his tastes ran to trashy only enticed her more. She'd opened the box in her bedroom and tried on the sexy clothes, ignoring the statue of *La Virgen de la Caridad del Cobre,* the patron saint of Cuba. The silver lamé top draped between her breasts. She hadn't worn anything this shiny since the tiara at her *quince,* her fifteenth birthday party. A matching flirty skirt hugged her hips two inches below her navel and flared to tease her thighs, plus the three-inch spiked sandals showed off her dark red toenails. The clothes had encouraged her to use exotic makeup that she'd never wear to work. Ray had also left instructions in his bold handwriting. *No panties. No perfume. No jewelry.*

She would feel naked without her gold chains and bracelets, never mind going commando as Ray had instructed. Without panties or bra, feeling positively wanton in the clothes, she shivered in anticipation.

They'd often played games where she told him no, and

one of the reasons she found him so compelling was that he
ignored her fake protests. He understood that she liked him
taking charge. He understood she enjoyed his domination.
But suppose she had really wanted him to stop? Would he
have backed off?

She didn't know.

Her uncertainty scared her, even as it turned her on, en-
snaring her in the dark sensuality she desired. They'd
hooked up several months ago. Each encounter had become
riskier, more intense until she craved him like no other.
When had he begun to make ordinary guys seem weak and
boring? When had she become addicted to his games?

It didn't matter.

If Ray came to her apartment and saw her dressed like
this, he'd know exactly what she wanted from him and
they'd never make the movie. She stared at the movie ticket.
She didn't want to go alone per his instructions. On opening
night, the line at the theater would be long. Men would stare
at her bare legs and the skimpy top, hoping she'd fall out and
give them an eyeful. Despite her irritation that she had no
idea when Ray would show, leaving her apartment and hitting the street dressed like he'd demanded excited her.

The notion of stepping into the public eye dressed this
scandalously heated her with so much anticipation, moisture
dewed between her thighs. She'd dated lots of men—but Ray
understood that although she longed for hot and wild, she
didn't permit herself to go there unless he pushed her into it.

Before she lost her nerve, Maria picked up her keys,
turned off the cell phone, and headed out the door. Ray always gave her exactly what she wanted—even if she
wouldn't admit it, not even to herself. He took control and
she reveled in every moment of playing the bad girl.

She'd spent her first thirty years making her parents
proud, finishing college at the top of her class, going to law
school, making junior partner at a prestigious firm, being the
dutiful daughter. Now, it was her turn to do exactly what she
wanted . . . or in this case what Ray wanted.

Unaccustomed to going without a bra, Maria was all too

aware of the bounce of her breasts as she stepped to the roadside curb in her heels. The cul-de-sac in front of her apartment was empty at this time of evening. Palm trees rustled in the breeze and the air smelled ripe with fresh mown grass. She was so ready to slip into her car, feel her skirt ride up her thighs, and let the leather kiss her bare legs. If only Ray were sitting beside her, watching her struggle to tamp down her excitement.

Maria used her remote to unlock the driver's door. Before she reached for the handle, someone stepped from behind the bushes and nestled his groin against her butt. She gasped and familiar sandalwood cologne wafted into her lungs.

"Ray?"

He closed his hands over her shoulders and nipped her neck, preventing her from turning around. A shiver of need raced down her spine. Feeling terribly naughty, she leaned into his kiss.

"Not here, Ray, the neighbors might see." At 9 P.M. the sun had set but it was at least fifteen minutes from true dark.

Just like always, he ignored her protest. Just like always, he pushed her a bit farther than their last "date." Keeping her trapped between his large body and her Lexus, still nibbling her neck, he placed his hands on the bare skin of her waist and lightly skimmed his fingers over her tummy.

His tone was rough, demanding. "Did you follow my instructions, *querida*?"

"Yes, Ray." He smelled so good, of sandalwood cologne and breath mint. She wanted to turn around, kiss him on the mouth, press her body full length against him.

"You followed *all* of my instructions?"

"*Sí*."

"You want me already, don't you, *niña*?"

Carajo, she did. Her heart pounded, blood rushed to her face. "Yes." She tilted her head back, allowing him full access to her throat.

He snuggled his hips against her, allowed her to feel his erection against her bottom. "It turns me on, knowing you are bare under that skirt."

"Good." She purred, knowing tonight was going to be so, so hot.

"Show me how much you want me."

At his demand, she squirmed with need, but the rational part of her said no. "Let's go inside."

He ignored her suggestion. "I brought you a special neck-lace." In the dark, he placed what felt like a three-inch-wide piece of leather around her neck.

"Now lace your fingers behind your head so I can attach your bracelets."

He'd never given her jewelry before. But she sensed that this wasn't ordinary. The choker around her neck constricted without being uncomfortable, but was a constant reminder of his possessive tendencies. Trembling, she did as he asked. He snapped more leather on her wrists, then attached her wrists to her neck collar.

She tugged, twisted. The straps held her firm. "Ray, I'm not sure . . ." He'd never tied her before. "Maybe this isn't a good . . ."

"You'd like the air to kiss your bare skin, wouldn't you? Would you like me to lift up your top?"

Madre mía . . . the idea set her pulse racing. She wanted Ray to bare her and with her hands tied, even if she wanted him to stop, he could do whatever he wanted. Shaking with lust at her helplessness, more dampness creamed between her thighs. Panting, trying hard to keep her hips from grinding against him, she bit her lip to keep from moaning.

His voice, rough in her ear, rasped. "Answer me, *dulce*."

It was almost dark, but was it dark enough? She told herself that if anyone glanced outside, they would see a man kissing a woman's neck—nothing more. If they looked real close, they would see the silhouette of her breasts straining for his touch.

He nipped her shoulder and desire pulsed.

She could only stand there and tremble, knowing she wanted him to follow through more badly than she'd wanted anything in her life . . . but unwilling to admit it. She should protest. The sane part of her said no, but the part that belonged to Ray said yes, yes, yes.

He waited and tension sizzled.

Her mouth went dry but she finally agreed. "Do it."

"*Querida,* have you forgotten the neighbors?"

Caramba, she didn't care.

Ray chuckled softly in her ear and raised his hand another inch beneath her blouse, his movement causing the material to rasp over her nipples. "Look over there. Is that the accountant staring at you?"

"What?" Adrenaline shot through her and Maria jerked her head toward the neighbor's apartment, frantically searching the upstairs and downstairs windows. She didn't see anyone watching.

Ray was toying with her and, nervous but even more aroused, she licked her lip. "No blinds moved. No one's watching."

"Maybe. Maybe not. A neighbor could drive up at any moment."

At his comment, her gut tightened. Beneath her feet, the pavement released the warmth of the day. As he raised her top until the material bunched under her arms and fully exposed her breasts to the night air, she flushed with heat. At the sheer decadence, she could no longer hold back a soft moan.

"Take me inside to my apartment. Please."

For his answer, he cupped one breast and tweaked the nipple hard.

"Ouch. That stings."

"You aren't into pain?" He pinched the other nipple.

"Ow. Ow. Ow." Even as she protested, heat blazed between her legs. She rose onto her toes, tipping her butt up to him, wanting him inside her, needing him to fill her. Oddly, despite the pain, she really, really wanted him to pinch her nipples again.

"Take what I give you. Already the sting is fading, but your lust grows. Tell me I'm right."

"*Sí.*"

"That's right, *cariña.* You're hotter now. Helpless and hot—and ready for me to bare your sweet ass."

"Don't make me wait."

"You like me calling the shots. I only give you what you want. Isn't that right?"

He placed his hands on her waist, lifted her, and for a moment she thought he was taking her inside and disappointment flooded her. He couldn't stop now. How dare he stop after he'd pushed this far.

She should have known better. Ray repositioned her, bending her over the hood of her car until her bare breasts and tummy pressed against cool metal. Then he raised her skirt.

She gulped, imagining how she looked to him. With her heels raising her ass in the air, her body bent over the car, he could see . . . everything.

"You have a lovely ass, *mi pequeña*." He stroked her gently, his touch a promise of so much more. "Perhaps I should leave you here and see who finds you." He stepped away.

"Son of a bitch. Don't you dare leave me here." She thrashed in an effort to stand upright.

With a throaty chuckle, he placed a hand on the small of her back. "Such impatience." When she heard his zipper, she realized he'd been toying with her again. He was going to give her exactly what she craved. What she couldn't ask for. What made her crazy with lust. Ray was going to do her right here in public . . . and he'd taken away her choices.

Any one of her neighbors could look out their windows and see her. Or a car could pull up at any time . . . she'd never felt so naughty. So helpless. So absolutely lusty and feminine.

When his hands closed around her throat, she tensed. He'd never tied her before. Never made love to her in such a public place before. But as his strong fingers closed about the leather necklace, terror flooded her. "What are you doing?"

"Don't worry, *querida*."

He squeezed, cutting off her air.

No. No. No.

She needed air.

And then he rammed his sex into her from behind. Rode

her fast, used her hard. She couldn't breathe. Her lungs burned. He was strangling her. He cut off her air supply, yet there was no pain. Only a rushing sensation as if she'd dived head first out of an airplane. Her stomach turned, flipped.

And he kept pumping into her, choking the air passage. Her vision narrowed into a dark tunnel. She thrashed, bucked her hips. Stars burst in her head, and she climaxed so hard her knees buckled.

She gasped for air, and realized that Ray had finally eased his grip on her throat. Air now filled her lungs and she took in greedy gulps as the last of the orgasm pulsed through her.

Wow. Lack of oxygen had rocketed her sensations off the chart.

Panting, she slumped against the car's hood, reveling in the after-spasms and drawing huge breaths of crisp air into her lungs. Never has she experienced such stunning pleasure . . . or such terror.

"I thought . . . I thought I was going to die."

"And you loved it, *querida*." He laughed low and throaty, caressing her shoulders, kissing her ear.

And after her heart stopped pounding, after he untied her, gently covered her breasts and sensuously lowered her skirt, she once again realized that he'd pushed her farther than she'd intended to go.

Despite her panic, she'd loved every second. *Dios mío*. Ray understood her better than she knew herself. Never would she have thought she would enjoy such madness. The man brought out a darker side of her she hadn't known existed. Her throat ached, her breath came in gasps. Her breasts throbbed.

She could have died.

She shouldn't see Ray again. Not ever. Maria knew it. She just wasn't sure she could resist him.

Chapter Eight

"HOW'S IT FEEL to be rich, Ms. Hansen?" A man holding a
Channel 28 mike stuck it into Dana's face. She swatted it
aside like an annoying mosquito and kept walking through
the terminal.

After landing at Tampa International Airport, Mandy had
hoped she and Dana could avoid zealous reporters as easily
as Zack had dodged them in L.A. But the moment they had
debarked the airside monorail and stepped into the terminal,
a news crew had swarmed around them. She didn't see the
bodyguards Zack had hired anywhere. Instead, photographers pointed their long lenses and snapped rudely while the
airport security paid little attention. In the circus-like atmos-
phere that made them the focus of an increasingly raucous
crowd that impeded their progress, Mandy's unease grew
and her stomach knotted.

She didn't like surprises. She didn't like being stared at as
if she were as rare as an albino gator.

A second reporter placed a delaying hand on Mandy's
shoulder. She shrugged it off and marched beside Dana.

"For them to be interested in us, nothing else important must have happened today. We aren't news. This is insane."

"And not very safe. I'd like to know how they found out which flight we were on." Dana kept her voice down, but Mandy picked up her concern. After Princess Diana's death had caused worldwide headlines, you had to be living in a tomato patch not to know that the press's vigorous pursuit could be dangerous. Mandy had heard reports of the paparazzi driving up on sidewalks to take pictures of celebrities like Jennifer Aniston and Paris Hilton. Although she and Dana weren't stars, their sudden wealth had most definitely placed them in the public eye.

Yikes. Mandy couldn't help but worry that if her picture showed up in the newspaper, that whoever had pushed her off the bridge might recognize her and find her again. *Stop it.* If she kept up that kind of thinking, she'd soon be worrying as much as her mother.

"Mandy!" A reporter called after her as they rushed across the terminal toward the escalators that would take them down two floors to the baggage claim area. At her name, Mandy turned and camera lights flashed. For a moment she couldn't see. If not for Dana's steadying grip, she might have fallen. The photographer moved in for a closer shot. "Smile for me, Mandy. Tell us how you plan to spend your winnings."

She wished she was wearing a hat and dark sunglasses. She even considered opening her travel umbrella and ducking behind it, but in this crowd, that was out of the question. Poking out someone's eye, accident or not, might make front page news. Would certainly cause a messy lawsuit. Instead, she held her closed umbrella in front of her like a weapon, ready to poke anyone who stepped within her space.

"How's it feel to win the lottery?" another reporter asked.

"Will you donate to the church?"

"How about to charity?"

Mandy rolled her eyes. "It's a damn circus." And she and Dana occupied center ring.

With determination they shouldered through the reporters onto the escalator. Narrow handrails forced the group to stop and jostle among themselves for the privilege of riding closest to them.

Dana tugged Mandy's wrist. "Keep moving. When we reach the bottom, bolt for the elevators."

Dana's plan had merit. Other travelers craned their necks and stared, curious to see what was going on. A quick look at the empty carousel revealed that their flight's baggage had yet to begin unloading. The idea of waiting even five minutes for their luggage while the reporters surrounded them and hurled questions had Mandy wincing.

But she hated to go home without her luggage and her presents for Gabby and her mother. "What about our bags?"

"We'll call the airline later and have them delivered." Dana dipped and swayed through the milling travelers, aiming for the bank of elevators. Mandy wondered why airport security didn't care they were being hassled.

Knowing her mother would understand and that Gabby wouldn't know the difference if she had to wait for a gift, Mandy nodded and drew Dana through an opening in the milling crowd. "Come on. Stay with me."

Out of breath, they arrived at the bank of elevators. One set of doors opened and two kids in backpacks hurried out. Mandy and Dana stumbled inside. Mandy slapped the "close door" button before anyone else could follow. She reached to press the button for the fifth floor of the parking garage.

Dana panted, slightly out of breath. "Press them all. If a reporter's watching, he won't know where we got off."

"Good thinking."

After they rose a floor and the elevator stopped and the door opened on the next level, Mandy tensed. She waited to see if reporters would try to join them and kept her hand hovering over the "close door" button. But three harmless-looking blue-haired ladies got on, chatting about the thunderstorm and how their wilting gardenias would perk up in the much-needed shower.

The conversation's normality soothed Mandy's frazzled

nerves. Over the heads and hats of the three diminutive ladies, Dana caught Mandy's eyes and grinned. "You having fun yet?"

Mandy rubbed her neck with obvious weariness. For the last week her life had taken on a chaotic quality she found upsetting. Her usual world, order and predictability, seemed to have shifted into random and scary.

While Dana seemed to be handling the pressure, the weariness in her eyes revealed that she'd had enough excitement, too. Of course, she wasn't also dealing with a potential killer or the effects of one bubbly baby, either.

"I'm looking forward to home and one of Sam's magnificent back rubs," Dana said.

"I'll take four of Gabby's sloppy kisses." The doors swished open on the fifth level, and Mandy peered out. No one seemed the least bit interested in them, and she relaxed. The three ladies got off. No one got on. "I know Gabby's too young to count. But last week every time I picked her up for a hug, she kissed both my cheeks, forehead and chin. That's four kisses every time."

"Maybe your mother taught her the pattern."

"Maybe." Her mother enjoyed showing Gabby new things. She'd already started teaching the baby her primary colors. Now, Mandy could afford to stay home if she wanted and enjoy her daughter's progress, too. All weekend she'd been trying to absorb the differences the Powerball money would make in their lives and figure out where a daddy might fit in. The money had been easier to deal with. No more financial worries—ever. No more making choices between paying off her student loans and saving for Gabby's education. She could even afford to buy her mother a place of her own. Buy a sports car and an SUV if she wanted. Thinking about the money had been *much* easier.

Ironically, Zack himself had made the process a little less painful than it could have been. She'd maintained an outward indifference to him and he'd continued to try to charm her, but except for the first night in the hotel bar, they hadn't spent a moment alone. Dana, too, had helped matters by never once mentioning Gabrielle while in Zack's presence.

But although she and Zack hadn't been alone, Mandy had watched him, listened to his exchanges with Dana. She'd forced herself to use every ounce of her lawyer's objectivity to decide how to best handle the difficult situation.

Two days later, the only thing she was sure of was that Dana was right to be worried about Zack. He hadn't been eating. His collar bones had stuck out in the V of his shirt, and he had worry lines at the corners of his eyes. He'd claimed to be waiting for his bruises and cuts to heal before taking his next dangerous assignment. While that reasoning was certainly plausible, both she and Dana sensed there was more to his story—parts he was unwilling to share. Dana had pushed him to open up, but Zack had met her with stubborn defiance, masked beneath charming smiles and quick wit.

Dana had been disgusted. Mandy had been relieved. Now *wasn't* the right time. Even if she'd wanted to tell him, she'd have had to tie him to a chair to get him to sit still long enough to have a conversation.

No, for the moment, Mandy saw no point in forcing any of them to deal with the upheaval her news would bring. Zack had promised Dana a visit home before he went undercover again. So Mandy would reevaluate when he got to Tampa. Maybe then he'd have resolved whatever was troubling him. Surely, meeting their beautiful daughter in person would take the edge off his shock—Mandy hoped.

The elevator doors swished open again, interrupting her thoughts. This time they were on an upper level of the parking garage. Tires squealed. A horn blared. Outside the parking garage, a lightning storm raged, lighting up the airport and stopping all incoming and outgoing flights. Between the thunderclouds that darkened the sky and the high winds blowing the rain sideways, they'd have a difficult drive home. At least, they'd landed before the storm had shut down the airport and none of the reporters had reappeared.

"Looks like we lost them." Dana reached into her purse for her car keys and cell phone. They'd driven to the airport together and Dana would drop off Mandy. "I'm calling to find out what happened to the bodyguards Zack hired."

Mandy just nodded, shoving away her memory of the incident with the silver pickup truck in the last parking garage
she'd been in. Instead, she willed the warm humidity to calm
her. They'd escaped the reporters. For the first time since
leaving the plane, she breathed in tropical air and confi-
dently stepped from the elevator, purse in one hand, umbrella in the other.

"What do you mean, Zack canceled our protection?" Dana
spoke into the phone. "There must have been a mix-up."

Mandy glanced at her friend to find her scowling.

"You'll be hearing from him. Trust me."

Dana snapped shut the phone, clearly irritated. "I don't
like this at all."

"I'm sure it will be fine once you talk to Zack," Mandy
hoped.

Dana didn't reply as they headed into the open-air garage
that revealed darkening skies. She winced at the rain that
slashed from the south and Tampa Bay, and directed Dana to
steer clear of the garage's sides where rain water blew in and
pooled at the edges.

"The weather's not too bad," Mandy said with forced
cheeriness. "Barring an accident on the interstate, we should
be home for dinner."

"Good, I'm starving."

For Dana a meal probably meant a short drive downtown,
perhaps to *Mise en Place* or Bern's Steak House, but for
Mandy, it meant eating with Gabby.

A clank that echoed behind her broke into her thoughts.

"Did you hear that?" Mandy glanced back over her shoulder. But she saw nothing unusual, merely a couple of senior
citizens rolling their luggage into the elevator.

"I didn't hear anything besides thunder." But Dana picked
up the pace, her heels clicking on the pavement. "What do
you think I should tell Mom about Zack?"

"What do you mean?"

"Did you notice how he changed the subject every time I
asked about his injuries? Damn closemouthed brother of
mine."

"You're worried?"

"Yeah," was all she said. Then added, "Mom will be, too."

Mandy nodded, still uneasy over the noise she couldn't explain. She peered down the row of parked vehicles and clutched her umbrella tighter. Thunder clapped and she jumped, her mouth dry despite the humidity. "Maybe we should go back."

"And face those reporters again?" Dana kept walking, her pace even faster. She'd just reached the rear bumper of her sporty Jag when a black Saturn pulled down their aisle and squealed to a stop, blocking the Jag.

Mandy tensed.

He's just going to roll down his window and ask for directions.

Maybe a reporter had caught up with them.

Or a photographer wanted their picture.

So why was she clenching her travel umbrella? Why were her calves and thighs tensed as if she might be forced to run for her life? Reminding herself that if her picture showed up in tomorrow's newspaper, it wouldn't kill her, she tried to relax.

But the window didn't roll down. Instead, the driver's door opened. A burly, African American man with a dark mustache and beard that didn't quite hide skin-deep acne scars approached. He wore a stained sweatshirt torn at one elbow, gold chains, and dark sunglasses. But it was the weapon in his hand that shot a shiver of terror down Mandy's back—a gun he pointed directly at Dana.

Terror for her friend pumped adrenaline straight into Mandy's veins. Her thoughts raced. The guy had made no effort to hide his face, so if he left them alive they could identify him. Perhaps he hadn't thought ahead. He could be all hyped up on drugs, but his eyes looked clear. Mean. Wild. Dangerous. But clear.

"Hand over your purses."

Oh . . . my . . . God. He meant to rob them.

Dana tossed her bag at his feet. "Don't hurt us."

Mandy had grown up in a rough neighborhood and

wouldn't make it easy for him. Unlatching her purse with trembling fingers, she turned it upside down and threw it, scattering the contents across the pavement. Her wallet flew one way, her lipstick and cell phone the other.

The thief's eyes didn't immediately focus on the twenty dollar bill sticking out of her wallet. He didn't seem to be after cash or jewelry. So this probably wasn't a random robbery.

He was after the lottery ticket.

And if he intended to steal it, he likely wouldn't leave anyone to contest his ownership. Ice shot down her spine and curled into her gut. Fear swelled up her throat.

She had to do something or they would die.

His gaze centered on the scattered contents of her purse and he scowled. She took a chance, slamming her umbrella down on his wrist.

Dana gasped.

The man shrieked and dropped the gun. "Shit, lady. You broke my hand."

With an umbrella? She didn't think so.

His injury didn't prevent him from yanking the umbrella from her grip and tossing it aside, where it snapped open and then refolded. She'd lost her weapon. And she hadn't hurt him enough to keep them safe.

Cradling his wrist, he picked up the gun and lunged at Dana as if she wore a red cape and he were a charging bull. Dana shifted to one side, ran out of room, and slammed into a neighboring car.

Mandy stuck out her foot to trip him, but he kicked her leg out from under her. She fell hard, banging her shoulder on the Jaguar. The coppery tang of blood filled her mouth.

Dazed from the pain, she teetered to her feet, determined to help Dana, who was nursing her arm and had retreated until her back was against the bumper of the next vehicle. Dana's voice turned fierce. "Take it all and leave us the hell alone."

The guy grabbed Dana by the hair, jammed the gun into her side while issuing orders to Mandy. "Gather all your crap into the bag."

The guy shook Dana with his good hand and yelled into her face. "What do you have to say now, bitch?"

"Do as he says, please." Face white, Dana spoke through gritted teeth.

Mandy fought down nausea. Behind Dana, her attacker glowered and Mandy tried to memorize his features. Brown eyes. Corn rows. Shaggy beard. Thick nose. Acne scars. Medium height and weight, in baggy jeans and tennis shoes, he looked strong, but average—until she caught his wild gaze that seemed to lack pity and any shred of humanity.

"Hurry." He glared, his eyes cruel, mouth spraying spittle.

Mandy groped for her phone, keys, and lipstick. Her wallet had flown open. Wind picked up the bills and blew them everywhere. She found a twenty smashed against a tire. A ten stuck under her umbrella handle. She grabbed the bills in shaking hands, but didn't spot the ticket on the ground with her cash. She'd been careful to tuck the winning ticket deep into her wallet, so it was likely still there. The ticket didn't matter. Their safety did.

Gathering the wallet with the rest of her things, Mandy placed them all into her purse. If she gave him what he wanted, would he let them go? Or would he shoot them because she'd fought back? Mandy wanted to resist, but how? What would Zack do if he were here?

Beat the guy to a pulp?

She didn't know karate.

Sweet-talk him?

Her mouth was so dry with fear, she couldn't speak. Couldn't think.

Just as she placed the last twenty into her bag, the elevator doors opened and reporters spilled out. At the sight of the press, their attacker snatched the purse from Mandy and shoved Dana against a column. Her head smacked the concrete with a sickening whack.

Then he rushed past, jumped into his car and burned rubber. Mandy didn't try to stop him. Instead she lunged and caught Dana, breaking her fall to the pavement.

God. She looked bad. Blood trickled from her mouth. Her face had lost all color. Had he snapped her neck?

Mandy eased Dana down to the concrete and cradled her head in her lap, slightly reassured by the rapid pulse at her throat. Gingerly, she smoothed back Dana's hair and her hand came away sticky with blood.

"Dana. Talk to me. Please." Dana looked too white, so pale and fragile.

"What happened?" A reporter stuck a mike in her face. Others gathered around. Photographers snapped more pictures.

Mandy's first thought was to slap away the mike. But she wanted whoever had done this to Dana to be caught and punished. Furious, thoughts whirring, she vowed to use the press, but first, Dana needed medical attention.

To her own ears, her voice sounded more like a plea than an ultimatum. "Call 911 and I'll answer your questions."

"I already did. And I called airport security, too," one handsome African American reporter said, proof that some in his occupation had human instincts. He even handed Mandy a clean handkerchief.

"Thanks." She dabbed the blood from Dana's eyes. Her eyelids fluttered.

Mandy bent over her, hope rising that she would recover with no side effects. "Talk to me, Dana. Can you hear me? Open your eyes and tell me you're all right."

Dana blinked, opened her eyes and spoke, her voice weak. "My head hurts."

"You hit your head. But you'll be okay," Mandy tried to reassure her. But she didn't like the way Dana looked. Fuzzy and confused.

"Were we in a car accident?" Dana asked.

"We were attacked. You bumped your head." *Please don't let her have amnesia.* They'd been through enough lately. The idea of seeing Dana so helpless made Mandy determined to protect her. Dana tried to sit up. Mandy shook her head and held her down. "Don't move—not until the ambulance arrives."

Dana frowned. "I don't remember—"

"Who am I?" Mandy asked.

"Sandra Day O'Connor."

"Very funny."

"You're Mandy. I'm Dana. That much I know."

Relieved that Dana seemed mostly okay, Mandy held Dana's confused gaze. "What's the last thing you do remember?"

"Running from the reporters. Exiting the elevator. The storm. Then . . . nothing."

More relief washed over Mandy. She'd heard that after car accidents, people with head injuries often couldn't recall the incident. If that was all that was wrong with Dana, then she was lucky. Their assailant could have shot her. He could have shot both of them. If the reporters hadn't been following them . . . she and Dana might be dead right now.

Mandy started to shake. Last week a truck had rammed her off the bridge. This week a different attacker seemed to have staked out the airport and waited for them. Maybe he'd even known the Jag was Dana's car. Although they'd been robbed and Dana was injured, the thief hadn't once mentioned the lottery ticket. Surely it couldn't be a coincidence that he'd chosen to attack them? That he'd picked them at random?

No way. Why hadn't he demanded they hand over the ticket if that's what he'd been after? What the hell was going on?

Would the man have shot them if the reporters hadn't arrived? Was this attacker connected to the man in the silver pickup truck or had he simply wanted to steal the lottery ticket? Were the two incidents unrelated? Mandy couldn't seem to put any pieces together—except that she'd been attacked twice, and both attacks had been connected to a parking garage. But it appeared that someone wanted to hurt her and she didn't know if she'd be safe until she found out who was after her.

As the reporters asked questions of their own, she realized no one had gotten a license plate number. With her short-term memory loss, Dana couldn't even give a description of the attacker or his vehicle.

But the attacker now had their cell phones, their credit cards, driver's licenses, and home addresses. Damn, he had her keys. He could get into her condo.

She had to call her mother. Change the condo locks. She hoped she could find a locksmith who was willing to work this late.

And money was once again a factor. Because the lottery ticket and her purse were gone.

Frustration and anger and fear welled. Although she tried to dial down the surging emotions, the facts were overwhelming her. Someone wanted her dead.

And they'd just lost 360 million dollars.

Chapter Nine

MANDY WOKE UP with a bad taste in her mouth and her head on a hard . . . leg? She scrambled to a sitting position and took her bearings. A television announced the morning news would come on soon. The weather was sunny. Life went on. Mandy was still in the hospital waiting room, where she must have fallen asleep. Only she'd been alone then, with the chairs empty, the frayed magazines and the sofa all to herself. Now she was no longer alone.

She blinked the sleep out of her eyes, the fuzz from her brain. "Zack?"

He captured her gaze in his. "After someone canceled the protection I'd arranged to meet you and Dana at the airport, Mom called me and I caught the red-eye."

Her stomach knotted. Zack was here. In Tampa. He'd made the trip he'd promised, sooner than she'd expected. Probably sooner than he'd expected, too. She wondered what he thought about that. With his tousled hair and circles under his eyes, he looked as if he hadn't slept on the plane, but he was still sexier than any man she'd ever met and her pulse ratcheted up a notch. As adrenaline rushed inside her, twisting her emotions into knots, she remembered . . . Dana.

It all flashed back at once. The attack at the airport, the stolen ticket. The reporters. Dana's ambulance ride to the hospital.

Oh . . . God. In the emergency room, Dana had seemed okay, but the doctors had taken her for more tests and had said head injuries were tricky. "Is Dana—"

"She'll be fine." Zack was quick to reassure her in a gentle voice that was rough around the edges. "Catherine and Sam are with her now." He handed Mandy a cup of lukewarm coffee. Their fingers touched and she noted the ridges in his nails, their shape so similar to Gabby's. Damn. Zack was in town—in the same state as Gabby. She chugged the coffee, needing the caffeine kick to engage her brain. More importantly, she required time to pull herself together.

Last night after the attack at the airport, after Mandy had spoken to the police, Catherine had heard that their attacker was now in possession of their driver's licenses and keys. She'd insisted that her mother and Gabby remain at her beach house in Clearwater on the Gulf of Mexico, where they'd be safe. Grateful, Mandy had explained to her mother the necessity of remaining out of town while Mandy stayed near Dana at Tampa General Hospital.

As it sunk into her sluggish mind that Zack wasn't likely to accidentally run into her mother and daughter, Mandy found the courage to question him. "How long are you here for?"

He raised one sexy eyebrow. "I'm staying as long as you need me."

That was what she expected. She'd thought she'd have a little time before he came to Tampa, enough time to figure out if and when she should come clean.

Turning from him to the coffee, she poured a hot refill from the pot and did her best to ignore the donuts. She couldn't afford the sugar in her system to mess with her already raw emotions.

Zack might be pure temptation but her reaction had to be

better managed than the last time he'd been here. Life was far, far more complicated now.

Mandy chose her words carefully. "Dana and your mother will be glad you're here."

Zack came up behind her, so close she could feel his heat. He leaned into her and spoke, his voice husky. "And what about you? Are you glad I'm here?"

She spun around so fast, the coffee spilled over the cup, a few drops burning her hand. "Don't toy with me, Zack."

"You could have been hurt last night." He picked up a napkin to dab at the coffee.

She snatched the paper from his hand and mopped it up herself. Damn. Why couldn't she pretend he didn't matter? For Gabby's sake, she had to get herself together.

"Last night was scary," she admitted. "I tried to help Dana but couldn't do more than hold her until the ambulance came. Now she's lying in a hospital bed."

"It's not your fault."

"Maybe it is. Maybe that man was after me and Dana only got hurt because she happened to be with me. I've been attacked twice this week." She fisted her fingers, then forced them open. "I want to find out what's going on."

"I will, and I'm not letting you out of my sight until it's safe to do so," he stated with an infuriating take-control attitude.

"And I'm quite certain that your mother asked you to come out here to help *her* and *Dana*," she countered, drilling him with her best fierce expression, "not me."

"You didn't used to be so independent."

"You didn't used to be so bossy." She drew in a deep breath, trying for calm, and released the air slowly. She wasn't being reasonable, and she knew it. She really wasn't ready to deal with him again. "I thought you were a professional. Act like one. Your family needs you."

Zack didn't flinch at her accusation. He didn't raise his voice. He simply stared at her as if trying to understand why she was annoyed. Obviously he wasn't buying her Your-family-needs-you-so-I-don't-want-you-with-me tactic. Instead he looked at her as if she was a code he had to decipher—except the look was far from impersonal.

For a moment his searching gaze seemed to penetrate her soul. What was he seeing? That she was rattled? That she had a secret that was about to mess with his life? She held his gaze but, damn the man, he only smiled.

"So," he said nonchalantly. "You want my professional advice?"

"Dana and your mother do." She didn't back down. She didn't budge. She didn't want anything from him. She couldn't afford to want . . .

"Mom's asked me to protect you 24/7."

Not even the caffeine helped that statement sink in. "Protect me? But—"

"Sam will watch out for Dana at home and she'll have protection, too. So will Mom. Right now, every lottery winner will have an armed bodyguard with them at all times." The teasing left his gaze. His tone was absolute, as if she had no choice, as if he had information she didn't yet possess.

She frowned at him. "Why me? Why aren't you protecting your sister or your mother?"

He threaded his fingers through his hair. "I asked the same question. But Mom didn't answer. She's barely holding herself together. She's already buried a son. The idea of losing another child must terrify her. Or maybe she thinks I don't have any objectivity where my own family is concerned. I didn't argue. I just agreed to do whatever she asked."

"But we no longer have the ticket. The danger's over, isn't it?" Mandy stared at him, sensing he hadn't yet told her all the news.

"Lisa Slocum's dead."

What?

Lisa was dead? Oh . . . God. Dead?

Zack plucked the coffee cup from her hand and set it aside. He steered her to the sofa and made her sit. Mandy didn't resist, just sank down, her emotions churning. Surely the lively twenty-three-year-old, a paralegal who'd intended to become a lawyer, couldn't be dead? No.

Lisa was encouraging her foster girls to keep up their schoolwork. She was going to attend law school. No more waiting for scholarships. The lottery win was going to make her dreams come true.

"Maria found Lisa's body this morning," Zack said gently. "Apparently, they carpooled to work."

The coffee in Mandy's stomach swirled in a sucking vortex of grief. She fought down nausea.

Lisa was dead.

And Mandy's hands trembled. "How?"

Zack slipped his hands over hers, and she held on, an anchor to cling to. "Forensics hasn't released a report, but Maria said her throat was cut. Her apartment was torn apart. Lisa had defensive wounds on her hands, indicating she fought back."

"Oh . . . God. If they were torturing her to make her give them the ticket . . . she didn't have it."

"We don't know what happened. Try not to make assumptions."

"Did they catch—"

He shook his head. "Detectives are dusting for prints and conducting interviews."

She stared at him, shock making it difficult to draw a good breath. "How do you know—"

"The DEA did the Tampa Police Department a favor last year. One of their guys is keeping me informed as a professional courtesy."

Just then the waiting room doors swung open and Mandy glanced up to see Catherine and Dana's husband Sam. Dylan Sawyer, Tampa's mayor, and Sam's best friend was with them. Catherine hurried toward her, but the men hesitated, their heads together, their voices low, apparently discussing important business. Although they kept their tones hushed, Mandy recognized Sam's tight expression, and guessed their business wasn't pleasant.

Catherine, impeccably dressed in a red power suit and white blouse, sank down beside them. She dragged a red-rimmed gaze over Mandy, then enfolded Zack in a hug. "Thanks for flying out."

"Of course, I'd come," he reassured her.

"After Lisa's murder, we really need you. And I missed you." Catherine gazed lovingly at her son and frowned at his fading bruises. "What happened to your face?"

"Nothing to worry about, and I missed you, too, Mom." Zack kept his arm slung over his mother's shoulder, his affection easy and genuine. Then he stood and offered his hand to his brother-in-law, Sam, who'd just finished giving Mandy a quick hug, then shook the mayor's hand. Catherine refrained from asking Zack more about his injuries but her worried gaze remained on the scar on his forehead.

While the men said their hellos, Mandy watched Zack. Stance casual, he nevertheless regarded Sam Hansen with a reserve he didn't bother to hide. Obviously, Zack didn't like Dana's husband, and she couldn't help but wonder why.

Sam was one of the best criminal attorneys in the city. While he wasn't one of Mandy's favorite people either, for Dana's sake she made an effort to get along and ignored his cocky nature. Shorter than Zack, Sam's broad shoulders, barrel chest, and custom-tailored suit attested to his success and position in the community. His clients were often wealthy, his cases media darlings, and his courtroom wins legendary.

As sole owner of his firm, he'd used his profits to invest in real estate throughout the city. He was on a first-name basis with powerful judges, the city planning commissioners, and the current Mayor of Tampa, a tall, reed-thin distinguished gentleman with steely blue eyes and bushy gray eyebrows, who was in the process of excusing himself from the family gathering.

But when the newscaster began a report about Mitch Anderson, a county administrator missing on his sailboat and Tampa Bay, the men halted to watch the newscast. Apparently Mitch's family had no idea he'd taken off in his boat and hadn't heard from him in two days. The Coast Guard had begun a search and the clip ended with Mitch's tearful wife, a baby in her arms, pleading with the public to keep an eye out for her missing husband.

As soon as the newsclip ended, the mayor left, leaving Sam standing in awkward silence with Catherine and Zack. No one looked like they knew what to say and she felt bad for all of them.

Sam was not an overprotective husband, but he certainly appeared concerned now. He hadn't shaved. His eyes were bloodshot. He'd chewed his unlit cigar until it had shredded. That he'd pulled strings to remain at Dana's bedside through the night and made certain she'd received top-notch care showed he was doing what he could to help. Mandy was glad for her friend's sake.

"Does Dana know about Lisa's death?" Mandy asked Catherine, who nodded.

"She saw the morning news. Because of her head injury, the doctors didn't sedate her, but she's holding up in her own way."

Sam released a sigh of exasperation. "Instead of resting, she's been searching her PDA, trying to find every case that links her, Mandy, and Lisa."

"I have that information at the office," Mandy offered. "Dana should rest. But why is she bothering with the cases when someone was after the lottery ticket?"

"You can't assume that," Zack told her.

Mandy hadn't thought to connect their attack with anything other than the 360 million dollar ticket. But when she thought about it, why would anyone have murdered Lisa early this morning? After the ticket had been stolen.

Perhaps Zack was right. The women all worked in the same office, and there might be some kind of connection between them besides the lottery ticket. A case. A client.

"Have you or my sister had any death threats?" Zack asked, clearly remembering the last time he'd been here.

Mandy shook her head. "But the cases we're working together are complicated. We've hired outside PIs and forensic accountants. Lisa coordinates our efforts. We'll have access to her records at the office."

"The chief of police promised me he'd put his best detectives on the case," Sam said. "He believes the attacks must be related to the lottery ticket. And Lisa's apartment was ransacked—either before or after her murder."

"Lisa might have been one of the winners but she didn't *have* the ticket," Mandy protested.

Zack frowned. "Her murderer may not have known that or that the ticket's been stolen. So he may still be looking."

Sam's voice was full of concern. "You all need to be careful. Close the firm for a few days."

"No, Sam." Catherine shook her head. "We have clients that can't wait. I've hired bodyguards to protect us."

"Mom," Zack said, "I'm not letting any of you risk your lives over—"

"I agree." Sam chewed his unlit cigar. "Let the police solve the case and you all stay home."

This was way too much protective testosterone for Mandy and the annoyed tilt to Catherine's jaw suggested that she felt the same way. Under normal circumstances, Mandy would have waited for Catherine to assert her authority, but she looked so tired.

"Lisa was murdered at home. What makes you think we'll be any safer?" Mandy asked. "And suppose they don't ever solve the case?"

Maria slammed open the door to the waiting room, her bodyguard beside her, who, after visually checking out the room, remained by the threshold. Maria wore her usual work clothes, a button-down shirt, slacks, and a sweater over her arm, as if ready for a casual day in the office . . . until Mandy looked into her dark brown eyes and recognized shock and anguish. Maria had found Lisa's body and the horror of what she'd seen remained in her weary eyes. She pressed her lips together and her voice wobbled. "Is Dana—"

"She's going to be all right," Catherine repeated.

"*Dios.*" Maria flung herself into a chair. "Sylvia said to tell you she's holding down the fort at the office, but we're to call her if there's any news."

Sam's cell phone rang. "Yes. I ordered five dozen white roses. My wife deserves the best." He hung up the phone. "I must be in court within the hour. But if you need me—"

Catherine nodded. "Thanks, Sam. The doctors should release Dana this morning. I'll stick around and take her home." She shooed Maria, Mandy, and Zack toward the door. "There's nothing more to be done here. Go home. Or go to work, but please be careful."

Maria stood, trembling slightly. "I've rescheduled my deposition. The judge delayed my afternoon hearing. I'm heading home."

"Take as long as you need, dear," Catherine squeezed her arm. "Have you spoken to Lisa's family?"

Maria's eyes filled with tears. "Assuming the autopsy will be done in time, the funeral's planned for tomorrow."

"Tomorrow?" Mandy wasn't ready to bury her associate. She still had trouble believing she'd died.

"She was Jewish," Maria said. "Her religion calls for the burial to take place as quickly as possible. It's their way of honoring the dead. Burials are postponed a day only if relatives cannot arrive in time and, in Lisa's case, there's only her foster family, who live in town."

"Did you know Lisa well?" Zack asked Maria.

Maria shrugged. "I know her parents died in a car accident when she was a kid and her foster parents are decent people. We talked about stuff during our drive to work. Why?"

"Most often a violent murder is committed by someone the victim knows. Did she have a man in her life?"

"An ex-husband, a jealous ex-boyfriend, and a new lover. I already told the police, why?"

"I handled her divorce," Mandy admitted, recalling that Lisa's ex-husband had given her the creeps. Every time she'd seen him, he'd been polite, but instead of looking at her, he'd seemed to look through her. He'd rarely spoken and when he had, he'd used a gravelly voice that she'd found disturbing.

"Anything unusual about the divorce?" Zack asked.

"Her ex is an attorney," Mandy volunteered. When Zack

didn't respond, she explained, "That means he knew his way around the court system. People owed him favors. He didn't have to pay one cent for his divorce, and he made sure his wife didn't have a penny to hire legal representation. We took her case pro bono."

Zack wasn't a lawyer, but clearly he understood about connections and pulling strings. His eyes sharpened with comprehension. "Was there anything else unusual?"

"You mean besides that the guy was into porn, the kinky kind?" Mandy replied.

Maria's eyes widened. "What kind of porn? Men? Children?"

"Snuff films." Mandy had the DVD titles in her files and that list had given her the clout to reach a fair settlement. Lisa had only been married four years, but she'd put her own education on hold to put him through law school. "He was smarter and more of a creep than the usual ex. It could be relevant."

Zack's eyes narrowed. "The guy gets off on watching women have sex and then being killed. Yeah, in light of Lisa's murder, I'd say it's real relevant. Maybe the cops will lock him up and this will be over soon."

To Mandy, Lisa's ex-husband hadn't seemed the violent type. He'd been so quiet, but she recalled other murders reported on TV and interviews where neighbors had claimed that the killer was quiet, polite . . . before he exploded and stabbed some poor woman fifty times.

Maria clutched her purse tightly and appeared to force out words, seeming like a shadow of her normally vibrant self. "I heard one of the cops at the scene mention that Lisa might also have been raped, but we won't know for certain until after the autopsy report."

Sickened by the violence, Mandy started to shake. Sensing her distress, Zack urged her toward the door. "The cops will want a list of those films and anything else we find out about Lisa's ex." He spoke over his shoulder to his mother, worry in his eyes. "Mom, you take care of Dana, and none of you ladies are to go anywhere without protection."

"You be careful, too," Catherine told him, her gaze following them as if she feared more trouble to come.

Maria exited with them and headed the other way. Mandy walked beside Zack, actually relieved she wasn't alone. Lisa's death, coming so soon after the attack, had left her feeling sad, bewildered, and distressed. What had happened to her orderly life? Who was doing this to them?

But with Lisa's murder, all their lives had changed. While she still wasn't clear why Zack had ended up protecting her instead of Catherine or Dana, she hadn't questioned Catherine, unwilling to cause her one more moment of distress. Mandy would cope with Zack.

As they walked through the hospital, past patients, visitors, and doctors in blue scrubs, she spoke quietly to Zack. "You believe the attacks on Lisa, Dana, and me are connected?"

"It makes sense. You handled Lisa's divorce. Maybe the guy who tried to kill you on the bridge learned he'd failed, and then he attacked you in the garage last night before he killed Lisa."

"He attacked Dana in the garage, not me. But the first man was white. Last night, the guy was black."

Zack took her elbow to steer her around a gurney with a sad little boy, being pushed by an intern down the brightly lit corridor. "Maybe someone hired both assailants and Dana just happened to be with you."

"Maybe." They exited the hospital into bright sunshine. Mandy was grateful to leave the chilly air of Tampa General Hospital. She breathed in the scent of salty air blowing off Tampa Bay, caught sight of a sailboat motoring under a bridge. Her entire life seemed out of kilter, yet for others, their day was ordinary. And poor Lisa . . . her life was over.

Sickened by her senseless death, Mandy ached for the woman who'd had such big plans, a woman with a good heart. She would be missed.

Zack matched Mandy's pace along the sidewalk, loosening the top button of his shirt as if unaccustomed to the summer heat. "Perhaps it's coincidence, but I think we simply haven't found the right connection yet."

Nothing seemed to make sense. A whirlwind of frustration and sorrow swirled around her, as cloying as the Florida humidity. "When I check my files on Lisa's divorce, maybe I'll find something else."

"Pull the cases you and my sister worked on together, too."

She appreciated Zack's take on what was happening. She thought it ironic that the career that was so instrumental in keeping them apart allowed him to analyze their situation with a trained eye. "Don't you think," she asked, "that after all the publicity we've had on winning the Powerball lottery, it's more likely we were attacked and Lisa was killed for the ticket?"

His assessing gaze raked the parking lot, taking in a young man on crutches, several couples, and a truck driver who was checking the tire on his vehicle before he turned to her. "It's possible the incident on the bridge wasn't connected to the attacks last night, and someone could have simultaneously sent men after Lisa, you, and Dana to grab the ticket. But slashing a throat is . . . personal, most likely done by someone who held a grudge, *and* someone Lisa knew."

Mandy looked at him, puzzled. "But you were the one who suggested there was a connection between our attack and hers."

Zack hesitated as if he didn't want to say more, then his eyes flashed and his tone roughened. "If those reporters hadn't followed you and Dana to the parking garage, you both might have ended up dead, too. And we have no idea who cancelled the security I'd arranged for you."

He was scaring her. Was someone out there watching them right now? She glanced down the street at a car driving slowly by, and shivered. The guy was simply looking for a parking space.

Relax. Zack would protect her, but she didn't know how he stood it. Living every moment as if it could be his last.

Once she calmed a little and thought about it, she realized the facts didn't add up. "The guy last night had a gun, and Lisa wasn't shot."

"Maybe the reporters showed up before he pulled the knife."

"Why would he do that? Isn't it easier to kill with a gun than a knife?"

"Easier? Yes." Zack's eyes darkened. "But some killers prefer to make death more personal, more terrifying. For all we know, the bastard only gets his rocks off when he uses a knife."

Chapter Ten

MANDY WALKED INTO the Catherine Taylor and Associates office building with Zack. Formerly a charming hotel with a wrap-around front porch that Catherine had converted into offices, the building had ample space for all the lottery winners—Catherine herself; three junior lawyers, Mandy, Dana, and Maria; their paralegal, Lisa, who pitched in as a secretary and who would never be coming back to work; and Sylvia Jacobson, who guarded the reception area. While they really needed another staff person, hiring someone had been put on hold for now. Even if they'd had the heart to start interviewing, who would possibly want to work here with the lawyers being picked off one by one?

The white-haired senior secretary Sylvia usually greeted Mandy with a motherly nod. It was part of her job to keep an eye on the comings and goings of the lawyers and clients. But when she saw Mandy, her eyes filled with tears and she hurried around her desk past her bodyguard to give Mandy a hug.

Since Mandy had seen Sylvia last—before her trip to California—Dana had been attacked, Lisa was dead, and they'd won and lost the lottery ticket. Sylvia pulled back from the hug. "You okay?"

Mandy spoke past the tightness in her throat. "I'm holding my own. What about you?"

"I'm a survivor, but it's been rough, dear. The police were here this morning. They've already gone through Lisa's belongings and taken her files. Feel free to go through anything they left behind." Sylvia returned to her desk and handed Mandy her mail and messages. "Doesn't look like anything that can't wait."

Zack insisted on checking Lisa's office before allowing Mandy to enter. The cops had made a mess. Law books were all over the room, the empty file cabinets open. Dust from fingerprinting was on the phone, the fax, and the keyboard.

Mandy accessed the server from a spare computer terminal. While the cops had taken Lisa's hard drive, all computer files backed up automatically on a daily basis to the server, so Mandy could still access Lisa's work. "I've found the cases that Lisa, Dana, and I have worked on."

She printed them out, tucked them in a file holder, and handed it to Zack. "Why don't you have a look?"

Mandy tried not to think about how she was invading Lisa's space. During the last year, the paralegal secretary had made the office her own with pictures of herself kissing a dolphin at Sea World with two of her foster girls in tow, a snow globe filled with a Halloween ghost—a present from one of her kids, a ceramic bowl full of Jolly Ranchers, and a pair of sunglasses tossed onto the desk as if she'd just left and would return momentarily.

Only Lisa was never coming back.

Zack began to read. Mandy liked the way he didn't ask questions before he finished, had forgotten how easy he was to be around while she was working. He had the ability to remain silent and fade into the background until he wanted to be noticed. Oh, he could turn on the charm, but he had a work ethic that went as deep as hers, allowing her to focus on the task at hand without distractions.

She pulled out additional files that she and Dana were

working on together and which Lisa had coordinated. Any one of them could lead to an ex-husband with a grudge. Or a dissatisfied client.

Zack had taken a seat on the couch. Sunlight spilled through the window and she noted the circles under his eyes, reminding her that neither of them had slept much last night.

Zack, however, still looked alert. His hand holding the file was steady. He sat upright on the couch without slouching, as if ready to lunge to his feet at the first sign of danger. But with only Sylvia answering the phone and her bodyguard in the reception area, the office was unusually quiet. Almost eerily so.

Mandy couldn't help thinking that she was glad Zack was there to protect her. She needn't worry over him finding pictures of Gabrielle in her office. Since she worked with his family, she'd always known the possibility existed that he might return at any time, and so she'd kept Gabby's pictures at home. Mandy might not know how he'd react if he learned about Gabby, but she could predict with utter certainty how he'd respond to a threat—he'd protect her with his life. That instinct seemed hard-wired into him, and she admired him for it as well as for the work he did.

Mandy hadn't had time to really absorb the fact that she and Dana could have died. Instead of losing possessions, they could be dead. Like Lisa. She and Dana could be lying on a cold slab in the morgue right now alongside—

Stop it.

Scaring herself silly would do no one any good. With determination, she headed across the hall to her own corner office. Zack stood and gestured for her to let him go first, taking the file folder with him and tucking it under his arm. He scanned the hallway, her office, even checking her coat closet before allowing her to enter.

Finally, she sat behind her desk, thumbed through her mail, then set it aside. Zack positioned himself with his back to the wall and opposite the doorway, with a casual air that suggested his wariness was routine.

Chilled by her thoughts of death, Mandy slipped into a

blue sweater she'd left on the back of her chair and reached to put her purse in her desk drawer. Except she had no purse. Or driver's license. She'd reported her stolen credit cards and new ones were being delivered to the office. But her purse and the rest of the missing contents had been taken last night along with the lottery ticket.

She was about to boot up her computer when Sylvia buzzed her intercom. "Mandy, Ben's here to take me to lunch. He wants to talk to Zack, first."

"Send him in." Ben was Sylvia's husband, a burly ex-cop now relegated to a wheelchair. But his handicap didn't stop him from staying busy or being a terrific husband. It amazed Mandy that the man seemed unfazed by his relatively recent handicap. After the tragedy, his personality hadn't seemed to have changed at all. He drove a van outfitted to accommodate his special needs and often stopped in to visit his wife at work. His eyes still twinkled when he looked at Sylvia. Seeing how happy they were after all this time had never seemed real to Mandy. No marriage could be that perfect. Surely no couple could be so devoted to one another?

But Ben still remembered every special occasion, every anniversary. He didn't seem to harbor any bitterness over his inability to walk. The man was just too perfect.

Ben wheeled himself to her office and Zack put down the file, stood, and the two men shook hands. Ben's gray hair was thinning, his eyebrows bushy over a tanned face. Mandy wasn't certain, but she believed the two men had met when Zack had been here before, since Ben was always finding excuses to come to the office, bringing his wife a sandwich, taking her to lunch, or running her errands. She sensed an immediate respect for one another between the two lawmen.

Ben greeted Mandy with a nod and came straight to the point. "Sylvia said the lottery ticket's been stolen."

Expression neutral, Zack closed the file and placed it beside him on the couch. "That's correct."

Mandy expected Ben to ask for details about the stolen ticket. Maybe, he'd suggest going after the thief.

"I'd like to tell the press." Ben's eyebrows knitted with

worry. "If we announce that none of the women have the ticket anymore, they should be safer."

Hmm. He'd surprised her once again by his unselfishness. Ben wasn't thinking about the lost riches, but his wife's safety. Mandy's, too. He had a point. No one in their right mind would bother attacking women who no longer possessed the winning ticket.

"You think an announcement will protect us?" Mandy asked, trying to think of a hole in Ben's theory and doing her best not to catch Zack's eyes to see what he thought. As much as she respected his opinions, she needed to come to her own conclusions. Besides, looking at him might reveal that she cared more about him than she wanted to admit—even to herself. So she went into attorney mode, running scenarios through her mind, uncertain if Ben's suggestion had merit. If his plan worked, they could all return to their routines. Mandy could practice law and have her mother bring Gabby home. Right now, normalcy sounded like heaven.

But one glimpse at Zack from her peripheral vision reminded her that things wouldn't be normal. Not the normal she'd known before this whole nightmare began. Not once she told Zack the truth.

"We aren't even certain if Lisa was killed because someone was after the ticket," Mandy said, too good an attorney not to punch holes in Ben's theory. "And I was pushed off the bridge *before* we won."

"What harm can it do?" Ben pleaded.

"I'll talk to Catherine," Zack promised, then found more holes in Ben's reasoning. "We have nothing to lose by trying, but even if we announce that the ticket's been stolen, there's no guarantee the killer will read the paper or hear the news, or that he'll believe it."

"Understood." Ben's voice softened. "Please thank your mother for providing the bodyguard for Sylvia. I would have phoned and told her myself but I didn't want to bother her at the hospital." He hesitated. "I heard Dana's going home and—"

"You licensed to carry?" Zack asked.

Carry? Mandy frowned, then realized from the bulge under Ben's arm he had a weapon holstered there.

Ben spoke over his shoulder as he rolled out of her office, "Permit's up to date. I never fired my weapon in the line of duty, not even when I got hit, but I still go to monthly target practice."

For all of Ben's sweet gestures, he remained a hard-edged cop through and through. He meant to protect his woman. Mandy realized that Zack probably had a weapon on him, too. Maybe several. She recalled he liked to wear one on his ankle and carried another at the small of his back, and he slept with one under his pillow.

They had yet to discuss sleeping arrangements tonight. Oh . . . God. She couldn't bring him back to her condo—not with a high chair in the kitchen and baby toys strewn throughout the living room. Zack would ask questions she wasn't ready to answer.

The mere idea of a hotel room brought back two-year-old memories of Zack's hot kisses, his powerful arms cradling her gently, his fingers in her hair inundating her senses. She didn't want to remember. But there was only so much tension her body could deal with in a day. As Ben left, she shut those thoughts down and pushed her concerns over sleeping arrangements to the back of her mind.

She could hear the water cooler cycle on. The fax machine spit out papers. The phone rang, but either Sylvia or the service would pick up. At the sudden intimacy, she could hear the beating of her heart.

She couldn't look at Zack sitting on the couch. She refused to dwell on the fascinating bit of sunlight that beamed onto the V neck of his shirt, revealing bronzed skin and a dusting of black curls. Instead she printed the files she wanted and scooped them up. "Why don't we discuss these over lunch?"

He stared at her, his eyes bright and interested. "Good idea. I'm starved."

Was he flirting again? She wasn't sure and she didn't like

her inability to read him. In many ways, he was the man she remembered, and yet, he seemed more serious, less ready to smile. Apparently, she wasn't the only one who'd changed. Zack seemed less carefree, more serious.

Good God, he could still turn on the charm. But he wouldn't push. She recalled he liked his ladies hot. And willing. She'd been both. No one had ever jazzed her up like Zack could with a mere glance. She'd never forget that he'd once told her that her skin was her best accessory. Sheesh— the way the man made her blood heat shouldn't be legal. Or possible. Not with everything that had happened. Still . . .

Stop it.

She couldn't dwell in the past. She had a crisis on her hands. Besides, it didn't seem fair to be reminiscing after what had happened to Lisa. Perhaps, thinking about Zack was her way of coping with the horror of her death. Perhaps it was normal to express grief by reaching out to someone. Only that someone could not be Zack.

She'd changed a lot in the last two years, too. She was more wary. Less likely to break her own rules.

She cautioned herself to remember.

Chapter Eleven

OVER TRADITIONAL CUBAN sandwiches—pressed ham, cheese, and Genoese salami from Italy, plus mustard on toasted and flattened bread—a Tampa specialty thanks to its mix of Cuban and Italian heritage—Zack surveyed Mandy. She'd slid into the booth at the restaurant, the files in her hands, almost as if she wanted an excuse to keep the conversation businesslike. Zack sipped his unsweetened iced tea. Could a boyfriend now be in the picture? Surely if that was the case, Dana, his mother, or Mandy herself would have told him.

Despite his worry over the safety of his mother and sister, the connection between Mandy and him seemed so natural, almost effortless. She was unlike any woman he'd known, with all that passion hidden under her practical nature. But as much as he liked to go with the flow, it was unlike him to take any interest in a woman when involved in a case. Yet Mandy had intrigued him, tantalized him, tested him, since they'd first met. Clearly she was still upset with him for pulling his vanishing act two years ago. But anger wasn't necessarily a bad thing. Anger meant she wasn't indifferent.

He wasn't sure why that mattered, but it did. Then again, it wasn't as if he'd exactly been stable lately. Ever since losing that little boy . . .

Zack tossed his napkin onto his plate. He kept his mouth shut and allowed Mandy to lead the conversation, more intrigued than he should have been. He hadn't had life signs in so long, but being around her again was proving to be exactly what he needed. Maybe he could learn how to cope with what happened to Todd.

She ate a few bites of her sandwich, then wiped her mouth with a napkin and pushed her plate and the untouched second half of the Cuban toward him. "Help yourself."

"Thanks." While he ate, she picked up the files and perused them again. He had the feeling she didn't want to look at him, didn't want to catch his glance. Was she as aware of him as he was of her? She was gorgeous. Stunning eyes. Cute nose. Pouty mouth. He easily recalled those lips kissing him, her mouth creating a burning fever that had made him throw away his good sense and get involved with a protectee. Made him think about getting involved again.

She sipped her tea, leaned over the files, but her eyes didn't scan as if she were reading. Instead, she stared, lost in thought. He'd give a week's pay to know what she was thinking. He was just about to ask when she said, "We have three cases in progress. Attorney–client privilege—"

"Be damned," he interrupted. "People are dying."

"But—"

"You're allowed to share privileged information with coworkers, aren't you?" he asked.

"You aren't—"

"I'm working for my mother and the firm."

She tapped her fingers on the table top, then nodded. "Fine."

Right now, he needed to dive into the records. He needed to take his mind off Mandy, check out the suspects by delving into the names, dates, and addresses in their files. Two years ago, against his better judgment, he'd allowed himself to get involved with her. Oh, yeah. He'd been some great catch. A guy who didn't stick around long enough to even say goodbye. But a man who'd thought about her way too often. He wouldn't make that choice again. In his line of work, such distractions got men killed. Or innocent kids.

"Last year, Dana and I took the case of a wealthy stock-broker and his stay-at-home wife, a mother of four children under the age of six." She summed up her cases without again consulting the files. "The husband mortgaged the house to the hilt, pocketed the bank's loan money, and cleaned out their joint bank account. He claimed he was broke and had to declare bankruptcy due to her spendthrift ways. We hired a forensic accountant who traced the hidden funds to a Bahamian bank. When we forced him to accede to her divorce terms, he was obnoxious. Livid."

"You think the stockbroker's dangerous?"

Her eyes flashed with a spirit he recalled from their short time together. "He'd threatened her to the point where she'd picked up the kids in the middle of the night and ran to her mother's house in her nightgown."

Zack could tell from her tone that she believed her former client's spouse was menacing but he had to remain objective. "Threats and theft are not proof he's dangerous."

"As I recall, the guy was some kind of martial arts cham-pion."

"Did she ever say explicitly that he'd hit her?"

Her lips tightened with a stubborn determination that added strength to her feminine features. She went silent.

"Well?" he prodded, wondering why she was having such a strong reaction to this case. If he had to guess, it was that she felt compelled to defend those who couldn't, or wouldn't, defend themselves.

"She was terrified of him." Mandy's nostrils flared. "She didn't want the money or the house. Or alimony or child sup-port. She just wanted to get away from him. He fought back by going after sole custody of the kids. He acted as though she was the love of his life—but he had a mistress. I couldn't let her divorce him without doing right by those children. She needed that child support and he was furious at the terms he had to accept."

"All right. We check out the stockbroker's whereabouts last night. Who else do you have?"

"Lisa was also in the middle of filing papers on a bitter child custody case. This one is ongoing and I can't speak to my client's spouse unless his attorney is present." She tossed her hair out of her eyes, but one lock fell forward over her cheek.

His fingers itched to brush her hair from her face—so he could touch the softness of her skin, watch her eyes dilate. Damn it. What was she saying? Oh, yeah, bitter child custody case. "I thought Florida awards joint custody?"

"Depends on the case. The standard is what is in the best interests of the child."

Zack was grateful his own parents had worked out their divorce in a civilized manner. He'd been in college and had chosen to stay near his father in California. Dana had gone to Florida with their mother. Although their parents had set aside their differences for the sake of their children, it had still been tough. Kevin hadn't handled the divorce well and had gotten involved with drugs. Two years later he was dead.

"This time, both parents are claiming the other one abused the baby—who isn't old enough to tell us which parent is causing all the bruises." Mandy didn't sound as adamant or certain about this client as she had earlier about the stockbroker.

Zack swore. "Surely the baby isn't going back and forth from parent to parent?"

"The child was taken out of the home and placed into foster care. A court-appointed special advocate now represents the interests of the child. The mother is fine with the arrangement. She says she'd rather lose the baby than see him abused."

"That sounds admirable."

"She didn't seem too upset that she couldn't see the little boy, either." Mandy's eyes darkened, and as a George Strait country song twanged over the restaurant's sound system, she tensed.

"So you don't believe her story?"

"I don't know. Their situation is heartbreaking. It'll take months to investigate and settle, and by then the baby will no longer remember either parent. The father is furious. He's a pediatrician and claims his wife is ruining his reputation. He says she has a record of mental instability."

"Is she unstable?"

"She's upset." He read doubts in her eyes. "She cries a lot and she's admitted to seeing a psychiatrist—an associate of her husband's whom she claims will take her husband's side in court."

"What do you think?"

"It's ugly and I'm not sure. In a divorce case, one or both partners often lie."

"Then what do you do?" He could tell that this particular case upset her. He'd once thought Mandy too soft to make a good attorney, but now he knew better. She had a core of steel beneath her vulnerable exterior, even when forced outside her comfort zone.

She shrugged. "It depends. I try to take only the cases I believe in." Her voice tightened with regret. "If a client misrepresents their situation, I make it clear I won't be the best person to represent their case, then I try to get them to seek a new advocate. If children are in danger, it makes it more complicated . . ."

Zack didn't want to think about injured children. Not when he didn't even have to close his eyes to see Todd. He'd never forget that little boy in his arms. The blood seeping from his mouth. His small body trembling. Confusion and fear in eyes that slowly clouded, until he just stared— empty—the life gone.

Zack gestured to the files. "Who else do you have that might display a proclivity for violence?"

"Lisa was overseeing a PI we hired to investigate a case. At first we thought the ex was only cheating, but he's using crystal meth. There's a possibility of HIV." Outrage made her words sharp. "The wife's being tested. However, the husband wasn't just careless about who he nailed. He quit his treatment program, stalked his wife to the women's shelter, and broke her jaw. She pressed charges."

"What's wrong?"

Mandy sighed. "He's out on bail."

"But he's dangerous."

"The jails are full. We've filed for a restraining order on the wife's behalf, but these guys never care about the law. . . ." She frowned. "Any or all of these men could be angry enough to come after us personally. Or the attacks might not have anything to do with work. Our names have been all over the papers and the TV news in connection with our winning the lottery."

He understood her frustration. "Investigations take time. The homicide detectives will check out Lisa's ex-husband and lover. Meanwhile, I'd like to discreetly investigate these other men from your joint cases."

Her eyes narrowed. "Won't the police do that?"

"My source said the police are overworked and the investigation is going slowly. They have several murder cases under investigation, and they're trying to track down the missing county administrator, Mitch Anderson. Official resources are stretched. Right now, their primary focus is on Lisa's ex-lover and ex-husband. Besides, if we check things out quietly, we protect the firm's clients. If possible I'd prefer that Mom's firm not take even more of a hit than it already has."

"Zack, I just want to go back to my life . . . the way it was."

"Not possible. Not until we find out who's after you. Neither you, Dana, Mom, or any of your coworkers will be safe until we catch whoever is behind the violence."

"We're dealing with *two* violent men."

"Perhaps the stockbroker or the pediatrician hired muscle to go after you. We need to talk to them as well as the guy on crystal meth."

She tapped her fingers on the table, then shoved to her feet. "I owe it to Lisa to find out what happened. We all do."

He wasn't surprised by her reaction. "So you'll help me?"

"What exactly would we be doing?"

He tossed money and a tip on the table and stood. "We talk to your clients' ex-spouses and their neighbors and friends to learn if they have alibis for the time when Lisa was murdered."

She raised a challenging eyebrow. "And if they don't?"

"We dig deeper."

Chapter Twelve

DANA STARED AT the windshield, at the lights sparkling on the bay as her newly assigned bodyguard maneuvered through traffic toward her home. Catherine had meant well, and Dana understood her caution after Lisa's murder and the attack at the airport. But the tight quarters of the Jag left her feeling suffocated and edgy, with not only her new protector, Tom Wainscott, but her mother and another bodyguard in the back seat. She remembered how hard Mandy had resisted personal protection and understood.

During the drive home, Dana fretted that she still couldn't remember the attack that had placed her in the hospital. Luckily, she'd only forgotten the few minutes right before she'd suffered her head injury, a common reaction to a concussion, her doctors had said. All she recalled was fleeing from the reporters in the terminal, riding in the elevator, and then waking up in the hospital.

"Mom," she said to Catherine, trying to ignore the two strangers now privy to the conversation. "Suppose I saw something important last night but can't recall it due to my amnesia?"

"That's unlikely. Mandy gave a description of the attacker and the vehicle to the police. You probably didn't see more than she did. Don't try to force the memory. The doctor said you need to relax."

"Easy for you to say," Dana snapped. Her head hurt. Lisa was dead, and she was worried about the other members of their firm—especially Mandy. "What did Mandy say after she learned you'd appointed Zack as her bodyguard?"

"I wasn't there," Catherine's tone remained mild, giving Dana little clue to what she was thinking.

Tom turned the car into Dana's driveway without their instructing him. The familiar angle iron fence surrounded an immaculate yard framed by ferns, snow on the mountain, and lilies. As always, the lush landscaping made Dana grateful to come home. She looked forward to sitting on her back porch under the granddaddy oaks covered in Spanish moss that draped the back yard set on a deep lot right on Tampa Bay.

"Stop, please, and let me grab the mail," Dana requested.

"I'll get it." Tom opened the window, took the mail from the box and handed it to her. She thumbed through bills, and at the sight of a thick manila envelope, the adoption application forms she'd requested, her mood improved. Sam spent too much time working and their marriage was suffering, due to his absences. She hoped children would renew his interest in coming home. Quickly, she hid the papers behind a magazine. She didn't want Catherine to guess at her intentions before she'd had a chance to talk over the process again with Sam and get him on board with her plan.

Tom tapped in the gate's security code as if he'd been a life-long visitor. Apparently, in her usual efficient manner, her mother hadn't missed a detail when briefing the bodyguard. The black metal gates swung open, allowing them to proceed to the home Sam had bought for Dana after he'd won his first major case—the acquittal of a hotel heiress accused of murdering her sister and the lover they'd shared. The juicy details had made national headlines for months, and the acquittal of his wealthy client had made Sam a multimillionaire.

He was so proud of his career, his powerful friends and their home, the sweeping lawns edged with split-leaf philodendron, the circular brick drive lined with royal palms. Sam was proud of Dana, too. And yet, she often wished she could go back to the time in their marriage where Sam had time to dote on her. Her only major disappointment in life was her inability to conceive and begin the large family they wanted. But for once she was grateful she didn't have children to leave motherless.

After two attacks, Mandy must be concerned that someone might find her, kill her, and leave her daughter parentless—a child who was the spitting image of Zack at that very same age. At first Dana had believed Mandy's story about an accidental pregnancy after a one-night stand. But after Gabby had been born, it hadn't been difficult for Catherine and Dana to count backward and figure out that Zack was Gabrielle's father.

Dana had tried to get Mandy to fess up. But Mandy wouldn't come clean. Dana hadn't wanted to put a strain on their friendship, especially when Mandy had been going out of her way to involve Dana and Catherine in Gabby's life. Family-by-love, Mandy had called them when she'd asked Dana and Sam to be godparents. Neither Catherine nor Dana had ever indicated to Mandy or Zack they knew the identity of Gabrielle's father, believing the two parents must work out their differences in their own time.

It was a difficult situation, Dana knew. Zack had channeled his grief over their brother's death into a crusade against the drug dealers. It was a noble cause, but one with a high price tag. He had no life. Only work. Dana ached for her brother, who didn't know he had a beautiful daughter. She also ached for her best friend, who hadn't gotten a chance to even try for a relationship with the father of her child.

But Dana knew her friend, and didn't think Mandy would

keep her secret forever. Not if it meant Gabby growing up without knowing the truth about *all* her family. Dana hoped, anyway.

She sighed. If nothing else the next few days were going to prove interesting, which was, no doubt, why Catherine had thrown Zack and Mandy together again. Her mother probably wanted to shake loose a few more truths besides who was after them.

The bodyguard swung the Jag under the circular portico and parked beside Sam's Escalade. Tom perused the grounds, then opened Dana's door. Her mother's bodyguard did the same for Catherine.

Sam and Dylan, the mayor, stepped through the elegant double front doors and headed toward them over a brick path. As their vehicle pulled up Dylan waved, got into his car, and drove away.

Looking handsome in his custom-tailored Armani suit, which set off his broad shoulders and powerful chest, Sam headed toward them with an innate confidence she'd always admired. Sam was a self-made man and proud of his success. He could be stubborn, bull-headed at times, but what others might call arrogance, Dana saw as self-assurance.

Catherine peered over her sunglasses. "Sam's here? I thought he had court today."

Well briefed, efficient, and quiet, their bodyguards stayed vigilant but relaxed, obviously recognizing Dana's husband. If Dana had to have someone dogging her footsteps, she appreciated Tom's cool efficiency.

"Sam must have finished early." Dana hurried toward her husband, anticipating his embrace and the chance to revel in the safety of his arms.

Sam's timing—as if he'd been waiting for their arrival— was impeccable as usual. He walked toward them, removing his jacket and loosening his tie. When he reached Dana, he gave her a much needed hug. "The judge heard what happened to you and delayed the trial a day."

"Tell him thank you." Dana kissed his lips.

"I suspect he wanted an excuse to take the day off to go

fishing." Sam's mouth curved into a pleased smile and his eyes warmed with pleasure.

"Maybe he wants to search for the county administrator," Dana said. "The mayor still hasn't heard if Mitch Anderson's been found?"

Sam shook his head. "Nothing yet."

"No matter the reason, I'm glad you're here," Dana told him, knowing he likely had a stack of messages and phone calls to return at the office and appreciating his taking time off from work.

"With Sam here to pamper you, I'll feel better about leaving." Catherine kissed Dana's cheek. "Bye. And don't forget the doctor ordered you to rest."

"I'll see to it." Taking over the way he always did, Sam placed a comforting arm around Dana's waist, nodded to Catherine, and dismissed Tom with a gesture, waving him to the guest house. He murmured in Dana's ear, "Let's get you to bed."

She groaned at the thought of another bed. "Why don't we sit by the pool?"

"All right. But no TV. No work."

"TV helps me rest." The background noise comforted her, but Sam never had understood that, yet to give him credit, he usually didn't object to her habit of turning on the TV in whatever room she happened to be in. He hadn't even protested when she'd asked the carpenters to mount a set on the back porch by the barbecue.

"All right. We'll talk by the pool." Sam's voice turned serious.

"Talk about what?" From his tone he clearly had a topic in mind. Sam was well connected in city politics and his many high-profile cases had earned him certain perks, allowing him to hear insider news. At the hospital, he'd been on a first-name basis with half the board of directors. Once he'd taken over, she'd had a private room, nurses hovering. It also meant that if the police turned up anything on their attacker, the police chief would likely call Sam himself. "What have you heard?

"Nothing on your assault."

"About Lisa?"

"No, honey. I'm sorry."

"The missing lottery ticket?"

"No luck there, either."

"Oh." Disappointment flooded her. Not so much for her-self. Sam already earned enough money that she didn't have to work. But that lottery money would provide security, lux-ury, and independence for her friends. But most of all, they were all living under so much stress from not knowing who'd attacked them or why.

The backyard was their oasis from the hectic pace of the office. The sea breeze from Tampa Bay never failed to invig-orate her and the trickling water that tumbled over a wall from the whirlpool into the lap pool soothed her almost as much as the TV would have done. The Florida heat felt good on her skin.

She set down the mail, eased into a chaise lounge, trailed her fingers into the pool water, closed her eyes, and let the sun soak into her bones. "Ah, that sun feels good."

Sam took a spot beside her but in the shade of several queen palms. "You aren't falling asleep, are you?"

Recalling that he'd wanted to talk about something, she opened her eyes and looked at him. Really looked. Usually his every hair was in place, his grooming immaculate. But the night with her in the hospital had taken a toll. He ap-peared edgy and worried, but also seemed uncomfortable showing his concern. Sam made all the right gestures of a loving husband, but he rarely said the words anymore. But then he hadn't been home in the middle of the day like this in years. Sam's parents were workaholics, too, and they hadn't shown affection either. She'd learned to accept that to him saying *I love you* meant he was showing vulnerability that he equated with weakness. What counted was that when it mattered, he was there for her.

"I'm okay. What is it?" She reassured and prodded, sens-ing his reluctance to say anything that might disturb her. "Why was Dylan here?"

"We'd planned to meet for lunch. When the judge delayed the case, I wanted to be here for you—so we linked up here."

"Is something wrong?"

"With Mitch Anderson missing, Dylan just needed my take on some legal matters."

Dana raised her eyebrow. Sam was a criminal attorney but he did have intricate knowledge about the working of local government. "You're doing too much. Between your law practice and your real estate ventures—"

"That's not what I wanted to talk about."

Something was wrong on his real estate ventures, Dana decided. Although he refused to worry her, she'd rather he confided than tried to protect her. Imagining what could go wrong was usually worse than the truth. She was about to ask, when he spoke. "Remember the race car driver accused of running over five people in Miami?"

"Ben Morrison?" She stared at Sam. "He wasn't just accused. He was guilty. They caught him on video tape, his vehicle slamming into those poor people."

"He claims his chief pit mechanic—who he'd fired the week before—messed with the brakes on his car. Due to the publicity in Miami, the jury pool was tainted. The judge changed the venue to Tampa—"

"So they want you on his case?" she guessed.

Sam nodded, his eyes shining with pleasure that he was *the* lawyer to bring in. Outsiders now recognized that her husband had all the right connections. She could see the battle light blazing in his eyes, his barely contained energy. He couldn't wait to be back in the limelight.

She kept her tone even. "You told me you wouldn't take another huge case this year." It meant hours of studying depositions, consultations with expert witnesses, and going over tactics. Taking a deep breath, she reached for the thick manila envelope. "Sam, I was hoping we could start the adoption process. It means filling out forms, parenting interviews, taking evaluations."

Gently he took the envelope from her hand and tossed it aside. He patted her hand, then locked their fingers together and lightly squeezed. "I don't want to adopt. I want children that come from my genes."

"We've been trying for five years."

"The doctors haven't found anything wrong with either of us. It'll happen."

"And if it does, we can have an even bigger family. We won't stop trying, but why not adopt, too?"

Sam's face tightened, and he released her hand. "All my brothers have kids and they don't support their families anywhere near as well as I do you."

Dana saw no reason to point out that the ability to conceive children had nothing to do with financial success or business acumen. To Sam, the inability to have kids was a failure, and he couldn't abide failure of any kind.

"I won't raise someone else's child," he snapped. "I want to raise my own."

She knew it was his hurt pride talking. "Sam, you adore Gabrielle. We're her godparents. If anything ever happened to Mandy, I'd be willing to raise Gabby as my own and so would you."

"Wrong." Sam stood and began to pace. "You adore Gabby because Mandy's your friend." At his cool tone, she bit her lip. "Mandy may not even know who the father is."

His accusation was unfair but she turned it to her advantage. "That's my point. I love Gabby for herself—not because of who supplied her DNA—and so do you." Of course she suspected Gabby's dad was Zack but she'd never reveal Mandy's secret to Sam. Her husband and brother didn't get along. She wouldn't give Sam any more reasons to dislike Zack. But she would not back down. While her husband's blunt refusal to adopt hurt, Sam would come around. He might argue. He might sound as if he'd never change his mind—but that was the brilliant lawyer in him. He adored Gabby. He just refused to admit it because he didn't want to lose the debate. He didn't want to face that they might never conceive.

"We've tried on our own. We've tried implanting your sperm in me as well as *in vitro*. So far, nothing's worked.

And I'm tired of the stress of trying. I don't like the hormones they pump into me. I want to make love when we feel like it, not when my temperature changes to signal ovulation."

"Adoption is not part of my future." Voice tight, he looked out into the bay, refusing to face her, but she could hear the pain in his voice. Sam had a grand plan. College. Marriage. His own firm. Real estate ventures. Success. Children. In every case except the children, he'd checked every goal off his list with ease. Unfortunately, his career had taken a toll on their marriage. They were so busy working, they no longer spent as much time together. In the early years of their marriage Sam often swept her away for a weekend, treating her like a princess. She missed those days and yearned to recapture the closeness by giving him children.

"Why not adopt?" she asked.

Sam finally turned to face her, his eyes sad, his tone weary. He knelt beside her and took her hand. "If you can't understand that I want a child from my DNA and yours, then I can't explain it."

"Filling out the applications commits us to nothing. The process takes months, sometimes even years. We can always change our minds later."

"I don't know."

"Please, Sam. Consider this for me. For us." She didn't mention they might have to look outside the United States for a baby. "We might as well get on the list."

Sam let go of her hand and bowed his head. Then he raised it and nodded, changing from argumentative to gentle acceptance. "All right. Whatever you want. But don't expect me to give interviews to social workers. Not until after the trial."

Relief washed over her, and her heart swelled with love.

Anyone else wouldn't have understood how he'd fought so hard and then given in so suddenly. But Sam was prone to abrupt changes of heart. He often fought vehemently, using his lawyer skills, but then conceded with grace.

She searched his eyes, grateful and pleased by his change of mind. "You really mean it?"

"Sure." He leaned over and kissed her forehead, then he picked up the adoption form and signed it. "If adoption is what you want, let's do it."

Chapter Thirteen

DANA, MANDY, AND Lisa had all worked on the stockbroker's divorce case last year. Mandy didn't look forward to speaking to her client's ex—and yet when it came to violent people all three women knew, the stockbroker topped her list. Mandy and Zack had driven to his office to speak to him but he wasn't there. His receptionist directed them to a local fitness center where the stock broker spent his lunch hour. Mandy and Zack walked around the block and entered a gym full of men. She ignored the stares that made her feel unwelcome. The guys jumping rope, jogging on treadmills, and riding stationary bicycles weren't showing any more skin than if they'd been on the beach. She'd seen no sign that said "men only."

Zack walked up to the trainer at the front desk as if he had a membership. "I'm looking for . . ." Zack waited for Mandy to help him out with the name.

"Damien Reed," she finished for him and tried not to stare at the tattoos on the man glaring at her. But it wasn't easy since he had so many of them, a biker babe with a big bust on his meaty biceps, a giant cross with a fire-breathing dragon on his chest, and a skull and crossbones on one side of his neck.

The guy jerked his thumb over his shoulder. "The stock-broker's fencing. He do anything illegal?"

Mandy let a friendly smile soften her face. "Why do you ask?"

"You look like cops."

"We're not." Zack took her arm and led her away before she asked more questions. He spoke quietly in her ear. "Will Damien recognize you as his wife's lawyer?"

"We've never met. All communication went through his attorney."

"Good. Let me do the talking."

She rolled her eyes at the ceiling. "I'm the one who makes my living by questioning witnesses."

She expected Zack to argue. Instead he laughed and shot her a charming grin. "All right, he's all yours."

Mandy's first glimpse of Damien was of a man with a rapier in his hand, lunging at air as he moved forward in choreographed advances and quick retreats, then repeated the moves. He wore a mask to protect his face but she could see his eyes and nose through a clear window. From the intense concentration of his stare at his opponent, she suspected he hadn't yet noticed them.

While one on-target strike with his rapier might be lethal, he certainly wasn't the same man who'd rammed her Beemer off the bridge. He was much bigger, his skin lighter than the man who'd attacked Dana at the airport. But even after the divorce, with a seven figure income, he certainly had the bucks to hire muscle to come after the women at their firm. While she couldn't judge his skill, his moves looked practiced, as if he might easily choose a knife to murder a woman.

"Sir. Are you Damien Reed?"

He removed his mask. "Who wants to know?" Sweat dripped down Damien's bald skull, over a ridged brow and past a nose that appeared to have been broken and reset crookedly. Diamond studs, at least three carats each, winked from the lobes of his ears. No wonder his wife was terrified of him. A solid six feet five inches, with powerful shoulders and abs of granite, he had the body of a professional athlete, not the conservative medium build she'd been expecting. "I don't give stock tips in the gym, lady."

"That's not why I'm here." Certain he'd clam up if she introduced herself as his wife's divorce attorney, Mandy made up a story. "My car was stolen last night and since I live across the street from you," Mandy lied, knowing from his file that he'd moved during the last two months and probably wouldn't have met some of the neighbors in his new apartment complex, "I was hoping you might have seen something."

He picked up a towel and slung it around his neck. "I didn't see anything."

"The police think my car was taken by my boyfriend early this morning, about 5 A.M." She pegged the alleged theft to the time of Lisa's murder. "My computer was in the car. Along with a spare set of apartment keys."

"Change the lock."

"I already have, but my laptop has e-mail information I'd rather keep private."

"What's your boyfriend look like?"

"He would likely have been wearing a suit. He's thin. About five ten. Are you awake that time of morning?"

"Yeah. I was jogging. And I didn't see him. What kind of car did you say it was?"

"A white Volvo."

"Sorry. You might want to talk to Mrs. Potter, the lady in 4B. She's already told me her son's a cop, as if she's afraid I'm going to steal her purse. She seems to know what's going on in the area."

"Thanks. I appreciate it."

Damien looked at her coldly. "Lady, why are you really here?"

"Excuse me?"

"Nobody tracks down a *neighbor* at the gym to ask if they saw someone break into their car. That's the lamest story

I've ever heard. If you wanted to know where I was early this morning, why didn't you just ask me?"

"So were you really jogging?" At the flash of triumph in his eyes, she kept her chin high and held his gaze. But she appreciated Zack taking a step closer.

Damien ignored Zack and glared at her. "I jog every morning, Ms. Newman."

Beside her, Zack tensed.

Ms. Newman? How had he known who she was? Had he had her followed? "You know who I am?"

"You see a man sweating in the gym and you think he doesn't have a brain? Why does my ex-wife want to know where I was this morning?"

She and Zack exchanged a glance, and Zack had the grace not to look smug. So much for making a decent impression. She shouldn't care what Zack thought anyway. "An attorney at our firm was murdered early this morning." Mandy gestured to the rapier Damien held. "Her throat was cut."

"So why are you here?"

"We're trying to keep our clients and their cases out of the news. The more you can tell me, the better I can do that. I'm sure if I told the cops that you were good with a sword, it wouldn't take them long to infer that you might not be averse to using a knife," Mandy bluffed. She had no idea if the police would think any such thing. Although Damien being the killer was a long shot, the more she could get him to talk, the likelier it was he might slip and reveal something critical.

"Fencing's a sport," he insisted.

"So is sharpshooting. If we were talking about murder from a bullet wound, don't you think the police would be interested in a hunter who had a motive? You must have hated us after your wife got more than she asked for in the divorce settlement," she prodded.

Damien wiped his arm against his forehead, attempting and failing to mop up the sweat with his wristband. "This is for competition. It doesn't even have a pointed tip." He gestured to men behind him advancing and retreating up and down the gym floor. They wore masks and fencing suits. Those with opponents scored points against each other with electronic equipment that registered the hits in beeps. The sword edges looked sharp but the tip had a tiny ball on the end that capped it. No one was hurt by the stabs—not even the ones that scored points. However, Damien Reed was good with a sword and had the brains to figure out who she was. He lowered his voice to a chilly whisper. "But if I were going to kill, I wouldn't use a knife. Too messy. I didn't kill Lisa."

Mandy fought down a prickle of unease. "I didn't say who died."

"Lisa Slocum's death is all over the news. So was the attack on you and Dana Hansen at the airport."

Was he covering a slip? Or telling the truth? Was it odd that he recalled all their names and was so well informed? Or was he simply a news junkie? She couldn't tell, but she certainly hadn't heard remorse in his tone. "You don't sound sorry."

He ran his finger along the edge of his weapon. "I've never met your associate. But since she worked at your firm, I can't say I'm all choked up over her death."

"Can anyone corroborate your whereabouts this morning?" she asked.

"Try Mrs. Potter," Damien sneered. "I can't leave the place without the old biddy knowing."

"Thank you." Mandy started to turn away. She noted that Zack covered her back, waiting until she took several steps before following.

Damien raised his voice so that she couldn't miss the angry edge. "And tell my ex . . . I'll go easier on her if she comes home of her own accord."

Mandy stopped, peered over her shoulder, lifted her chin and stared at Damien. Oh God. Had her client gotten back together with her ex? "Was that a threat?"

He didn't reply, just shot her a sly smile and slashed the

air with his rapier. Sheesh—no wonder his ex-wife had been frightened of him. But the woman was no longer Mandy's client. Unless she hired Mandy again, there was nothing she could do.

Zack snorted as they walked away. "That went well, don't you think?"

Mandy sighed. "I suppose you could have done better?"

"I would have used a more direct approach."

"Easy for you to say now." They walked outside into the bright sunshine. The bumper-to-bumper traffic along Dale Mabry Highway sent choking fumes their way. Famous for traffic, wall-to-wall concrete, and strip malls, the sprawl attracted shoppers but there were so few trees; if it weren't for the heat, sunshine, and humidity, they could have been in Any City USA.

Once they reached the car she'd leased until the insurance company processed her claim, she opened all the windows to release the worst of the steaming heat. The steering wheel was hot, and she didn't look forward to returning to Damien's neighborhood to check with Mrs. Potter to verify his whereabouts.

But as much as she wanted to return to her law practice, she couldn't—not until they found out who was hurting her coworkers. Looking for the culprit in her stack of files seemed an exercise in frustration. However, Mandy would not give up. Not with all their lives riding on finding out what was going on.

When a man in a parked car opposite them rolled down his window, she tensed. Zack's hand eased to his weapon. But the smoker only wanted to let some fresh air into his vehicle, then flicked out his cigarette butt.

Before the assault at the airport, she wouldn't have noticed the stranger in the parked car. But now little things spooked her. Soon she'd be flinching at the sound of a stranger's voice.

She pulled into traffic, thinking she was more suited to working in her air-conditioned office, not pounding the streets for murder suspects. Until she recalled poor Lisa.

Mandy had no right to complain when they would bury the paralegal tomorrow.

MRS. POTTER DIDN'T depict the professional Mandy had expected to find living in Hyde Park. One of Tampa's oldest and most prestigious areas, the neighborhood was full of upwardly mobile professionals. With Damien's apartment complex offering charming one- and two-bedroom garden-style residences featuring wrought iron gates and manicured lawns, he didn't seem to be suffering financially since his divorce. Located a short walk from terrific shops, entertainment venues, specialty restaurants, and art festivals, the area was convenient to downtown Tampa and his Dale Mabry office. The white-haired, lanky lady who opened the door to 4B was dressed in a clingy T-shirt and yoga pants and had to be in her sixties. This time Mandy decided to let Zack work his charm.

He spoke politely. "Good afternoon, ma'am."

She began to shut the door. "I'm not buying anything."

"We came to ask about your neighbor, Mr. Damien Reed."

"That maniac." Ms. Potter hesitated, then curiosity got the better of her. "What's he done now?"

Zack smiled pleasantly. "We were hoping to confirm his whereabouts this morning at 5 A.M."

"Who are you people?"

"I'm an attorney investigating a case." Mandy handed her a business card.

Mrs. Potter glanced at the card. "Mr. Reed was out."

"Jogging?" Zack asked.

Mrs. Potter snorted. "He was riding his damn Harley."

"You're sure?"

"Of course I'm sure. Every time he comes back or leaves, he wakes up the entire neighborhood."

"So he was out?"

"Yes."

Zack prodded for more information. "Do you know where he went?"

"I have no idea. He left around 2 A.M." Ms. Potter shut the door and clicked the lock, ending the conversation.

Zack frowned at Mandy, his eyes puzzled. "Why would Damien send us to talk to Mrs. Potter when he knew his story wouldn't hold up?"

She shrugged. "You're obviously accustomed to dealing with criminals covering their tracks—not vindictive husbands. Nothing can be more squirrelly than dealing with people after love turns to hate."

Zack cocked his head as if considering her theory. "So Damien sent us on a wild goose chase out of spite?"

"Or damaged pride. Or depression that comes from anger. Or pain. People often don't act rationally about matters of the heart. Maybe Damien just wanted to waste our time. Or get back at Ms. Potter."

"I was surprised he was callous enough to admit he didn't care that Lisa was dead," Zack told her, taking in the garden blooming with tiny white flowers and ferns which surrounded a stately magnolia. "But if he were guilty of killing her, it's unlikely he would have admitted knowing about the murder."

"It's been on the news," she reminded him.

"Still, in my experience most criminals are habitual liars and don't ever admit knowing anything." They left the upscale apartment building and headed back to the car, which was for once parked in the shade under towering old oaks.

"Maybe he enjoyed the thought of sending us in circles. Or maybe he's taunting us. The way he played me, pretending not to know who I was when he obviously recognized me, suggests he's cunning. Not that stockbrokers are usually dummies."

"He's taunting us with the knowledge that he lied." Zack spoke as if he was thinking out loud and gave her a sideways glance. "I thought the DEA had some tough characters to deal with, but even they don't often terrify their own wives."

"The guy's twisted. He likes to mess with people, harass them." They headed back once more to her car. "But that's why I love going to court. He can't bully the judge."

Zack stopped at her car. "You like taking on scum like him, don't you?"

"When I got through wringing Damien dry of his hidden assets, his wife was able to pay for her kids' living expenses and maybe have enough left over for music lessons and summer camp. Raising her children alone can't be easy, but his child support payments will help." She opened the car door and got inside. "And for me, there's satisfaction in justice."

Chapter Fourteen

THE INVESTIGATION INTO the Dana–Lisa–Mandy cases was totally unsatisfying to Mandy. She and Zack had been unable to verify the stockbroker's alibi, and the wife beater who was out on bail wasn't at his last known address in Palm River. His landlord had evicted him for non-payment of rent. The neighbors hadn't seen him. His mother had hung up on Mandy's phone call.

"I'm ready to call it quits for the day," Mandy admitted from the front seat of her car, as she drove out of the Palm River neighborhood, a mix of custom waterfront homes on the river and fixer-uppers that had once been run down but with the skyrocketing price of real estate in the bay area, had become attractive again to first-time buyers. With their huge yards and quiet streets, it was a safe place to raise a family . . . or a good place to hide from the law.

Zack regularly checked the side mirrors to watch for a tail, but he hadn't mentioned seeing anything out of the ordinary. Her stomach growled and she was too tired to care where Zack and she would spend the night. Hungry and exhausted. Not a terrific combination for good decision-making. She pulled onto the highway and stayed in the slow lane. "I need a break. How about dinner?"

"We've a better shot at catching the pediatrician at home tonight than at the office tomorrow, where his patients will give him an excuse to avoid us." Zack's reference to the third case on which the three women had worked together, made her realize he wanted to keep going. But it was difficult enough for her to believe the pediatrician's wife's accusation of child abuse, never mind that the doctor could have killed Lisa.

Beside her Zack buried his eyes in the file. He obviously had more stamina than she did. And here her mom thought *she* was a workaholic. But his determination showed concern, didn't it? That was a good sign. Not for her so much, but for Dana and their daughter.

"My stomach's growling at me, complaining that I only ate a half sandwich for lunch. I don't think well with hunger pangs, and I need a ladies' room." Without saying more she pulled into a restaurant. If he wanted to work without food or sleep that was his prerogative. However, Mandy wasn't out to prove that she could keep up with him.

She knew better, recalling how he'd made love to her for hours. Zack had certainly known how to please her. His combination of playful and erotic sexiness had left her totally satisfied, until he'd gotten up and run on her treadmill the next morning. She'd watched him work out, admiring his tan chest dusted with a triangle of hair. Zack wasn't built like a weight lifter, more like an Olympic swimmer with long, lean lines. He had a gorgeous body. His legs had pounded a steady rhythm and his cute butt had tempted her into drawing him back into bed.

Two years passing had only served to hone his muscle tone. As he stepped in front of her to open the restaurant's front door, she'd had to force her gaze from his butt. Grateful he hadn't noticed her interest, she sniffed at the wafting scents. "Smells good."

He grinned. "I'd forgotten how much you like to eat."

She wondered what else he'd forgotten. Although they'd

spent the day together, they'd spoken little about themselves, saying almost nothing about the past. She hadn't felt the strain of being with him again for several hours—until just then, when he'd made a personal comment. She could have sworn he'd done it on purpose.

Zack could change from all business to all personal with chameleon-like skill. When he ratcheted up his intimate side and boosted the charm that made her so aware of him as a man, it was with a suddenness that unsettled—that made her recall the shimmer in his eyes when he teased, the burn when he taunted.

With just a sentence he'd brought back images of their night together. Damp skin, ragged breathing, lots of kissing. The best kisses ever. When she met his direct gaze, she saw fierce determination, as if he was bent on breaking down every barrier she'd attempted to raise. A sudden flush of heat warned that the banked embers connecting them could ignite at any time.

He grabbed a booth. They ordered chicken quesadillas with guacamole and sour cream, and she excused herself to go to the rest room. He insisted on accompanying her, and while he stood outside the door, she ran the water and made a quick call to her mother. Gabby was fine and both baby and grandmother were enjoying the beach as much as possible, considering the circumstances.

To reassure her mother, Mandy told her she had a bodyguard, promised to be careful, then headed back to Zack. Their soft drinks had arrived with a basket of warm chips covered by a napkin. She plucked out a chip and dipped it into hot salsa.

She had questions about this man that needed answers. There was only one way to get them. "So how long will the DEA let you stay here in Tampa?" She ventured farther into the realm of the personal before she lost her nerve.

"That depends." Zack leaned forward, his gaze on her lips causing her mouth to go dry.

She sipped her cola to wash down the spicy chip and hot salsa. "Depends on what?"

"On why you're interested."

Mandy swallowed hard. She should have known Zack wouldn't mince words, and scrambled for a plausible reason for her interest. She certainly didn't want him thinking she intended to pick up where they'd left off two years ago.

"Dana's been worried about you," she said, latching onto the first reason that made sense. "After seeing you in California, I understood her concern. I wanted to know . . . how life's been treating you."

She wanted to know if he had any room in his life. For Gabby.

He eyed her with a gaze that saw too much and the silence grew. Then he nodded and said simply, "I can stay as long as I'm on administrative leave."

"I don't understand."

"My last case had complications." He bit into his chip, his thoughts apparently going inward. Then he added, "A child, a six-year-old boy, Todd, died."

"You were involved?" She tried not to sound shocked, didn't think she'd managed it by the way his expression grew distant.

"His mother sold drugs. It was my job to befriend her. She was a prostitute and a low-level snitch who led me up the drug supply chain."

The waitress returned to see if they needed a refill and Zack fell silent. Mandy didn't need to ask if talking about this was hard for him. A muscle in his jaw twitched and he avoided her gaze. She swirled a chip into the salsa and gave him time to continue if he wished.

Finally he said, "Neither she nor Todd was supposed to be at the warehouse when the bust went down. But she was a junkie who needed a fix."

"I don't understand." What kind of mother would . . .

"She'd towed Todd along with her at three in the morning to work the sympathy angle from a dealer known to have a soft heart for children."

Mandy put down the chip. She couldn't eat. She wasn't certain if she wanted to hear this story, but at the same time, she needed to. Who knew when she might see Zack again after they found Lisa's killer?

He stared at her, his face hard, almost painfully composed as if he could hide how much he cared. "Mother and son were in the warehouse when the DEA moved in. We cut the lights. Inside, everyone hit the deck. It was dark. Shots were exchanged. Todd had a metal toy, a robot I'd given him." He swallowed hard, his Adam's apple bobbing, his face tight, his eyes full of regret. "In the confusion, one of the agents mistook the robot for a gun and shot Todd. Until the lights came back up, he didn't know he'd shot a kid, not an adult."

She heard the regret, the sorrow, the grief over his part in the operation and she ached to comfort him. But she didn't know what to say. *It's not your fault* sounded trite. "And you blame yourself."

"If not for me, he wouldn't have been in the warehouse that day. You see, earlier that morning, I'd tossed his mother's drugs down the toilet—with the intent of protecting her from the bust that was coming—not for her sake, but the boy's."

"You were protecting her?" Had he had feelings for this other woman? A junkie?

"After the DEA nailed the dealers, we would have rounded her up during the mop-up operation. I didn't want Todd to lose her. She was all he had. Todd looked after her as if he was the adult and she the child. He adored her. But she didn't think about him. She needed her fix . . . went to her dealer. And Todd died."

She placed her hand on top of his, sad that he hurt so much, but a tiny part of her encouraged that he had wanted so much to protect the child. "Saying I'm sorry doesn't seem adequate."

He didn't appear to notice her touch. His voice was raw with emotion. "Administrative leave is standard procedure after a death. If they clear me, I'll be called back to take on another case."

"Is that want you want?"

"The DEA shrink said what happened is similar to falling

off a horse. I have to climb back on—or the fear of falling, of getting someone else killed, will paralyze me." His thumb rubbed the back of her hand.

So he *was* aware of her touch, which gave her the courage to speak some of her thoughts. "And you are buying into that?"

Zack jerked up his head. "What do you mean?"

"Is this shrink on a DEA retainer?"

His eyes narrowed. "Probably. So what?"

"Did you ever think his job is to slap a bandage on your mental wound and send you back into battle? That he doesn't give a damn if you heal or if the wound leaves scars?"

Zack only shrugged. "Doesn't really matter. I'm committed to my work, and I'm never having kids."

His out-of-the-blue statement took her off guard, knocked the breath out of her lungs. Her hands started shaking.

Zack noticed. "After Todd died, his mother overdosed. She couldn't take the pain or guilt or shame of living, of going on without him."

Surprise and anger pushed away her shock. "So you feel so awful about the boy's death that you don't want to have children of your own?"

"Something like that."

"You are so wrong." She wanted to take away his pain. She wanted to shake him. Instead she used the best line of reasoning she could muster, her determination to change his mind surging as high and furious as a hurricane's high tide. "So you shouldn't date because you might fall in love, marry, and get divorced?"

"Been there, done that."

"It's like saying you shouldn't make friends because they might disappoint and hurt you. It's as if you're unwilling to feel *anything* because some feelings might be bad."

For a moment fury flashed across Zack's face. She watched a war waging until he finally shook his head. "You weren't there, Mandy. That little boy died in my arms."

No doubt seeing Todd die, and the mother's overdose had

brought back all the agony of losing his brother. At the sight of the pain in his eyes, the twist of his lips, the muscle tensing in his jaw, Mandy recognized a bigger obstacle than work to his becoming a father. Zack had never healed his grief. Now Todd's death had only reopened the wound. No wonder he looked so drawn, so tense. He might act like his usual charming self, but he was forcing his smiles and laughter. Dana had known.

"I am sorry," she said.

Zack downed half his drink in one long swallow, then carefully set the glass back on the table. Mandy ached to tell him to stay here and to take up a less dangerous line of work so he could heal his wounds and she could tell him about their daughter. But he was hurting too much now to throw that at him. As much as it hurt her, knowledge of their sweet daughter would only feel like a burden to him.

As a family law attorney, she of all people knew that fathers had legal rights. Keeping Zack from his daughter would have a bearing in any custody case and if Zack ever took her to court he could use her actions against her. Yet, he'd just told her he didn't want a child.

But she knew Zack wasn't dead inside. Shocked, grieving? Yes. But he had too much fire in him to remain indifferent, too much courage to close himself off. He was no longer the same idealistic young man she'd met, but she wasn't the same light-hearted woman, either. Two years had changed her from a breezy girl to a dedicated mother. Those same years had given him a maturity that went beyond twenty-four months of normal living. He'd been through . . . hell.

She hated keeping Gabby from him. A father had the right to know he had a child. The baby had a right to meet her father. Keeping the secret weighed on her. Especially since Mandy's own life might be in danger. Perhaps if she told Zack about Gabby, perhaps if he met his daughter, he'd change his mind.

"After I'm cleared, I'll return to work. I'll be fine."

"Is that what you still want?" She pushed the chips and salsa toward him.

Her cell phone rang and he never got a chance to answer. He looked relieved.

She dug out her cell and answered. "Hello."

"It's me, Dana. Lisa's funeral's at 10 A.M. tomorrow."

"How's your head?" Mandy asked.

"Good. But, it doesn't seem right for me to be so happy when poor Lisa . . ."

"We could all use some good news. What's happened?" Mandy wondered from the upbeat lilt in Dana's tone if the police had found the lottery ticket. With all that had happened—the assault, Lisa's death, and dealing with Zack—she hadn't had time to grieve over the loss of the ticket, of what it meant to her future as well as the other winners.

"Sam's agreed to sign the adoption application."

"That's wonderful." As much as Mandy would like to have heard the cops had caught their attacker and/or Lisa's murderer, or even good news about recovering the ticket, she still was happy for her friend. She wanted to hand her phone to Zack so he could hear his sister's good news. But recalling their conversation, she thought better of it. "I'll tell Zack."

"Thanks. Bye."

"You'll tell Zack what?" he asked, eyes burning into her.

"Sam's agreed to adopt."

He rolled his eyes. "Oh, yeah. There's an awesome concept."

"Don't spoil it for her, Zack. A baby is what Dana wants. Children mean the world to Sam. At least pretend to be happy. Please?"

He lifted his glass in a salute, his voice deadpan. "It'll be a stretch."

Chapter Fifteen

AFTER DINNER, MANDY had called Liam Seegar, the attorney of Dr. Brad Meriman, the pediatrician accused of bruising his baby. Lisa, Dana, and Mandy had all worked on the doctor's wife's divorce case. Since their client had accused him of abuse, he fit into the possibly violent category. Luckily, she'd worked with Liam before and had found him to be reasonable and open to mediation.

Mandy had been upfront with the other attorney. "I'm trying to protect our clients and their spouses and keep this divorce situation private. If Dr. Meriman could answer a few preliminary questions for us this evening, I'd appreciate it."

The pediatrician's attorney had agreed to join them at his client's house that evening, and by the time Mandy and Zack arrived in Apollo Beach, a waterfront community south of Tampa where the residents lived a relaxed Florida lifestyle, she could see by the car parked in the driveway that Liam had already arrived.

The pediatrician opened the front door to his spacious two-story home on a canal and escorted them into his home office, where he had a pot of coffee waiting along with a plate of fresh-baked sugar cookies. Mid-thirties, with spiked blond hair and blue eyes, he stood about five and a half feet tall and seemed harmless enough. Mandy couldn't decide if he was trying to manipulate them into believing he was a genuinely nice man who'd never hurt a baby, as his wife accused, or if he was exactly what he seemed, a professional saddened by divorce and the terrible accusations against him.

Liam Seegar, a heavy-set blond wearing a khaki pinstripe suit and a soft green shirt, but no tie, shook her hand and Zack's. "This is highly unusual."

"I know. Thanks for coming. I really appreciate it," Mandy spoke with sincerity.

"I wouldn't have agreed, but . . ." Obviously he didn't want to say more about the murders.

"Thanks for helping us out," Zack added.

Liam seated himself by the window. The doctor sagged into a brown lounge chair and Mandy and Zack sat opposite him on a plush leather couch. A cat curled up on an upholstered piano stool. Dr. Meriman pulled a Yorkshire terrier into his lap, sharing his cookies with the dog. She noted that Zack casually but carefully checked out the room, almost as if expecting an ambush. She'd seen nothing to disturb her, only the usual framed degrees on the wall, pictures of his soon to be ex-wife and baby, and a library of leather books. Nothing odd—nothing to suggest this man was capable of hurting his own son. Or of killing Lisa in a murderous frenzy. Or of hiring men to attack Dana and Mandy—no matter what kind of papers she'd filed on his wife's behalf against him.

"Doctor, can you tell me where you were this morning between 5 and 7 A.M.?" Mandy asked.

He didn't look at his attorney to see if he should answer. He didn't hesitate. "I was at Brandon Hospital until 3 A.M. last night and I came directly home and went to bed."

"Can anyone else confirm that?" Zack spoke in a businesslike tone.

Dr. Meriman sipped his coffee. "After the late night,

I slept longer than usual this morning and was walking out the door when my housekeeper arrived at eight. But except for Brutus," he patted his dog, "no one was home while I slept." He put down his coffee cup and leaned forward. "My son . . . he's . . ."

"Fine," Mandy assured the man. With the pending child abuse charges against him, she supposed it was natural for him to think something might have happened to his baby and wondered why he hadn't immediately asked about the safety of the son the state had taken away from him and his wife. Still, she sought to reassure him. "This has nothing to do with your baby."

The doctor's eyes filled with pain. "Do you know how difficult it is for me to be separated from him? I can't sleep without taking a pill. Every time I close my eyes I fear he'll end up a statistic."

The man sounded genuinely concerned about the baby. Could his pain have turned to violence? She sensed nothing threatening in his tone, demeanor, or conversation. Nevertheless, for the baby's sake, she followed the law and established procedure. "The court must decide what's in the best interest of the child."

"Why can't I have supervised visits with my son?" he asked.

His question shocked her. His attorney looked surprised, too. Previously, Meriman's attorney had indicated the doctor considered supervised visitation insulting and beneath him. Yet, right now, his reasonable behavior was contradicting what his spouse and Liam Seegar had told her. His wife had claimed the doctor had no interest in the baby and had abused the child after the baby's crying had disturbed his sleep. According to Mandy's client, after she'd reported his abuse, he'd retaliated and accused *her* of abuse—so the state had taken the child away from both parents. Mandy wanted to make certain she understood what he'd said and reiterated, "If the judge okayed it, you'd agree to supervised visits?"

"You don't have to answer that," Liam replied.

"It's humiliating, but yes. I would agree to do almost anything to see my son."

She couldn't imagine being separated from Gabby for weeks, or the out-of-her-mind fear she'd have if her daughter were placed in a foster home. Although most families did wonderful jobs with the children they housed for the state, some did not. Last year a case where a family locked up and starved the kids had made headlines. Seeing that his baby was well cared for seemed a reasonable request to her. "I'll see what I can do. Liam, if you call me next week—"

"I'll do that."

"Thank you," the doctor said.

Zack remained silent until they returned to the privacy of her leased car, but he had a puzzled glint in her eyes. "What just happened back there?"

She started the car, adjusted the AC to cool her face. "What do you mean?"

He checked the street, then his gaze settled on her. "Dr. Meriman's *wife* is your client. Why would you do him a favor?"

"Why not? It's not like seeing his baby under supervised circumstances will hurt Mrs. Meriman."

"But she certainly won't like it," he countered.

"The parents are adults. They need to act with maturity for the sake of their child."

He rubbed his jaw. "Didn't you just get through telling me over dinner that not everything in life is fair?"

"I didn't say it was. But," she shot him a grin, "there's no reason not to try and make things right. Why should Dr. Meriman have to worry more than necessary? I'm a family law attorney because I want to help people at a time when they might not be thinking clearly, when they are hurt, when the decisions they make can affect how they live for many years."

"Are you always this passionate?"

"Yes," she answered before realizing he was teasing her, and she couldn't help but smile. Pulling out of the driveway, she steered and headed past more custom-built homes toward the interstate, her frustration spreading as wide as the smoke from the Teco stacks, a coal plant that generated electricity for the area. "Do you realize we've spent the entire day searching for clues to who might have killed Lisa and come after Dana and me, and we've come up with zip, zero, zilch."

"You may chalk up our work as a bust, but it's a rare investigation that turns up evidence on the first day." Zack's tone was mild.

"But we couldn't verify the stockbroker's or the pediatrician's whereabouts during the time of Lisa's death, nor could we find the drug addict. As far as I can see, we've wasted our time . . ."

"Time you could have better spent on your cases?"

"Time where I actually help people and earn a living."

"But you can't return to earning a living until we catch these people," Zack reminded her.

"I know. I know. But I have a life, a schedule, that I've worked hard to mold. Is it selfish of me to want that when poor Lisa is dead?"

"Of course not. You'll get your life back. You just have to be patient." Zack sounded so certain.

But he was used to living like a nomad. He didn't have a child waiting for him to come home. Mandy's whole life was on hold. Gabby and her mother were at the beach. She couldn't even sleep at her condo tonight. Not with Zack for her bodyguard. Before she freaked, she reminded herself things could be worse. She could be dead right now.

By the time she'd cruised up the on-ramp to the interstate, she managed to ask casually, "So where are we going now?"

"Mom has a furnished rental house in Brandon that's currently vacant. She's offered it to us."

"Really," she said, wondering if Catherine thought she'd be safer away from her home. Mandy didn't ask. Whatever the reason, Catherine had just solved her problem about Zack walking into a condo full of baby paraphernalia.

If Mandy could just focus on the next problem—spending the night with Zack—could she trust him not to make a move? Could she trust herself not to welcome it, if he did?

Chapter Sixteen

ASPIRIN, SUGGESTED BY her doctors, helped ease the pain of Dana's head injury. Tonight, she wanted to put the attack at the airport behind her. She'd had food catered from Wright's Gourmet, and ordered Sam's favorites, a veggie relish with pickles, olives, and a dill dip; Brie, covered with almonds, apple slices, raisins, and apricots and fresh bread rounds; and turkey tetrazzini with water chestnuts, white sauce, and smothered with aged Vermont cheese. For dessert, his favorite carrot cake. She hadn't felt up to cooking or going out, but she'd wanted a special evening for the two of them. She'd set a table on their bedroom balcony, which overlooked the pool and their waterfront view of Tampa Bay. She'd planned a romantic dinner with a sunset and had dressed up the table with a fine lace cloth, silver, and her favorite china. She'd lit candles, and a bottle of Sam's preferred Pinot Noir awaited him in a copper ice bucket.

She'd been warned not to consume alcohol after her concussion and had iced a bottle of mineral water. Sam had come bounding up the stairs after working out in their home gym, glanced at the dinner table, and entered the shower. "Give me ten minutes."

"No hurry."

While Sam showered, Dana channel surfed and picked out clothes to wear tomorrow for Lisa's funeral. By ten in the morning, the sun would already be high enough in the sky for the temperatures to soar into the eighties. She picked out a black cotton dress, sandals and a purse, and laid out a silver belt and earrings. She'd already ordered flowers from the firm as well as from Sam, then canceled them after learning Jews didn't send flowers to funerals. She settled for a card and a donation to the foster system on Lisa's behalf, but she wished there was something more she could do.

Lisa had been so young and so enthusiastic about her work. Her family was flying in for the service and her friends from school would be there tomorrow. She'd died horribly, violently.

And Mandy had been attacked twice. Dana once. The incidents couldn't be mere coincidence. They had to be connected, but just thinking about it made her head throb. Dana rubbed her forehead, opened a bottle of aspirin, and poured the cold mineral water into her glass. She was swallowing the aspirin when Sam emerged from the master bathroom, wearing shoes, slacks and a dress shirt, his damp hair combed.

Tie in hand, he strode to the mirror and placed it under his collar. "Sorry dear, I just got a phone call. I have to meet the lead attorney on the Morrison case."

So it was starting already. "Can't you delay the meeting until after we eat?"

Sam came up behind her, placed his hands on her waist and kissed her neck. "I'd rather skip dinner and try to come back early."

Early for Sam meant sometime before midnight. Disappointment flooded Dana. Recently, she'd spent too many evenings alone, and after the attack last night, she didn't want to be by herself. "It's a shame to waste the food. I'll call Mom and see if she'd like to join me."

"Good idea." He kissed her cheek. "Got to run."

Although she wished Sam could stay, she realized he'd missed a lot of work recently. While he'd been wonderful today, she shouldn't have to be in the hospital to gain her husband's attention. She hoped things would change once they started a family. But meanwhile, she consoled herself with the knowledge that if she told him she'd needed him to stay, he would have been there for her, just like she was certain he'd be there if they had the children he wanted.

Dana phoned Catherine but was sent straight to voice mail. Her mother must be on another call, so Dana text messaged her. Waiting for her mother to call back, Dana lay down on the bed to watch the news. But she must have been more tired than she'd thought because she dozed off.

When she awakened, it was dark. In the light from the television, she could see that the ice around the wine had mostly melted and condensation drizzled down the outside of the copper bucket.

Dana heard footsteps on the stairs and she shoved herself to a sitting position. "Sam? Is that you?"

No one answered. "Tom?" Her bodyguard was supposed to make intermittent rounds along the yard's perimeter. After each inspection he came inside and remained downstairs. However, if there was a problem, he might have come up to the second level. But if he was here, why hadn't he answered when she'd called out?

Adrenaline and fear wiped away the last dregs of sleep. Her head pounded but there was no time to take another aspirin. Dana rolled off the far side of the bed, grabbed her cell phone and crawled toward the closet. Heart pumping hard, blood pumping too fast, she brushed a trickle of sweat from her eyes. At the sound of another footstep, she trembled.

Someone had sneaked past her bodyguard. They were coming upstairs. For her.

What should she do?

Dana wanted to scream for help. Instead she dialed 911. At the damn busy signal on the network, she swore in frustration.

Blinking back tears, Dana listened hard. The rustle of clothing on the stairs warned her she didn't have much time.

Perhaps Sam hadn't heard her call out his name and he'd breeze into the room at any moment and they could laugh over her silly fears. But in the meantime, she wished she had a solid weapon. A baseball bat. A fireplace poker. A gun.

What the hell was wrong with her? She had a gun in the closet—one she knew how to use.

Thankful for the thick carpet that covered the sound of her mad scramble, she opened her closet. Didn't dare flick on the light.

Where was the gun? Her hands knocked a hanger to the floor and it clattered. Her mouth so dry she wondered if she'd be able to talk if her call ever connected, she peeked through the wooden slats. A shadow loomed, emerging from the dark stairwell.

Unable to find the gun, she again dialed 911, her hands quivering, her heart dancing up her throat. Again the network wouldn't put her call through.

Damn.

She picked up a wooden hanger, the best weapon she could find, and peered through the wooden slats once more. The shadow lengthened, enlarged. Someone padded into the bedroom without hesitation. A woman's silhouette.

"Dana, did you fall asleep?"

"Mom?" Heart still stammering, Dana exited the closet.

Catherine flicked on the light. Both women blinked. Stunned, Dana banished her fear while her mother frowned at the wooden hanger that Dana held in her hand like a club. Catherine's worried eyes took in Dana's ebbing panic. "What's wrong?"

"I called out and when no one answered . . ."

"I didn't hear. I thought you might be sleeping."

Dana sank onto the bed and dropped her head into her hands. "I thought . . . I thought someone had snuck in."

Her mother sat next to her on the bed, smoothed her hair and rubbed her back like she'd done when Dana had been a little girl. "It's okay. You're fine. When I returned your call, you didn't answer."

"I fell asleep."

"I thought you might be in the shower so I just came over, figuring we'd have dinner together. Tom's downstairs. He let me in." Catherine stood and gave Dana a few more moments to regroup. "Are you hungry?"

"Starved." The idea of food, of normality sounded great. But first she popped another headache pill.

The sun had already set over the bay. The candles had burned down and the food was no longer piping hot. But they reheated the meal downstairs in the kitchen, then brought it back up, to enjoy some privacy from the body-guards who could otherwise overhear their every word. When they finally settled on the balcony to eat, Dana sighed, still on edge. "Between the attack last night and Lisa's death, I'm as jumpy as a defendant about to hear the judge pro-nounce sentence."

Catherine blotted her mouth with a napkin and waited for a noisy boat to speed by before speaking. "I'm half tempted to close the firm until—"

"You can't. We have clients who need us."

"I know." Catherine waved her to silence. "We have a duty to our clients. But I also have a duty to Mandy, Maria, Sylvia, and you and Zack." She smiled at the mention of her children. "Especially you and Zack."

"We could close for the rest of the week but that wouldn't necessarily make us any safer. Until someone cashes in that lottery ticket, we'll all be targets."

"What's the time limit to cash in?" Catherine asked, spearing an olive with her fork as if it were Lisa's murderer.

"Thirty days. Much too long to close the firm—although I wouldn't mind if Zack and Mandy stayed together until then."

Catherine sipped her wine. "Don't get your hopes up. Zack's so much like his father . . . he wants to save the world and doesn't mind risking his life to do it."

The frogs chirping in the cattails and the water lapping against the dock and seawall soothed Dana's nerves as much as her mother's presence and discussing family. "Zack's got some of you in him, too." Dana dipped her celery into peanut sauce and enjoyed the sweet crunchy taste. "Have you seen the way he acts around Mandy? He plays it oh-so-casual but the rest of us might as well not be in the room."

Catherine rolled her eyes and eyed the Brie and sesame toast. "Lust does not a marriage make." Generally her mother avoided high carbs, determined to keep her elegant shape, but this time she gave in to temptation.

Dana changed the subject. "I want to share some good news. Sam's agreed to apply for adoption. I want to try for siblings, maybe a boy and a girl, but two girls or two boys would be fine, too."

Catherine broke into a wide grin of delight. "That's wonderful." If her mother had any concerns about Sam's taking so long to agree to adoption, she kept them to herself. She raised her wine glass and clinked it to Dana's water glass. "Good for you, dear."

"Thanks, Mom."

A shout followed by a heavy thud downstairs interrupted their meal. In a flash, Dana's good mood evaporated and her fears returned as if they'd never really left.

Dana exchanged a frightened glance with her mother and whispered, "You heard that, right?"

"Shh." Catherine raised her finger to her lips, her face paling.

Dana shoved back from the table and turned off the light. She returned to her mother's side, grabbed Catherine's hand and a dinner knife and tugged her toward the closet, determined to find her gun.

From downstairs, she heard the sound of a fist smacking flesh, a soft moan and an oof, the sound of air leaving a man's lungs. It sounded like—a brawl. A whizzing noise—maybe a gunshot—then more loud thumps, like a body keeling over and knocking into a table or overturning a chair. Then nothing.

Silence.

Oh . . . God. Where the hell was her gun? She tossed aside shoes, purses, scarves, belts.

A car's headlights shined through the window. A car was turning into the driveway. Dana peeked out. Sam was coming home, heading straight into the danger downstairs. While she prayed the two bodyguards had started a fight with one another, she doubted that men so well trained would be so undisciplined.

Dana wanted to hide with her mother in the closet. But how could she let Sam come inside to face . . . she didn't know what without trying to warn him?

"Mom, call 911," Dana whispered, praying her mother's phone would get through.

"Why not warn Sam?" her mother asked.

"If his cell phone rings, it could make him a target." Her fingers finally closed on the gun. She switched off the safety and prayed she was making the right decision. Leaving the bedroom, she headed for the stairs. Once she reached the landing she could peak over the balcony, figure out what had happened and hopefully find a way to warn Sam—all while remaining out of the line of fire.

Catherine yanked her back and whispered. "No. You can't go down there."

"Sam's home." No way could she hide while he strode into danger. Dana shook free of her mother's grasp, pressed the dinner knife into her hand, and left her mother behind.

Knees trembling, heart hammering, gun in hand, she hesitated on the upstairs landing. The wooden stairs creaked, but she could avoid the noisy spots if she took her time and kept her head. Holding her breath, she proceeded, listening and estimating how much time she had before Sam entered the house.

The car's engine was too quiet for her to hear it in the garage. She'd made it down four stairs before she picked up the sound of another thud.

Had her mother's call to 911 gone through? How long would it take for help to arrive?

At a creak above her, Dana turned to see her mother

following. Damn. She should have realized that no way would Catherine allow her to head into danger alone.

Praying that her mother had gotten through, that Sam wouldn't enter the house but go down to the water as he sometimes did, and that the cops were on the way, Dana kept her hand on the banister to guide her. The laundry room door opened.

Sam was heading into the kitchen.

She swore. Dana had to hurry. Should she call out? Warn Sam to turn and flee? If she did, would he listen? It was more his nature to charge ahead.

She swallowed hard. Strained her eyes to see. Every light was out except the fluorescent lamp in the fish tank that cast eerie reflections through the marble foyer.

When she peered into the den she glimpsed a short man with long hair hanging out of a baseball cap before he scrunched behind a column. She recalled the description of Mandy's attacker—the one who'd rammed her car off the bridge. Dana would bet her law degree this was the same guy. In a reflection from a framed painting, she could even see that his hair was light. He held a gun.

From the sound of Sam's progress behind the intruder, he'd stopped in the kitchen and opened the fridge. Light reflected into the living room. All the trespasser had to do was turn around to see Sam in the kitchen.

Dana wished she had a clear shot from her position. If she proceeded, the shooter would see her. Should she shout now? Or wait until she was certain Sam wasn't where he could be so easily shot?

Fear seemed to make her hearing acute. Sam twisted off a beer cap and threw it into the trash.

Shut the fridge door. The light had to be making Sam a perfect target.

Dana held her breath. Waited. The ticking seconds passed like days. Which way would the intruder go? Advance toward her? Retreat toward Sam?

If she was lucky, he'd flee out the front door. But if he chose Sam, she planned to creep up on his back. Shoot him.

But the intruder ignored Sam. Crouching, he zigzagged through the den, his steps light and quick. It was so dark, she still didn't have a shot.

There was no time to retreat. No time to hide. And she didn't know where he'd hidden.

She faced the den, sweat beading into her eyes, heart pounding. There. The intruder lurked in a shadow. She aimed. Too late.

Eyes glinting, his arm was already raised. His gun trained. On her.

God.

Icy fear slashed her.

Several things happened, seemingly simultaneously. The intruder pulled the trigger. Someone slammed into Dana, knocked her into the wall, then pressed against her. She dropped her gun and it skidded across the floor out of reach.

A bullet whizzed past Dana's head. Molding chipped and splinters shot into her neck.

Sam flicked on the light. "What the hell?"

Dana recognized the person who'd slammed her out of harm's way, the person covering her with her own body—was her mother.

In the same instant the lights had come on, the intruder spun, aimed, and fired at Sam. Eyes wide with surprise, Sam staggered, his gaze dropping in confusion as if to see if he'd been hit. Sagging to his knees, Sam flung the beer bottle with his good hand at the gunman. He missed, the bottle breaking as it hit marble. Glass shattered.

The shooter dodged the glass as he scrambled down the hallway toward Dana. Using all her strength, Dana shoved her mother aside, scooped a bronze statue off a table and flung it. The statue flipped backwards, the base striking the gunman in the nose. He cursed in pain, clamped a hand over his face, turned to shoot again. Catherine stuck out her foot.

The guy stumbled, slipped, and got up. Police sirens wailed.

In a running crouch, the shooter finally fled out the front door, stringy blond hair beneath his Devil Ray's baseball cap

flying behind him. Dana's glance into the living room revealed two bodies and she shuddered. Food churned in her
stomach. From the angle of Tom's neck and the stillness of
her mother's bodyguard, Dana didn't need a medical degree
to know they were dead.

Those poor men had died . . . to protect her. *Dear God.*
She closed her eyes and swallowed hard.

"You okay?" Catherine asked Dana.

She didn't mention the headache that had swooped back
with a vengeance. Not at the sight of Sam trying and failing
to stand.

While her mother went to the door to greet the police,
Dana hurried toward her husband, praying he was all right.
Then she saw the blood. Too much blood. All the air in her
lungs whooshed out. She couldn't breathe. Clammy and
sweaty at the same time, Dana fought to stay calm. "Sam?"

Ignoring her nausea, the spilled beer and the glass shards,
Dana dropped to the floor beside Sam, who lay on his back
in a pool of blood. Damn it. Why did all the people she loved
keep getting hurt?

"Sam. Talk to me."

"I'm hit."

Although she was holding him, she couldn't even see
where he'd been hit. "Mom, Sam needs an ambulance."

"I'll tell the police," Catherine called back from the front
steps.

Sam's eyebrows knitted in pain. His breath was ragged.
But he grabbed Dana's hand with surprising strength. She
leaned over him and he whispered, "Call Mandy and Zack.
Warn them."

"The cops will catch the guy."

As if fate wanted to mock her, she heard the roar of a boat
speeding away and out into the bay. She feared that by the
time the police notified the Coast Guard or brought in search
helicopters, the killer would be long gone, hidden in any of a
dozen nearby parks, inlets, or mangrove swamps.

"Warn them," he insisted, his face racked with pain.

"Okay, Sam." Dana hadn't thought to warn anyone and

hoped the police would catch the man who'd just run out the door and escaped in the boat. She was too worried over her bleeding husband to think of much else besides getting him help. But even in serious pain, Sam was thinking about others. "We'll warn everyone. Don't try to talk anymore."

Sam lifted his head, his eyes glazed with pain, his voice raw. "Tell Zack to kill the son of a bitch."

Chapter Seventeen

SYLVIA JACOBSON WASHED salad greens at the sink. Between Ben inside and the bodyguard parked out front by the street, Sylvia felt safe and grateful to be home after a trying day of fielding phone calls at the office. After work, she'd stopped to nurse her grandson, who was running a fever. She'd helped her daughter rub the boy with alcohol and he'd finally fallen asleep, his fever down. So she'd gotten home much later than usual, but she could sleep in the next morning. Catherine would close the firm during the funeral, but Sylvia suspected tomorrow afternoon would again be hectic.

Ben rolled his wheelchair up to the kitchen counter, took a knife from the drawer and started chopping carrots. Head bent, his thinning gray hair a reminder of the many years they'd been together, he appeared lost in thought. While he seemed the same since his accident, she sometimes wondered if he put on a cheerful front for her sake, although he hadn't let the wheelchair slow him down.

Working side by side in the kitchen, without a need for words, was one of her favorite activities. However, from the ticking muscle in his tan jaw, she knew Ben had something on his mind and it wasn't the late hour of their supper that was bothering him.

It wasn't like Ben to keep things from her but he'd been up to something lately. He disappeared for hours and came home exhausted. When she asked where he'd been, he told her he'd taken up wheelchair basketball, but when she'd asked to watch a game, he'd refused, telling her the guys would feel uncomfortable.

Ben chopped and diced for a few minutes before he looked up, his deep blue eyes filled with concern. "Why don't you take off the rest of the week? We could start your vacation early."

She wished she could have set his mind at ease. That old saying, *once a cop, always a cop,* was so true. Ever since the lottery win and the trouble, Ben had stuck close to her side. She loved having him around, not just for his companionship but for his keen insight. "I can't leave the rest of the girls in a mess. They need me."

"I need you." Ben placed the carrots in a bowl and began to slice celery. She handed him radishes, olives, onions, and red bell peppers to dice while she made fresh salad dressing, adding sage from the plant growing next to her sink. She'd mix in cooked chicken and the late night supper would tide them over until morning.

"Ben, you saw what it was like today. With Lisa gone," she choked up, "everyone has to pitch in until . . ." Sylvia wiped her eyes. "Until we find Lisa's replacement and hire some office staff."

"Perhaps now would be a good time for you to retire," he suggested gently, setting down the knife.

"I can't. The winning lottery ticket's gone." She sniffed, holding back tears that would upset her husband. "Dana and Mandy were lucky they survived."

Ben chopped harder, attacking the vegetables. "We have my pension, your social security, and our savings and soon I'll be earning more building Web sites. It'll be enough."

She wiped her hands on her apron. "But if I work another two years, we'll be able to build a cabin on that land your father left us in the mountains. You know the doctor said it's good for you to get out of the summer heat that makes your joints swell."

"The cabin isn't necessary to my well being—you are." Ben plucked the bottle of oil from her hand, set it aside, and tugged her onto his lap. "I'm worried about you."

"I'm fine." Sitting on his lap in the wheelchair, she snuggled into him, loving the feel of his strong arms around her. After so many years of marriage, she still enjoyed nestling against Ben's warmth, savoring the spice of his aftershave and the comfort of being able to count on him in a crunch. "You take such good care of me."

He smoothed her bangs from her face. "I have a bad feeling about what's going on at the firm. Between the assaults on Dana and Mandy, and Lisa's death, half of the lottery winners have been attacked."

"It is scary," she admitted.

"The evening news stations cooperated and picked up the story that none of you ladies have the ticket anymore, but we can't let down our guard. The killer may not have heard that the ticket's been stolen."

"My phone hasn't stop ringing all day. Lots of people heard on the radio, too."

"It's also possible that the attacks aren't because someone's still searching for the ticket."

"What do you mean?" She looked into his concerned eyes and realized how lucky she was to have him. Another man would be bemoaning the loss of the money, probably focusing on trying to get it back. But Ben's concern was for her. She rested her head on his shoulder and hugged him.

"It's also possible that whoever stole the ticket doesn't want anyone left alive who can contest ownership."

"So they can claim all the winnings for themselves."

"Yes."

She lifted her head from his shoulder. "Surely the police would question anyone who shows up with our ticket?"

"Of course they would. But after past snafus with allegedly stolen tickets, the new Powerball lottery commission rules state that possession equals ownership. So anyone who has the ticket can cash in." Ben stroked her cheek. "What do you know about Maria?"

"She's smart and has a new boyfriend. Why?"

"Because she and her boyfriend could be prime suspects. You and Maria are the only winners who haven't been attacked. Since I know *you* aren't trying to kill the other lottery winners, maybe she's—"

"You've forgotten Catherine."

"Catherine would never hurt her own daughter. But suppose Maria—"

"No. That girl worked her way up from nothing. She's so proud of her law degree." Sylvia had been a cop's wife long enough to know that most violent crimes were committed by men. "Besides, I can't picture any woman using a knife to kill poor Lisa. Men kill with that kind of rage—not women."

"Have you met Maria's boyfriend? Maybe the two of them plotted together to . . ."

She sighed. "I hate thinking in this direction. But Maria has been real secretive about the guy. She's known as the good girl, the overachiever, the one always trying to please her parents and her boss. She even graduated first in her class. Never been in a lick of trouble. She just doesn't seem like the type to hang out with dangerous men."

"Perhaps you're right. Meanwhile, none of you are safe. Someone's targeting the lottery winners or people in your firm."

"Seems like it," Sylvia admitted.

"I don't want anyone coming after you, too. I couldn't bear to lose you."

"That won't happen. Not with you here to protect me. You're still a good shot and you don't go anywhere without a gun." She'd seen him hide a holster in his wheelchair.

"I'm not in the same shape I once was."

That was her Ben. He never complained about his handicap. Not once. After the accident, he'd expected to die. Now he considered every day, every year a bonus. He'd retired rather than work a desk job, but he was taking some computer

courses and learning to build Web sites. Soon he'd be earning as much as he always had, maybe more. He played
wheelchair basketball, tutored three of their grandchildren,
and organized police fundraisers. He had more activities and
friends than anyone she knew, but he always put her first.

"Honey, with you here to protect me, there's no reason to
worry." Ben was her hero. He might be at a disadvantage due
to his paralysis, but he was smart and often that counted for
more than strength or mobility. "I have no doubt that if anyone attacked, you'd shoot them. I just wish the other girls
were as lucky. Dana has Sam, but Catherine, Mandy, and
Maria are all alone."

"Mandy's got Zack protecting her and he's nobody's fool.
I like the look of that boy."

"Zack's hardly a boy. When you were his age, we already
had three kids."

Ben smiled. "I was an early starter, but who could blame
me when I lucked out finding a pretty wife like you?"

Back then Ben couldn't keep his hands off her. He still
couldn't. She shoved down her grief over the recent troubles
and managed a grin. After so many years, they'd both
learned not to allow bad things to steal their happiness. "Did
you notice at the office today that when Zack was watching
Mandy he had a gleam in his eyes?"

"Don't start with your matchmaking. I know you want the
entire world to have what we do, but not everyone is so
lucky."

"Sometimes they are," she teased. "Didn't I do a good job
finding Roxie her Dennis?" Roxie was their youngest daughter and Sylvia had met her future son-in-law, their vet, when
she'd taken their dog for a checkup. One look through his
thick glasses into those warm brown eyes and she'd known
he was the right man for her Roxie. The two of them were
expecting their third son any day now. "I think Mandy and
Zack could be good together."

"Uh-huh." Ben didn't argue. He'd been married long
enough to know that Sylvia had a sixth sense when it came
to matters of the heart.

"Maria's new guy is keeping her happy, too. She seems bubbly lately. Like some man is doing a good job in her bed." Sylvia unfastened the top snap of his jeans.

"Distracting me with sex isn't going to work this time."

"Uh-huh," she agreed. "I wouldn't think of doing such a thing." But her hand moved lower.

"I mean it, Sylvia. Let's go away next week. Catherine can hire a temp to answer the phones."

"I do more than answer the phones. I type—"

"I want you someplace safe. Someplace I can have you all to myself."

"Why wait until next week? You can have me right now."

Sometimes there were advantages to a wheelchair and to knowing her husband almost as well as he knew himself. Ben might have put on a few pounds. His hair might be thinning. He might not be able to walk, but some things never changed. He always wanted her and he didn't mind the wrinkles around her eyes, or the body that had birthed seven kids or that she wasn't as spry as she once was.

They still knew to please one another. They still knew how to love.

Sylvia sighed happily as Ben rolled them toward the bedroom. Beneath her cheek, Ben suddenly tensed. He spoke in a whisper. "Did you hear that?"

"What?" She listened to the air conditioner cycling on, Ben's breath in her ear, and the neighbor's dog barking.

Ben eased her from his lap and pulled his gun. "Get down. Stay away from the window. Someone's in our backyard."

Sylvia's mouth went dry. Their yard was fenced, the gate locked to keep kids from their pool.

No one should be there.

"Should I call for help?" she asked. The phone was back in the kitchen and since Ben was home, her bodyguard remained outside in his car.

"Stay where you are," Ben ordered in a calm, but firm, voice.

He raised his gun to the window sill, peered through the pane into the darkness. Clouds blocked the moon.

"See anyone? she whispered.

"I'm waiting for my eyes to adjust."

She peeked over his shoulder. "There."

A man merged with the shadows between the Canary palm and the giant lily plants she was so proud of. Clouds parted and moonlight glinted on a gun. He fired and the bullet smashed into the side of the window sill, spraying splinters.

She jerked back with a gasp.

Ben didn't hesitate. He shot right through their bedroom window.

The trespasser howled, ducked behind a tree.

"You got him." Sylvia placed a hand on her husband's shoulder to steady her nerves. She had never seen a man shot before.

"I nicked him. But he just hightailed it over the fence. I can't fire another shot and risk it going into the neighbor's yard."

"He's getting away?"

Ben headed towards the kitchen and the phone. "I'll call it in. Maybe a black and white will pick him up."

Chapter Eighteen

"THE COPS ARE hot on my ass," Nick Vizzi panted into his phone. His nose still smarted. The bitch may have broken it with her statue-throwing trick.

"Did you complete the job?"

"Shit, no. You forgot to tell me about the two bodyguards. Took me a while to take them out. The women must have heard the commotion and called the cops. Then the husband came home and to get out of the house, I had to shoot him."

"What a fuck-up."

"Someone must have figured out where I was going next and warned the cripple and his old lady. They shot at me before I even got inside." He refrained from mentioning that he'd fired from outside, reluctant to go inside after the previous screw-up.

"What about Mandy Newman?"

"I'm not icing her unless you triple my fee."

"Listen, you little motherfucker. We had a deal. You can't change our arrangement."

"Damn straight I can. I didn't figure on bodyguards and cops."

"The cops are your fault. You took too long."

"Yeah, well, you try taking out two trained bodyguards without making a sound."

"You used a silencer?"

"Does a hooker fuck for cash? Of course I used a muffler, but bodies make noise when they hit the floor."

"Has anyone seen you?"

Nick hesitated. "I'm wearing a disguise. It was dark. By tomorrow my hair will be short and a different color."

"You got hit?"

"Just a scratch, boss."

"You leave any blood behind?"

"That shit don't matter. They got to match the blood to something, and they ain't gonna find me if I don't want to be found."

"So far as I can see, you haven't completed one assignment. Now you want me to pay extra?"

"This wasn't a one-person job." His nose had swelled to twice its size. Tomorrow, he'd have two black eyes. His ear burned. The cripple had blown off the lobe. From the sting, he guessed he'd have to down a shitload of vodka to dull the pain. "I told you this many hits in one night would be tricky."

"You told me you could pull it off."

"Your pissing info was wrong."

"I don't spoon-feed my—"

"You said I had to deal with only women, that no one would be armed. Look, the heat is on. If you don't want to pay my price, find someone else. I've had enough of this shit." Nick was ready to fold for the night.

But if he didn't complete the job, word would get out—sure, he'd always find more work—but he might have to lower his asking price which was never a good thing, especially the way his new lady was hitting him up. She liked pretty things.

"All right," he conceded. "I'll do the lawyer lady for double, not one cent less."

"Agreed. This time, don't fuck up."

Chapter Nineteen

ZACK AND MANDY hadn't made it out of the restaurant parking lot before his phone rang. "Dana?"

"Sam's been shot."

Zack's protective instincts shifted into overdrive. He'd already lost one brother. He couldn't lose Dana, too. "Are you okay?"

"Yes. I'm on the way to the hospital."

"What happened?" Zack asked, then turned to Mandy. "Sam's been shot." He put the conversation on speaker phone so she could listen. "Mandy and I can both hear you now."

"How are you?" Mandy asked.

"Mom and I are fine and safe, but our bodyguards are dead." Her voice trembled and she sucked in a breath before continuing, "The police are doing their thing and the press have shown up." Dana sounded exhausted. After her attack last night and now this one, it was a wonder she could carry on a rational conversation. His sister was one tough lady.

But neither Sam nor she was equipped to take on trained killers. If her bodyguard was dead, she was vulnerable. So was his mother. "We'll head over."

"No, Zack. Take Mandy to the rental house." Resignation and weariness flooded Dana's tone. "The police are protecting us and there's nothing here for you to do."

"Tell me what happened," he requested softly, wishing he hadn't answered the phone so gruffly, wishing she would accept his help.

"Someone broke into our home. They killed . . . our bodyguards. God . . . Those men were so young—" Her voice broke. "Mom's going to take care of the funeral expenses and help them out financially."

"Good. Have the cops come up with anything?"

"They haven't given us any answers yet, but at least the police are keeping the press away."

"Where were you and Mom when the bodyguards died?"

"Eating dinner on my upstairs balcony . . . those men died trying to save us . . ."

Fear iced through him. His mother and sister had been in the same house with a killer. Likely, they'd been the targets since Catherine and Dana were both lottery winners. Yet, it was Sam who'd been shot. Had the killer intended to go after them all?

"Dana, I'm so sorry you had to go through that. Make sure Mom hires more bodyguards."

"But—"

"I want you both to be as safe as possible."

"How badly is Sam injured?" Mandy asked.

"The paramedics said the bullet went through the fleshy part of his arm. He hurts but they've assured me he'll be fine. He insisted that I warn you. The shooter might be coming after you next—can you hold on? Sylvia's calling me."

"Sure," Zack agreed. Sam's assessment was probably correct. But right now, no one knew where he and Mandy were. Or where they intended to hide. Dana had been at home, a sitting duck, easy to find. Zack would have to make other arrangements for his sister and mother. The firm was going to close so they could all go into hiding. He'd insist.

Protective instincts at full bore, Zack ached to go to the hospital. His mother and sister needed him. But Dana had insisted he shouldn't—perhaps she wasn't thinking that clearly after all. He should be there.

"Oh . . . my . . . God." Dana came back on the line. "Someone just climbed over Sylvia's fence and fired at them. Ben returned fire and thinks he nicked him. The police are searching the neighborhood as we speak."

Mandy's shoulders sagged as if she couldn't take any more bad news. "Is Sylvia okay?"

"She's fine. I should call Maria. She's the only one of us who doesn't yet know what's happened."

"We'll do it," Zack offered. "You just take care of Sam and Mom." *Until I get there.*

"Ben thinks the guy is coming after Mandy." Just let him try, Zack thought as a feral need to protect her hammered through his blood. "Sam told me to tell you to shoot to kill."

"That won't be a problem."

Dana paused, then spoke. "Mandy, there's one other thing you should know."

"What?"

"The man who shot my husband wore a baseball cap and had stringy blond hair."

Mandy's head jerked up. "You think he's the same guy who rammed me off the bridge?"

"Sounds like it, and I don't think the people we care about are safe, either," Dana said. "Do you understand what I'm saying?"

There was a beat of silence and Zack waited, knowing more was going on here than he knew.

Mandy finally shook her head, as if shaking off a daze. "I hear you. Don't worry. I'll take care of it."

"Take care of what?" Zack asked.

Mandy waved him off. "Not now. What about Sylvia's trespasser? Did they get a good look at him?"

A siren in the background blared and Dana spoke loudly to be heard over the noise. "No."

"How far apart do you and Sylvia live?" Zack asked.

Dana was almost shouting so they could hear her over the siren. "Sam's shooter fled by boat. It's possible he left here and went straight to Sylvia's house. We can call and talk later. You've got to warn Maria and her bodyguard."

"I'm calling her right now." Mandy already had her phone out and was dialing. She didn't reach Maria, but her bodyguard answered and promised he'd stay vigilant.

Zack was filled with adrenaline with no adversary to punch. At the idea of someone stealing into Dana's home, attacking her and his mother, his fury escalated. He needed to hide them. But they wouldn't listen. His mother and sister intended to stay with Sam during his surgery. He didn't want them alone. Their bodyguards were dead and if the killer returned, they weren't protected. "Dana, we'll be there in half an hour."

"No, Zack. Dylan's coming over right now and will stay with Mom and me. The police have us protected. No one could get past them. Take care of Mandy. Promise me."

He'd never heard Dana sound so stubborn and Zack supposed that Dylan, as Mayor of Tampa, could pull more strings to help Dana and Sam at the hospital than he could. Still, he found it odd that Dana didn't want him there. "I'll call you back." He hung up and looked to Mandy for answers. "Either Dana isn't thinking clearly or she believes it's more important for me to protect you than her and my mom."

"I don't know why she'd think . . . that." Mandy might have started her denial in a convincing manner, but then red suffused her face as if she knew exactly what Dana was doing. Mandy wasn't a good liar. Her hands clenched the steering wheel. She glared off into space, unseeing of the other cars in the parking lot.

At that moment the killer could have walked right up to the car and pounded on the window and she looked as if she'd tear him apart with her bare hands. Talk about silent rage—Mandy could do it as well as he could, maybe better.

"What the hell is going on?" Zack didn't feel clueless very often. But right now he was up to his neck and about to go under.

Mandy closed her eyes tight as if she was in agony, then

she opened them. Voice tight, she agreed. "We need to talk. But not here."

He hesitated, stemming his burning inclination to drive straight to the hospital. But obviously something was going on that Mandy and Dana hadn't told him. Did Mandy have an ex-lover who was stalking them? Had the firm handled the divorce of a serial killer who'd gone free? Whatever was going on . . . he didn't appreciate being kept in the dark.

"Please. I don't want to talk . . . here."

"Fine." Zack opened his door. "But you're in no condition to drive." He walked around the car and opened the driver's door. As he slid behind the wheel, Mandy moved over, then dialed her phone. She spoke woodenly, as if her thoughts were far away. "I'm trying Maria's phone again. She really needs to keep it on—even during a hot date."

They reached the rental house in ten minutes. Zack didn't need directions since he'd stayed there for a few days the last time he'd been in town. He'd thought the ranch style home with a two-car garage and a fenced yard in a sleepy neighborhood was a perfect place to disappear, until he noted the neighbor's curtain move aside. The man watched Zack use the automatic opener on the garage door. After pulling Mandy's vehicle inside, he closed the door behind them. While she gathered the items she'd purchased during a quick stop at the mall on the way home, he headed toward the door that led into house.

"Wait here until I check it out."

She mumbled something under her breath and began moving packages from the trunk to the door. He stepped inside, flipped on a light. Nothing moved. Or made noise.

He sniffed and the air seemed clean of body odor, sweat, and perfumes. He only smelled furniture polish, bleach, and floor wax. He passed by a laundry area and checked to make sure it was empty, then explored the three bedrooms before entering the living and kitchen areas. Again, they were empty. With all the blinds shut, the house seemed cozy. His mother had furnished it with items she'd restored from garage sales along with a few antiques. Zack found no sign of anyone in the master bedroom or bath and after making sure that all doors and windows were locked and that no one had hidden in any of the closets, he rejoined Mandy and helped carry her things inside.

He flipped on the living room lights. A tan overstuffed couch sat opposite a matching recliner, a dining table rested in a corner, and several framed tropical prints of women drinking tea hung on the walls. Baskets filled with magazines, books in a floor-to-ceiling armoire, and several decorative candles gave the rental a homey feel. He flipped on the ceiling fan and adjusted the thermostat lower.

Mandy chose the recliner, not the couch. Perhaps she didn't want him that close to her. Zack was too edgy to sit. Something was wrong and if it affected his family's safety or his ability to protect her, he wanted answers. Pacing along the draped sliding glass doors and past the kitchen counter, he pivoted and caught Mandy's gaze. "All right, what haven't you told me?"

She met his eyes and looked away. "I've decided now is the time."

"For what?" he asked, more sharply than he intended. But he didn't like guessing games. "Who was Dana worried about?"

"My daughter." She spoke softly, her voice almost devoid of any emotion.

"You're a mother?"

"Yes."

Zack scowled at her, still not sure he'd heard right. "You have a daughter?"

"Yes."

"And a husband?"

"No."

"An ex-husband?"

"No." She raised her chin and locked gazes with him, her eyes proud, defiant. She tightened her muscles, almost as if she expected him to explode. "Just me and my baby. That's why Dana is so concerned about our safety."

Zack folded his arms over his chest, sensing there was

more, and not sure what to make of this unexpected development. "What's the reason for the big secret?"

She looked away, shifted in her seat, folding her legs under her. "We haven't kept in touch."

He winced at her accusation. "Dana and Catherine never said a word, either."

"And how often have you spoken to them? Did you ever even ask about me?"

The truth of her words angered him. "Looks like there was no need. You didn't waste much time after I—" He suddenly stiffened, his eyes narrowing on her, adrenaline suddenly rushing through him hard and hot as a thought occurred to him. "How old is your baby?"

Chapter Twenty

MANDY SWALLOWED PAST the lump in her throat. One answer and she'd no longer have to wonder how Zack would react to finding out he was a father. How ironic was it that she'd been worried about Zack's work and its impact on Gabby, and she was the one placing her daughter in danger.

The time for truth had come. There wasn't a doubt in her mind. Zack's emotional state and her fears about forcing him into their lives no longer mattered. Only Gabby mattered, and if anything happened to Mandy, she wanted Gabby to have at least one of her parents.

"My baby's first birthday is in three weeks."

She held his gaze as Zack mentally calculated. A year. Then another nine months. Shock registered in his eyes, but his voice was flat when he said. "It's mine?"

"*She* has no father's name written on her birth certificate."

"But she's mine?" He spoke in that same level tone, but the question reverberated like a shout in her mind.

She took a deep breath and let the air out in a rush. "Yes."

His face hardened and a muscle in his jaw ticked. "You're certain?"

"Don't insult me." She'd imagined a lot of scenarios when this moment finally came, but she'd never imagined such raw frustration boiling to the surface. Zack looked as if she'd clubbed him with a gavel.

"Why the hell didn't you tell me?" He choked on the words, his voice breaking with frustration. "Why didn't *anyone* tell me?"

This was on her head. No matter how angry he was, she wouldn't allow his family to take any blame. "Dana and Catherine don't know. I didn't want to tell them until I'd told you first." She rubbed the back of her neck. "I just told them I had a one-night stand and they took me at my word. So don't blame them."

And that was the truth. No arguments there, and Zack knew it, judging by the rattled-to-the-core look he shot her.

He sagged onto the sofa as if all his hard muscles and bones had melted. "I have a daughter?"

She allowed her face to soften. "Her name is Gabrielle."

"I have a kid?" Zack looked a bit green and asked again, "Why didn't you tell me?"

She wondered if he was going to keep down his dinner. Hopefully, he just needed time to adjust to the idea. She didn't want to say more before he'd absorbed what she had just told him. Standing, she entered the kitchen to get him a glass of water, but perhaps a shot of whiskey might be better.

Mandy poured a healthy-sized shot and thrust it into his hand. He downed it in one long gulp and his color began to return. "I'm sorry. I shouldn't have asked if you were certain the baby—"

"Gabrielle."

"—was mine."

"You most certainly shouldn't have."

He raised his eyes from his empty glass to her. "It's just the thought of you with someone else . . . stung."

She hadn't expected *that*, and her pulse raced. She read the confusion in his gaze and realized he was probably too shocked to even know what he was saying. Zack wasn't the jealous type—to be jealous implied he had feelings for her.

"I understand you're upset." But she was upset too. That he could think she wouldn't know who the father of her child was . . . honestly. She could barely control the edge to her voice when she said, "You asked me why I didn't tell you about Gabrielle? I had several reasons. Good reasons."

"Really?" He folded his arms across his chest, and waited as if he had a right to demand answers.

"There was no simple solution. You made it loud and clear when we got together that we had no future. The last thing I expected was to get pregnant. I *shouldn't have* gotten pregnant—it wasn't as if we didn't take precautions."

He just raised a dark eyebrow and waited for her to continue. Her palms started to sweat. Damn. She made the pretense of smoothing her slacks to dry them off.

"The night Gabby was conceived, you told me that your first marriage failed because you couldn't commit to a relationship, that a DEA agent's career and family life didn't mix."

"I was trying to be honest that night. Before we made love, I wanted you to know there could be nothing permanent between us."

"Does that explanation ease your conscience over you leaving for California and never calling me?" she asked, admitting that his callous behavior had hurt, and recognizing that her hurt, too, had factored into her decision.

He scowled. "*You* should have called *me*. You should have told me you were pregnant."

"It wasn't as if I could just pick up the phone, Zack. I'm nobody to you. I couldn't just tell the DEA to have you call me. I would have had to go through Dana—which would have meant telling your family that we slept together and that I was pregnant. I didn't want to do that to your family or you."

"But you were pregnant with my child."

"So what's your point? You'd already made it clear your commitment was to your work."

"The point would be I'd have known I was going to be a father."

She shrugged. "Like I said, the situation wasn't easy. And

it wasn't as if I intended to keep Gabby a secret forever. I wanted to wait until the right time to tell you."

He narrowed his gaze. "We were just together in California."

Mandy spread her hands in entreaty. "I thought about telling you, believe me. But after seeing you . . . you were hurt. I didn't know at the time you'd just lost Todd, but I knew something was wrong. I didn't feel right about dropping this bomb in your lap."

"I could have handled it."

"But I didn't know that. You'd told Dana you'd come home soon for a visit. I decided to wait until then."

"Are you done with your *explanations*?"

By his tone, she knew he wasn't buying her reasons for her decision. Taking a deep breath, she tried again. "I'm sorry. Waiting seemed best for all concerned."

"For you, anyway."

"Not only for me. For *everyone*." She'd expected him to be upset, but he was angry. "Why was my decision so hard to accept?"

He didn't answer, but met her gaze, and the accusation in his eyes hurt. "Are you done?"

She gave him credit, he'd heard her out. "Yes. I'm done."

He looked weary, too hurt, revealing that for the moment the fight had gone out of him. "I need some time to think. The last thing I expected was to come home and find out I'm a father."

"You don't have to be unless you want to," she said gently, hoping to ease some of the burden by letting him know he still had choices.

"You don't think I want to be a father? Or you don't think I can be a good one?"

He closed his eyes as if he really didn't want to hear an answer, and in that moment Mandy understood that the anger beneath his shock wasn't directed at her. "That's not what I meant. Of course; I think you can be a good father." *If* that's what he chose. She kept that thought to herself. "That's why I'm telling you now. Someone's trying to kill me. If Gabby loses me . . . my mother would do her best, but it would be better for Gabby to have a parent in her life."

His brow furrowed and he seemed to consider that. "Where's the baby now?"

"At your mother's beach house."

"Your mom's taking care of her?"

Mandy nodded.

"Does anyone else know where they are?" he asked, concern evident in his tone and demeanor.

She shook her head. "No one knows besides me, you, Catherine, and Dana. I thought Gabby would be safe but after what's happened to Sam and Ben, I'm not sure anymore."

He shoved his fingers through his hair and his expression hardened around the edges, the look of a man intimately acquainted with the underside of life. "She's safer than we are. That beach property is titled under a corporation. No one can connect it to us."

Mandy was surprised that she needed reassurance. She hadn't realized how much the burden of single parenthood had sat on her shoulders. She made every decision about Gabby, was always worrying that if something happened to her, her daughter would be parentless. Sure, her mother loved Gabby, but she was a grandmother, not a mother. Suddenly the prospect of sharing the responsibility of Gabby's upbringing held some promise.

Revealing her secret had lifted a burden from her heart. Mandy's inherent sense of right and wrong had been stretched to the limit over keeping this secret. Now that she'd told Zack, would he want to see Gabrielle? Would he want a role in her life?

Only a few hours ago, he'd clearly told her that he didn't want children. Would he resent Mandy for putting him in this position? Would learning the truth about Gabby add to his struggle over Todd's death? Was he sorry he'd come to Florida and learned the truth?

"Do you have a picture of Gabrielle?" He said her name as if tasting a new dish, a bit hesitantly.

She shook her head. "Not with me. My purse was stolen at

the airport. But she has your eyes. Even the same ridges you have on your fingernails."

"She's happy?"

His question surprised her. He was thinking of Gabrielle and her heart warmed a little.

"She's happy and loved."

Zack's voice lowered to a steely whisper. "It may be best if I stay away from her, have no part in her life. I don't want to hurt her."

"Because of your work?"

"I'd be in and out of her life at best. You told me how tough it was being raised without a reliable father."

She wanted to say *whatever* in a light tone as if his decision didn't matter. But she couldn't. Mandy wasn't indifferent, not when his choice would affect all their futures. But Zack had to make his own decision and live with it. So did she.

Not responding was more difficult than she'd ever have imagined. He could have so much if he'd change his line of work. He'd miss out on if he refused to be a father to Gabrielle. But that would be his loss. All her earlier thoughts of sharing responsibility evaporated. She certainly wasn't giving up any part of Gabby's childhood to a man who didn't appreciate what a privilege being her father would be.

Her feelings were twisted and conflicted. Becoming a mother had changed her into someone she wouldn't have recognized two years ago. She was stronger now, yet so much more vulnerable.

She had no words for Zack right now. She was having enough trouble coping with her own see-sawing emotions and overwhelming disappointment.

"I'm tired," she said. "I think I'll turn in."

Standing, she headed toward the bedroom closest to the garage. The house had a split-bedroom plan and she'd let him have the master suite. Right now small and cozy and as far away as she could get from Zack sounded good. At least now that he knew about Gabby, Mandy could openly call her mother and check in.

But it was too late to make a phone call. Both Gabby and

her mother would be asleep. Mandy took a quick shower, changed into the long T-shirt she'd bought at the mall, and turned back the covers of the single bed tucked in the corner. A tall wicker chest and a matching dresser with a mirror hanging over it cast shadows on the walls. When she turned off the light, the leaves on overgrown shrubs outside the window next to the bed brushed gently against the glass. She slipped into bed, trying to accustom herself to the strange sounds, the too-hard pillow, and the stiff T-shirt. Although exhausted, she didn't know if she could fall asleep.

When she shut her eyes, Mandy again saw the look on Zack's face when she'd told him about Gabby. She'd seen wonder, fear, confusion, and pain. Which emotion would override the others?

How would his decision affect their lives?

She couldn't predict if Zack would ever understand why she'd kept Gabby a secret, or what he'd do once he got over the shock. She locked her hands behind her head and stared at the ceiling, then rolled to her side. She'd never slept well in strange places. With Zack in the house, she couldn't relax. Her leg muscles twitched and she squashed the pillow, trying to shape it into something comfortable.

Zack's soft knocks on the door startled her. She hadn't heard his footsteps.

"You still awake?" he asked.

For a moment she wanted to pretend she was asleep, but curiosity got the better of her.

"Yeah, I'm up."

She lifted her head but could only see his silhouette in the dark as he opened the door and stepped inside. The room seemed to shrink. The air electrified.

He didn't approach her but leaned against the doorjamb, his posture stiff, awkward, almost as if he had come against his will. She suspected if not for the fact that Dana and Mandy were in danger, he'd be packing his suitcase and heading back to California.

"Tell me about Gabby," his voice was throaty, low. "What's she like?"

That he'd asked almost melted her heart. Less than an hour ago, he'd told her he should stay away from Gabby. Yet, here he was, asking her about their daughter.

Obviously, Zack was no coward, either. Oh, she'd always known about his daredevil stunts and reckless activities but she wasn't talking about physical bravery, but emotional courage. Some men could risk their lives much more easily than they could admit to their feelings. She'd seen enough divorces to recognize that some men simply didn't have it in them to commit to anyone else. Those who tried and failed left devastated families behind.

But despite his failed marriage, she refused to believe Zack was one of those men. She'd seen him with his sister and mother. That he'd come across the country when they'd needed him proved he was capable of loving relationships.

She cautioned herself that in another fifteen minutes he might change his mind again. But surely his inability to stay away was a step in the right direction.

She propped her head on the pillow and spoke quietly. "Gabby smiles when I walk into a room. She likes a quick hug, a bunch of fast kisses, and then she wants me to put her down so she can explore. She must pull or push herself into a standing position a hundred times a day, then plops back on her bottom. Sometimes, she takes a few steps while holding onto her playpen. But usually she's so impatient to get to wherever she's going that she crawls."

"She sounds like a handful."

"Oh, she's full-time all right. Mom watches her while I'm at work."

"You all live together?"

"The arrangement is best for Gabrielle. Mom handles the child care and I pay the bills."

Darkness made talking easier, draining away some of the former tension, and there was no judgment in Zack's tone. In fact, he continued to speak in that throaty soft voice. "Am I remembering wrong? I thought you and your mother didn't have the greatest of relationships. Didn't she always hover and worry—"

"Let's just say we've both chilled out some. She's so loving with Gabrielle and now that I'm a mom, I understand how easy it is to worry."

"I'm glad you aren't raising her alone."

Mandy turned onto her back. "If we'd collected the lottery winnings, I would have lightened my caseload to spend more time with Gabby."

"You wouldn't have quit working?"

"I like what I do."

She avoided saying she'd have purchased another home for her mother if she could have afforded it. The ticket was gone, so there was no point in thinking how great it would be to have her own space. Right now she had the satisfaction of knowing her daughter was loved and well cared for. She just wanted her to be safe.

In the distance, she heard a crackle or a hiss. Before she could ask Zack if he'd heard the odd noise and what it could be, he lunged toward her.

Sprawled on top of her.

The mattress bounced. His weight pressed her down, his hips sinking between her thighs. "Don't move."

"Hey—"

An explosion cut off her protest. The blast wasn't like those she saw on television. Her ears hurt. Acrid smoke curled into the room, tickling her throat and making her eyes tear. She couldn't breathe. The light in the bedroom went out.

Suddenly Zack's weight lifted from her a bit as he rose onto his elbows. She gasped in air.

He drew his gun. "Stay still. Don't move. That was a grenade."

A grenade? "It sounded like a transformer blew."

"I'm not taking any chances. The explosion sounded as if it came from the master bedroom where I left the light on. If someone's found us, they'd have expected us to be in there."

She peered toward the hallway. From the flickering of light, it appeared that the master bedroom was on fire. "We need to get out."

"We need to stay here."

"Zack, this is no time to fool around." She tried to edge out from under him.

Again, he whispered into her ear. "If the guy who threw that grenade throws another one in here, the safest place for you to be is under me, with the mattress protecting your back."

A part of her warmed at the thought that he was willing to place himself between a live grenade and her. But those other bodyguards had died protecting Dana and Catherine, and Zack could all too easily lose his life. Then Gabby would be orphaned. But Mandy disagreed with Zack's assessment. "The house is on fire. The safest place to be is anywhere other than this room."

"Wrong. He's probably waiting outside. If we come out, he'll pick us off."

"How do you know?"

"Because that's what I'd do if I were him."

"You've got to be kidding me." She didn't know what to believe and kept her voice as low as his. Her heart pounded so hard he had to feel her pulse with his chest pressed against hers.

"Damn it, Zack," she whispered. "Why don't we roll to the floor and pull the mattress on top of *both* of us?"

"Since this bed's in the corner and it's dark, if we stay still, whoever's outside can't see us. But if we flip the mattress, there's a good chance they'll pick up movement."

Zack was the expert and she should probably listen to him, but her every instinct screamed to escape. "So we just stay here?"

"Eventually, he'll come inside."

"You're scaring me." She didn't like this one bit. "We should—"

"Shh. We're done running."

"Now is no time to be a hero," she hissed. "Gabby needs me. I can't risk my life while you play hide and seek with a killer. Let me go."

She squirmed, he pressed her down. With him lying on

top of her she couldn't help noting his erection. "What the hell are you doing?"

"Sorry, sweetheart—"

"I am not your—"

"If you keep squirming, I can't help my reaction to you— I never could."

They could be dead in five minutes. But his body didn't seem to be taking their predicament too seriously. Zack was too close.

He smoothed her hair with his hand. "I understand that you're scared—"

"Terrified."

"It's going to be okay. Try to relax."

Sure. Like she could relax when a killer was hunting them? Mandy didn't want to know how Zack remained so calm. She didn't want to become immune to terror like he apparently had.

"So what's the plan?" she asked.

"I already told you, we wait for him to come inside and find us."

"Oh that makes me feel so much better." She groaned and tried to think past her fear. "Why are you so certain the killer will enter a burning house?"

"Look down the hall. The flames are almost out." Zack shifted slightly, wedging tighter between her legs.

"If that explosion was a transformer blowing out and not a grenade like you thought," she frowned at him, "then the fire would go out as the wire went to ground—"

"Shh." A light shined on the window and she braced for another grenade, this time one that might land right next to them. Zack must have felt her tense because he whispered, "It's only a flashlight beam."

"He's coming?"

"It might be another minute. Try to think of something else."

Like that was going to be possible. "Let's call the police."

"The neighbors probably already have. If the cops come

in with their sirens wailing, he might slip away. Wouldn't you like this to be over?"

"Of course, but . . ."

He snuggled, his long legs wrapping over hers, his arm against her breast.

"You're crowding me."

"Sorry. I'm getting into shooting position." He aimed his right hand and the gun at the door. "Once he enters the house, the tiniest sound will warn him. We'll need to hold perfectly still. Stay quiet."

"You're using us for bait."

"I'm keeping us alive."

Without Zack's weight pressing against her, she would have been trembling and icy. His heat helped keep her teeth from chattering but she felt trapped, scared.

"Za—"

His mouth came down on hers. Damn him. Despite her raw nerves, despite her irritation, despite her fear, his kiss made her breathe in his spicy scent. Memories she'd forgotten washed over her. Memories of other kisses as hot as this one. Memories of need. Of desire so strong he'd haunted her dreams for almost two years.

He pulled back quickly. "If anything goes wrong, I didn't want to have any regrets about—"

The sound of creaking wood, probably caused by a footstep, stopped him in mid-sentence. Even as fear pummeled her, she could feel Zack's hardness. Knew he wanted her despite the danger, despite the real possibility they might die.

Her head was spinning.

Zack's body was primed for sex.

And a damn killer was in the house.

Chapter Twenty-One

Down, boy.

Zack sure as hell didn't need distractions right now. But it was his own fault that he was now all hot and hard. When she'd been threatened, he hadn't thought, just reacted on pure instinct. When he'd lunged onto the bed and covered her body with his, his motive had been purely protective. But once her soft curves molded against him, once her sweet scent stirred his senses, once he'd felt her heart pounding against his chest, he'd shifted from protective mode to hook-up mode in less than a nanosecond.

He'd kissed her—despite the explosion.

While it wasn't as if she hadn't dropped her own grenade tonight in the form of a baby girl, two years of trying to deny his physical needs was no excuse for his reaction to her. He needed his focus, now—even if she had a way of making him come unglued, of making him forget the reason they were in bed together.

He'd swallowed a groan and torn his mouth from hers before he could savor that she'd kissed him back. Their kiss had been no more than a tease to remind them both how good they could be together, then he'd used all his honed discipline to back off.

But it cost him. He'd paid as he'd hardened to a painful state. At least he didn't expect to have to walk or fight. The best defense was to let the killer come to them. All Zack had to do was wait, aim, and pull the trigger.

Except he was lying on top of Mandy. Her breath smelled like coffee, her hair like strawberries.

And now they were connected for life. They had a child. He still couldn't quite wrap his mind around the concept. When Zack thought of Mandy he thought of hot sex, all-nighters—certainly not about motherhood and a baby.

He'd never been so confused, frustrated and hot—all at the same time. At least when the killer showed—Zack could take out some tension on him. Zack would have preferred to use his fists, to beat the living crap out of anyone who'd threatened the three women in his life—his mother, his sister, and Mandy. Yet, he couldn't take any chances of getting it wrong—not with so much at stake.

So he tried to ignore the painful throb. He tried to dump everything from his mind, a daughter he hadn't known about, Mandy with her delicious body and her sexy mouth.

Focus.

Lives were at stake. His, and Mandy's, and all the other lottery winners. Although Zack practiced on a target regularly, it was dark now, and his usual targets didn't shoot back. In addition, he was prone and every time Mandy breathed, the mattress moved slightly.

A hinge squeaked as the killer stalked through the house. Then he fired two muffled shots into what sounded like the master bedroom. Obviously the guy was nervous. He'd be more on edge when he discovered no one was in the master bedroom, that the grenade hadn't done the job.

Beneath Zack, Mandy tensed. He wished he could say something to calm her fears, pat her shoulder, squeeze her hand. But once he heard bullets smack into walls, he figured it was time to move. Staying between her and the door, he changed positions, remaining careful to stay below window sill height—in case of a second shooter. Turning onto his side, he steadied his shooting wrist with his free hand and waited.

A bead of sweat dripped into Zack's eyes. He'd been shot at before. He'd had to wait before, but he'd never had to worry about the safety of a woman he cared about. . . . *Cared* about?

Don't go there.

The killer was likely moving down the hallway, stopping, probably to look in the third bedroom. He couldn't be certain. Zack heard nothing.

Come on. Don't stop.

With the door open, he'd appear suddenly.

Zack breathed in a deep silent breath, steadied his hand. Waited.

Mandy didn't make a sound. She didn't move. Didn't take a breath. Either she was doing exactly as he'd asked, or fear had paralyzed her. At the moment, either way worked for him.

What was keeping the guy? Did he suspect something? Had they made a noise that had warned him?

Zack heard the killer's clothing scrape against a wall.

Amateur.

Don't get cocky, Zack reminded himself. An amateur's bullet in the heart was just as deadly as a professional's. If the guy got off one lucky shot . . . it could kill either of them. Besides, although neither Dana nor Ben had indicated this was anything but a one-man hit, there was still a possibility there could be two or three men out there. No way would he go stalk a killer and leave her vulnerable, not while there was the possibility of a second assailant.

Jeez. A snail moved faster.

Was their assailant in pain from Ben's shot? The cop thought he'd nicked this guy, maybe he was hurting, tired, angry, not thinking clearly.

Or just plain scared.

It was one thing to hide like a coward in the bushes and throw a grenade into a building or shoot people in their bed.

It was another to enter the premises and scout out every dark room for a target—one that might shoot back.

Or was he simply so confident of the kill that he wanted to appreciate the moment? Some men got off on other people's fears. Some men liked the actual killing since it made them feel powerful. Some did it for the money. But most men killed out of an uncontrollable rage.

This was likely his third attempt to kill tonight. He'd already killed two bodyguards, shot Sam, trespassed at Sylvia's, and he'd possibly killed Lisa. It would end now.

Zack would wait as long as it took.

He just prayed Mandy wouldn't move. The slightest rustle of clothing could give away their position. So far, she was acting like a pro—if he discounted her reaction to his kiss. A steamy, heart-pounding, knock-your-pants-off kiss that had left him smoking hot.

Concentrate.

A lunging foot step into the doorway was Zack's only warning. The shooter's silhouette loomed.

Zack took the head shot, drilling him. The guy's head snapped back, his legs buckled. The gun in his hand fell to the floor. Zack put a second bullet in his heart before he hit the floor.

From the terrible smell, Zack knew the guy was dead. Sam had gotten his wish.

With each fired round, Mandy had flinched, but she hadn't made a sound. He'd half expected her to yelp. She hadn't. But now, she was trying to shove him off her, trying to sit up.

"It's okay. He's dead." He gathered her into his arms, and rocked her against him, relieved that she wasn't trembling, although her skin did seem a bit cool. "It's all right. Close your eyes. Let me get you into some fresh air."

"I'm fine."

"You don't sound fine. Give yourself a few seconds," he spoke low and easy.

She pulled back and kicked her feet. "Put me down. I want to see him."

Zack hesitated, and listened hard. He heard nothing, no

sound of breathing or steps to indicate someone else might be in the house. However, he was quite certain that there was messy brain spatter against the wall, as well as blood from two bullet wounds. "It won't be a pretty sight."

"I've seen grisly crime scene pictures." Her voice shook, but she didn't sound hysterical.

"A picture is different from—"

"I need to know he's the same man who ran me off the bridge," she insisted.

"All right." Zack put her back down on the bed. "Stay there and I'll find a flashlight." He'd take a quick peek down the hall to assess whether they really were safe.

Chapter Twenty-Two

"THAT'S HIM." MANDY eyed the dead man sprawled on the floor, trying to focus past the neat bullet hole Zack had drilled between his eyes, beyond his broken nose and the bloody wound from a recently missing earlobe to his facial features. "He's the guy who shoved my car off the bridge." The stringy blond hair and his cold eyes that remained open in death made her certain of his identity.

He'd fallen onto his back, and gladness that he could never harm anyone again mingled with relief that she couldn't see the exit hole, which would be much larger than the neat red circle on his forehead. He looked so young, too young to die, too young to be in the business of taking lives. She reminded herself he'd killed two bodyguards, shot Sam, and had likely killed Lisa.

Blue and red lights of cop cars flashed in the yard, signaling that the police had arrived. One moment she was fine, the next her stomach heaved. She lunged for the bathroom, making it to the commode in time to lose her dinner. Shaken by the fact that she wasn't as professional as she'd thought, she brushed her teeth and turned around.

She only saw concern in Zack's expression as he matter-of-factly handed her a damp towel. "Let's get you outside for some air. I didn't want you to go through—"

She blotted her mouth. "It wasn't the sight of him. The smell set me off." She shuddered. She didn't think she'd ever forget the stink of gunpowder mixed with the metallic reek of blood and feces.

"Police," a deep male voice shouted.

"DEA agent Zachary Taylor here," Zack spoke in a strong voice. "This is my mother's house. I just shot and killed an intruder. I'm placing my weapons on the floor and my hands behind my head. I'm here with Mandy Newman, an unarmed civilian." He placed the weapon he'd fired on the floor next to another one he pulled from his ankle holster and a third from the small of his back, then turned to her. "Put your hands up. We don't want to make the cops nervous."

"You certainly don't." A cop entered the room, his gun drawn. Bald, lean, and tough, the black cop appeared about forty years old. He had the face of a pro, cautious, yet not jumping to conclusions. "I'm Officer Denby. Hold still and easy."

"Zack Taylor," he said again. Mandy kept her hands behind her head, where she'd placed them earlier at Zack's instruction. Zack spoke in a normal tone as if he'd done this many times before. "Officer, all of my weapons are on the floor."

She let Zack take the lead, wondering how he could be so calm. She was shaking. Yet, she was glad the killer was dead. Before tonight she would have been certain that if she'd been holding the gun, she would have fired, too. Now she wasn't so sure.

Intellectually, she was glad the man was dead. Yet contradictorily, his death sickened her. She was appreciative Zack was beside her, clearly well versed in handling shootouts.

"Sir, you said you're DEA? You have any ID?" Officer Denby asked.

"It's in my wallet. Right rear pocket." Zack didn't move. He appeared to be waiting until the officer told him to get his ID.

"Slowly, sir. Take it out, please." The officer kept his gun aimed at Zack, but he didn't take his gaze off of her, either.

Zack plucked out his wallet, flipped it opened, and held it up. Officer Denby verified the credentials and then reholstered his weapon. "All right. Lower your hands. The neighbors called in a disturbance."

"They probably heard the explosion from the grenade the deceased threw in the bedroom window."

"You don't know his name?" Denby asked.

Mandy spoke for the first time but she didn't sound normal. There was a quiver in her voice that she couldn't control. "He's the same man who tried to kill me last week. He followed me from the parking garage and—"

"Well, I'll be damned." Denby's eyes narrowed in recognition. "You're the lady that went over the Harbour Island bridge?" The officer focused almost solely on her, and for the first time since he'd walked into the room, the tension eased from him. In fact, he looked almost happy.

"Yes."

"And you won the lottery?"

"Yes." She supposed the media deserved some thanks for once. Denby had obviously seen her picture in the newspaper or on television and knew she'd been a target.

"You're the winner who lost the ticket?"

"You know a lot, Officer Denby." Zack kept his gaze on the cop, his tone easy.

"The mayor's been pressuring the chief, who's been after us for answers. I might get myself promoted for this." He gestured to the dead man, then radioed for a homicide detective.

Mandy refrained from saying that Denby hadn't done anything. He'd arrived after Zack had shot the killer.

"Sir, leave your weapons where they are for now," he instructed Zack, but his I'm-on-your-side attitude suggested that his instructions were due more to proper procedure than to suspicion they'd done anything wrong. Another, less experienced cop might have been more suspicious and accused them of murder, instead of self-defense. "I'll return the unfired guns if your statements check out. Ma'am, if you could step around the body without touching it, forensics will be grateful."

Zack held her hand and she tried not to look directly at the body. Still, blood was starting to congeal and the man's skin tone had grayed. Holding her breath, she stepped over him and didn't look back. Once they reached the living area, she realized she'd been holding her breath and had to consciously draw air into her lungs. The house reeked of smoke but the air was better here than in the bedroom.

Another police officer arrived. This man was younger than Denby and in superb physical shape. The two men conferred quietly and she couldn't hear what they said. Then the new policeman, a homicide detective, took Zack into the dining room to talk while leaving her with Denby in the living room.

At Denby's request, she sat on the couch and summarized the past week, starting with the incident at the bridge, continuing with the attacks that had led up to the moment Denby had arrived. Meanwhile forensic teams entered and began working, taking photographs, measuring blood splatter, gathering DNA evidence, and examining the body. Finally a team carried out the dead man in a black body bag. He'd end up at the county coroner's, where an autopsy would be performed.

"Ma'am," Denby asked, "there's only a few points I need cleared up. After you thought the grenade exploded, why didn't you immediately leave the building?"

"It wasn't a grenade?"

He shook his head. "A transformer blew and caused the fire."

So she'd been right. But Zack had been right, too. The shooter had been outside, waiting to pick them off. After the explosion, terror and adrenaline had made her certain running as fast and as far away as possible was the right thing to do. If she'd been alone, she would have fled and she shuddered at the idea of the shooter sitting outside, waiting to pick her off as the flames outlined her silhouette.

"Zack said if we ran out, the killer could shoot us too easily. He said our chances were better if we waited for him to come to us."

"Smart man. And if the shooter's gun matches the bullet that struck Sam Hansen, maybe all your troubles are over." Someone from forensics handed Denby a piece of paper. He read it, then told her, "Looks like a recent bullet wound struck the deceased in the ear."

"That would tie him to Ben Jacobson, too."

"According to forensics, we've now got a blood sample from Mr. Jacobson's backyard fence. We'll have to wait for lab results to tell us if the blood types match." He paused, then looked up at her. "We also found ID in the deceased's wallet. Looks real enough. Ever heard of Nick Vizzi?"

"Nick Vizzi?" The name sounded familiar. She was about to say she needed to check her files and then she remembered and started to shake. "Nicholas Vizzi was married to Terry Vizzi, one of my clients. I represented her in their divorce about eight months ago. Oh . . . no."

"What?"

"Lisa and Terry were friends and Lisa referred Terry to me. Do you think Nick Vizzi killed Lisa because she befriended his ex-wife?"

"I don't know, ma'am."

She started thinking in lawyer mode. "It fits. The crime scene was violent—as if the killer was in a rage. But his divorce was completed six months ago. Why would he come after us now?"

Denby closed his notepad. "We may never know. The homicide detective will follow up. It would be best if you didn't leave town."

His tone pulled her from her thoughts of the crime. "Officer, my daughter is in Clearwater. If it's now safe, I'd like to go get her and bring her home."

"That shouldn't be a problem."

Mandy's head was spinning. She wanted to call Dana and find out how Sam was doing. She wanted to go get her baby. And she no longer needed to stay close to Zack. They could go their separate ways without Zack meeting his daughter. Yet, despite Zack's earlier words, out of a sense of fairness, she longed to give him a chance to meet Gabby.

After the police left, Zack phoned a cleaner to take care of the mess from the dead body as well as a contractor to board up the house. While she waited for him to complete the arrangements, he gathered her things from the room so she wouldn't have to go back in there, a gesture she appreciated.

Zack could be so thoughtful—when he wasn't being . . . Zack. After all they'd been through, she still hadn't forgotten that he'd said he didn't want any part of Gabrielle's life. It hurt—even if his decision let her keep Gabby all to herself.

She'd known better than to expect anything else—but Mandy always had hoped . . .

An hour later she and Zack both got in her car. She pulled out of the driveway. "Where can I drop you off? Do you want to go to the hospital or to your mother's, or Dana's?"

Zack turned his head and frowned. "This isn't over."

What? She pulled over to the side of the road and shut off the car to give him her full attention. "Nick Vizzi's dead. What do you mean, it's not over?"

"Remember the guy who assaulted my sister at the airport?"

Like she could forget the black man with his deep acne scars and dreads. "What about him?"

"He's still out there."

Frustration zinged through her. "But he was after the ticket. He's got it. We'll probably never see him again."

"I'm not betting your life on probably. Or my daughter's." He leaned toward her . . . too close. "I'm calling for more protection, but I can pretty much guarantee that the security company won't be able to put anyone in place until morning. I'll take you to my mother's beach house, and we can both keep an eye on our daughter."

Our daughter.

She could feel his words in the pit of her stomach. Maybe it was the husky tone of his voice when he said it, but the words evoked a reaction far too potent for a man who'd claimed he didn't want to be involved. "I thought you said you should stay out of *our* daughter's life."

"I said I wasn't sure."

She recalled him lying on top of her in that bed, his too-quick hot kiss, his arousal. He was doing it again, turning on that charm. She was reacting to his protectiveness and re-strained herself from leaning into his scent.

"I'm not leaving her safety or yours to chance."

She let out a long sigh. "You're saying you're still my bodyguard?"

"Yep." He spoke in an intimate tone that was way too sen-sual. Leaning closer, until she could practically feel the heat radiating from him, he brushed a curl of hair from her cheek. Their eyes locked and he caressed the curve of her ear.

She told herself to slap his hand away, to start the car and drive. But she couldn't seem to make her limbs move. It was as if his gaze had frozen her hands to the steering wheel.

She trembled and he was sitting too close not to notice.

"Are you afraid of me?" he asked.

"No." But she was lying. She didn't want to respond to Zack. She didn't want to think about his kissing her. Even when her life had been in danger, the blood had roared in her ears and her response troubled her as much as it stimulated her every sense. With Zack around, she was too alive, too aware. Of him. She smelled his male scent mixing with the leather car seat and it intoxicated her. Sure she was drunk, drunk on his charm. Damn the man, he acted as if he knew exactly how much she wanted his mouth on hers again— only for longer. As far as she was concerned, their last kiss was nothing more than a teaser.

He chuckled. "So if I kiss you, you won't run away?"

"*I've* never run away." She angled her chin, proud her tone sounded mocking. "You're the one who left for California." Her words ruined the mood. Tension spiraled into silence. When he said nothing, she turned the conversation back to business. "How much longer will you stay?"

"Until you don't need me anymore." He sounded far from pleased by the idea.

"Thanks for being so specific," she snapped, thoroughly irritated with him but a bit more pleased than she'd have liked that she didn't have to say goodbye just yet.

Besides, she was too tired to argue with him and herself too. "I should call Dana and let her know—"

"The only phone call we're making is to the security company. You drive. I'll make the call, and make damn certain we don't pick up a tail."

"We'll have to drive back tomorrow for the funeral." She kept trying to give him an out. He didn't take it.

"At this time of night, there shouldn't be any traffic. The sooner we leave, the sooner we'll get there."

Chapter Twenty-Three

"MOM DOESN'T KNOW you're Gabrielle's father," Mandy reminded Zack as she parked the car at Catherine's beach house, her stomach in knots, "and for now we should keep it that way."

Another man might have been insulted. Zack chuckled as he opened her car door. "I'll follow your lead."

Mandy sighed, both looking forward to him seeing Gabby and dreading it. "Just remember that Mom's not going to be thrilled when I show up in the middle of the night with my bodyguard."

"I'm guessing she'll be happy to see you. She's probably been worried."

"Mom is the queen of worriers. But she doesn't like surprises."

She stepped out of the car and the salt tang of the Gulf of Mexico carried across the beach, the sea breeze tangling her hair. She couldn't wait to kick off her shoes and dig her toes into the sand, but even more she wanted to see Gabby.

Yet, she held back. Zack was going to finally meet Gabrielle. Her nerves kicked in and as much as she wanted to go inside, she wondered if bringing Zack here was a mistake. Once he'd seen her, how could he not love her?

Overwhelmed, confused, she stalled to get a grip on her emotions, reminding herself that Zack was too damn good at his job to ever give it up. He'd probably leave and life would go on—like always. Was that what she wanted?

Or life might change drastically. Mandy gulped. For so long she'd wished for this moment and now that it had arrived she wondered if it would be a disaster.

The beach house stayed dark, but the outside lights suddenly came on. Zack's expression turned wary in the space of a heartbeat.

Mandy frowned. "Mom's a heavy sleeper. There's no way she could have heard us way out here. The motion detectors must have picked us up."

Mandy used the key Dana had given her to open the front door. Outside lights lit the foyer and she headed down the hallway to the master bedroom, leaving Zack behind. "Let me tell Mom we're here. I'll be right back."

Mandy walked into the elegant master bedroom without her mother waking. She didn't bother turning on a lamp to approach the canopied bed. Placing a hand on her mother's shoulder, she gently shook her. "Mom. It's Mandy."

Hair in pink curlers and wearing a bright green and purple flowered nightgown, her mother turned over, her voice full of sleep, her eyes still closed. "What's wrong?"

"Nothing. I'm just letting you know I'm here with my bodyguard. We'll see you in the morning. Go back to sleep."

"Okay." Without opening her eyes, her mother rolled back over. Mandy pulled up the blanket to her shoulders and hoped her mother would remember their conversation in the morning.

She left the room, shutting the door behind her and almost bumped into Zack in the hallway. He reached out to steady her, his fingers warm, his touch gentle. "Sorry. I didn't want to let you get too far away."

"Zack, there are extra blankets and a pillow for the couch in the hall closet. I'll take the guest bedroom."

His tone was whispery soft in her ear. "I'd like to see Gabby."

"She's sleeping and while both she and Mom are heavy sleepers, if we do happen to wake Gabby, she'll be excited to see me and won't go back to sleep for hours. You can wait until morning, can't you?"

"All right. But I'm too keyed up to sleep," he muttered. "How about a walk?"

A moonlit walk. On the beach. His invitation tempted her. What could be more romantic than Zack, darkness, and lapping waves? Her pulse escalated. She shouldn't. "You go ahead."

He shook his head. "I'm not leaving you alone. We both go. Or we both stay. I understand if you're tired. It's been a long day."

Mandy should have been exhausted, but she wasn't. She doubted she'd fall asleep for hours. She'd only refused because she didn't trust herself with Zack. But he was being so decent. "On second thought a walk sounds like a great way to unwind."

She grabbed her key and they locked the front door behind them. They walked around the house to a wooden deck that led through sea oats to the beach. When her eyes adjusted to the darkness, she could see moonlight sparkling off the black water of the Gulf of Mexico.

A light breeze caused canvas umbrellas to flutter in time to the waves rolling onto the beach. She breathed in a deep tangy breath. Zack took her hand, twining his fingers through hers.

Holding his hand felt right. She recalled him protecting her with his body when he feared a grenade might come through the window. As much as she told herself he was simply doing his job, she knew she meant more to him than sheer duty. She'd felt his erection. While she might dismiss his reaction to her as simply a male responding to a female, she couldn't forget his urgent kiss. Or his words afterward that had told her that if they'd died, he'd regret not following his instincts.

She suspected Zack felt close to her because of the night

they'd shared and the child they'd made. Danger had brought them together again, and even knowing Zack would likely soon leave, she couldn't deny him or herself in that moment.

She curled her fingers around his. They reached the water's edge and she kicked off her shoes, wanting to feel the powder-soft sand between her toes and the water foaming over her ankles. She wanted to forget that a killer had come after her today. She wanted to forget that her time with Zack was limited.

Just this once, she didn't want to think about the past or the future. She wanted to live in this moment. The breeze carried his male scent to her and reminded her of those hours when they'd created Gabby. So much had happened since then— and yet that elemental connection was still there.

And now they had Gabby connecting them, too.

They walked hand in hand, not talking. As if they each feared words would spoil the peace of the moment. A boat motored offshore, its bow lights a soft glow on the horizon.

They had the beach to themselves. Even the condos, hotels, and mom-and-pop motels that lined the beach were dark at this late hour, their balconies empty.

"We shouldn't go far," Zack said.

He was thinking about Gabby's safety. She looked up at him, wishing she could see his expression better in the darkness. But all she saw was the silhouette of his firm jaw, the set of his broad shoulders, and the outline of his wide chest. When he didn't say anything, she brushed a lock of wind-blown hair from her eyes. "Is anything wrong?"

"No one's following us. It's just that . . ."

"What?"

His voice sounded hungry, husky. "This is the first time we've been alone, where we haven't been following up a clue."

"And?"

"And I want to . . ."

"Yes?" She tipped up her chin.

"To kiss you again."

At his admission a thrill slid down her spine and curled in

her stomach. But he didn't move so much as an inch closer. He let go of her hand. When she realized he wasn't going to kiss her, disappointment flooded her. Refusing to let the conversation die in an awkward silence, she tugged his hand. "Come on. You need to cool off. Let's go swimming."

She tugged him into the water. He splashed beside her. "We aren't dressed for swimming."

"Our clothes will dry." She began to run, picking up her feet, sprinting into the cool waves, eager to duck under the water and escape her disappointment. She'd been so ready for Zack to kiss her and wondered why he was fighting his instincts.

Did he think if he kissed her again, she'd ask him to stay? Did he fear if he kissed her again, he'd want to stay? Or did he feel that he shouldn't lead her on because he fully intended to leave again?

She didn't know. But as the water reached her waist, she dived under, letting the salt water wash away her disappointment and worries. When she surfaced to find Zack right next to her, she splashed him. He retaliated, but she'd anticipated his move and shifted sideways. But then he leaped after her. His hands gripped her waist, lifted her up and she was certain he intended to toss her back into the water. But he let his hands slide up her sides.

And then his mouth closed over hers in fierce possession. He kissed her as if he couldn't stop himself. As if nothing was more important than him having her against him, her mouth under his. Zack tasted of salt and lust and need and she wrapped her arms over his shoulders, threaded her fingers into his hair.

When Zack had kissed her on the bed, he'd rushed. But this time, he took his time. He kissed her thoroughly, and his scent combined with the sea water to tantalize. Mandy forgot that she was standing fully clothed in the Gulf of Mexico. She forgot that Zack and she had so many things to work out. She forgot the two years they'd been apart.

Kissing Zack made her pulse race. Zack brought out Mandy's lusty side. With him she felt safe to let go, to kiss him back, to enjoy the moment. On her own she was serious and practical, but with Zack she relaxed, laughed, and had the freedom to be more feminine, more passionate. She remembered this feeling, so completely special, a feeling that had only happened with Zack. Now that she was finally back in his arms and kissing him, she enjoyed snuggling against him, pressing her chest against his, feeling his heart pound.

And she wanted more. She wanted to unbutton his shirt and remove her own clothing. But Zack placed his hands on her waist and gently broke their kiss. "I shouldn't have done that."

"You're right. It was terrible," she teased.

"I meant . . ." He ran a hand through his hair and let out a disgusted sigh.

"What, Zack?" Her pulse pounded. Her mouth went dry. She wanted him to explain. To tell her what he was feeling—or at least what he was thinking.

"We should go back to the house."

"Whatever." She felt like throwing up her hands in disgust. But she didn't. He'd kissed her—although he hadn't wanted to. For now, that would have to be enough.

Except it didn't feel like enough. She'd wanted more than a passionate kiss from him. Settling for less was difficult, especially when she already knew how good they could be together. But she refused to push Zack, he would come to his own conclusions in his own way.

However, she didn't mind nudging a bit. When she got back to the beach, she unbuttoned her shirt.

He grabbed her wrist. His voice came out raw, letting her know he was hurting, too. "What are you doing?"

"Peeling down to my lingerie. It'll be more comfy."

"But someone might see." He sounded totally exasperated and she hid a tiny grin of satisfaction.

"It's dark." She shimmied out of her jeans and spun around. "And my bra and panties look like a bikini, don't you think?"

Zack grabbed her hand again and tugged her along the beach. "I don't know. I'm not looking."

Chapter Twenty-Four

ZACK HAD LOOKED at Mandy's body, of course. She'd looked good. Damn good. It was all he could do to resist pulling her back into his arms for another kiss. But he had no right to lead her on. So they'd returned to the beach house.

Despite the cool shower he'd just taken to wash off the salt from their swim, Zack tossed on the pullout sofa in the living room. He couldn't sleep and told himself the bed was uncomfortable, but the real reason was quite different. He remained wide awake because of Mandy. It didn't matter how many times he told himself she was a mother, he thought of her as sexy and available. Maybe if he saw their child, it would serve as a permanent reminder that he and Mandy were more than two single adults who were free to act out their selfish impulses.

Besides, he'd been kept out of the loop for long enough. He didn't want to wait until morning to see his daughter. He tied on a bathrobe Mandy had loaned him.

Mandy had disappeared into the guest room and her mother slept in the master bedroom. Since there was only one other spare room, he had no difficulty finding Gabby's room. The door had been left cracked open. He paused outside in the hallway, sensing that once he stepped over the threshold, he'd be entering new territory from which he could never return.

He should retreat to his lumpy sofa bed. Instead, he advanced, leaning forward to peer through the crack. But not enough light came through for him to see anything beyond the darkness.

At the moment of truth, he had second thoughts. Perhaps this wasn't a good idea.

Should he go back to sleep, get up early tomorrow morning when the bodyguard arrived, watch the house from outside and wait for Mandy to exit? With his career, he had no business having a child. Some DEA agents had families, but those who worked undercover took enormous risks with their lives and were absent for long periods of time. He couldn't be a good father and a good DEA undercover agent.

He should leave.

But what could one look hurt? Zack couldn't stop himself from pushing the door open wider until he could see better. Light from just outside shined in through the window and lit up the crib.

She slept on her side, her round face peaceful, sweet and innocent. Baby smells hit him, lotions and powders. Her yellow pajamas reminded him of summer sunshine.

Gabrielle was his daughter. His child. She didn't look like him. Thank God. She was gorgeous. So small. Although he tried to deny a connection between them—he couldn't quite do so. He longed to touch her, talk to her, get to know her. But he had no right.

"Want to hold her?" Mandy asked softly from the foot of the crib, shocking him by her presence. She wore a long T-shirt she must have borrowed from her mother. Her feet were bare, her hair still damp from her shower.

It was a measure of how upset he was that he hadn't noticed Mandy standing in the shadows. He'd seen his daughter for exactly ten seconds and already he was losing his instincts.

He shook his head and kept his tone low. "I don't want to wake her."

"Sorry. I misled you before."

"Why?"

"I had to get used to the idea of sharing her. She's a very heavy sleeper. She won't wake up to a dog barking, a fire engine siren, the sound of a TV or us talking. Mom once knocked over a lamp in her room and Gabby didn't wake up." Mandy leaned over the crib, slid her hands under the baby, picked her up and cradled her in her arms. Her face softened with love and Zack caught his breath. They looked so right together. Mother and daughter seemed two halves of a whole, complete.

Mandy stepped toward him and held out the baby. He should walk away. But strangely fascinated, he couldn't muster the willpower to leave, couldn't help wondering what it would be like to hold her—just once.

Zack tried to make a cradle out of his arms. "I've never held a baby."

"Rest her head in the crook of your elbow and support her back and bottom with your arm."

"She weighs so little." He was surprised how natural it was to hold her against his chest. The baby seemed to curve into all the right places. He marveled at the softness of her skin, the perfection of her tiny mouth, her button nose, her rounded cheeks, the fine hair on her scalp. As Mandy predicted, she remained asleep.

"Her weight has more than doubled since she was born."

Gabrielle sucked her thumb contentedly. Zack didn't understand what was happening to him. Ever since Mandy had told him about the baby, Gabrielle had seemed more abstract than real. But now that he was holding her, hearing her tiny breaths, feeling her move, taking in her warmth, it hit him that she was a person, an individual, who could love and be loved, who would grow up and make decisions that stemmed from her past.

For the first time he considered how she might feel about growing up without a father. His parents had been

divorced—and that had been tough. Look what it had done
to Dana. She'd been starved for male attention, and she'd
fallen for a man who made her feel feminine. Would his sister have made the same choice if his father had been around?
Zack didn't know.

But he didn't like the idea of this vulnerable baby growing
up with thoughts that her father didn't want her. Zack hated
the idea of causing anyone pain, especially this beautiful
child.

The dryer beeped, signaling their clothes were done.

Mandy reached for Gabrielle and he was reluctant to hand
her back. As if sensing his hesitance, she grinned. "You can
hold her again and feed her and change her in the morning if
you like."

His head spun. He'd almost said, "I don't think so." But
the words wouldn't come out past the tightness in his throat.

He handed over the baby and headed for the laundry
room, appreciating that Mandy didn't ask questions. He
pulled on his jeans, slung his shirt over his shoulder, and recalled that his workout shorts had been destroyed in the fire
along with the rest of his things. In the morning he'd ask his
mother to bring a suit to her office in Tampa, so he could
change before the funeral.

Zack ached to go for a run on the beach or for a real swim
to clear his head. It was wrong to come into Gabby's world,
get to know her, then leave for undetermined amounts of
time. Better she never knew the pain of missing her dad—
especially since he came to Florida so infrequently. But he
refused to leave Mandy and Gabrielle unprotected.

"Give me a minute." He opened the door onto the balcony
that spanned the entire waterfront side of the beach house
and cleared the porch furniture to one side, making a space
on the deck about ten feet by ten feet under the stars. With
the waves lapping gently on the beach, the breeze in his hair,
he sought to center himself.

After a few quick stretches, he began shadow boxing, jab,
punch, counterpunch, and follow-through, the drill he'd
practiced for many years. Usually he kept his mind involved.

Hands up, quicker, faster. Spin, repeat. But tonight, his punches had no focus, no heat. He kept thinking about Gabrielle, how little she was, how much she needed care.

How he'd soon be gone. Undercover. Out of touch for long stretches of time. He'd already missed the first year of her life. It was quite possible that he might not see her again until she was three. Four, or even five.

He started adding kicks between the punches, not so much a conscious decision, simply his muscles knowing what to do from long practice sessions. As he spun, performing a spinning back kick followed by a lunging jab, he glimpsed Mandy stepping onto the balcony and closing the door firmly behind her. If she wanted to see what the father of her child was really like then he'd show her how much he didn't belong in a family environment. Zack could kill with his hands, his head, his feet. Even one finger could be lethal since he was an expert at knowing where to strike.

Since the day his brother had died, he'd honed his skills, devoted his life to taking down the drug dealers, the cartels. While he'd had some success, he could only put a dent in the supply chain. Drugs were simply too profitable for criminals to ignore. When they made it to the streets, kids like Kevin died.

Zack moved so fast his hands became a blur. His kicks could knock out a muscular thug before his opponent pulled a trigger—even if his gun was already in hand. The trick was being within striking distance.

Zack could cover distances quickly. Keep his balance. Attack.

And right now he'd rather be dealing with an enemy than with thoughts about his daughter.

"She got to you, didn't she?" Mandy asked.

Of course, she hadn't. Zack was in total control of his body, mind, and emotions.

When he didn't answer, continuing his routine, Mandy spoke quietly. "Wait until she smiles at you. Once she recognizes you and looks forward to you picking her up, she holds up her arms and practically jumps into your hands."

"Stop it."

"She's learned to give wet, sloppy kisses. She likes to kiss my forehead and nose and cheeks. Four kisses every time. I sometimes wonder if she's taught herself to count."

"Don't. I know what you're doing—" Mandy had sounded so innocent, but she wasn't.

"I'm telling you about Gabrielle."

He followed through with a knife-hand strike that stopped just short of her neck. Mandy didn't so much as flinch. So he looked her straight in the eye and spoke with determined ruthlessness. "She's a beautiful little girl. It's too damn bad I won't be around to watch her grow up. She shouldn't have a father like me."

She spoke quietly. "Gabrielle might think differently—"

He shook his head. "I've already thought about what it's going to be like for her to grow up without a father around. But even if I were to be involved in her life and she could handle the long absences, there could be consequences, dangerous consequences. I don't want you or her to fear that a simple phone call from me could endanger your lives. The people I hunt have sophisticated equipment. If they ever broke my cover, they'd try to use Gabby against me. I won't ever put her in danger or myself in that position." After realizing his admission revealed how much he cared, he practically growled at Mandy. "Why aren't you in bed?"

"Why aren't you?" she countered. When he glared at her, she rolled her eyes at the sky. "I stayed up to put the rest of the clothes in the dryer, then I checked on Gabrielle."

Mandy might have kept secrets from him but there was no denying her loyalty to her baby. "It can't be easy raising her by yourself."

"Mom's been here for me."

Her words might imply he hadn't been, but there was no disapproval in her tone. But if Mandy had told him about her pregnancy would he have been there for her? He didn't know. He was a different person now than he'd been two years ago. Back then, he'd seen the world as good or bad, now he'd learned there were many shades of gray in be-

tween. Todd's mother had loved her child, yet she'd gotten
him killed—with Zack and the DEA's help. She hadn't been
able to live with that knowledge. Zack was fairly certain her
overdose had been deliberate—she'd shot up triple her limit.

"Your family have also been great," she continued. "They
accepted what I told them about a one-nighter. So I don't
know if they suspect you're Gabby's father. I do know that
I've gone out of my way to include them in Gabby's life, and
they've gone out of their way to be included."

"I'm glad." He had to ask. "You never considered ending
the pregnancy?"

"I thought about it, but I couldn't . . . She was part of
me . . . part of us. That night may have been a one-night stand
to you, but to me it was more. Maybe I shouldn't have felt that
way, but I did." Mandy looked away, as if fearing she'd exposed too much. Clearly, she had some feelings for him.

"I'm willing to provide child support."

"That's big of you, Zack." Pain flashed in her eyes for a
moment before she cut him out as effectively as if she'd put
up a bullet-proof shield. She leaned on the balcony railing
and stared at the gulf.

Zack joined her and placed an arm over her stiff shoulders. "We need to keep on protecting her. It'll be difficult for
a little girl to understand her daddy might have to go months
without seeing her. I'm trying to do the right thing."

"I know." She nodded.

She looked so sad that he suppressed his churning emotions
and drew her into his arms for a hug. His anger wasn't at her,
but himself—for getting her into a position where she'd become a single mom. For putting himself inside a vise.

Mandy came to him easily enough, seeming to understand
his turmoil. Or maybe she needed comfort. He held her
close, threaded his hands into her hair, marveling that despite everything, they could still want each other. Just like on
that long-ago night, when their need for each other defied
reason. When they were in each other's arms there was no
past, no future. Only now.

She stood on tiptoes and kissed his mouth. What started

as a sweet kiss added fuel to embers that needed no more than a spark to flare into smoldering heat. For a moment the image of Mandy holding his baby seared his mind. A thought flitted through his head that his desire for her was wrong, that she was a mom now. The thought went up in flames. She was a mom, yes—one steaming hot mama. In less than a second, all his pent up anger broke into desire and flooded back tenfold. Blood in his body rushed south.

He tore his mouth from hers, ground his pelvis into her, making certain she understood the full ramifications of what her kiss had done to him. "What do you want from me?"

He thought she'd pull back. But instead she met his gaze and he could see desire softening her expression. "Nothing. Everything. Right now—if that's all you've got to give."

"You're sure?"

"Oh, yes."

He narrowed his eyes. "Tell me exactly what you want."

He hadn't thought her lips could look so sexy, but hers pouted at his challenge and shot a sizzle of heat to his core. Her voice wafted in the sea breeze, soft and provocative. "I want everything you can give me. Your hands, your mouth, your—"

He didn't need to hear more. Angling his mouth over hers, again, he took what he wanted, raked in everything she gave. Mandy knew how to give. She'd always been that way. Once she made up her mind, she didn't hold back. She participated fully, meeting him more than halfway.

She opened her mouth, dipped her tongue between his lips, flirting, then invited him to enter hers. He placed one hand on her back, the other on her butt, drawing her closer until they stood chest to chest, hip to hip, thigh to thigh.

Zack, who prided himself on finesse—had none. It had been too long. He wanted her so badly he burned. He tugged off her shirt. She wasn't wearing a bra, only panties. From her lips, to her neck to her collarbone, he traced a path to her nipples. He helped himself to a long hard pull from each breast, and took satisfaction as they turned to hard points and her breath grew ragged.

Then her fingers dived into his hair and she jerked him back with a painful tug. "Zack. Stop."

"Stop?" He ground his teeth, his mind whirling with confusion. How could he stop?

But she'd sounded frantic.

Eyes wild, she gasped. "Have you any protection?"

"Huh?"

"Condoms?"

"In my bag." He swore. "The one that burned in the fire. Don't you have—"

She shook her head, a muscle in her neck pulsing. "Nothing. None. Zip. I haven't been with anyone since you. I'm not in the habit of—"

"It's okay."

"It's not okay," she practically wailed.

When they'd first met, he'd never expected her to be so passionate given the straight-laced image she presented to the world. The night of Gabby's conception, she'd told him she'd never had a fling and he'd been charmed by how self-conscious she'd seemed until he'd reassured her that he loved how she let herself go with him.

He lifted her chin. "Tomorrow we'll buy a whole damn case. In the meantime, we can make do." He hooked his hands into her panties, slipped them over her hips, her knees, her ankles. She looked as good as he remembered. Mandy had a tiny waist, womanly hips, terrific legs and shapely toes that she'd painted passionate purple.

He looked into her eyes to tease her but his breath caught in his throat. Her pupils had grown huge. Her nostrils flared.

He spread her hands on the railing. "Do you have any concept of how lovely you look?"

"I've gained a few pounds since Gabby—"

"You're stunning."

"Show me," she whispered, parting her thighs, arching her back, an action that caused her breasts to rise. Zack loved the way she loosened up when they were alone together.

He kneeled between her legs, let his hot breath tease her

curls. She tilted her hips toward his mouth and he covered her breasts with his hands. At the same time, he slipped his tongue into her heat. At his first lick, she cried out in joy.

Just out of her shower, she tasted like the first raindrops before a storm. Tension in her gathered. Her thighs quivered—hot, wild. She was so ready for him.

He'd barely tendered a few licks when the first orgasm ripped through her. She shivered right into his mouth.

"Ah, Zack. More. More. A little more," she panted, her breath raspy, needy.

Sensing the first explosion was only the tiniest ripple in an onslaught of needs, he licked harder, faster.

"Ah, Zack. Yes. Yes."

The sound of her coos rewarded him. She bucked her hips, unable to hold still. He tweaked her nipples, holding her there, determined to give her everything she could take.

As much as he enjoyed her taste, he still ached to plunge into her. He settled for skimming his fingers down her stomach, sliding them between her moist nether lips, first just his pointer finger, then another, and another.

He maintained constant pressure with his tongue, licking and flicking her core, pleased to focus on her sensitive spots while she swayed and jerked.

Finally, she creamed into his mouth and hands, her hips gyrating. Her fingers twisted into his hair.

"Please," she whispered.

"Please what?"

"I need you inside me, Zack."

"We can't—oh, yes. We can." He pulled back.

Her eyes popped open, frantic and searching. "What do you mean?"

He chuckled wickedly. "I forgot about the condom in my wallet."

"You forgot?" Her voice was mock-angry.

His only excuse was that with Mandy around, he never seemed to think too clearly.

"Come inside with me."

"You go. I need a moment to cool off."

"You're certain?" He didn't want to leave, but his wallet was just a few steps inside the living room.

"I'm fine."

He placed his hands on her hips. Turned her around to view the ocean. Meanwhile he had the most delicious shot of her ass, high and round and firm. "Why don't you watch the view until I come back?"

She glanced over her shoulder at him, her eyes dark and questioning. "Zack?"

He swatted her bottom. "Don't turn around or you'll spoil the surprise."

"It had damn well better be worth waiting for," she threatened, but her tone was more needy and tormented than threatening.

When he opened the sliding glass door, she whispered, "Hurry."

He suppressed a chuckle. "How long will you wait for me, Mandy?"

"Not too damn long," she muttered.

"I'll be right back."

"Okay," she turned to look at him again, "but promise me that you'll make it worth the wait?"

This time Zack didn't hold back his laugh. "Now that's a promise I'm sure to keep."

Her voice turned throaty and playful. "One more thing."

"Yes?"

"Don't forget to bring back the massage oil in my bathroom." She grinned at him, the moonlight revealing her brazen smile. "Get going."

"Yes, ma'am."

Zack took one last mental picture of her standing on the balcony, waiting for him as she gazed out to sea. Walking in his state was painful, but he still moved quietly.

He found his wallet on the coffee table, opened it with shaking fingers. *Please, let it be there.*

Chapter Twenty-Five

MANDY LOVED THE feel of the sea breeze skimming her bare flesh. Even more she liked the way Zack made her feel so sexy—as if she was the only woman in the world—because he acted as if there was no place he'd rather be. When he centered all his magnificent intensity and focus on her, she changed into a different woman—one that was bold and brazen and unafraid to ask for exactly what she wanted. She liked herself when she was with Zack. For some reason she was more confident, bolder, sexier.

Although Zack had already given her pleasure, she recalled from their night together that he was capable of so much more. He anticipated her needs with extraordinary skill. When Zack stroked her, he performed magic. The night of Gabrielle's conception she'd asked how he had known what she wanted without her saying the words. He'd told her that he paid attention. Listened to her breathing patterns, the hitch in her moans. Watched the tremble of her flesh, felt the tension in her muscles. He read her body like sheet music, interpreted the rhythms, and then played her like a maestro.

Her entire being certainly hummed with anticipation and when he returned, she looked over her shoulder to see him pick up the garden hose.

Her pulse sped and she licked her bottom lip. "What are you doing?"

"You splashed me when we were swimming." He shot her a playful look that tingled right down to her toes. "Now it's my turn."

She spun to face him and held up her palms. "Zack, that water's going to be cold."

"You said you needed to cool off." He sprayed a little water on his hand. "It's perfect for what I have in mind."

She braced for water but Zack didn't spray her. Instead he held up the massage oil, the condom, and a tiny bottle she didn't recognize. "Mission accomplished."

"What's in the bottle?"

"I found some White Flower in the medicine cabinet." He set aside the hose, opened the fragrant cocoa butter and scooped some cream into his hand. He spread it out a bit, then opened the tiny bottle and shook a few drops of the liquid into the cocoa butter.

"White Flower?" She sniffed.

The peppermint scent was sharp. As he mixed the concoction she had no doubt he intended to smooth it over her skin. At the thought of his hands trailing over her body, her stomach clenched, her nipples tightened.

Zack raised an eyebrow. "The oil comes from a Chinese flower and is mixed with eucalyptus, lavender, and peppermint. It's great for minor aches and pains."

"And?"

"It's good for other things, too. The massage oil has a bit of a bite." He placed one hand on each of her shoulders and began to rub. "What do you think?"

She closed her eyes and leaned into his massage. "Mmm. Your hands feel wonderful. I'll give you a few hours to stop that."

He nuzzled her neck, nipped lightly. His bite's tiny sting spread over her shoulders as he rubbed the concoction into her flesh. Warmth from the White Flower settled into her shoulders, shooting delicious heat through her skin and straight into her bones.

"That's good stuff," she murmured.

"It gets better."

She opened her eyes. "Really?"

"Oh, yeah. Wait until you feel what it does to the rest of you."

She laughed. "I'm all yours tonight. Or at least for what's left of it."

"I'm a lucky man."

He smoothed the lotion into her arms, ran his hand over her biceps and forearms and wrists. She hadn't known that a hand rub could be so erotic. Perhaps the reason he felt so good was because she was standing there nude, her muscles soothed, her bones melting, totally relaxed, yet all too aware that he intended to totally cover her in lotion. Several places on her skin were already demanding attention.

He had yet to touch her breasts but as if of their own accord, they swelled and ached for his clever touch. She tried to be patient, wished she could demand that each part of her wait its turn so she could fully enjoy him rubbing her fingers, her palms, and her sensitive finger joints. But she kept thinking where else he intended to apply the heat. Private places.

He was proceeding so slowly. After spending a lot of effort on her shoulders and arms and hands, he gave her plenty of time to soak in the heat. She kept tensing and he kept releasing the knots.

Impatient, she reached for the cocoa butter. He nudged it out of her reach.

"Hey, I want to put some on you," she complained.

"Later."

"But . . . but . . . why?"

His tone soothed, caressed, provoked. "Because I want you to only think about my hands on you."

"Oh." She swallowed hard.

"Will you do that for me?"

She fisted her hands on her hips. "If I agree? Then you'll let me do the same to you?"

"Oh, yeah."

He'd agreed too easily. She eyed him suspiciously, but it was difficult to think when his hands bypassed her breasts and rubbed the lotion into her belly. Somehow she now knew he was going to skip putting lotion on the parts her bikini would have covered.

Sure enough, he soon moved on to her thighs, her knees and shins, her ankles and toes. The sensation was odd, yummy. Her entire front except for the areas he'd deliberately avoided was warm. The rest of her front and all of her back remained cool.

She felt cherished, adored, beautiful. As he stroked and caressed he was clearly enjoying himself.

"I don't think I truly ever understood the meaning of sweet torture—until tonight," she admitted, her tone low and husky.

"Good. Turn around, please."

She faced the sea as he requested. The wind had begun to kick up the waves, matching the growing froth inside her. She parted her legs, hoping to entice him back to her throbbing center. But he began with her shoulders and slowly, ever so slowly worked down her back.

"My butt's cold," she hinted.

"Is that so?"

"Uh-huh. Would you mind putting a little of that lotion there?"

"That will be a real hardship," he teased. But he began smoothing the heat into her bottom, kneading muscles that made her sigh in delight. And oh, the heat was making it difficult to remain still.

She peered over her shoulder at him. "Did you mix extra White Flower there?"

"Why?"

"My skin is so hot."

He grunted. "Too hot?"

She laughed. "There's no such thing. But the heat is making

my lower half throb." She began to turn around. "You missed some spots on my front."

He stopped her from turning. "Patience."

She snorted. "I'm not the patient sort."

"All right then, I'll hurry."

But he didn't. His hands caressed the back of her thighs, her calves, the bottoms of her feet. Satisfaction purred in his tone. "Now, please turn around."

Surely he would soon place that wonderful potion on her breasts? But he'd picked up the hose that she'd forgotten about, a wicked gleam in his eyes. "You splashed me in the water. Now it's my turn."

He turned the spray on very low, to a light mist, and he trickled water over her breasts.

"I don't think . . . ahhh."

The heat on her body, the cool air and water trickling on her nipples had her so sensitive that she could feel each ripple of water drip over her hot flesh. She could tell from the arrogant twist of his lips to the glowing glint in his eyes that he knew the hot and cold was driving her wild. He knew she was about to come unglued.

"So, talk to me, Mandy. Which would you prefer? A little lotion on those beautiful breasts or a little water spray between your legs."

"Uh . . . both. I want both," she demanded.

He chuckled. "Your wish is my command."

He shoved the sprayer's nozzle between the straps on the back of a chair, aiming directly between her legs. The force was enough to tease, to provoke, to excite, but not enough for release. Finally, he began to smooth the heat into her breasts.

"Look at me."

"Why?" She sucked in a breath and locked gazes. He let her see his desire, his need, his excitement and it made her want him all the more.

"I want to watch every emotion flicker in your eyes." He tweaked her nipples. She gasped. He raised an eyebrow. "You liked that."

"Uh—"

"You did." He tweaked the tips again. "I can see your eyes dilating."

She refused to lower her gaze. "If you don't get that condom on, I'm going to tackle you."

"But then you'd miss my kiss. You do want another kiss, don't you?"

She'd never wanted anything more in her life. "Damn you, Zack, kiss me, right now."

"Sure." His mouth angled over hers. His hands left her breasts and she missed the contact. Leaning into him, she slid her oiled body again his hard chest. At the same time she unzipped his jeans and shoved them to the floor.

She pulled back her mouth long enough to ask, "Where's the condom?"

He took care of it, then held up the cocoa butter. "Put some on me."

Happy to comply, she scooped some from the jar. As badly as she wanted him inside her, she figured it was her opportunity to take the initiative. She applied the White Flower to the cocoa butter and slowly, sensuously smoothed her palms down his hips, his thighs, the insides of his legs.

When she reached his balls, he sucked in air and then released his breath on a long, low hiss. "Be careful."

"Sure."

He spoke between gritted teeth. "I mean it. The area is rather tender at the moment."

She giggled and kept rubbing the lotion into the area. "You want me to stop?"

"No."

"You sure I'm not hurting you?"

"No." He was beginning to sound desperate. He clenched the railing so hard that his knuckles paled.

"Oh, Zack. I'm so glad we're doing this. I'm having fun." He groaned. "You are so bad."

"You like me bad." She squeezed a little harder. "Don't you?"

"I . . . like . . . you . . . any way . . . I can . . . get . . . you."

"Mmm. Kiss me, again. Please." She kept her hands right

where they were on his balls, stroking, tugging, caressing.

Zack leaned forward, his arms encircling her. His kiss revealed mounting frustration. Slashing need. Burning lust. She let him have her mouth, but she didn't stop caressing. His flesh beneath her fingers warmed, heated.

He groaned into her mouth.

Then he placed his hands on her waist, lifted her onto him, and lowered her slowly. He felt totally delicious and with a gasp of pleasure at his fullness, she wrapped her legs around his hips.

His hands clutched her bottom, his fingers teasing the sensitive skin in her crease. Forced to release her hold of him, she wound her hands around his neck.

"Comfy?" he asked.

"Oh . . . my." Heat flamed where their bodies joined.

"What?"

"Some of the White Flower is . . . ah . . . ah . . . ohh. It's inside me."

He grunted. "I . . . can . . . feel it, too."

As the temperature rose, he thrust into her and the wondrous blaze swept through her like wildfire. Delicious warmth suffused her from the inside out. Every area he'd caressed seemed connected.

She burned. Wanted it to last forever. She needed release now. Right now.

Her head was spinning. Her muscles tensed. Her nerves gathered. She was so close. Tipping her hips, she created friction where she needed it most.

"Come with me," he demanded.

She exploded and Zack covered her mouth with his to muffle her scream. The shock wave rippled through her, reverberated, then ripped again, leaving her so satiated, that if Zack hadn't been holding her, she would have collapsed.

When her heart rate finally approached normal, when she opened her eyes and took in her surroundings, she found that Zack had lowered her to a chaise lounge. She sprawled on top of him and his fingers lightly trailed up and down her back.

In the moonlight, she lifted her head. "Wow."

"Yeah."

"You were marvelous."

He grinned. "You weren't so bad yourself."

She snuggled against him. "You know the last time we did this—"

"—the condom broke. I think we're okay this time," he squeezed her shoulders.

"Last time . . . was it this good?"

Zack brought out her adventuresome side. She had never made love outdoors. She'd never made love with hose spray and cocoa butter and White Flower. But it was Zack who made her heart hammer. Zack who excited her. Zack who always seemed to know how to push her buttons.

"It must have been. I haven't hooked up with anyone else in two years," he admitted.

"Me, either." She sighed contentedly against him. Just this once she didn't want to think about the future. About Zack leaving for California. She didn't want to think about what she would say to her mother in the morning.

She just wanted to take these precious moments and revel in them. She didn't understand why the physical connection with Zack was so strong.

However, she did understand why she found him so irresistible. Zack could focus better than anyone she knew. When he turned all his incredible energy in her direction, she felt intoxicated. Her blood hummed. Her pulse accelerated. There could be thirty people in the room, but her attention would be on him.

She even liked the tender way he held her afterward. He didn't rush for a shower or bed. He caressed her, cuddled her, finishing what he'd started with a gentle tenderness that made her feel appreciated.

Morning was going to arrive all too soon.

Chapter Twenty-Six

"HOW'S YOUR HEAD?" Sam asked Dana. "Are you sure you feel up to attending the funeral?"

"I'll be okay." Dana gazed at her reflection in the bathroom mirror, wincing in three mirrors as she hit a sore spot with the brush. Hair covered her egg-sized bruise, but it still throbbed. She took an aspirin for the pain and washed it down with a glass of water.

Sam came up behind her, held her hair off her neck with his good arm and kissed her behind the ear. "No one will blame you if you decide to stay home."

"I know. But I need to pay my respects. It's the least I can do." Dana put on her favorite teardrop pearl earrings—a birthday present from Sam. "Lisa was so young. She died so violently. It's horrible."

Dana hugged Sam, careful not to touch his arm, which remained in a black silk sling that managed to look sexy. He'd always been her rock and she was grateful he'd accompany her today. His phone rang and he broke the embrace, reached into his pocket and answered the call. "Hello."

Even from a distance, Dana could hear a burst of sound

and recognize Dylan's voice, before Sam said, "Calm down."

He walked away, talking in a low voice that sounded worried. Dana heard him mention Mitch Anderson, the missing county administrator.

She didn't understand why Sam had suddenly gotten so thick with Dylan lately. And his sudden interest in politics worried her. Didn't he have enough to do between his thriving law practice and his real estate investments? She understood he had big dreams, but it almost seemed as if he'd moved into Mitch Anderson's position as advisor to the mayor.

Turning back to the mirror, Dana checked her blush, then added lipstick. She probably had her own list of voice-mail calls to return but simply didn't have the energy. Perhaps her sorrow over Lisa had sapped her energy. Or perhaps she hadn't recovered from her head injury yet.

Usually Dana felt calm in her bedroom. She loved the cream wallpaper, the matching carpet and coverlet. Between the eggshell-colored oak furniture and the monotone creams, the room's decor soothed her. But Sam, dressed in a black suit, black shirt, and black shoes had disturbed the harmony.

She turned around to put on her dress and caught sight of him as he returned to their bedroom. His brows had furrowed into an angry line. Worse, his face had reddened, a sign his blood pressure was high.

She zipped her dress. "What's wrong?"

"Nothing." He masked the frown but the furrows in his forehead remained.

"Sam. You might as well tell me. Otherwise, I'll worry." She picked up a string of pearls to place around her neck.

"The chief of police called to tell me that Nick Vizzi—"

"Who?"

"The man who shot me."

"Right."

Sam shot her an odd look. It wasn't like her to forget names. "The medical examiner finished his autopsy."

"That was fast."

"I pulled strings."

"And?"

"Vizzi didn't kill Lisa."

Dana dropped the pearls. "They're certain?"

"Yeah. Lisa managed to scratch the killer. They found skin under her nails that didn't match Nick's."

"So whoever killed Lisa is still out there?" Dana bent and picked up the pearls, her stomach churning.

"I'm afraid so. We'll have to tell the others."

Chapter Twenty-Seven

MARIA FINISHED BREAKFAST to find a white box with a big red bow on top of the morning newspaper that her body-guard had placed beside her on the kitchen table. She opened the card and smiled, knowing it was from Ray before she recognized his neat handwriting. "For the funeral."

Heart thumping, she carried the box into her bedroom. She hadn't seen Ray since the night they'd done some grind in the street, right up against her car. Right from the first time they'd met at a club four months ago, Ray had seemed unusually sensitive to her need to push the envelope sexually but with the assurance of a safety net. In the last few days, as if sensing her hesitancy, he hadn't called. He was a master at balancing her need to feel safe with her love of surprise and experimentation.

She opened the box, expecting to see something totally inappropriate to wear to a funeral. But Ray had sent her a black hat, a dark gray suit, a pink blouse, dark thigh highs, pumps and an exquisite set of delicate lace lingerie. The panties, a thong and bra set, were soft sexy and exactly her size. Everything fit as if she'd tried on the clothes and picked

them out herself. In addition, the dark gray suit fabric com-
plemented her tan. He'd even included a clutch purse.

She looked perfectly respectable but felt naughty in the
underwear—which was surely his intention. Maria locked
the front door behind her and her bodyguard just as Ray
pulled up to the curb. She was surprised but pleased to see
him; he looked yummy, dressed in a navy suit that brought
out the sparkle in his eyes.

He strode up to her as if they had a date. "You look
lovely."

"Thank you for the compliment as well as the clothes."

His tone was low and husky. "I like dressing you. I like
knowing that I picked out every stitch of clothing that
touches your skin."

He didn't seem to care that they weren't alone and his intimate words in front of her bodyguard made her uncomfortable. "Ray, what are you doing here?"

"I'm escorting you to the funeral. Did you think I would
let you go alone?" Ray's gaze turned to the bodyguard.
"You're hired protection?"

"Yes, sir."

Maria had no idea how Ray had known. Another man
would have assumed she had a date or was with a friend. So
how had Ray known this man was here to protect her? If she
hadn't been seeing him for months before Lisa's death, she
would have refused to see him at all. When she'd considered
whether he could have had anything to do with the attacks
on the lottery winners, common sense told her that if he was
really dangerous, she would have known it long before now.

"What happens when you sleep?" Ray asked the bodyguard.

"My replacement will arrive in eight hours."

Ray raised his eyebrow. "And if Maria requires privacy?"

Heat rose to her face. "Ray!" It was bad enough she
couldn't resist Ray's combination of mystery and passion,
he didn't have to announce it to a stranger. Maria had
never in her life been obsessed with a man. She'd always
been a good girl and had told herself Ray was simply a fling,

her walk on the wild side before she settled down with Mr. Right. But Ray surprised her, intrigued her, and he was just the right combination of sensitive and tough to fuel her fantasies.

"I have plans for you tonight, *amor mío*." Ray placed a proprietary hand on the small of her back and escorted her to his car. Over his shoulder, he spoke to her bodyguard. "There's no back seat but you're welcome to follow. We're heading to the cemetery."

The bodyguard looked at Maria and she nodded. Then she slipped into the front seat of Ray's car.

Ray slid behind the wheel and started the car. He looked so handsome and she adored the soft leather seats of his Porsche. However, she didn't like his assuming she was free.

"Maybe I had other plans."

"Then cancel them." He didn't seem the least concerned. "You'll have a better time with me."

His voice implied the sex would be hot. She raised her hand to her neck. Although his strangulation had left no marks on her neck, she still recalled her terror and the explosive orgasm that had followed.

The mix of danger and pleasure called to her like a drug. She'd worked hard to get a good education and she deserved some fun. But she had to be careful. For all she knew, Lisa could have died because of an illicit sexual relationship.

"I don't know." Maria couldn't recall the last time she'd wanted something as much as Ray's lovemaking. Just thinking about going another round with him elevated her pulse. Moisture seeped between her thighs.

"I have special plans for us. Afterward, I thought I'd take you to my place."

The idea intrigued her. She didn't even know where he lived. They'd met at a club and he kept his life private. He'd told her little about himself. She didn't know what he did for a living or where he worked. He just sent her gifts and showed up—usually with no warning, like he had today. She'd often wondered if he was married, or hiding the fact that he lived with his mother—because Ray had a sensitive side, like showing up to accompany her to the funeral, as well as a darkly sensual side.

His offer to let her see where he lived, find out more about him, tempted her. Yet going into his territory scared her and excited her. She supposed if she brought her bodyguard, it would be all right. She'd have him wait outside. Just his presence should be enough to stop Ray from going too far. Besides, if Ray had wanted to kill her, he'd already had plenty of chances.

Chapter Twenty-Eight

"NICK VIZZI WAS a private eye who worked both sides of the law," Ben explained to Sylvia at their kitchen table, his voice raised a bit to be heard over the glazier's bangs as he replaced their shot-out bedroom window. "Apparently, last night I nicked Vizzi's ear. When he went after Mandy, Zack killed him."

Sylvia shivered and sipped her coffee. Ben's old contacts in the police department were all too eager to inform him of news. She worried about him missing the excitement now that he'd retired. "I'm glad Vizzi can't bother anyone any more. But what did you mean when you said he worked both sides of the law?"

"He was a good snitch. He knew stuff coming down on the streets." Ben smeared strawberry preserves on his wheat toast, his expression thoughtful.

"You knew him?" Sylvia asked.

Ben nodded. "Vizzi was useful. He tipped me off occasionally, but he also skirted the law, installing illegal security systems for those who wanted to know if their phones were tapped."

"Did he have any personal reason to come after us or Mandy or Lisa or Dana?"

"I don't know, but Catherine Taylor and Associates handled his divorce. Maybe he held a grudge. Maybe it was coincidence." Ben frowned. "But Vizzi didn't kill Lisa. The DNA didn't match." He chewed his toast, washed it down with fresh-squeezed orange juice.

She didn't remember Nick Vizzi or his spouse. But her memory wasn't infallible.

"Vizzi always had money problems. Although he had a rap sheet as long as my arm, he wasn't violent."

Sylvia rolled her eyes. "He tried to shoot us. That's violent."

"However, I could see him scheming to steal the winning lottery ticket. Maybe he had a partner."

"The man at the airport who attacked Dana?" Sylvia raised her eyebrows. She didn't want Ben back on the street investigating. In a wheelchair, he was simply too easy a target. "Maybe you should suggest your theory to Zack," she said. "Let him look into it."

"You want me out of it, don't you?" Ben smiled at her, his tone gentle.

"Yes. If I'm being selfish, I can live with that—as long as you're safe."

Chapter Twenty-Nine

GABBY SAT IN her high chair, playing with her cereal. While Zack found his daughter's every movement fascinating, an undercurrent of tension in the kitchen kept distracting him from his own breakfast.

Mandy's mother sighed, her smile vanishing the moment she'd joined them in the kitchen and noticed Zack and the bruises on his face. Even without the bruises, he'd probably still have that stay-away-from-my-daughter effect on mothers. One look and they usually figured out he was bad news. But Mandy's mom shot him a curious glance. "I've waited two years for an explanation, it's time to 'fess up."

"What do you mean?" Mandy shoved to her feet, her back to the beach and the blue water of the Gulf of Mexico.

Zack pushed back from the table, too, intending to give the women privacy. He didn't need to be here for this conversation.

But before he made his getaway, Mandy's mom said, "I've got eyes, Amanda. I may not have gone to some fancy law school, but I can see what's in front of my face. Gabrielle is the spitting image of Zack." Her mother's piercing eyes found hers. "I can also count backwards."

Mandy's shock showed in her eyes. Apparently Gabrielle looked so much like him that Mrs. Newman had known the moment she'd seen him that he was the father. Zack didn't say a word, unsure where the conversation was heading, but positive he didn't want to be here. He was grateful Gabby was too young to understand the conversation, because a lot of the blame was his. So he didn't move as uneasiness slicked over his skin.

"And as much as I love Gabby, I'm too old to watch two kids."

"Two kids?" Mandy gasped.

Lord. Zack prayed her mother hadn't awakened and heard them making love on the balcony last night. Mandy was extraordinary . . . someone special. The effect she had on him was like a drug. Addictive. No way could he have kept his hands off her—especially after she'd made it clear how much she wanted his touch. Damn, they were good together.

"From the sparks flying off the two of you this morning, it looks like you're about to make another baby on the kitchen floor."

"Mom. It's not like that."

Did what they'd shared show on his face? Obviously, around Mandy, keeping his expression stoic was just not happening.

Since Mandy's mother had figured out Gabby was his, Zack suspected that Dana and Catherine must also know the truth. He couldn't help feeling bothered that he was probably the only one who hadn't known. He understood Mandy had had her reasons, and he didn't have anyone to blame but himself for dropping out of everyone's lives . . . but damn it—he still felt as if he was standing on the outside of a conspiracy.

His phone rang and Zack couldn't have been more relieved. He answered the call and took it into the living room. When he returned, the women were no longer arguing, although the tension was arcing through the room.

"That was Ben." Zack slipped his phone back into his pocket. "Why don't we go for that walk on the beach and I'll fill you in," he suggested, hoping Ms. Newman wouldn't choose to accompany them.

She didn't. But it wasn't much of a walk. Even with Mandy and him each holding one of Gabrielle's hands, the baby kept stopping to look at the oddest things. A broken sea shell. A stick. Seaweed.

Zack didn't mind. He found his daughter attractive. To her, the entire world was one big adventure. To see her laugh at a stray piece of paper the wind tossed along the beach made him smile and lightened his mood. She'd happily accepted him and his bruises without any wariness—as if she expected the best of everyone because she'd always been well treated—unlike Todd, who had flinched every time Zack had raised his hand to do something innocent, like reach for a newspaper. He couldn't have been more grateful to Mandy for seeing to this precious little baby's welfare. It was too damn bad he couldn't be around to watch her grow up.

"Sorry about the drama back there," Mandy said once they'd walked down to the water, far enough away from the beach house to be out of her mother's hearing range. Then she gave up on the walk and sat in the sand next to the baby. "What did Ben say?"

The morning light bathed her face in a golden glow and although neither of them had had but a few hours of sleep, the contented look in her eyes pleased him. For a few hours, they'd forgotten the killer. Over breakfast Sam had called to tell him that Nick Vizzi hadn't murdered Lisa—so her killer was still out there, still dangerous. Then Ben had suggested Zack might want to search for any connection between Vizzi and the black man who'd attacked the women at the garage. Perhaps an investigation might even lead him and Mandy to the missing lottery ticket.

With the warm water from the Gulf of Mexico gently lapping at their feet in the still morning, Zack didn't want to answer Mandy's question. He watched fishermen returning from their early morning hauls with their catch and a sailboat following the coast. Finally, he broke the peaceful moment and explained Ben's theory on investigating Vizzi as Gabrielle tried to eat sand.

Gently, Mandy pulled the baby's hand from her mouth. "Gabby, no. Sand is dirty."

"Dir-tee?" Gabby looked at Mandy and grinned, then picked up more sand and threw it at her toes.

Mandy brushed a stray lock of hair from her eyes and glanced at him over Gabrielle's head. "Do you think it's odd that Vizzi used to work with Ben?"

"Vizzi was a paid informant. He worked with several police officers."

"It still seems like a strange coincidence."

"What are you saying?" Zack asked, uncertain where she was going.

"I'm not sure."

But Mandy's suspicions had Zack thinking. "You know if Ben had hired Vizzi to steal the ticket and knock off the other winners, he and Sylvia would claim a larger portion of the lottery winnings."

"Ben and Sylvia plotting murder? No way. I know them well. Like them. Ben's a fantastic cop. No one ever has a bad thing to say about the guy. Sylvia's the grandmotherly type, adored by everyone at the firm. Neither of them seems to have a greedy bone in their bodies. Their behaving like murderers doesn't wash or make sense. If Vizzi had succeeded in killing me, Gabby and my mom would inherit my share."

Zack frowned. "Who's to say Vizzi wouldn't have gone after them next?"

"Although I think your scenario is far-fetched, I'm glad Mom and Gabby are at the beach house and not my condo." She shivered. "I'll feel better when their bodyguard shows up."

Realizing his words had upset her, he placed an arm over her shoulder. "There's no point in anyone going after your mother or Gabby while you're alive—and I intend to keep you safe. Besides, it's just as likely someone's targeting members of the law firm out of a personal grudge."

"But you don't think so?" she pressed.

"I'm trying to think of every possibility. A good investigator doesn't eliminate any suspect until the evidence clears him."

She disagreed. "I still don't believe Ben and Sylvia could have hired Vizzi. And don't forget, Vizzi came into Ben's backyard to shoot Sylvia, maybe Ben, too."

"So Ben claims. But we don't know why Vizzi was there. Maybe Vizzi came to see Ben, his boss."

"But Ben shot him."

"What better way for Ben to cover his tracks than to kill the guy he'd hired to do his dirty work?"

Mandy pulled a hat from her back pocket and placed it over Gabby's head to protect her from the sun. "Anyone could have hired Vizzi. Like Damien Reed, the stockbroker, or even the pediatrician. Or Vizzi could have been working alone."

"True. But as you pointed out, Ben already knew Vizzi. Now Vizzi's dead because Ben warned me he might be coming. That's a good way to shut a man up, have him killed."

"But Sam told Dana to warn us, too. It was the decent thing to do." She sighed. "And there's so much money. Why would a good cop kill to get a larger share? Ben doesn't have a good motive."

"Three hundred and sixty million dollars is a very good motive. Don't Ben and Sylvia have seven kids and twice that many grandchildren? Perhaps he'd rather share with his family than the other lawyers at the firm."

"Do you believe your theory?" Mandy asked, her brows drawn into a frown.

Zack shrugged. "Everyone's a suspect until we figure out who killed Lisa. For all we know, Vizzi planned to take out Sam, Dana and Catherine, Ben and Sylvia, then you and me. That wipes out a lot of winners and some of their heirs. Lisa was all alone—maybe that's why she was the first victim."

"Lisa may have died without a will, but Catherine intends to see that Lisa's share goes to her foster parents." Mandy wiped sand from Gabrielle's mouth. "Even if one of the lottery winners, their family, or someone they hired is trying to kill the rest of us in order to keep a bigger share of the lottery, there are still holes in your theory."

"Because Vizzi rammed your car off the bridge before anyone knew you'd bought the winning ticket?" Zack asked.

"Exactly."

Zack stared at the horizon. "Vizzi's still our best lead. After the funeral, why don't we check him out? See if we can find a link between him and any lottery winners or the guy who attacked you and Dana at the airport."

"Won't the police—"

Zack shook his head. "My source at the department told me the police department is focusing its efforts on tracking down an ex-boyfriend of Lisa's. Right now he's the prime suspect in her murder."

"I like that theory much better than one of us turning on the others out of greed." Mandy fluffed sand, which had landed there during one of Gabrielle's misfires, out of her hair. Zack appreciated her easy companionship with the child. Mandy didn't fuss or worry about the sand. She simply enjoyed her daughter and kept her safe, stopping her from eating the sand but letting her enjoy playing in it.

"Apparently," Zack said, "Lisa's boyfriend had a temper. During an argument with his mother he put his fist through a wall. When a former girlfriend broke up with him, he dragged her out from behind her station at the hair salon into the parking lot. He slammed his fist into her car's windshield and the police had to break up the argument."

"Have the cops brought him in for questioning yet?" Mandy's voice rose in frustration.

"They can't find him."

"If one of us has stolen the ticket and hired Vizzi to come after the rest of us, then none of us are safe."

"Ma-ma-ma-ma-ma." Gabby stood, using Mandy's shoulder to steady her shaky upright position. The baby bobbed up and down on her toes, her eyes bright with excitement.

"What is it?" Mandy asked.

A flock of sea gulls had landed on the beach and her daughter tried to step toward them but fell back on her bottom. Undeterred, she crawled towards the birds with such determination that Zack laughed. "I wonder what she'd do if she caught one."

Mandy grinned. "Hopefully, we'll never have to find out."

Mandy's mother came out onto the deck and motioned for them to leave the beach and return to the house. About a hundred yards away, she couldn't have overheard their conversation, but from her stiff posture, she looked tense.

Zack spoke gently. "I think your mother wants us to come inside."

"She want to talk to *me*—alone."

He raised his eyebrow. "How do you know?"

"She gave me her I-want-to-talk look over breakfast."

"Really?"

"Yeah. She wants to grill me about you."

That was one conversation he could avoid. "Do you want to go to the house while I stay with Gabrielle?"

Had he just tried to avoid one bad situation by jumping into another? He'd actually offered to spend alone-time with Gabby.

Damn. Mandy and Gabby had come to mean a lot to him in a short time. Walking away was going to be hard . . . but Zack recalled his brother's funeral, and reminded himself he could do hard things.

Mandy bit her lower lip, dusted sand from her hands, and stood. "Thanks for the offer, but we should all go. I'll delay a private conversation with my mother for as long as possible."

Was she trying to give him more time to come to terms with fatherhood before talking to her mother? He didn't know his own mind so how could she explain anything to her mother? Zack realized he'd put Mandy in a difficult position—and not for the first time. While he admired her, he couldn't let his growing feelings distract him from his work responsibilities.

He was here to protect her.

He gazed down at the smiling child beside him. *Protect Mandy and his daughter*. "Since Vizzi wasn't the man who attacked you and Dana at the airport, until we're certain there's no further danger, it's a good time to move your mother and Gabby and their new bodyguard."

Chapter Thirty

EVERY MEMBER OF the firm had come to the funeral to say goodbye, and for the first time all the lottery winners were together—which meant the press was there but the police kept them back behind barriers. Catherine; Dana with her husband, Sam; Sylvia and Ben; Mandy and Zack; and Maria with her new boyfriend, Ray, congregated in the synagogue. Mandy had never met Ray before, and although his manners were impeccable, she didn't like the way he kept Maria to himself, as if he was jealous of her friends.

Mandy turned her attention from her coworkers and their dates to the rabbi, who began to recite a blessing, "*Baruch atah Hashem Elokeinu melech haolam, dayan ha'emet.*" Blessed are you, Lord our God, Ruler of the universe, the true Judge. Witnesses repeated a shorter version of the same blessing. Psalms were recited, then a eulogy and the memorial prayer, *El Maleh Rachamim*, was said.

Sadness welled inside Mandy's heart. Lisa had been so full of life, yet there were so few people here to mark her passing. A few foster kids. Her own foster family. All sitting in chairs in a row up front and wearing torn black ribbons to

mark their grief. There were people from the firm, a couple
of girlfriends from college.

While Mandy didn't judge a person's importance by how
many people turned out for the funeral, she regretted that
Lisa hadn't had time to make more friends. To fall in love
again. To start a family of her own.

Lisa had always had a bright smile, pitching in when
needed and staying late often. Mandy remembered her ready
laughter, her confidence, as well as her determination to help
women in desperate need of legal counsel as well as her foster kids. Now she was gone.

Tears made her vision swim. Beside her, Zack threaded
his fingers between Mandy's, lending comfort and strength.
For now, she could lean on him. There might not be a future,
but there was a right now, and she could live with it. The
DEA would soon call him back to work and the possibility
he'd have to leave again was all too real—but for now, he
was with her, and she vowed to make the most of their time
together.

Lisa Slocum's plain pine casket was wheeled out of the
room accompanied by the recitation of the Twenty-third
Psalm. Short and solemn, the ancient ceremony was over in
about twenty minutes. As per Lisa's written wishes, the burial would be a private ceremony, attended only by her foster
family.

Mandy joined Zack and his mother, sister, and brother-in-
law outside the synagogue. Although Sam had remained beside Dana during the ceremony, the moment they passed
over the threshold into the hot sunshine, he was on his cell
phone. Eyes worried, his voice low, he walked away as if not
to disturb them, or to give himself privacy—Mandy couldn't
say which. Dana didn't seem to mind Sam abandoning her.
She stood beside her mother, the bond between them close.

Ray, tall, dark and expensively dressed, seemed eager to
draw Maria away from their group, but she pulled her arm
from his and joined them, dabbing at her eyes with a hanky.
Ray spoke in her ear; then, his long strides eating up the pavement, he headed for his gleaming Porsche. Mandy assumed

Maria would catch up with him in a few minutes, but thought his antisocial behavior strange.

Meanwhile, all the bodyguards kept a careful watch on their charges, but gave them room to speak among themselves in a shady spot outside the synagogue. The press seemed to have disappeared. As head of the firm, Catherine, wearing an elegant black suit and hat, thanked them for coming and then announced, "As all of you have heard, the police have not yet apprehended Lisa's killer. I'll leave it up to each of you to decide when to return to work. If you need time off, please notify our clients. Sylvia's agreed to come in for the rest of the week, so coordinate your schedule with her." She squeezed Sylvia's shoulder. "Thank you for volunteering."

Sylvia pulled a fistful of pink message slips from her purse and handed them out. Mandy had three. Nothing that couldn't wait.

Maria placed hers in her purse without reading them. She glanced over at Ray, sitting behind the wheel of his car, then back at Catherine. "I'm taking off the rest of the week. I'll be back Monday."

"That's fine." Catherine patted her shoulder and made a casual reference to Ray. "I'm glad you won't be alone."

"How long have you known him?" Zack asked.

Maria refused to meet his eyes. "A while. Ray wants to meet all of you, he just didn't want to intrude . . ." Her attempt to made excuses for Ray fell flat, but clearly his standoffishness had made her uncomfortable.

"It's okay," Catherine said to Maria. "We all have to get through this in our own way. But it might be best if you didn't spend time alone with people you don't know well." She looked at her children and Mandy. "That goes for all of us."

Sam hurried over and pulled Dana aside. He spoke in a low and urgent tone. Dana's eyes narrowed and her lips tightened. Mandy couldn't hear what he'd said, but Dana explained, "Mom, Sam's got to meet the mayor for lunch. Can I catch a ride home with you?"

"Sure." Catherine agreed easily, but her gaze followed Sam, her expression thoughtful, a touch of worry in her eyes.

Car tires squealed, drawing everyone's attention to the Porsche. Apparently, Ray didn't intend to wait any longer for Maria to join him. He sped away in his Porsche, tires smoking and leaving behind the reek of burnt rubber.

"Ray's always having emergencies." Maria's excuse sounded as lame as Sam's meeting with the mayor. "He knows my bodyguard can take me home."

Mandy was picking up tension from everyone. She turned to see Zack's expression and caught him staring at Ben. The ex-cop had rolled his wheelchair down the sidewalk and he was conversing with two uniformed police officers.

Ben pivoted on one wheel, then joined them. He made no secret of his conversation. "They need me downtown."

"They do?" Sylvia didn't look happy.

"They want me to ID Vizzi's body." Ben tugged Sylvia to his level and kissed her before Mandy could question him. But why would *he* have to identify the body? Vizzi had had identification on him and an announcement had been made. Ben's statement didn't make sense and she eyed him with renewed suspicioun, almost certain he was lying to his wife. Ben patted Sylvia's shoulder. "Don't worry, sweetheart. It's just routine. I'll meet you back at the office within an hour or two."

Worry in her eyes, Sylvia grabbed Ben's hand to keep him from leaving. "Why can't someone else do it?"

"Vizzi's mom is an alcoholic and isn't answering calls. No friends have come forward. None of the other cops knew him as well as I did." Ben sounded too cheerful, which struck Mandy as odd. Was he glad Vizzi was dead? Or glad to be reuniting with his police buddies? Maybe he liked feeling useful. Or maybe Ben was lying and going someplace else. Was it possible the accident that left him in a wheelchair had changed him more than anyone had realized?

Mandy hated being suspicious of everyone, but right after a funeral was not the time to question anyone. Not even

Ray—who's behavior seemed as oddly antagonistic as Ben's did too cheerful. And why was Sam running off with the mayor and leaving Dana alone?

The only dependable male in the bunch was Zack, but even he wouldn't stick around for long. That's one reason Mandy had avoided any private conversation with her mother. Between the last few days of danger, making love to Zack during the night and introducing him to his daughter, and knowing he intended to leave soon, her feelings were raw. Zack's presence and Lisa's funeral had given her a way to dodge her mother's questions.

So she'd made certain Zack and Gabrielle were with her from the moment they'd awakened until they'd left for the funeral. Putting off talking to her mother until after Zack left for good seemed Mandy's best option. She'd sensed her mother's impatience with wanting to know more about their relationship, but Zack wouldn't be here much longer. There would be time to sort out her feelings and make explanations later, after Zack returned to California and the DEA.

Chapter Thirty-One

AFTER THE FUNERAL, Dana took her mother to lunch. Their two bodyguards shared a table nearby but not so close that they could overhear their charges' conversation. Pleased to have an opportunity to have time alone with her mother, Dana ignored the menu. She sipped her water, then cleared her throat, deciding to plunge right in.

"I'm worried about Sam."

Catherine closed her menu and removed her reading glasses. "Is his arm bothering him?"

"I don't think so." Sam hadn't complained about the bullet wound. In fact, he seemed rather proud of his sling. "He's just been gone a lot. He's spreading himself too thin. His criminal practice and the real estate deals eat up a lot of time, and now every other phone call seems to be from the mayor."

"The mayor?"

"Dylan's been relying on Sam for advice since Mitch Anderson disappeared. Even when Sam's home, he's distracted."

Catherine angled her head. Her piercing green eyes held

Dana's in that penetrating way she had of coercing witnesses to tell the truth in court. "Sam's always been distracted and he's always been gone a lot. What's different now?"

Leave it to Catherine to pinpoint the problem. Dana sighed, appreciating her mother's insight. Catherine could get to the real problem because she asked the right questions. Dana recognized she was too emotional to think clearly—especially when it came to Sam. He'd literally swept her off her feet when they met. Their romance had been a whirlwind and led to marriage a few months later. Those first few years had been everything she'd dreamed. But recently . . . the spark was gone and she wasn't certain exactly what had happened or why. Was Sam just preoccupied with work? Was she? Or had the strain of trying to conceive a child taken the romance out of their love life?

"The only time Sam seems happy is when he's with his high-powered friends, the mayor, the chief of police, and now he's befriending some of the Tampa Bay Buccaneers on the golf course."

"So?"

"He used to be happy like that with me," Dana admitted, feeling inadequate but not knowing where she came up short. She was intelligent, attractive, and interested in him. What had gone wrong?

"You've been married eight years. You can't expect him to be as infatuated with you now as he was when you were newlyweds." As usual, Catherine was practical.

Dana frowned. "It's not the sex. It's little things. He tells me he's exhausted, but he refuses to come home early from social events. The other day, he told me he was working late at the office and I found a restaurant receipt in his pocket."

"And?"

"While it's not unusual for Sam to eat with a colleague and then return to work, he told me he'd ordered in. Bar drinks were on the tab, Sam's Pinot Noir and a piña colada."

Her mother could put clues together faster than any detective. "You think he was with another woman?"

"Why else would he lie to me?" Even asking the question made her heart ache.

Catherine took Dana's hand as she had when Dana was a little girl and had fallen off her bike and skinned her knee. "What does your heart tell you?"

"I don't know." This hurt so much worse than a scrape on the knee. Dana hated the fear, hated the uncertainty, hated living with suspicion. "A few weeks ago, before we won the lottery, before Mandy was shoved off the bridge, before Lisa died, I walked into the room and Sam was on the phone. He stopped talking when he noticed I was there. But he had this ferocious glint in his eyes that made me uncomfortable."

"Did you hear anything suspicious?"

"I'm not sure. I heard him say, 'I haven't told her anything. I can slip away.' " Dana closed her eyes, then opened them slowly.

"Oh, sweetie. Why haven't you said anything until now?"

Dana didn't try to pretend a toughness she didn't feel. She let out her uncertainty. Her hurt. "Sam's kept secrets from me before—it's not that unusual in his line of work."

"So why was this time different?"

"Sam's been distracted lately. On edge. Now that he's finally agreed to adopt, I'm not sure if it's fair to bring a child into a shaky marriage."

"Did he say anything else?" her mother asked.

" 'Meet me at the Bay Star in thirty minutes.' "

Catherine's brow arched in confusion. "What's the Bay Star?"

"I looked in the yellow pages. It's a hotel near downtown. Sam didn't come home until dawn."

"Did you hit the automatic redial on the phone to see who he'd called? Or check caller ID?"

Dana shook her head. "I was too upset to hit redial. I checked caller ID on his phone when he showered but he'd erased the history. The next morning when I asked him where he'd been, he said a client needed bail. I also checked his credit card receipts but there was no room or meals charged at the Bay Star."

"He could have paid cash." Her mother gestured to the waitress to leave them alone. "If he's having an affair, do you really want to know?"

"Yes."

"You're certain? Lots of men have flings and then return home. There may be no need to upset your entire life over one indiscretion."

"If he's cheating, I don't think having a baby or adopting one is going to fix the problem."

"All right. I had to be sure you were sure. If that's what you want—"

"It is. I won't spend my life with someone I can't trust. I don't want to wonder where he is when he goes to the store for a pack of gum, or if he's working late with the mayor or with another woman. I can't live like that."

"We can hire a private investigator."

"I've thought of that—but suppose I'm wrong? Sam knows every decent PI in town and if he hears about what I'm doing—that will be the end of our marriage."

"So *I'll* hire someone from out of town. You don't do anything. That way, if by chance he does find out, he can blame me."

"Thanks, Mom. But he won't believe you went behind my back."

"Sure he will. I'll tell him I wanted to make certain your marriage was a solid one before I included him and the children you intend to adopt in my will."

"It would be better if he never knew."

"Agreed."

Relieved that she'd confided in her mother, Dana was ready to move on to a more pleasant topic. "Now how about lunch?"

Chapter Thirty-Two

"MOM AND GABRIELLE have settled into Orlando with their bodyguard," Mandy told Zack, before hanging up her cell phone and tucking it back into her purse. Then she slipped the strap over her shoulder and kept the purse close to her side. Nick Vizzi's neighborhood in Mango consisted of old trailers with sagging roofs, rusted-out cars, and weed-filled yards and reminded her of the poor areas where she'd lived growing up. "Mom mentioned she might take Gabrielle to Sea World but I told her to stay inside and keep a low profile."

Zack guided her around a broken lawn mower that blocked the sidewalk. "You're right to tell them to lay low and stay out of crowds until this is over."

She jerked up her head. "You think my mother and Gabby are in danger?"

"We don't know. So far only firm members, their bodyguards and spouses have been targeted, but it's better to play it safe. She can go later."

"Maybe we can all visit Busch Gardens. Gabby adores zebras and lions." Mandy left unsaid the thought that they could visit the local amusement park *if* Zack remained in town. With her thoughts focused on the potential danger, it was difficult to make plans. But she had to stay alive—for Gabby. Whoever was targeting Mandy and her associates seemed determined to keep killing. Shivering, she rubbed her arms, knowing they had to find and stop the killer . . . before he found her again.

"Vizzi's place looks abandoned, but I want to knock on the door. Maybe someone's home."

"There's no AC or lights on." Mandy edged closer to Zack and lowered her voice. She'd grown up in places similar to this one and didn't like the reminder. A group of teens had scattered when they'd driven up the street, leaving the cloying stench of weed in the air. Across the potholed road, a curtain in a window moved. It could be a fan or a nosy neighbor, or someone hostile with a gun aimed at them.

Winding between the weeds growing through cracks in the overgrown sidewalk, she felt exposed, like a target, and had to remind herself that Nick Vizzi was dead. But if Ben was right, he could have a partner. Zack could knock on the door and the man who had stolen the ticket might open it and confront them.

"Maybe this isn't such a good idea." Mandy tugged on Zack's elbow. "Are you sure we can't leave the investigating to the cops?"

"We'll be fine. I've got your back."

"Maybe Sam could use his influence with the mayor to apply some pressure on the police."

They'd reached the door and it wasn't closed. Zack banged on the trailer's side. "Anybody home?"

"Go away," an older woman shouted at them, her tone more weary than hostile. "Nicky's dead and I ain't got enough cash to turn on the lights, never mind pay his debts."

"Ma'am. We're not bill collectors," Zack told her, his voice firm and polite.

"Get out of here. Didn't you see the 'no trespassing' sign? This is private property." The woman slurred her words.

Mandy didn't want to go inside. She didn't want to talk to

the woman, but from the determined look on Zack's face, he was prepared to camp outside her door in the hot sun until the woman came out or agreed to let them inside.

"Would you answer a few questions for ten bucks?" Mandy offered.

"Fifty."

"Ten." Mandy remained uncompromising. "Twenty if the information's useful."

"And who's to say what's useful?" The door creaked open. A heavyset woman wearing a stained house dress, her beady eyes narrowed in suspicion, waved an almost empty beer bottle. From her body odor, Mandy guessed that she hadn't washed in a month, and the sour smell of beer on her breath suggested she'd been drinking since sunup.

The trailer's occupant stood between piles of stacked newspapers and a fake palm tree strung with Christmas lights. Several cats rubbed against her swollen ankles but she seemed oblivious to their attentions.

"Do you live here with Nick Vizzi?" Zack asked.

"I'm his mama, Angelina Vizzi. And I ain't saying another word until I see some cash."

Mandy dug two tens from her wallet and held them in the air. Angelina tried to grab them and missed. She stumbled into the trailer doorway, then righted herself with a heavy heave of her bosom.

Mandy waved the bills in front of Angelina's nose. "We're looking for an associate of Nick's."

"An associate?" She took a swig from her beer. "Oh, you mean one of the punks he hangs with? Got a name?"

"He's black, has dreads, and has lots of acne scars." Mandy described the man who'd stolen the ticket and held her breath, hoping Angelina wouldn't exhale again in her direction.

"You're looking for Moose."

Mandy handed Angelina one of the ten dollar bills. "Moose? Does he have a real name?"

"None that I ever heard." Angelina stuffed the bill into her bra and burped.

"Where's Moose live?" Zack asked.

"Don't know."

"Does he have a job?" Mandy asked.

"Yeah, terrorizing good honest folk." Angelina's face began turning red. "Come in. I needs to sit myself down."

Mandy did not want to enter the trailer. It smelled bad
enough from the doorway. She heard tiny animals scurrying,
lizards, palmetto bugs, or field rats, although the cats would
probably chase away rats.

Before Zack or Mandy responded, Angelina hiked up her
dress to her knees and sat on a messy stack of newspaper.
Mandy fought to keep a pleasant expression. She knew what
it was like to be poor, yet she'd never seen a trailer or a
woman in such horrible condition. Perhaps Angelina had
gone on a drinking spree after hearing about her son's death,
but filth like this took years to accumulate.

Angelina looked ready to pass out. As promising as the lead
on "Moose" sounded, they couldn't be certain he was the man
they were looking for. Mandy wanted to bolt. Her stomach
soured. Just standing in the doorway was making her itch.

"Where can we find Moose?" Zack asked.

Angelina dropped the beer but the bottle didn't break. The
cats lapped up the spilled liquid. She was too far gone to notice, but even in her alcoholic haze, her eyes focused on the
money Mandy still held. "Moose and my boy. . . . My boy is
dead, you know. I had to identify his body."

Mandy couldn't think of anything worse than having to
ID the body of a deceased child and her heart went out to
Angelina. No wonder she was drinking. At the same time,
her statement bothered Mandy. Hadn't Ben said *he* was go-
ing to the police station to identify the body? So he'd lied to
Sylvia. But why?

"Where can we find Moose?" Zack prodded.

"He hangs at Cherry's, the neighborhood pit stop."

"Pit stop?"

"Booze. Pills. Whatever you want, you can get it at
Cherry's. It's around the corner and up the street a ways.
Moose hustles pool there most nights."

Mandy offered the rest of the money. "Thank you."

Before Angelina could take the bill, her eyes closed and she slumped to the floor. Mandy placed the remaining ten dollar bill on top of a newspaper pile and under a string where Angelina would easily find it—when she came to.

"Think we should call 911?" Mandy asked Zack.

"She'll sleep it off. And I don't think she'd appreciate your concern." Zack backtracked down the sidewalk and took her hand again. "You did real good with Angelina."

"Thanks." Mandy appreciated the praise. "You think Moose is our guy?"

Zack shrugged. "If you see him again, will you recognize him?"

Mandy recalled his violent eyes and shivered. "Yes."

Zack placed his arm over her shoulder. "We can't go to the neighborhood hangout dressed like this." He grinned at her and the way his eyes twinkled, she just knew he was about to say something outrageous. "We need to buy you something ugly so you can be inconspicuous." He patted her butt. "And add extra padding to your hips so if Moose is there, he won't recognize you."

"What about you?"

"I'm be modeling black leather pants and a Stetson."

She snorted. "That's never been in style."

"Exactly. I want to draw attention—the wrong kind."

She frowned. "Why?"

"Because I'm hoping there's a pool table in there and that they see a sucker coming."

"How will losing at pool help us find Moose?"

"We'll be outsiders. We can't go in asking questions. Moose recognizing you could get us shot."

"So—"

"Men who win money at pool drink lots of beer. Lots of beer loosens tongues."

She glanced sideways at him. "And what am I supposed to do while you're losing?"

"You keep your eyes peeled for Moose."

"What if he recognizes me?"

"He won't. Not if we dress you right." Zack grinned one of those charming smiles that made her itch to slap him or kiss him—she never could decide which.

"Zack, I don't know. Moose got a good look at me in the airport parking lot."

Zack chuckled. "Trust me, darling. You're going to look so ugly no man will look at you twice."

She stared at him, stomach twisting. The idea of coming face to face with a killer unnerved her. "Maybe you should go without me."

"I need you to eyeball the guy."

Yikes. Zack had her so distracted she couldn't think straight. But she didn't like this plan. She had a very bad feeling she couldn't explain.

Chapter Thirty-Three

SYLVIA HAD PLANNED to stay at the office all afternoon. But when her daughter called in tears to tell her that she'd caught Sylvia's twelve-year-old grandson, David, smoking pot, Sylvia had locked up the office and left with her bodyguard. The answering service could take messages. Family problems were always more important than work.

Before she abandoned the office, Sylvia phoned the police station and asked to speak to Ben. But no one had seen him. They patched her through to the morgue, but he hadn't shown up there, either.

She stepped outside, wondering where he was.

Ben had always been good with their children and grandchildren. His straightlaced no-nonsense and nonjudgmental talks had always set their kids on the right path. Years ago, after he'd caught one of their underage boys drunk, he'd taken him to the county jail to watch an alcoholic dry out. The vomiting, dry heaves, and shaking had done the trick. The teenage bingeing had stopped.

She could use Ben's help now. She'd left her cell phone at home. She rarely turned it on even when she had it with her, using it only for emergencies—unlike her eldest grandson who didn't even have a land line and carried his cell with him all the time.

Progress could be a good thing, she supposed. Between the faxes, computers and cell phones, iPods, DVDs, and satellite TV, she felt old. Stepping to the curb, she resolved to find a way for her and Ben to move to the mountains and a simpler lifestyle—even if they never recovered the lottery ticket.

Meanwhile she turned to her bodyguard. "May I please borrow your cell phone?"

"Sure."

She dialed Ben, and tried again fifteen minutes later, hoping he might be home. But no one answered.

Chapter Thirty-Four

ZACK AND MANDY bought clothes, ate pizza, and then checked into a hotel. It was too early to hit Cherry's and they hadn't slept much in days. It was a measure of how badly he needed sleep that he didn't think about lovemaking. Okay, so he did think about it, but he put aside his hunger for her. They both required sleep if they were to function with any kind of intelligence.

Zack pulled the blackout shades to block the sunlight, and the air conditioner's hum muffled the noise of traffic. After a solid eight hours of sack time, Zack had showered and was good to go. Mandy took a turn in the bathroom to shower and change, but stayed behind the door so long he became concerned.

Zack knocked. "Mandy? Everything okay?"

She cracked open the door. "I'm trying to decide if my mother would recognize me in this get-up."

Zack chuckled. "I wouldn't have asked you to do this if I didn't think it was safe." As he caught sight of her, he stared. She looked nothing like herself. She wore a dull brown wig, and thick glasses that he'd decorated with duct tape until she

looked nerd perfect. In addition, her baggy blouse and overstuffed padding at the waist and hips of her jeans threw her
shapely proportions out of whack. The scuffed Salvation
Army sandals were the finishing touch.

She opened the door wider and he restrained a laugh. She
tugged her blouse out and it flopped over the padding around
where her waist used to be, exactly where it was supposed
to. "Do I look natural?"

"No one but me will know how dazzling you really are."
He smiled.

"It won't be funny if this wig falls off." Her tone snapped,
but the fire in her eyes told him she'd been pleased by his
comment. She cocked her wide hips, placed a fist on her
waist, and her bulging tummy quivered. "You sure you want
to be seen in public with me?"

"I'd rather stay here and keep you all to myself," his voice
turned husky. "But we need to find Moose and that outfit will
keep you safe. Remember the last time he saw you, you were
your gorgeous self. He won't recognize you in this."

"Fine." She dabbed at her too-red lipstick with her pinky
and he almost groaned. Somehow he suspected the evening
was going to be much harder for him than her. Because even
though they'd disguised her beauty, he continued to think of
her the way she was—gorgeous.

When she brushed past, he inhaled her perfume and this
time he did groan. She turned around, her wig brushing his
face. "What?"

"I wish I had a camera. The sight of you in that disguise is
one I'm never going to forget."

Shoving his Stetson onto his head, he followed her out the
door, appreciating her being such a good sport. Most women
would have complained about making themselves so unat-
tractive, but Mandy didn't seem to care. He liked that she
had the self-esteem not to worry about her looks, that she
was focused on the job to be done.

He prayed that they would see Moose the moment they
stepped into Cherry's Bar. But when they arrived, the joint
was hopping with wall-to-wall people, the cigarette smoke

thick, the local band playing loud and raunchy rock, the dance floor full.

Although many women wore less than stylish clothing, none looked quite as nondescript as Mandy. With her mousy brown wig, the thick glasses, and the padding beneath the out-of-fashion clothing, she should have no difficulty avoiding attention. Mens' heads turned and their eyes moved right on by her as if she didn't exist.

If anyone asked, she was Zack's pain-in-the ass cousin. When a massive, dark-haired biker dude with bulging biceps approached Mandy, Zack stiffened.

"Buy you a drink?" he asked Mandy, his eyes unfocused as if he'd begun his drinking binge that morning.

She squinted at him. "I guess."

"Great," Zack muttered and headed for the pool tables at the far end of the bar. He ordered a beer, placed his back against a wall where he could watch the action on the tables as well as Mandy. In her dark clothing, she blended into the crowd. Biker Dude didn't seem to mind her extra padding.

At least the guy was protecting her from the rest of the losers, and Zack would protect her from him—even if Biker Dude was huge. Not many guys would willingly tangle with Zack—not unless they'd had too much to drink, not unless they were stupid, not unless they thought a gun would win them the girl. Since Zack knew a dozen ways to take down the big guy, he kept a casual pose, nursing his beer, watching from under the brim of his lame hat, but inside he was as tense as a drug addict making a buy.

Experience told him the night could turn ugly in a heart beat. Yet, he sensed they were in the right place. The bar was blue collar, a mix of races—black, white, and Hispanic. Zack's clothing made him stick out like a pretty hawk among doves. He'd added an ostentatious fake Rolex and a thick gold chain around his neck to draw more attention. He waited to be hustled.

It took only five minutes.

"Hey you," a white man with an ugly scar on his forehead addressed Zack. "You know how to use a stick?"

Zack sipped his beer, then set it down and moved forward too eagerly. He took mincing steps, puffed up his chest, and held out his hand to shake. "I'm Robert Kingly. Pleased to meet you. It's swell of you to invite me." Zack refrained from wincing as he used the word "swell."

"Billy Bob McAllister."

Billy Bob, a redneck in jeans and a T-shirt that said "Eat Me," elbowed his Hispanic friend in the ribs. They were taking Zack's bait. Now all he had to do was lose fast, ply them with liquor, and hope their conversation would lead him to Moose. Zack lowered his outstretched hand, picked up a pool cue and smoothed out a ten dollar bet on the table's edge. While the boys racked the balls, he gazed at the dance floor.

As the band played a decent version of *If Bubba Can Dance (I Can Too)* by Shenandoah, Mandy and Biker Dude shouldered through the crowd to the dance floor. What was she thinking? She was supposed to keep a low profile. She kept her head down, her shoulders slumped and studiously stared at the floor as if embarrassed to be out in public.

One skinny, pimply faced teen tried to cop a feel but Biker Dude smacked him aside. The red-faced kid stumbled away and tried to retrieve his dignity at the bar. No one asked him for ID, yet he had to be underage.

Meanwhile, Mandy began to sway. While she danced, she moved around the room, checking out men's faces. She stopped in front of one black man, and Zack broke into a sweat.

"Hey, you. It's your turn, cowboy."

Zack forced his eyes back to the pool table. His opponent had already broken the rack and pocketed three solids. Zack was way behind. He picked a difficult shot when an easy one was just sitting there. He aimed a bit off. But just as he eased forward on the stick, Mandy whipped around, catching his eye. His cue struck the white ball straighter than he'd intended and a striped ball ended up in the corner pocket.

Damn! How could he concentrate with Mandy's spinning on the dance floor, checking out the men to see if any of them were the killer? Maybe this wasn't such a good plan. He clenched the cue stick, reminding himself she was doing what he'd asked—but she'd obviously forgotten the maintaining-a-low-profile part.

Zack sauntered around the table as if he'd expected his shot to go in. This time he tried a fancy behind-his-back bridge shot. Luckily, he missed and could sit out, nurse his beer, and worry about Moose recognizing Mandy.

As long as the wig stayed on, she should be fine. He finished the beer and motioned to the barmaid that he needed a refill. When she brought it, he handed her ten bucks and told her to keep the change. She smiled at him, interest in her eyes despite his off-the-wall leather slacks and silly hat, but his gaze returned to Mandy.

The music turned slow and she'd placed her arms around Biker Dude's neck, who bent his head to catch her whispering in his ear. Then he threw back his head and guffawed. Zack suspected she was pumping her dance partner for information and told himself to trust her instincts.

"You going to play or what?" Billy Bob prodded.

Zack missed his next four shots in a row. He needed to lose his money as fast as possible, pump these players about Moose, and take Mandy out of here.

Zack bought a pitcher of beer, while his opponent sank the eight ball in the side pocket and won his ten dollars. Zack took out a twenty, signaling that he intended to up the stakes and play another game. This time he racked and broke. But two balls went in. Just to make the guy sweat a little, he sank two more balls.

When he looked up, he saw that Billy Bob had helped himself to Zack's beer. He pretended not to notice. However, the swift guzzling of his beer must have blurred Billy's vision or caused his hands to tremble. He missed. Zack muttered a curse and missed, too.

Three men at the bar spoke loudly among themselves, drank heavily and eyed Mandy. Zack would have preferred to wait longer before he tried to get friendly with his pool buddy but he sensed trouble brewing. "I heard a guy by the name of Moose is the best stick man around."

"Is that so?" Billy Bob eyed him across the pool table. "Where'd you hear that?"

Zack frowned as if trying to remember. "Maybe one of the barmaids."

"That's odd because Moose don't shoot the table, he's into darts."

No one was throwing darts. Had Angelina deliberately steered him wrong? Or was she too grief stricken over her son's death to remember correctly? Zack licked the chalk dust off his finger and measured his shot. "Darts are for pussies."

"Don't let Moose hear you say that." Billy Bob openly emptied the beer pitcher.

"Why not?" Zack gestured for a refill and not only missed, he sank his opponent's ball for him. He forced his grin into a grimace, and at the sound of wild cheering and clapping, he stole another glance at Mandy.

His lower jaw dropped. She was dancing chest to chest with Biker Dude. What the hell? Zack snapped his teeth together so hard they clicked. His shoulders and neck ached as he attempted and failed to relax tensed muscles.

"See that biker and the ugly chick with glasses?" Billy Bob planted one end of his stick on the floor and stared at Mandy.

"So?"

"That's Prancer."

"Prancer because he likes to dance." Billy Bob must have read Zack's doubting expression. "Didn't say he was any good at it."

"What's your point?"

"Moose ain't near as big as Prancer but last week he knocked Prancer out. It was a helluva fight."

Zack poured Billy Bob another beer. "Moose and Prancer had a disagreement over a dance partner?"

"Naw. Over darts. The dart landed right in the metal that separates the bull's eye from the ring around it. Weirdest thing I ever saw. The shot cracked the metal."

"Is that why Moose isn't playing tonight, he's hurt?" Zack guessed.

"You don't listen so good. Moose won the fight. Tossed Prancer over the bar. Never seen anyone that bad."

Prancer didn't looked badly hurt to Zack, but he kept the conversation going. "So how come Prancer is back in Moose's territory?"

"You sure ask a lot of questions."

"Usually the loser slinks away to lick his wounds and the winner sticks around to relive the moment," Zack commented, hoping for more information.

Billy Bob grunted, which could mean Moose was in the bar right now, but Zack suspected not or he would have said so. Clearly, Billy Bob had lost interest in the conversation. He moved back toward the table and Zack was about to try to sucker another player into revealing information about Moose when a glass pitcher shattered on the bar.

Mandy screamed. Bodies surged forward and Zack lost sight of her. Heart surging up into his throat, adrenaline pumping, he shoved, ducked and wove through the mass of kicking, punching and shouting bodies.

He should never have allowed her to come in here—not even in disguise.

He should never have left her alone.

The band ducked for cover but someone slammed the juke box on its side and it began to play. Fists flew. Chairs smashed into heads and over the bar. A window shattered. The lights flickered and went out.

In the smoky darkness, someone kicked Zack's shin, a head smashed into his arm. He dodged a flying body. Pulse racing, he shouldered through the surging mass of humanity toward where he'd last seen Mandy.

Finally, he reached the bar.

But she was gone. So was Biker Dude.

What a disaster. Fear pumped adrenaline straight into his veins, lending him strength.

Zack frantically searched behind the bar and several overturned tables. Mandy wasn't in the restroom either, and his fear escalated by the minute. Had someone grabbed her? Was she hurt? In danger? Questions churned in a maddening

rush. Had their inquiries about Moose landed in the wrong
ears? Had Moose sneaked in and retaliated? Or had Biker
Dude swept her outside? He needed answers and the knots in
his gut only served to remind him that if anything happened
to her it was all his fault. He'd brought her here, promised to
protect her and failed.

He'd been so certain Mandy would be safe. So sure he
could protect her. But the fight had happened too fast. Angry
at himself, terrified she'd fallen into the killer's hands, he
sprinted into the parking lot as police cars drove up, their red
and blue lights flashing.

When he didn't find her in the crowd of bystanders, he
broke into a sweat and sprinted to her car. A cursory glance
revealed that the vehicle was empty. But as he neared, Zack
spied Mandy scrunched beneath the dash on the passenger
side. *Thank God.*

The pounding pressure at his temples eased. She was
okay, just hiding.

When she spied him, she straightened. "About time you
got here."

"I've been looking for you everywhere," he admitted, sliding behind the wheel, his nerves still rattled. He couldn't recall ever having been quite so shaken. He'd been prepared to
fight and even though he now knew she was safe, his adrenaline surge kept his blood rushing, his emotions spinning.

"I scooted out a side door to avoid the fight as well as
complications with the Harley guy." Her voice was soft,
breathless as she removed the wig and glasses. "I was beginning to think he'd find me before you did."

She'd been smart to leave. He would have said so, but his
throat was too tight. He glanced at her again, to reassure himself she was okay. In the reflection of the red and blue police
lights, Mandy's chest rose and fell enticingly. The pulse at
her throat told him she wasn't as calm as she appeared.
Catching his glance, her eyes widened and her nostrils flared.

Mandy scooted over and flung her arms around his neck.
"I was so scared."

Her heart thumped against his chest. Still, she was more

in control that he was. Right now, his hands trembled and he clenched his thigh to hide his reaction. He was a wreck.

His defenses had never been lower. She smelled temptingly spicy, like hot apple pie, vanilla, and cinnamon. No wonder the biker hadn't cared what she looked like—not when she'd smelled so good.

Zack had never been so aroused. Gritting his teeth, he drove straight to the hotel. Luckily, it wasn't far. With Mandy draped over him, he felt as if he was going to explode before he even ripped off their clothes.

Burning with need, he parked, led her to the hotel and into their room. He locked the door. She'd taken exactly one step inside when he slapped his palms on either side of her head, trapping her between his arms. She lifted her mouth and that was all the invitation he needed to plunder, to ravish, to take what she offered.

Zack thrust his tongue between her lips. And tasted mint, orange juice, and a hint of vodka. She groaned and pulled him closer, winding her arms around his neck and pushing her hands into his hair.

He never recalled removing his stupid leather pants or her clothes and padding or donning protection. Somehow in his raging fever to have her, he got the job done. Too needy to bother with foreplay, he thrust into her, savagely pleased to hear her soft moans of pleasure.

She clasped her legs around his waist and he rode her up against the door, with no finesse, with no thought of anything but having her. Holding her. Helping himself to every inch of her tempting flesh. Mandy. Sweet Mandy. She was driving him insane. Tormenting him with her silken flesh and feminine heat. God, she felt good. Slick. Hot.

Her low-pitched gasp of pleasure slammed into him. Her husky murmur urged him faster. Deeper. Her fingers clutched him back but it was her passion that chained him sweetly.

Driven by need so strong, so primal, he gave himself up to her. "Mandy. Mandy. Mandy." He roared in pleasure and found release.

When the rush ebbed, when his thoughts stopped whirling, he realized he'd just lost all control. "I'm so sorry."

She panted, still clinging to him. "If I had the strength, I'd slap you for saying that. How can you be sorry?"

"But—"

"It was good."

"But—"

"Zack, I didn't do anything I didn't want to do." She kissed his mouth, her lips tempting him all over again. But this time he carried her to the bed. He took his time, showing her with actions what he couldn't say in words, knowing he would never be the same.

Chapter Thirty-Five

MARIA PARKED HER car in front of a two-story house—
Ray's house—in an upscale neighborhood. It was the first
time she'd ever been here, and despite the bodyguard who
would accompany her to the front door and watch from outside, her nerves were rioting. For once the clothing Ray had
sent—comfortable sandals, a sparkly top, a silver necklace,
and a short ruffled skirt—had nothing to do with the desire
screaming through her veins.

She walked across the paved driveway and glimpsed a lake
in the back yard. The house perched at the top of a tiny hill,
keeping it safely above the flood line. The beautifully manicured yard and the well-tended house didn't look like one a
pervert would live in. The peaceful setting should have reassured her. But not even the sweeping green lawn and lovely
landscaping highlighted by two massive royal palms stopped
her from trembling. Ray had something special planned.

Lisa's funeral this morning had reminded Maria that life
could end at any time. Yet, she rang the doorbell with an eagerness that she didn't try to deny.

"Welcome." Looking handsome in black slacks that

hugged his narrow hips and a dark gold shirt that comple-
mented his eyes, Ray took her hand, leading her across the
threshold. She left her bodyguard outside.

The entrance opened into a mirrored foyer lit with a glass
and crystal chandelier. Maria stepped onto a highly polished
hardwood floor. Even as she kissed Ray, she noted two stair-
cases with white handrails behind him, one going up, the
other down.

"You have a cellar?" she asked, never having heard of one
in the Tampa area.

"The house was built in the nineteen fifties during the
height of the Cold War. The basement was built to serve as a
bomb shelter."

She recalled the lake behind the house. "Does it flood?"

"Not since I've been here. I've turned it into a playroom."
He raised an eyebrow. "I was hoping you'd like to see it."

She cocked her head to one side. "And if I said no?"

"You won't." His eyes glinted.

He sounded all too sure of himself and her heart pounded
with excitement. Always he gave her more pleasure than
she'd ever dreamed. She tried to inhale deeply but her chest
was too tight, leaving her shallow sips of air.

"But if I did say no?" she pressed.

Ray locked gazes with her. He raised his hand to her
cheek, caressed her jaw, her lips, her collarbone, then slowly
unfastened the top button of her blouse. "I didn't think *no*
was in your vocabulary."

Maria tossed her head to keep the bangs from her eyes.
"There are some lines I'm not willing to cross."

He took her icy hand in his warm one and raised it to his
lips. "*Amor mío,* it's time for you to learn the truth."

"You're married?"

Ray chuckled and his eyes twinkled. "Time to learn the
truth about yourself."

"I came to your home to learn about *you*."

"And so you shall, *dulce*. Come." He tugged her toward
the stairs.

She could have pulled away. Or shouted for her bodyguard. She didn't. She was perfectly safe. Besides, she wanted to see Ray's playroom, but even more, she wanted to discover what he'd planned. He really was the most creative lover she'd ever been with.

The stairs dropped for five or six feet and then they changed directions on a landing and doubled back. At the bottom was a door. Ray removed a chain from around his neck and unlocked the door with an old-fashioned skeleton key.

Her mouth went dry. She didn't know what to expect. Her heart pounded. Heat suffused her.

When he'd mentioned a playroom, she'd conjured dark, dirty, and creaky. But the room she stepped into had spotless limestone floors, track lighting that left no portion of the room in shadows. He'd even painted the walls an inviting dusty rose.

Ray shut the door behind them and it took her a few moments to figure out what she was seeing. At first, she thought he'd outfitted the playroom as a garage or a workshop or a home gym, but then she looked more closely. The pegboard wall held an assortment of objects from rods to chains with manacles on the ends to feathers. She stared in fascination and a bit of fear, uncertain of the use of most of the items in his collection.

She saw paddles, whips, hoods, blindfolds, gags, clamps, and dildos, plus dozens of devices she couldn't name. She spun around and headed for the door.

"I'm not into pain."

She'd leave. Right now. She had no idea what all this stuff was, but the cage and the whips scared her into realizing that if she screamed from down here, her bodyguard wouldn't hear her.

"I know you don't like pain." He didn't try to stop her from leaving. His tone remained gentle, challenging. "Tell me what you like. The choice is yours."

Dios. Fearing he might have locked her in, Maria placed her hand on the knob. But the door opened. If she wished, she was free to leave. He'd really meant the choice was hers.

She hesitated. "This is scary."

"Scary turns you on." He placed a hand on a rack like device. It was made of metal and padded with leather manacles to hold the arms and feet in place.

The rack didn't appear to have a purpose that she could see. "How does that work?"

"The straps restrain your hands and feet, then I do what I wish with you."

She gulped and pointed to something that looked like a pommel horse used in gymnastics, but it came with an assortment of straps and buckles. "And that?"

"For spankings. You would not like it." He gestured to a basket-like device hanging from the ceiling. "Now this is more your style."

She couldn't make sense of the straps, didn't understand why the harness hung from a rope attached to a pulley. "How does it work?"

"Take off your clothes and I'll show you." He lowered the harness and ignored her, not even watching to see if she disrobed.

"Tell me how it works first."

"Ah." He opened the basket. "You sit here. These straps support your legs, these your arms."

"And then?"

"You're like a spider caught in my web. I will give you much pleasure."

She shook her head and strode to a nice padded table covered in latex. The smooth material and the lack of all metal called to her. Smoothing the soft material, she shivered in anticipation as if knowing her fate was here.

"The quiet table interests you?" Ray joined her and placed an arm around her waist. "You like?"

"What would we do?"

"You lie on the table. I wrap the latex around you until you cannot move."

She sucked in her breath. Heat flushed her cheeks. "And then?"

"The material is silky soft. Smooth. I caress you."

"And?"

"You won't be able to move. Some women find the loss of control . . . erotic."

She bit her bottom lip, recalling how Ray had bent her over the hood of the car, how she couldn't move, how turned on she'd been. This would be like that but . . . "We would make love?"

His fingers caressed her waist. "*Sí*. There are holes in the latex. You'd be completely at my mercy. You'd like that, *querida*, wouldn't you?"

Moisture seeped between her thighs. Her entire body trembled with eagerness. She'd come here for adventure. Even the name, the *quiet table*, enticed. She nodded, afraid her voice might crack if she spoke.

"Let me turn down the lights a bit while you get naked for me."

Hands trembling, she kicked off her shoes and unbuttoned her blouse. While Ray had already seen and tasted every inch of her body, she'd never undressed in front of him unless he was undressing too. Or unless he was caressing her.

Feeling decidedly wicked, she removed her panties and bra and placed them on a chair.

"Your jewelry, too."

She unclasped the silver necklace, removed earrings and a ring. "Now what?"

He pulled back the black latex and it was like peeling Saran Wrap from a casserole dish. Underneath, more latex covered the padded table. He patted the plush leather. "Hop on and lie down."

She expected the material to be cold but it was warm, soothing. Ray handed her a blindfold. "Put this on. It's to protect your eyes from the pressure of the latex."

"I won't be able to see?" She gulped.

"Without your other senses, you'll be able to focus much better on my touch."

She placed the blindfold over her eyes and he adjusted the pads to make certain she had them centered. "It's spooky sitting here without clothes on—especially since I can't see you."

"Hmm."

He began wrapping her feet and calves, each leg separately. The latex felt like smooth silk. All of a sudden the table split, opening her legs wide and he enveloped her legs up to her knees and thighs in the latex. She felt him cover her hips and tummy in one sheet, another piece covered her breasts, her neck, her arms and hands.

She felt cozy, comfortable as she sank into the padding.

"Open your mouth."

"Why?"

When she spoke, she'd parted her lips and he placed a rubber ball between her teeth and secured a strap behind her head to hold the gag in place. She shook her head, telling him no, but Ray paid no attention. Then he encased her head.

"Easy. Breathe through your nostrils."

Like she had a choice. Her heart hammered. She couldn't see. She couldn't talk. She couldn't so much as quiver a muscle and at the realization, excitement jolted her.

"So how do you like being at my mercy, *querida?*

She couldn't answer, not even to groan past the ball in her mouth. Fear mixed with excitement and arousal. What would he do? Only the flesh between her legs was exposed.

When she felt his light brush strokes through the latex over her breasts, her muscles tried to jerk . . . and couldn't. *Dios*. Delicious sensations poured through her. She couldn't squirm, couldn't encourage, couldn't plead for more.

Her heart raced. Ray's touch through the latex was indescribable. The binding seemed to increase sensation and the material spread each caress evenly so she had difficulty determining where and what and how he was caressing her.

Hot ribbon-like streams of sensation rippled through her. She sucked in air through her nose, wishing her chest would expand, wishing with every cell in her brain that she could talk and tell him how good he felt and that she needed more.

One minute, or five minutes or maybe ten minutes later, she was frantic for release. If her mind could have conveyed the message, she would have begged, sobbed, promised him anything.

But she'd made her choice.

When she'd submitted to his domination, she hadn't known the consequences could be this erotic. She hadn't known anything could feel so good.

As if sensing she might be about to break, he ceased caressing and stroking her breasts. Her hard nipples pressed against the latex and . . . she held her breath, hoping, praying, frantic for the release she craved.

Her muscles tightened. Her stomach knotted into a tight ball of desire.

She'd heard nothing, except her own breath. Surely he wouldn't leave her filled with frustration? Burning.

Ray.

Please.

More. More. More.

But he'd seemed to have abandoned her. Tears seeped beneath her eyelids into the padding.

And then she felt the slightest brush of air between her legs and tears of frustration turned to tears of joy. Ray understood. He knew what she wanted.

Chapter Thirty-Six

"SAM'S NOT CHEATING," Catherine told Dana over the phone.

"How do you know?" Dana walked with the portable phone into her kitchen where her new bodyguard couldn't overhear her conversation, a weight lifting off her shoulders.

"The PI has followed Sam constantly. He hasn't met with a woman for breakfast, lunch, or dinner. He spends a lot of time holed up with the mayor. Apparently the county administrator still isn't back and it's thrown the local government into a legal tangle that Sam's trying to help the mayor sort out."

Relief washed through Dana and she sipped her first cup of morning coffee. "It's only been a few days. Can we be certain?"

"These people are pros. They examined Sam's credit card bills, phone records, and personal bank statements. He hasn't charged anything suspicious like jewelry, flowers, or women's clothing."

"What about the Bay Star Hotel?"

"Nothing."

"Maybe she's paying." But even as Dana said that, she

knew better. Sam was too much of a male chauvinist to allow a woman to pay for anything.

"He has no hidden assets, no secret apartment that he's bought or renting. The PI followed the money trail back six months. Sam might be a workaholic but he's not cheating," her mother repeated.

Dana sank onto a bar stool. "All right. Call them off. I don't want Sam to—"

"You don't want Sam to what?" Sam strode into the kitchen and kissed Dana on the cheek. He shouldn't have been home. But he was. *Deal with it.*

Her pulse leapt. How much had he heard? What could be worse than a wife who didn't trust her husband? If Sam found out what she'd done, he'd be hurt and furious. "Mom, I'll call you later."

Dana hung up and smiled at Sam, hoping she looked calmer than she felt. "I don't want you to worry about me," she improvised.

"I know. The doctor's cleared you to travel and we don't even need your bodyguard anymore." Sam took Dana into his arms with a grin. "Especially not where we're going."

"Sam?" Dana read his happy mood and her heart lifted. Obviously Sam hadn't heard much of her phone conversation and he didn't seem the least bit suspicious. She hadn't seen him this excited in a long time. When they'd first met, he was always surprising her with theater tickets, flowers, a trip out of town. "Where are we going?"

"How about here?" He handed her a picture of a crescent white-sand beach that framed turquoise water. A lovely contemporary beach house overlooked a private cove with a boat dock, water vehicles, and an inviting tiki hut.

"It looks wonderful." After her harrowing week, she could think of nothing better than spending private time with Sam in some romantic getaway.

"The house is on a tiny island in the Bahamas. I've hired a jet to take us to Walker Cay. From there, we set sail for Shell Island. I've rented the house for a week." He twirled her around. "Can you be ready to leave by noon?

Dana's eyes widened. "Noon? Today?"

"Yes, today." Sam swatted her butt. "Get a move on. Just think, we can be swilling Bermuda Triangles and watching a glorious sunset by evening."

The last time Dana had drunk spiced rum, peach schnapps, and orange juice over crushed ice, they had been on their honeymoon in St. Croix. She'd always loved the beach but Sam preferred going west on vacation. He liked to ski at Vail or Aspen. But he'd obviously booked this island spot for her.

Dana peered at him, a dozen thoughts flying through her head. She hated to leave the firm and her mother with all the turmoil and, yet, she'd been dreaming of livening up her marriage and now that Sam was willing, she certainly didn't want to nix his grand plan. Besides, she'd already cleared her schedule for this week, why not take advantage of it?

"What about your big case?" she asked.

"I'm taking this week to devote to you."

Dana checked her watch. She had less than two hours to pack, but she could manage. Grinning, she pirouetted toward the walk-in closet, looked back over her shoulder and teased, "Bet I can pack faster than you can."

Chapter Thirty-Seven

LAST NIGHT AT the bar, Mandy had picked up more useful information than Zack had, acquiring the name of a business, Franklin Construction, where Moose worked as well as his home address from Biker Dude. An hour ago, Zack had followed up her lead from their hotel room to learn Moose's former residence had turned out to be a dead end. A new family lived in his old trailer. Apparently, the landlord had had to evict a squatter before they'd moved in. Unfortunately, the police had no record of a legal eviction taking place, stymieing Zack's attempt to find Moose's legal name.

Zack hoped to have better luck with Moose's work address this morning. Mandy still wore some of her disguise, the duct-taped glasses on her forehead and the wig, but had ditched the padding, claiming it was too hot.

He was driving her car on the way to the construction company to ask about Moose when his mother called. "Dana and Sam are flying to the Bahamas for a week," Catherine told him. "All clients have been contacted and know we're closed until further notice."

"Isn't the Bahamas trip kind of sudden?" Zack asked, leaning back in the car seat.

"Sam surprised her and Dana was so happy. As much as I'd like her to relax, get pregnant, and give me grandkids, I'm concerned."

Now there was a loaded statement if he'd ever heard one. Zack wasn't going to tell his mother that she already had a grandchild—that wasn't a conversation he wanted to have over the phone. He didn't want to discuss Dana's marriage or her desire to have children, either.

Zack clenched the phone tight, but tried to keep his tone loose and easy. "Mom, it's been a stressful week for all of us."

"What about you, Zack? How are you holding up?"

Was her question a veiled reference to his and Mandy's relationship? He wasn't going there and deliberately misunderstood her question. "Mandy and I learned that Vizzi knew a black man named Moose. He may be the guy who stole the lottery ticket. His description matches the one Mandy gave to the police. He works for Franklin Construction. We're going there now to see if Mandy can identify him as the thief."

"If she can, you call the police. Don't handle things yourself."

Zack refrained from rolling his eyes. "Yes, Mom."

"Don't you *yes-Mom* me."

"Okay."

"Zack, don't patronize me. I mean it."

Zack snorted. "You do realize that I'm agreeing with you and you're not satisfied?"

"I know you, Zack. Your save-the-world complex worries me. Your face still has bruises from—"

"We're here." Zack pulled onto the interstate. "Got to go, Mom. Love you."

Beside him in the passenger seat, Mandy raised an inquisitive eyebrow and the glasses slid down onto her nose. Zack rubbed his brow and let out a long sigh. "I know. I know. I shouldn't have lied about being there already, but she's not going to be happy until you're working safely back at the firm—"

She shoved the glasses back up and eyed him. "Nothing wrong with that."

"—and I'm in a career she considers safe. She'd love it if I opened a shoe store."

Mandy laughed. "Somehow I find it difficult to picture you selling shoes." When he didn't say anything else, she gave him a sideways glance. "Have you ever considered another career besides the DEA?"

No, not since Kevin had died. "When I was a kid, I wanted to work as a spy for the CIA."

"Now *that* would be safe." Mandy's sarcasm was teasing, but he sensed that beneath the facade of light conversation, she was searching for more. But he wasn't ready to have a discussion about his future. He still felt torn between his career and his child and this woman who deserved more than he might be able to give.

So Zack kept the conversation light. "When I was a teen, I wanted to be a race car driver."

"We're on a roll here. Didn't you ever want to do anything that wasn't life threatening?"

"No."

"Do you need excitement to feel alive?" she asked, her tone curious.

"I'm not an adrenaline junky. But I like doing important work. When I stop tons of cocaine from coming into the country and put the dealers behind bars, I save lives."

She bit her lower lip. He had to give her credit. She didn't try to change his mind by mentioning Gabrielle. But although she didn't say anything, he did have a daughter now. As long as he continued his undercover work for the DEA, he couldn't be a father to Gabrielle.

Zack felt trapped. Yet how could he ever regret being that sweet little girl's father? He recalled holding her hand on the beach. Watching her throwing sand at her toes and then chasing the sea gulls—that golden moment was one of the most perfect in his entire life.

And being with Mandy again—it was better than he'd ever imagined.

Yet, every time he made a bust, every time he stopped containers full of drugs from entering the country, he saved lives. Zack took satisfaction that he did his job well, that his superiors appreciated him, that the other agents respected him.

He hadn't a clue what he intended to do.

Chapter Thirty-Eight

FRANKLIN CONSTRUCTION DEVELOPED large tracts of land, turning acreage into subdivisions. They did it all, land clearing and site preparation, underground utilities, paving and home building. If Zack and Mandy had known Moose's legal name, searching for him would have been easier.

But Franklin's office staff only had the legal names of their employees and the field people who might know Moose by his nickname were spread out among five surrounding counties. With three thousand employees, the company was so large that most employees didn't know the others.

After striking out in the office, Mandy and Zack had donned hard hats. They'd strode over to the shop where loaders and backhoes were hoisted onto bridge cranes for servicing to ask about Moose. None of the mechanics knew him. They also asked several dump truck drivers, a field team, maintenance and inventory control, as well as a fence crew. Nothing.

Two hours later Mandy's shoulders slumped in discouragement. "Maybe we're doing this wrong."

"I'm open to suggestions." Zack removed his hard hat and wiped his brow.

"We don't have his real name but we do have his last known address. Maybe the computer can do an address search and come up with his name."

Zack grinned. "That's a great idea. Let's go talk to Franklin's computer guru."

A hundred bucks and fifteen minutes later, they learned that Carl Francisco Roberts, aka Moose, was a grader operator who hadn't been to work in over a week. However, now that they had his legal name, Zack called a contact at the DEA and learned more.

As they headed back to the car Zack told Mandy, "Moose served time for vandalism when he was just ten years old. He now has a rap sheet as long as a novel."

Mandy thought about what kind of childhood had created such a monster. Although he'd probably had it rough, so had most of the kids she'd grown up with. They hadn't turned into killers. Everyone had a choice. Along the way, Moose had made bad ones.

Zack opened her door for her. "He moved from petty theft to armed robbery to fencing stolen goods. He mostly stayed out of jail thanks to some excellent defense attorneys, the latest of which is none other than my brother-in-law."

"Sam's good at what he does." She sighed, slipped into the hot seat of the car, tossed the glasses onto the dash and removed the wig. She fluffed her hair and recalled hearing Sam speak passionately about how every citizen deserved a legal defense and a fair trial—but she wondered how he'd feel if he'd helped keep the man free who'd hurt Dana and who'd murdered Lisa. "I wonder if Sam ever defended Nicholas Vizzi."

Zack shook his head. "If that had been the case, I'm certain Sam would have mentioned it after Vizzi shot him."

"True."

Zack got in and started the car. His ring tone sounded and he pulled out his cell and checked caller ID. "It's Mom, again."

He automatically turned on the speaker phone so Mandy could listen. Catherine didn't mince words. "Maria was attacked last night."

"Oh, no." Mandy paled, her shoulders sagged, and she raised her hand to her mouth.

Zack remembered Maria from the funeral. Even with the sad occasion, she'd had that special spring in her step and a light in her eyes that suggested she was in love. "What happened?"

"She went to Ray's house and her bodyguard waited outside. He's dead, his throat cut. A neighbor noticed his body in the bushes while walking her dog this morning and called the police. The cops arrived to find Maria in the basement. It was filled with all kinds of sexual items—apparently she and Ray were into kinky stuff. Maria was tied to a table, swathed in black latex. She'd been sliced up pretty badly but she was alive. She's on the way to the hospital as we speak."

Zack had never ruled Ray out as a suspect. Perhaps they'd been searching the wrong trail for clues. "And Ray?"

"He's in pretty much the same shape as Maria." So much for Zack's suspicion of Ray. He wouldn't have cut himself badly just to create an alibi. "The police think Ray fought off the attacker and that's why he and Maria are still alive, but we won't be certain unless he survives to give a statement." Catherine's voice cracked. "I can't believe this is happening again. I wish Sam and Dana hadn't left the country."

Zack tried to console his mother. "Maybe Dana will be safer there."

"I called to let her know what's going on, but she didn't answer and must still be on the plane. I left a message and I'm calling Sylvia next."

"All right. Mandy and I are tracking down Moose, aka Carl Francisco Roberts. His fingerprints are on file since he has a record. If the police find anything at Maria's crime scene, maybe they'll get a match."

"I'll let them know." Catherine cleared her throat. "Be careful."

"You, too."

"Now what?" Mandy asked, her voice determined—even if it shook a bit.

"We find Moose. I'm pulling in every favor I can. If Moose uses a credit card or a cell phone under his real name, my friends at the DEA will be able to pinpoint his location."

"And then what?"

"We let the police handle it after that." Zack turned to her, knowing from the fear in her eyes that she needed reassurance. "I'm not putting you in any more danger. Last night, when you disappeared on me, I realized that . . . I should never have asked you to come to the bar. I shouldn't have left your side."

"If you'd been with me, I'd never have coaxed Moose's address and place of work from his friends." She seemed to choose her next words very carefully. "When all hell broke loose in that bar, I got out fast."

"You did the right thing." But he was still kicking himself for letting her go into a dangerous situation and not being right next to her to protect her. That she could take care of herself—wasn't the point. He could have lost her, and if anything had happened to her, he would have been devastated. Not because she was his assignment, or because she worked for his mother or because she was Dana's best friend. Not even because she was the mother of his daughter.

Because he didn't want to lose her.

Chapter Thirty-Nine

AFTER HEARING ABOUT Maria, Mandy insisted on calling her mother. Fearing a trace, Zack refused to let her use her cell phone—not even from their moving car. However, he stopped at a truck stop to use a pay phone. Mandy didn't know why she was so concerned about Gabby but she didn't question her instincts. She needed to know her baby was safe.

"Hi, Mom. Is everything okay?"

"We're both exhausted after the drive on I-4 but settled in. I was just about to put Gabrielle down for her nap. Will you be joining us in Orlando soon?"

"I don't know."

"You avoided me this morning. You do understand that I only want what's best for you."

"Mom. I know. Zack says I can only talk for three minutes."

"Why?"

"He's just being cautious. I need you to be careful, too. Listen to your bodyguard. Don't talk to strangers and if you see anyone suspicious—"

"I'm not a child—"

"Call the cops."

"What happened?" her mother's tone sharpened.

Mandy's stomach churned at the horror. She could barely force out the words. "Maria and her boyfriend were attacked last night. Her bodyguard was killed. We don't know if Maria and Ray will live."

"Amanda, I want you to come join us right now."

"Mom, I've got to go. I love you."

"Then act like it. Come stay here with us where it's safe."

"Bye, Mom." Mandy hung up the phone, wondering if she should listen to her mother and feeling guilty for ending the call so abruptly. She hated that her mother would worry. But no one would be safe until she identified Moose and the police locked him away.

Zack hung up from a second pay phone in the parking lot of the truck stop. "Moose bought a plane ticket for Fort Lauderdale." He grabbed her hand and tugged her toward the vehicle. "We can hitch a ride on a DEA flight that leaves Tampa International at 2 P.M. If we hurry, we can make it."

Mandy rubbed her head with her free hand. Should she go with Zack? Or return to her mother and daughter? If Moose was the killer and he was on his way to Fort Lauderdale, then she didn't need to worry about Gabby's safety. And this might be her opportunity to identify him for the authorities.

Zack drove her to the airport, weaving in and out of traffic. She didn't dare distract him with conversation. While he didn't drive more than ten miles an hour above the speed limit, the intensity in his eyes told her he was concentrating, focused on driving.

They arrived at the airport and ran to catch the plane. If the flight had been a regular one, and they'd had to buy tickets, check luggage, and go through security, they would have missed their flight. But Zack flashed his DEA badge and an official whisked them through a long hallway and directly onto the tarmac.

Mandy had expected a smaller-than-commercial aircraft, but at the sight of the four seater, she slowed to a halt. It was one thing to accompany Zack in the hopes of spotting Moose, but ever since she'd become a mom, Mandy had curtailed perilous activities—like flying in a plane no bigger than a postage stamp. "That's our plane?"

"It'll be fine. We might even land around the same time as Moose. That'll give us a chance to tail him."

"You go on without me."

Zack shook his head. "I still need you to identify Moose."

"Take his picture and fax it to me."

"That's too cumbersome. He might slip away again and go so deep undercover we lose the chance to nab him."

"What about old pictures?"

"The only pictures we have of Moose are when he was arrested. He was bald, then, and sporting a thick mustache."

Mandy spoke her thoughts out loud. "The man I saw wore dreads and was clean shaven."

"The chance of you recognizing him is better if you see him again in person." Zack's tone was gentle, almost pleading. "We'll stay back. I'll keep you safe. I promise." Zack tugged her toward the plane.

Mandy didn't know which scared her the most, the idea of meeting Moose, or getting on that flimsy plane. Her heart thumped in her chest and her mouth went dry.

Once Zack opened the door and helped her inside, she realized he would be sitting up front next to the copilot. From his position, Zack wouldn't even be able to hold her hand to help her get through the flight.

Stomach knotted, she tugged her seat belt tight.

Chapter Forty

SYLVIA DECIDED TO take matters into her own hands. If Ben wouldn't tell her where he was spending his free time, she would follow him. In fifty-two years of marriage, he'd been her rock. So why was he refusing to tell her what he was up to?

At home, he seemed more tired than usual, but he was still her Ben. He'd made her an omelette with onions and orange peppers this morning and cleaned up the kitchen. Then he'd puttered around the house, fixing several sagging cabinet doors with the new hardware he'd bought last week.

After lunch, she'd told him she was tired and intended to nap. Ben casually mentioned that he was heading out for a game of basketball. She nodded and proceeded to the bedroom, certain no one would play basketball in the summer mid-day heat in Tampa. Well, maybe kids might. Certainly grown men had better sense. Suspicions on alert, she waited for him to leave, and the moment his van—which had been outfitted so he could drive it—turned the corner, she grabbed her keys, headed to her car, and followed her husband with her bodyguard beside her.

Ben always drove five miles an hour below the speed limit, and it took her only a few minutes to catch up. She stayed far enough back to keep her eye on the big blue van, but hopefully not so close Ben would spot her. When he drove right by the park and the empty basketball courts, her stomach lurched.

Ben had always been steady. He'd never looked at another woman. Hadn't gone through a mid-life crisis. She recalled with unease that Ben had also disappeared the night of Lisa's murder. He hadn't even seemed shocked by the news when they'd heard what had happened to Dana and Mandy, or when Sam had been shot. At the time, Sylvia had told herself he was a cop, that he was accustomed to violence, death, and murder.

But Sylvia had worked with these women. She'd eaten lunch with them. Shared family stories with them. She'd known how much Lisa had wanted to help other kids in the foster care system. She was aware that Maria was excited by the new man in her life. She'd overhead Dana talking to Catherine about Sam's business problems. These women were her friends. One was dead. All of them were in danger.

Her reliable husband was lying to her and missing. Sylvia's worries escalated. What was he doing that he couldn't share with her? Why was he being so secretive?

Chapter Forty-One

ZACK SAT IN the copilot's seat and awkwardly reached back to pat Mandy's knee. He could see her over his shoulder and from her pale face and firmly compressed lips, she clearly didn't like small planes. Perhaps he should have sat next to her, but he'd wanted to be available to work the plane's radio if any messages came through.

At this altitude, his satellite phone might work—or it might not. He'd instructed a colleague at the DEA to try to track Moose after he deplaned in Fort Lauderdale. If Moose ate a meal or rented a car or booked a room in a hotel with his credit card, Zack would know. However, if a friend picked him up or he had his own car parked in the airport garage, Moose could disappear on them again.

Unfortunately, Zack didn't have any physical evidence to tie Moose to Lisa's murder. While Vizzi had shot Sam and attacked Sylvia and Mandy, that didn't mean Vizzi's friend was guilty, too. But it was a big coincidence that the two men had known one another and that Moose matched the description of the man who'd attacked the women at the airport. The forensics team was searching Ray's playroom for DNA evidence but until they processed their results and found solid proof to link Moose to the crime scene, Zack and Mandy were on their own.

Thankfully the sky was clear of common summer thunderstorms and the flight remained smooth. They were about twenty minutes out of Fort Lauderdale when Zack's ring tone sounded. Caller ID said it was from the DEA. "What's up?"

"Carl Roberts, aka Moose, isn't staying in Fort Lauderdale. After he got off the plane, he paid cash and booked another flight to Freeport. His new flight arrives in the Bahamas within the next few minutes. So far he hasn't reserved another connecting flight, a hotel, or a car rental."

"Stay on it."

Zack turned to his pilot, his throat tight. Moose was flying to Freeport and his sister was in the Bahamas. Coincidence? He didn't believe it. This private aircraft was slower than commercial transportation but it would still fly them to the Bahamas faster than landing, dealing with security, and finding another flight. "Can we reroute to Freeport without stopping to take on fuel?"

"The Bahamas?" Mandy leaned forward, her eyes unhappy.

The pilot's gaze dropped to his fuel gauge. "No problem. Let me inform the tower."

Mandy tapped his shoulder. "Zack, I don't want to leave Gabrielle for too long."

"I know."

"Suppose Moose lands and gets on another plane? We can't follow him around the world."

"It's unlikely he'll catch another flight from Freeport."

"Why not?"

"If he were going to South America or Europe, it's much easier to connect in Miami. Remember, he has no idea we're following him. He's taking a direct route to his destination, not covering his tracks."

"He paid cash."

"That's probably habit."

"If you say so." Mandy still didn't look pleased, especially as she spied the looming Atlantic Ocean on the horizon.

He squeezed her knee and thought hard. Dana was in the Bahamas. Moose was on the way there. He didn't believe in coincidences. He'd eventually have to tell Mandy that he suspected Moose was stalking Dana, but for now, she was having enough trouble dealing with the tiny plane. Besides, there was nothing she could do for his sister—except fret. "We'll be back tomorrow, okay?"

"And if I said no?"

"Please, Mandy. The island's not that big. Give me a day in Freeport. We'll find him, then you'll ID him and we call in the cavalry."

"All right, but—"

Zack's phone rang again. "Hold that thought." He put the phone to his ear. "Hi, Mom. We're following Moose to the Bahamas."

"Thank God." Catherine sounded close to hysteria and Zack's stomach clenched. His mother spoke in a rush. "I think your sister's in big trouble. You've got to get to her."

"Whoa." Zack pushed his fear for Dana aside. He had to think clearly, choose the best option and he couldn't allow his emotions to interfere. "Slow down. Start at the beginning."

"Dana told me she overheard a conversation that Sam had on the phone."

"A conversation with who?"

"She didn't know. She heard Sam say he'd meet someone at the Bay Star. Dana thought it was a hotel and he was having an affair. But, the Bay Star isn't a hotel—it's a boat."

"Huh?"

"The *Bay Star* is Mitch Anderson's boat—remember our missing county administrator? Apparently he hasn't been seen since the very night Dana overheard Sam's conversation."

"So?"

"Anderson just floated up in Tampa Bay. With a bullet in

his brain. His corpse was found on his boat—named the *Bay Star*." Zack sucked in his breath, his mind screaming with adrenaline. Damn. Damn. Damn. Dana had heard Sam say he'd be at the *Bay Star* the night Mitch disappeared? And the guy had just floated up in Tampa Bay? "It gets worse. The medical examiner pinpointed the time of Mitch Anderson's murder as the same night Dana overheard Sam say he was going to the *Bay Star*. The night he didn't come home."

Sweat broke out on Zack's forehead. "It's still circumstantial evidence. You really think Sam had something to do with Mitch's murder?"

"For all I know Mitch killed himself. But I'm not willing to bet Dana's life on Sam's innocence. If your sister overheard Sam's conversation, she could have become a threat to him."

"How?"

"All Dana had to do was go to the police with her suspicions and Sam's reputation would be shredded. You know how proud he is." Catherine paused. "Sam could have hired Moose—"

"We don't know that." Zack was arguing more to draw the suppositions from his mother's sharp brain than from real disbelief. In his heart, he suspected Catherine was right. That meant Dana was in real danger. As more adrenaline jolted his system into overdrive, Zack dialed back his fear. He had to stay impersonal in order to help his sister.

"It fits," Catherine's voice broke. "Sam's bringing Dana to the Bahamas. Moose is going there."

"Moose may be following Sam and Dana."

"You aren't listening," Catherine's voice snapped with frustration. "Sam knew the *Bay Star* would eventually turn up with Mitch's dead body. No way would Dana miss the news and she'd immediately connect the conversation she'd overheard with Mitch Anderson's death. Sam knew Dana would be suspicious of him having something to do with Mitch's murder."

"But Sam himself was shot. And Mandy was the first one attacked."

"She was Dana's friend and Dana might have talked to her about what she'd heard. Besides, Dana couldn't be first on his list, it would draw too much attention to Sam."

Zack wished he could poke holes in his mother's theory, but she was damn smart. "Where exactly is Dana?"

"I don't know. She didn't tell me where Sam was taking the private jet. She's in the Bahamas somewhere—"

"The FAA can track her flight. We'll find her." But would it be in time? Zack had never liked Sam but he'd never thought him capable of murder. He should have known better. Anyone was capable of murder—under enough duress. "I assume you've tried to call?"

"Both Dana and Sam. There's no answer."

"We're on the way to Freeport now. Try not to panic. I need to get off this phone and make some arrangements." If Dana and Sam's phones were turned on, the DEA could pinpoint their location. "I'll let you know the moment I hear anything. If Dana happens to call—"

"I'm praying she will and I'll let you know."

Chapter Forty-Two

SAM DIDN'T WHISK Dana away often, but when he did, they traveled by private jet. After Dana had packed her bags, she'd never touched her luggage again. A bevy of people had carried her suitcase from the limo to the jet, where Sam had arranged for catering to deliver a magnificent meal for them. He'd even had champagne chilling on ice.

He hadn't been this attentive in years and his attention to detail warmed her heart. He'd even remembered that lilies were her favorite flowers and a luxurious vase of them created a delightful aroma during the flight. After a delicious meal of phyllo triangles filled with spinach and feta cheese, stone crabs dipped in butter with bacon and chive potato pancakes and raspberry mouse aboard the plane, they'd landed in Walker Cay. They didn't stay on the tiny island long. It was still early afternoon when a captain and crew of a chartered yacht sailed them from the marina to Shell Island.

In the sloop's bedroom cabin, Dana changed into a swim suit, determined to take advantage of the sunshine to work on her tan. On deck, Sam sat beside her in the shade under a Bimini top, close enough to hold her hand.

"Happy?" Sam handed her a strawberry daiquiri.

She accepted the drink with a grin. "This is my idea of perfection."

Sailing. Sun. And Sam all to herself for a few glorious days. What could be better? Dana had no idea what awaited her on Shell Island but was perfectly willing to leave the arrangements in Sam's capable hands. She sipped her drink and then set it aside. Between the deep turquoise waters, the dolphins playing off their bow wave, the soft flap of the sails in the wind, and the gentle rocking of the boat as they sliced through the water, Dana's eyelids grew heavy. It had been too long since she'd felt safe enough to fall into a deep relaxing sleep.

Chapter Forty-Three

SYLVIA FOLLOWED BEN onto the interstate. He drove north, exited on Fowler Avenue and headed toward the University of South Florida, an interesting area of shopping centers, suburbia, and industrial properties. The traffic in this part of the county was bumper-to-bumper with frequent stops at traffic lights.

Where was her husband going?

He drove in the slow lane and signaled a turn with his right blinker into what appeared to be an older shopping center's entrance. But the pavement curved behind the stores and led to a warehouse. There were no signs on the modest gray metal building to indicate what might be inside.

She waited around the corner for Ben to lower his wheelchair ramp. He rolled from his van to the building and stopped at the third door from the end. He didn't knock, but opened the door and entered as if he'd been there many times before.

Sylvia waited ten minutes, curious to see if he'd come back out. He didn't.

She parked, then walked to the warehouse with her bodyguard and hesitated. It was very likely Ben would be on the other side of that door. He'd learn that she'd followed him, that she didn't trust him. Once she stepped across the threshold, there could be no going back.

Sweat broke out on her brow and beaded at her nape beneath her hair, but she had to know what he was hiding. With determination Sylvia placed her hand on the doorknob and tugged. Inside was a messy office with no receptionist or phone. Stacks of folders slumped on a table next to an open newspaper, a half-eaten tuna sandwich, and a glass of lemonade with lipstick on the rim.

Sylvia saw nothing on the walls to indicate who paid the rent. One connecting door led to a bathroom, the other to a long, narrow hallway. Taking a deep breath to steady her nerves, Sylvia and her bodyguard walked down the hallway toward a room near the end.

As she reached the room, she heard a woman talking. "Ben, sweetie. Hold on tight. Push deeper. Deeper. Give me more of that. Yes. Right there. Lovely."

What the hell? Pressure gathered in her chest. Sylvia didn't know what she'd expected to find, but it certainly wasn't Ben with another woman. Although some disabled men resorted to prostitutes, Ben had no such need.

The door to the room contained a Plexiglas window that cast blue and greenish reflections from the room into the hallway where she stood. Sylvia was about to shove open the door, but instead moved closer to the window and stared.

Inside, Ben stood between two parallel bars, holding himself upright with his arms. Tiny pieces of tape held wires to his legs, chest, and head. He hadn't been here long, but he was sweating with effort, his breath labored.

A woman sat behind a computer screen. She typed a keyboard and issued another command. "A little step with the right."

"Ow. I got a shock that time," Ben complained.

"I'll turn down the current. Try another step with your right leg."

Sylvia's eyes widened as Ben *moved his right foot* an inch forward. *Oh, my God.* Ben was standing and holding most of his weight on his hands but he had slid one foot forward. The effort cost him. No wonder he came home drained.

Why hadn't he told her he was participating in an experiment or some kind of therapy?

As soon as the thought struck, she knew the answer. Bless his heart, Ben didn't want to raise her hopes. After all, the doctors had told them he would never walk again.

"Left. Come on, Ben. Think. Dig deeper. Use what you can."

Sylvia stared. Oh . . . Lord. His left foot moved.

Tears rolled down her cheeks. She'd never been so proud of Ben in her life.

Ben would tell her when he was ready, and she would honor his decision. Wiping away her tears, she hurried away. She spoke softly to her bodyguard. "We were never here. Understand?"

"Yes, ma'am."

On the drive home, she vowed to keep her husband's secret until he was ready to reveal it.

Chapter Forty-Four

AFTER ZACK HAD repeated his conversation with Catherine, Mandy sat stunned and horrified in the plane's back seat. Sam a murderer? It was insane. Although Sam had sometimes been aggressive and domineering, she'd always attributed his bullying tactics to his type A personality and determination to get ahead. She'd never have thought he'd resort to murder. Never.

At first Mandy had difficulty believing that Sam had had anything to do with the country administrator's death. She'd pegged Sam as hardworking, well connected and determined, honorable—until she recalled how worried Sam had been recently. Once Mitch Anderson had disappeared, it seemed like every time she'd seen Sam, the mayor had been at his elbow, at the hospital after Dana had been attacked, even at Lisa's funeral. Had Mitch's presence prevented Sam from getting close to the mayor, so Sam had killed him? She didn't know.

If Dana had somehow become a threat to Sam, he would have had reason to want her dead. But as a criminal attorney, Sam knew how difficult it was to get away with murder—

especially if he was married to the deceased. So had he hired muscle to kill Dana for him?

After Zack hung up the phone, she tapped him on the shoulder. "Even if Dana overheard Sam's conversation and Sam decided to get rid of her, why not arrange a simple accident? Why would he have targeted the lottery winners?"

Zack answered immediately, his tone grave. "When Vizzi pushed you off the bridge, you hadn't won the lottery, yet. But Sam knew even then that if Dana was murdered he would be the number one suspect. Accidents are difficult to arrange. If even the tiniest suspicion occurred, the police would be all over Sam. However, with a serial killer, the police would have lots of suspects. They wouldn't look as closely at Sam. So he hired Vizzi—"

"We don't know that—"

"I'm theorizing, but it fits. Suppose Sam hired Vizzi to take you down first. Then, later, when Vizzi hit Dana, it would look as if the murders were connected to the firm."

"But Vizzi shot Sam."

"There could be several explanations. The most likely is that Vizzi was a subcontractor, working directly for someone—maybe Moose—whom Sam had hired to take care of his dirty work. Sam would have wanted to distance himself as much as possible from the murders. Vizzi probably didn't know Sam was the person paying his fee."

She supposed anything was possible. If Sam was behind the attacks, he could have given Dana and Mandy's flight information from their trip to California to the press and cancelled the bodyguards Zack had hired. He'd have known where to send Vizzi to attack Zack and Mandy at Catherine's rental house. "And the stolen ticket?"

"After you won the lottery, Sam switched gears. Since he's already wealthy, going after the ticket and the lottery winners cast suspicion even farther from him. Why not steal and keep the lottery ticket, too? He could pretend to find it later in Dana's things, and claim a bigger share after everyone else was dead."

"But the lottery winnings would go to the heirs of the deceased."

"True. But if Dana was dead, he'd inherit her entire share. It's also possible that Moose stole the lottery ticket and never gave it to Sam. Moose could be heading to the Bahamas to kill Dana and Sam."

Had Sam hired killers to do his dirty work? Had he planned that methodically, that carefully? Mandy shivered and rubbed her arms, sick with worry over Dana. "So you think Sam originally hired Moose?"

"He was Moose's lawyer. Sam may know facts that implicate Moose in other cases—enough to use as blackmail. How difficult would it have been to make a deal?"

"And then Moose could have hired Vizzi."

"Exactly. Theses are all possibilities, but right now I'm more interested in finding my sister before Moose catches up with her." Zack frowned. "If Moose is Sam's hired gun and their plan is to kill my sister, Sam could claim the "lottery killer" followed her to the Bahamas."

Her head spun. Zack was making too much sense for him to be totally wrong. Dana was in trouble and they had to warn her and stop the killer. "So why aren't we calling in the cavalry?"

"I already did—right after I hung up with Mom," Zack told her. She realized she hadn't been listening closely. She'd been too upset over Dana being in danger. "My friends," Zack added, "at the FBI are on the way, but we have a head start."

She read between the lines. Oh, God. It might come down to Zack and her rescuing Dana. "How can we find her?"

"The DEA is searching with their high-tech equipment."

"You have agents in the Bahamas?"

"A few, but none I can tap—since this mission hasn't been authorized. But we're following the money trail from the states." His phone rang. He muttered thanks and turned to the pilot. "Can you land on Shell Island?"

"Let me check." The pilot spoke into his radio.

"Where's Shell Island?" Mandy asked, her heart jumping

into her throat. It was bad enough flying in a tiny plane. Now they might land at a substandard airport.

"Shell Island is not too far from Walker Key, where Sam hired a yacht to take them to the house he rented this morning."

"How do you know?"

"Sam's bank wired the money to a real estate agency that rented a house to him. The island has about thirty private homes and the airport was too short for the jet to land. Luckily this plane is smaller."

The pilot spoke up. "I don't know yet if the airstrip is long enough for this plane."

Mandy closed her hand into a fist and raised it to her mouth. She wasn't going to think about how Gabby wouldn't have any parents if this plane crashed. Not with the clouds streaking past the windows, so thick the wings disappeared entirely. Not with the electronic beeping of the various instruments, the only sound she could hear above the roaring in her ears. The only thing she would think about right now was that Dana needed them. They couldn't let her down.

"Time might be of the essence," Zack pressed the pilot. "Sam and Dana may have stopped to snorkel or fish or swim but we can't count on that."

"What makes you think that he hasn't already . . . hurt her?" Mandy could barely get out the words. Zack met her gaze with a level stare that assured her that while he had to be as anxious about his sister as she was, he was thinking clearly—like a DEA agent.

"Sam will probably want to establish a strong alibi while he pays someone else to do his dirty work. That's been his method so far."

She prayed he didn't change tactics and suppressed a shiver. Dana trusted Sam. And she didn't even know she was in danger.

Mandy had to force herself to breathe. Looking out the window distracted her—but then wished she hadn't. When had the blue skies darkened? The thundershower appeared localized, but the plane seemed to be flying into a dark spot while the rest of the sky remained blue.

Below, the wind kicked up white caps and she saw several sailboats heading for shore. The powerboats were more difficult to see, but they left a wake that could be spotted from the plane. She couldn't help wondering if Dana was down there staring up at them, praying for help. Or was it too late?

Oh please . . . let her live.

Mandy refused to believe anything except that Dana was still alive. They *would* arrive in time to save her. She wouldn't let a defeatist attitude creep in with the rain that now battered the plane.

Damn it. Why didn't the pilot know if they could land on Shell Island yet?

Chapter Forty-Five

"MARIA. WAKE UP," Catherine pleaded softly from the side of her hospital bed. She shouldn't even be in ICU. But last year Catherine had helped out Dr. Warren with her divorce and now the doctor was returning the favor by allowing Catherine to visit.

"You can't talk long," Dr. Warren warned. "My first responsibility is to the patient."

"I understand."

Although Catherine was terrified that Dana was in terrible jeopardy, she hadn't any hard evidence to convince the authorities. Hearsay and supposition were not enough for them to start an international search for Moose and Sam. But if Maria could regain consciousness and if she could ID either Sam or Moose as her attacker, then Catherine could muster official support for her, Zack, and Mandy.

Since Ray was in an even deeper coma, Maria was her best chance. And she'd do anything to avoid losing another of her children. Not a day went by when she didn't think about Kevin. She couldn't lose Dana, too. Catherine leaned over the bed. "Come on, Maria. Wake up."

Maria's eyelids didn't flicker.

Catherine took her hand. "I know it's easier to sleep, but my daughter needs you, Maria. Please. Wake up."

"Dana. Dana's in danger," Maria muttered.

"What do you mean?" Catherine wondered if the drugs were making Maria hallucinate. But when Maria slipped back into unconsciousness without supplying the evidence she needed, tears slid down Catherine's cheeks.

Chapter Forty-Six

"WE CAN LAND on Shell Island," the pilot shouted as rain sluiced the windshield. "If I use every inch of tarmac, the runway's long enough."

"What does that mean?" Mandy asked.

"It means he has to set the wheels down as close to one end of the runway as possible to have enough time to brake," Zack answered, his tone tight.

The pilot handed him a head set. Zack placed it over his ears. Between the thunder and the rain, Mandy couldn't hear the conversation. When he removed the headset his eyes were grim. "The DEA used Sam and Dana's cell phones to locate them. Sam's at a bridge tournament in a restaurant."

"And Dana? You spoke to her?" Mandy prayed she was with Sam. In public. Still safe.

Zack's eyes hardened. "She's at the south end of the island but not answering her phone."

The fear in Zack's eyes told her there was more. "What else?"

"A man matching Moose's description hired a motor boat to take him from Freeport to Shell Island."

Mandy clenched the seat arms so hard she cut off her circulation. But no matter how often she told herself this was not happening, it was. This was the exact scenario Zack had predicted. Sam setting up an alibi while he sent Dana off, easy pickings for a killer.

Moose was here. With Dana's partial amnesia, she wouldn't recognize him.

"We have to try and land," Mandy whispered.

Zack nodded and faced forward. "Set her down."

As if the weather understood the urgency of the situation, the shower stopped as suddenly as it had begun. The storm clouds dissipated. When they broke through the mist, Mandy leaned forward to see the land below.

Shaped like a crescent moon, the island was dotted with two-story homes, their roofs glistening white in the sunlight from the rain runoff. The waterfront homes themselves were painted soft pastels, pink, turquoise, and aqua with a variety of multihued shutters and wooden docks that housed an assortment of watercraft. She saw no cars on the island, not even a real road. The southernmost part of the island appeared desolate.

When she spied the landing strip, her hopes plummeted. It was too short and unpaved. Even if the pilot set them down perfectly, they could not possibly stop before they ran out of runway.

But they were going in.

Mandy leaned forward to grab Zack's hand. Trees rushed by and at the end of the runway, she glimpsed the ocean and rocks. If they didn't stop in time, they'd crash into the sea. She closed her eyes, too scared to think or breathe.

They hit softly and she opened her eyes. The pilot jammed on the brakes, the force pulling her forward until the seatbelt strap cut into her hips. Then they skidded and bumped. She prayed her seatbelt would hold.

Using her free hand, she braced herself and never let go of Zack with the other, clinging to him as if he could control the crazy fishtailing of the plane. One moment they were upright, then they skidded and tipped.

Finally they righted and slid to a halt in a cloud of dust. Mandy coughed until her eyes teared. But they'd made it. They were alive. "Thank you. Thank you. Thank you, for getting us down alive," she said to the pilot. Zack popped open his door, climbed out, then helped her down.

At the sight of how close they'd come to the rocks and ending up in the sea, her legs weakened. But then she thought of Dana and strength surged back.

"Now what?" she asked.

Zack took her hand. "Dana's at the southern tip of the island, or at least her cell phone is. I have her GPS coordinates. Let's go find her."

Chapter Forty-Seven

DANA WOULD HAVE been happy to stay with Sam and play bridge. But her husband knew how she loved to snorkel, and he'd insisted that she go with the guide he'd hired to take her to a reef just offshore on the island's southern tip. Disappointed that they wouldn't be together, but appreciative he'd arranged an adventure, she kissed Sam goodbye and left with the guide, who introduced himself as Moose. A black man with deep scars from acne, he didn't speak with a local accent. In fact, he sounded as if he were from the southern part of the United States.

Moose wasn't talkative and Dana didn't mind. He'd picked her up from the restaurant in a golf cart, snorkeling gear for a bigger group in the back. The ride had been short and silent, slightly uncomfortable, actually. She kept thinking she'd met him somewhere before and should remember him.

But she was more concerned that a second thunderstorm might catch them. However, the dark clouds had blown offshore and dispersed. When they reached a sandy spit that gently sloped to the water, she could see that the storm had left the emerald green sea calm and the inviting pinkish white beach dotted with shells.

The roar of a plane took her attention from her swim. She craned her head and looked back over her shoulder. Sam had told her only tiny planes could land here since the runway was so short. However, the pilot must have landed without problems because she heard no crash, saw no sign of smoke.

Dana set her sights on the coral reef in the cove below. From her elevation, she could make out the dark emerald of the reef that bisected the lighter waters of the rest of the cove. While the variety of shells on the beach would have been a collector's dream, Dana was eager for a swim. Her passion was for the colorful sea life and diverse coral.

Moose drove the golf cart straight down to the beach and parked above the high-tide mark. Dana hopped out, peeled down to her swim suit, and then grabbed some gear. As she dipped her mask into the water and cleaned it and put flippers on her feet, she looked forward to swimming off the tension of the last few weeks. Sam had read her mind perfectly, understanding how much she'd needed the soothing balm of this vacation, knowing how she'd enjoy hitting the water while he played bridge. They both liked to unwind with activities, then spend a romantic evening together.

They'd hired local guides on other trips and all of them had been chatty. Moose worked silently and efficiently and when he placed a belt around his waist and sheathed a gleaming knife, she asked, "What's the knife for?"

Moose picked up a spear gun, too. "You never know when a shark might turn aggressive." He spit into his mask. "You forgot to remove your earrings. Sharks are attracted to shiny things."

"Thanks." Dana reached up for her diamond studs, a fifth anniversary present from Sam. She placed them in the dry pouch that hung from her hips. The pouch carried extra sunscreen, a spare key, cash and a credit card, a habit she'd started after a thief snatched her purse from a beach on Aruba. "All set?"

Moose gestured to the water. "I'm right behind you."

She ambled into the warm water and Moose followed. The sea lapped at her thighs, then her waist as she walked out farther. Dana stopped to pull the mask over her nose and eyes, placed the snorkel into her mouth and dived in. She was immediately rewarded by the refreshing buoyancy of the salt water. It had been much too long since she'd taken a tropical vacation—or any vacation. She only wished Sam's arm hadn't been in a sling so he could enjoy the reef, too.

Moose was a poor substitute. He really didn't have the personality for a guide.

But with the reef in plain sight, Dana didn't require directions. Violet fan coral and yellow and purple striped fish led her onward. Bright sunlight made it easy to see about four or five feet below the surface. But the former storm and previous wave action had clouded the deeper water.

Content to stay near the surface, she took in the view. She caught several glimpses of Moose, who lagged behind, his dreads floating wildly around his scarred face.

His image bugged her, and again she thought she should have recognized him. She turned her head and really looked at him, but no matching likeness came from her memory. However, Dana suddenly recalled Mandy's description of her assailant in the parking garage, black, with scars from acne and dreads.

No.

There had to be thousands of men matching that description, particularly here in the Bahamas. Still . . . at the recollection of his spear gun, the lethal-looking knife, and how unsuited he seemed to his job, fear tugged at the back of her throat and she gasped for air through her snorkel.

Don't panic.

She could be jumping to conclusions, her tired mind playing tricks on her.

Her gut said otherwise, especially since Lisa had been slashed to death with a knife.

Dana's brain might try to rationalize that her assumptions were all a big mistake, but her pulse raced. Oh, God . . . had

Moose tracked her here and somehow convinced Sam to hire him?

She was in trouble.

Her only advantage was that Moose didn't know she suspected the danger.

Dana was a strong swimmer and put a little more distance between herself and Moose. She wasn't certain how far a spear gun would shoot. She didn't want to find out.

Was if just another coincidence that Moose had positioned himself between her and the shore?

Self-preservation made her spit water out of her mouth before she choked. Sam couldn't have known the danger he was putting her in by hiring Moose.

He couldn't have.

When a harpoon whooshed by her and struck the reef, Dana could no longer deny the truth. Moose wanted her dead.

And she was alone. Without a weapon. No way to call for help.

Fear lodged in her gut. And her muscles seemed to go on the fritz. Moose was gunning for her. Hunting her.

When a second harpoon missed her shoulder by inches, Dana's anger surged and fueled her determination—even as tears burned her eyes.

If she wanted to live a little longer, her only choice was to swim out to sea, lose Moose, and somehow make it back to shore.

Chapter Forty-Eight

A DEA AGENT had located Dana's cell phone and passed on the coordinates to Zack. With no transportation available, Zack and Mandy had no choice but to sprint on foot to the island's southern tip.

Loose sand and clumps of grass made running uneven and difficult. Zack seemed to have no difficulty maintaining a quick pace, but Mandy's side burned and her lungs ached. Although she did yoga when she had time, she obviously needed more aerobic conditioning.

"Zack, go on . . . I'll . . . catch up," Mandy panted, unwilling to delay him one second when she knew Dana was in danger. Just a few critical moments might make the difference between her living or . . .

"I'm not leaving you." Zack slowed his pace.

"But Dana needs you."

"Moose could double back and find you alone." Zack's eyes narrowed and his tone was grim.

Mandy forced air into her lungs and tried to find a running rhythm. The bright sun and the warm temperature didn't help. Only the knowledge that Zack wouldn't go ahead without her and her fear for Dana kept her going.

When they crested a hill, she got her second wind, or maybe it was the sight of the empty golf cart on the beach that spurred her on.

Where was Dana? Mandy didn't see her friend. Or Moose.

The beach appeared deserted but she redoubled her efforts. Zack must have thought it was now safe to leave her and surged ahead. By the time she'd collapsed to a halt, he'd found Dana's cell phone in a backpack she'd left in the golf cart.

Two sets of footsteps in the sand clearly led from the beach into the water.

Zack peeled off his shirt, kicked off his shoes. He kept the gun holstered at the small of his back and another at his ankle.

Without hesitation Mandy removed her shirt and slacks, leaving her free to swim in her bra and panties. Already out of breath, she didn't need any extra drag.

Zack lunged toward the water just as she glanced at the golf cart full of gear. "Zack, wait."

Digging into the gear at the back of the cart, she found and tossed him a mask, snorkel, and fins, then retrieved a set for herself and raced after him, trying to put on the mask, while carrying the fins to the water and juggling, then dropping a fin.

She wouldn't do Dana any good if she panicked. Or fainted from lack of air. Forcing herself to slow down and breathe, she picked up the fins and tucked them under her arm, pulled the mask in place. She walked out until she was up to her chest before putting on the fins.

By the time she started swimming, she could see Zack ahead of her, his fins churning a white frothing wake as he aimed for the reef. At first the change from running to swimming was a good switch for her body. But breathing through the snorkel took effort and her arms quickly tired.

Thankfully, the fins kept her going. She searched for any sign of Dana, but the reef twisted and curved and she could be behind the next bend or half a mile away. Mandy spied spiny sea urchins whose quills reminded her of a porcupine and took care not to touch them or the red fire coral that could burn the skin on contact. At the sight of lobsters waving their claws, a moray eel backing into its hole, and a ray skimming the bottom, she shivered at the hostile environment.

Mandy preferred to do her swimming in a pool where there was no chance of a jellyfish sting or of being eaten. Luckily the tiger sharks were small—although she supposed they could nibble on a finger or toe. *Yikes.* If she wasn't careful, she'd scare herself into heading back to shore.

Where the hell was Dana?

Forcing her legs to kick harder, Mandy tried to keep up, but Zack was by far the stronger swimmer. However, all of a sudden he stopped and gestured for her to stop, too.

Squinting through her mask, she tried to see what he saw. But she tilted her head and sucked water through her snorkel. Coughing, she had to tread water for air. It took several moments to regain her composure, blow the water from the snorkel and duck back under.

On the surface, the water had appeared serene, warm, and balmy. In the distance a sailboat flew a bright red spinnaker and ran downwind. Above her head, sea gulls swooped and dived.

Her breathing back to normal, Mandy searched for Zack at the spot where she'd seen him last. When she couldn't find him, her heart sped and she gnawed the snorkel between her teeth. Why had he stopped? Where had he gone?

Before she could begin to guess, she spied a dark silhouette in the water. Peering closer, she noted yellow swim fins. At first, in the distance she thought it was Zack and started swimming closer, but then she realized the darkness wasn't caused by lack of light, the swimmer had dark skin. A headful of dreads.

Moose!

Terror froze her limbs. He was swimming right toward her, a knife in his hand.

Chapter Forty-Nine

HORRIFIED, ZACK PEERED through his mask. About fifty yards away, his sister thrashed, blood clouding the water around her in a pocket so thick that he couldn't even determine the location of her wound. Dana. Heaven help him. His little sister was dying, bleeding to death right before his eyes, and he tamped down a silent howl of fury.

Zack couldn't afford to wallow in emotion. Dana's only chance to live . . . was Zack.

But saving Dana . . . meant leaving Mandy. His heart wrenched.

He glanced over his shoulder to see Mandy gamely following, then focused on Dana. Her flailing slowed, her body went limp. She might have already suffered a mortal wound, but if Zack didn't reach her soon, even if sharks weren't attracted to the blood in the water and about to start a feeding frenzy, she would most certainly drown.

Zack had no choice. Forging ahead, he kicked toward Dana, arms cutting through the water with desperation. His lungs ached for air but he barely noticed his discomfort. Dana wasn't moving. She didn't appear to be holding her breath or breathing. He had to get her to shore fast, get some air into her lungs.

Zack finally reached her, placed an arm over her shoulder and across her chest and surged to the surface. He couldn't wait to perform CPR until he got her to shore, she'd be dead. He felt for a pulse. It was weak, but there. He spun her around until she faced him, pinched her nostrils shut and then awkwardly placed his mouth over hers, trying to push air into her lungs. But her head lolled and they both sank.

Come on, Dana. Breathe. Breathe. Breathe.

Again, he lifted Dana's head above the water, but since she wasn't breathing, it wasn't doing her any good. Kicking madly to keep both of their heads above the surface, he again tried to force air into her lungs.

This time she coughed, spit out water but never opened her eyes, an indication of her weakened state and loss of blood. Nevertheless, as she began to breathe, relief washed over him.

Then she thrashed, inadvertently smacking him. "No. No."

"Easy, Dana." He saw the knife slash that began at her temple and opened all the way to her ear and winced. Moose had to be out here somewhere close by, and Zack was as worried about Mandy as he was about Dana. Where was Mandy?

Zack stayed calm, talking soothingly to his sister. "It's Zack. I've got you, relax."

Maybe his words got through to Dana or maybe she'd sunk back into unconsciousness. She went limp again. Zack started to swim her toward shore, floating Dana on her back, kicking hard with his fins and spitting out salt water from sea spray.

By now Mandy should have swum beside him. Where was she? Where was Moose?

He scanned the surface but didn't see anyone. Ducking his mask and head underwater, Zack looked right, left, toward the reef. He swore. Moose was swimming straight for Mandy, his arm outstretched with a twelve-inch blade . . .

Swim. Damn it. Swim.

Mandy didn't move. She seemed frozen in place, bubbles rising from her snorkel, the only indication she was alive.

Didn't she see the danger? Why wasn't she swimming away?

Zack couldn't shout to warn her or to give instruction and he couldn't let go of Dana or she'd drown. Torn at the terrible choice of helping Mandy survive a killer's attack or rescuing Dana, Zack didn't hesitate.

By God, Moose wasn't going to kill either one of them.

Moose swam closer to Mandy.

Zack grasped for the gun at his waist—but the holster was empty. Lost, during his swim. He plucked the back-up gun from his ankle holster, but he couldn't fire underwater. The bullet would lose momentum, only travel a few feet.

Treading water, holding Dana above the surface with one hand and waiting for Moose to surface so he could shoot him with the other took supreme concentration. The wave action kept changing the angles.

Moose surfaced for air. Zack fired. Missed. And swore.

Moose swam within ten feet of Mandy. If he came any closer, Zack feared he might miss Moose and hit her.

Fear rode up onto his shoulders and weighed him down.

Mandy suddenly revived—as if Moose's nearness had jolted her into action—and she turned toward shore and swam with furious strokes. Moose surfaced and pursued. He was gaining on her.

Zack held his breath, fired twice more and this time, he hit flesh. Moose's body curled into the fetal position. Blood spurted. Zack didn't know where he'd struck. He didn't care.

Mandy could now swim to shore free of pursuit. Zack placed the gun back in the ankle holster and focused on carrying Dana to shore. Exhausted, he finally put his feet down on sandy beach and Mandy helped him tug Dana to safety.

It was a measure of Zack's exhaustion that he had no breath to speak. He sat beside Dana, gasping.

And Moose lunged out of the water.

Chapter Fifty

WHEN MOOSE REARED out of the water, blood streaming down his arm, fear iced through Mandy. For a moment, she could only stare in terror. But Zack, cool as James Bond, reached for his gun and fired.

The bullet splashed in the water about two feet in front of Moose, and he halted in waist-deep water. Eyes wide, blood running down his arm, he stammered, "Shh-shark."

A large fin veered toward him.

He took another step forward.

Zack fired again and water spattered Moose in the face. Zack then raised his gun and leveled it at Moose's chest. "I won't miss the next time."

"Please." Moose shook and craned his head over his shoulder, his eyes wide in fright at the sight of the large fin swimming toward him. "Don't let it eat me. I'll do anything. Wear a wire. Nail Sam for you."

Zack cocked his head as if to consider. Mandy held her breath. Moose may have slashed Lisa to death, may have killed Maria and Ray. He'd definitely just tried to kill Dana and Mandy. He deserved to die . . . and yet, she didn't want to see a shark tear him apart, limb from limb.

Zack's eyes burned with fire and resolve as he glared at Moose. "You change your mind, I'll make sure you end up as shark bait, not in some air-conditioned cell." Zack pulled out a pair of handcuffs from his jeans. "When you reach the sand, turn around and drop to your knees."

Moose scrambled out of the water, just as the shark swam by. Despite the bullet wound in his arm, he didn't hesitate to drop and place his hands behind his back. Zack handed Mandy the gun. "If he twitches, shoot him."

"No problem."

Zack snapped the cuffs closed with an efficient motion that told her he'd performed the task many times before. But she had never before seen Zack under pressure. He'd rescued Dana, saved Mandy from Moose, caught the killer, and made a deal with him that would put Sam away forever. But now that she'd seen Zack in action, she realized he was too good at his job to ever give it up. And a tiny piece of her died.

Zack used the phone he'd left on the beach to check on the DEA chopper. Then he smoothed Dana's hair out of the open wound on her face. "Medical help's on the way."

Zack held out his hand to Mandy. She shrugged into her shirt and then without hesitation took Zack's hand. Together they waited for the helicopter.

"I'm sorry I left you behind in the water," the words came out of him torn and ragged. "But Dana would have drowned if—"

"It was a terrible choice to have to make." She didn't know what else to say to reassure him.

"I knew Moose was out there. I promised I'd keep you safe."

"You did. I'm fine."

"I left you unprotected."

Mandy leaned forward and pressed her lips to Zack's cheek. "I would never have forgiven you if you hadn't saved my best friend."

"And I wouldn't have forgiven myself if I'd lost you."

Chapter Fifty-One

TO MANDY'S SURPRISE, Moose had actually kept his word. In return for sentencing consideration, Moose had fully co-operated with the authorities. He'd worn an FBI wire and tricked Sam into implicating himself and admitting he'd hired Moose—right before Sam had tried to shoot him.

Apparently, Sam had intended to clean up all the loose ends. With Moose dead, Sam could claim he'd shot the man who'd murdered his wife and Lisa. If not for Zack, Sam would have been a hero, instead of a ruined man.

From her hospital bed, in a room opposite Maria's, Dana had just listened to Sam's taped confession. Watching her face had been painful for Mandy. Upon hearing the confirmation that her husband had planned to kill her, tears had brimmed in Dana's eyes and fallen to her cheeks. But she'd taken Mandy's hand, lifted her chin, and told her she'd be fine.

Mandy knew if anyone could recover, Dana would. She had a loving family to support her. Mandy would do whatever it took to help her through it. If Dana needed her— she'd be there.

Maria and Ray would also survive, but would have to suffer through several plastic surgeries to minimize their physical scarring. The horrible experience had brought the couple even closer together, and when Maria recovered consciousness, she'd been able to tell them that while Moose had slashed them, he'd bragged about killing Lisa. Mandy was glad Moose would be locked away forever.

Head stitched from temple to ear, Dana closed her eyes, wiped away her tears, and looked at her brother. "So Mitch Anderson found out that Sam and Dylan had faked the environmentals on the property they intended to sell for a county school?"

"Yes. The mayor also had a conflict of interest in trying to sell property to the county. When Mitch tried to blackmail them, the argument turned heated. Sam and the mayor killed him. To hide what they'd done, they dumped the body in the bay," Zack filled in the details. "Sam and the mayor are both in jail, where they'll spend the rest of their lives—if the judge doesn't sentence them to death."

Mandy's heart broke for her friend. She couldn't imagine what she was going through. Her husband had conspired with the mayor to sell polluted land where a school would have been built. When Mitch had been ready to blackmail them or reveal the truth, Sam and the mayor had killed him.

Dana raised her hand to her bandaged head, her pain-filled eyes staring out the window. When a sob escaped Dana's lips, Mandy tugged on Zack's hand. "Perhaps we should discuss this later."

"No." Dana lifted her chin, her tone strong. "I want to hear it all. Tell me."

Zack nodded and settled on the bed beside his sister. "When you overheard Sam talking to the mayor about the *Bay Star*, he knew that you'd eventually learn about Mitch's death and figure out that Sam had something to do with it."

"So he decided to get rid of me before I could cause a fuss?"

"I'm afraid so. We found evidence in his office accounts that Sam hired Moose. Moose admitted he hired Vizzi," Zack explained.

"And Sam had them go after the other women at the firm to cover his tracks and make it look like a serial killer?" Dana surmised.

"Exactly." Zack's tone was gentle.

Dana frowned. "So the killings had nothing to do with the lottery ticket?"

"Apparently not," Mandy spoke softly, aching when Dana closed her eyes and inhaled deeply.

"Poor Lisa . . ."

Mandy grabbed Dana's hand and squeezed tight. The bed sank as Zack sat down and wrapped a strong arm around his sister. She rested her head on his shoulder, but didn't open her eyes when he said, "None of this is your fault, you know."

Mandy hoped Dana would be able to make peace with her feelings about the man who was supposed to have loved her.

Dana opened her eyes and turned to Mandy. "Sam just used the lottery ticket to confuse everyone. I'm sorry," Dana's voice weakened, her face almost as pale as the bandage around her head. At least the scar would be hidden by her hair.

Mandy knew Dana didn't want pity and tried to sound upbeat. "Hey, what matters now it that you, Maria, and Ray can get well."

Dana closed her eyes. "I think I'd like to be alone now."

Mandy looked at Zack, worried about leaving Dana. She'd been through so much, but Zack seemed to read Mandy's thoughts. Zack took her arm and led her from the hospital room. "Dana's strong. With time, she'll be fine and she'll have both of us to help her."

"*Both* of us?"

Mandy stopped in the hallway and blinked. She couldn't have heard right. "Zack what did you say?"

"Marry me."

Stunned, Mandy eyed him, wondering if she'd wake up tomorrow and find she had dreamed the entire conversation. "But the DEA. Your work?"

"I went into the DEA because I thought I could prevent

what happened to Kevin from happening to others. But that was only part of the reason. Another part was for revenge against the drug dealers. I wanted to pay the dealers back. Now I'm done with revenge—Kevin wouldn't have wanted that. He was a family guy. He would have wanted me to be with you and Gabby."

"What about what you want?"

"I've been thinking about opening a private investigation firm in Tampa. Mom can throw enough business my way to keep me busy. And I bet if I ask Ben, he'll help out."

"Won't you miss the DEA?" Although all her dreams seemed to be coming true, she had to be certain that Zack knew his own mind.

"Other agents can step up to take my place. No one else can be a father to Gabby as well as I can. You're both more important to me than a job. I think I've always known I loved you, I just couldn't admit it—not to you, not even to myself."

Happiness and contentment suffused her. Zack was the only man she'd ever loved. And now they were going to be together. Always. "Yes, Zack. I'll marry you."

Chapter Fifty-Two

One week later

"GO. GO. GO." Gabby toddled across the foyer to Mandy, then clung to her leg, demanding that she be allowed to accompany her mother.

Zack leaned down, scooped up their daughter, tossed her into the air, and caught her. Gabby screamed in delight. Mandy's heart swelled with joy. She'd never dared to hope that she could have both Zack and Gabby full time.

Even her mother was smiling. "Zack, you'll spoil her rotten."

Zack wore a broad smile. "A little attention—"

"A little?" Mandy arched a brow but couldn't keep from grinning. Zack had enough energy to wear out an eleven-month-old. He was willing to play with Gabby whenever she climbed into his lap, or smiled across the room at him, or brought him a book. Oh, yeah, Zack was a soft touch where his daughter was concerned.

He tossed her again. "Gabby's such a good girl—"

"Good girl," Gabby repeated with a giggle.

Mandy took Gabby from Zack and finished his sentence with a bribe. "Such a good girl that she's going to have strawberries with peanut butter."

"Eat." Gabby reached for her grandmother, who carried her to the kitchen.

"We could have brought her with us," Zack complained, looking over his shoulder as if he couldn't bear to be separated from his child.

One of them had to be reasonable. "I'd rather not take Gabby into the rain." Mandy reached for her umbrella. "You ready?"

They were meeting Dana and Catherine for lunch, then picking out wedding invitations and hiring a photographer. If they had time, they'd even shop for rings, but she didn't care about jewelry. Zack was finally hers. She only had to look at the love in his eyes to feel deliciously happy.

Zack opened the front door for her, and Mandy stepped onto the covered stoop. Thunderclouds blackened the sky. Wind from Tampa Bay slanted the rain sideways. Zack swept her into his arms and brought his mouth down on hers.

Mandy leaned into the kiss. Between visits to the hospital and playing with Gabby, she and Zack hadn't had much time alone. The surging rush in her heart matched the wild elements around them. Zack's kisses never failed to accelerate her pulse.

When he finally pulled back, his eyes dancing with heat, she grinned, enjoying him and the knowledge that they were so good together.

A wind gust sprayed them and Mandy popped open her travel umbrella. A piece of paper floated out. A rectangular piece of paper spun into the air, floated down, and settled briefly on the stoop.

"Zack, look," Mandy pointed, tossed aside the umbrella and stomped on the paper, then bent to pick it up. "It's the lottery ticket!"

"Huh?" Raindrops trickled over Zack's face, angled over his cheekbones. His eyelashes collected water droplets.

"It's the winning ticket." She waved it in his face. "The

ticket was inside my umbrella all this time." Mandy threw her arms around Zack's neck. She recalled the night of the attack at the airport, flinging her purse upside down and papers going everywhere. The ticket must have flown into her partially open umbrella and she hadn't used it since.

Moose hadn't stolen the ticket. She'd had it all along.

Oh, my God. They still had plenty of time to cash it in. It looked as if all their luck was changing. She couldn't wait to tell Maria—she'd been through so much. Sylvia could retire. Lisa's foster parents would get their daughter's share.

Mandy could buy her mother her own place, send Gabby to the best schools, help Zack open his business. None of them would ever have to worry about money again. Catherine and Dana would be thrilled.

She grinned at Zack. "We're rich."

With a chuckle, Zack clasped his hands around her back and spun her on the stoop. "I was already rich. I have you."

Solar Heat

TALK ABOUT UNLUCKY missions. Everything that could go wrong *had*. One moment Azsla and her crew of four "fugitive" slaves had been on course for Zor, the next the starboard engine had thrown a rod through the hull. The spaceship had jolted, causing mechanical failure and damage, turning their systems inside out, slamming her crew into unconsciousness. The cosmic whammy had dealt them one hell of a beating, and she thanked Holy *Vigo* for the lifelong supply of salt that gave her strength and enabled her to remain alert.

The ship was currently powerless and drifting toward the portal that was supposed to have transported them to Zor and freedom. The lights flickered. With a snap of a toggle, Azsla cut the blaring alarm. She didn't need a news flash to know that unless she altered their course, the forces sucking them into the black portal would now squash them flatter than a neutron particle.

Azsla, concerned the backup system hadn't automatically

come on line, initiated emergency procedures and flipped open the auxiliary engine panel. Twisting the manual override, she thrust the handle to starboard. But the reboot mechanism was also on the fritz. When no lights or controls came back on, licks of alarm shot down Azsla's back. Mother of Salt—a double cosmic whammy.

Keep it together. She'd drilled for emergency situations. Only this was no drill. They were in trouble. Bad trouble. And fear ignited in the pit of her gut like a retro rocket on nitro.

She checked her watch, then estimated the triple threat of time, distance, and mass. At the inescapable result—certain death—her scalp broke into a sweat. As a First of Rama, Azsla had been entitled to a life of privilege and all the strength-building salt she could swallow. But what should have been a life of luxury on Rama had been destroyed by a slave rebellion. And so she'd agreed to spy on the slaves to prevent future uprisings. She'd always known her mission required sacrifice and she'd accepted the danger of pretending to be an underfirst, a lowly slave, in order to assess what kind of weapons Zor was developing against Rama. But to succeed, she had to get to Zor.

Right now, that didn't seem likely. Or even possible. She glanced around at her still unconscious crew. She'd always thought she'd understood the risk of covert operations. When her superiors had cooked up this mission, she'd volunteered. After training for over half her life, the decision hadn't been a hard one. Fifteen years ago when she'd been thirteen, a slave uprising on Rama had killed her parents and ruined her home. Some 200,000 slaves had escaped her world and resettled on the planet Zor. Eventually the Firsts had regrouped and regained control, but life as Azsla knew it was over.

After losing everything, her existence had gone from street orphan to ward of the state. When the corps offered to train her as a weapons specialist and promised her a shot at stopping any chance of another slave rebellion, they hadn't had to ask twice. As a First she'd understood, even as a teenager, that as long as Zor offered safe haven to slaves, all Ramans stood in peril, their way of life threatened. Aware that no Raman had ever succeeded in totally suppressing *Quait,* a First's ability to dominate, she'd undergone grueling years of training. She'd accepted she might never succeed—but she had achieved the impossible. Sort of. As long as she kept her emotions in check, her *Quait* didn't take over and Azsla could prevent herself from overpowering the will of her crew. Reining herself in tight, she could now pass as one of them.

If her crew sniffed out her real role, they'd sabotage the journey to Zor. Slaves might be weak, but they were fanatical. Dangerous. They placed little value on life, even their own. To find out what the Zorans were up to, Azsla had to be just as ruthless. And knowing any one of them would turn on a First to keep her away from Zor reminded her to keep up her guard. Always. While it had been surprisingly easy to leave behind her regimented existence where no one would miss her, she'd never considered that engine failure might kill her in this tin can before she'd even landed on Zor.

One by one, the systems went down. Artificial gravity failed. The air grew stale. And it was freezing cold, as if the heat wasn't just turned off in the past few moments but hadn't been on since liftoff three days ago. Azsla gripped the command console to maintain her position at her station and ignored the white air puffing from her mouth, the prickly bumps rising over her flesh, her body-racking shivers. Gravity failed. She clutched the console to maintain her position. Her unconscious crewmen floated away from their consoles as the ship lost gravity.

"Anyone awake?"

Frozen, shocked, possibly injured, none of her crew answered. Apparently, they'd all stalled out on her. Yet, they weren't dead. Kali, her second-in-command, drew in choked breaths. Rak, the chief engineer, flailed on the ceiling, seeking leverage to alter his altitude.

Knowing she had mere moments to divert the ship, Azsla stayed put. If she couldn't change their course, the wormhole would devour the ship, leaving nothing, not even scattered debris, to mark their passing.

"Report," she repeated, her voice lowering an octave as if ashes filled her mouth, her cold-numbed fingers flicking the damaged control toggles, frantic to restart the engines. Surely Jadlan or Micoo in the sleepers had been jarred awake? Or had they ditched protocol, abandoned their posts, and ejected in their escape pods? Azsla had no way of knowing, not with her instruments off line, but as always, she cut her crew some slack, all too aware that none of them had her superior intellect or physical strength. After all, they were slaves.

Taking stock, she assessed their predicament with as much presence of mind as she could summon. Instant depressurization had collapsed the aft stabilizer. Her ship now spiraled end over end—straight toward hull-crushing forces that would terminate her mission—unless she found some miraculous way to steer clear.

Azsla ripped open the panel's cover to examine the wiring. The reek of burning plastic singed her nostrils. Smoke filtered into the cabin and fear scratched along her skin like claws, ripping and shredding, threatening to tap out her last reserve of *Quait* control. Damn her crew. They should have responded by now.

Not that she was even close to normal. Her fingers trembled and she despised her own weakness as much as that of the underfirsts who hadn't responded to her plea for information. Trying to fight down the fear, and with her gut doing a slow churn job, she battled fresh panic.

Easy. She was beginning to hate the empty brutality of space. Not that she was bitter. Sweet *Vigo,* people were supposed to live on planets where they didn't have to breathe recycled air, where every little mechanical failure wasn't life threatening, where a stray piece of dust didn't create lethal havoc with her ship's systems.

Trying to buy herself a little relief from pounding panic, Azsla attempted to dial down her emotion. She cornered it, squashed it. Beat it into submission. *Pretend it's just another drill.* After ten years of keeping her cool and suppressing her

Quait, her spontaneous instinct to dominate should have been under control . . . yet, as the port fuel tank exploded, her natural inclinations to overpower kicked in. Hard. Every cell in her body ached to reach out and make the crew work as one. But even if she reverted to instinct and could use her *Quait* to save all their lives by forcing them to fix the ship, her crew would then learn that she wasn't one of them. If they didn't kill her, she would wind up returning home in defeat. Sure, mind scrubbers could erase her crew's memories, but the corps didn't accept failure. Azsla would never get another shot at returning to Zor.

But the aching instinct to survive at any cost began to burn. Sizzle. Her blood boiled with the need to take charge . . . for the sake of self-preservation.

She was about to lose it and take over the will of every underfirst on board. With no time to talk herself down slowly, she popped a *tranq,* swallowing the pill without water. Immediately, the fire eased. The seething boil cut to a manageable simmer—thank you, *Vigo.* Of course, later, if she lived that long, she'd pay for relying on the *tranq.* If her superiors ever discovered she'd resorted to artificial tactics, it would put them off—enough to shut her down, boot her from the corps. But with the metal hull groaning, official consequences were the least of her problems.

The portal was sucking them in. Thanks to the *tranq,* her *Quait* settled and the need to dominate abated. Finally, praying to save the ship from annihilation, she struggled to route the last remaining battery power into the bow thrusters.

Her fingers manually keyed in instructions, and she regained her normal tone of voice. "Kali. What's doing?"

Kali groaned, opened his eyes, shoved off the ceiling and buckled into the copilot's seat. He slapped his flickering monitor. "Navigation's a bust. Hyperdrive's nonoperational. Engineering's off line. Life support's nonfunctional. Time to bail?"

Unless she could alter their direction, they'd have to abandon ship or be crushed four ways to summer solstice. However, the portal would draw in the sleeping pods, where, as long as the emergency batteries maintained the pods' shielding, they'd be shot through to Zor. Hopefully someone at the other end would pick up an automated distress signal—if not, they would drift in space, frozen. Forever. Not an appealing option, but neither was instant death.

Azsla jerked her thumb toward the safety pod. "Hit the air lock."

Although her crew often disappointed, she wasn't cruel enough to dash their hopes and reveal they had little chance of survival, never mind escape. Of course, the corps never intended for her crew to achieve the freedom they sought. On Zor, they'd be rounded up by other spies and sent back to Rama in chains as an example of what happened to slaves who attempted escape.

Kali unsnapped his safety harness, snagged Rak off the ceiling, and swam toward the rear. "Captain, you coming?"

"Just messing with the bow thrusters." She didn't exactly lie. Although she had little hope of cranking out a course alteration with the bow thrusters, she used the excuse to stay at the helm to secretly shoot the logs and a report of the disaster back to Rama, a last-ditch effort to inform the corps of their predicament. Notifying home was a calculated risk. Her crew believed they'd escaped Rama, when in actuality the government had allowed them to leave in order to insert Azsla into their midst. If any of them caught a whiff of what they'd consider betrayal, there was no telling if she could handle them after swallowing that *tranq*.

"Captain."

At Kali's sharp tone, Azsla stiffened. Had he seen her dispatch the log? Despite the *tranq,* she couldn't conceal the edge to her voice. "Yes?"

"Ship temperature's approaching freezing. The hull's breached. Shields are failing. We need to leave, now."

Relieved her cover remained intact, Azsla skimmed her hands over the keys, robbing the remaining power from every system except the pods. "I'm right behind you."

Kali soared through the control cabin into the ship's bowels. She heard him pop open the pods along with the terrified voices of her crew. So the others had awakened. She shouldn't be thinking about them. Slaves were easily replaced. Weak. A waste of salt.

And yet . . . this crew had trained hard. Not as hard as she had. But then they didn't have her abilities. Still, they'd done what they could with what they had.

Finally, she shunted the last of the power into the boosters.

Done. She turned and shields began to go down. The injured hull squealed in agony, the tearing of metal a death knell. Diving for the escape pod, she overshot her mark. Kali snatched her by the ankle, saving her from a painful smack into the bulkhead.

"Thanks." She seized a handhold and righted herself. He'd already stuffed Jadlan, Micoo, and Rak into the pods and ejected them through the air lock.

"Ready to bounce?"

"Absolutely." Totally on board with the plan, she slapped the button to open her sleeper. Kali slid into the last remaining pod.

She tensed her muscles to do the same. Only her pod didn't open. "What the frip?" she swore. All hell was about to come down on the ship and she nailed the button mechanism again with her fist.

And got zip. Zero. Zilch. The canopy refused to budge. Her high-pitched gasp shamed her and she hoped Kali put it down to the cold that seemed to have frozen her bones.

This was insane. Surely every freaking system on the ship couldn't fail . . . unless someone had sabotaged the mission. But who? If the slaves had known about her mission, they would have killed her, or died trying. They wouldn't have vandalized the entire ship. And she had no other enemy. The corps wanted her to succeed.

The delay didn't seem to faze Kali. Instead of ejecting, he moved smoothly, climbing from his pod. "Let me." Picking up a wrench, he slapped the release button.

"It's no good." She pointed to the hull that had caved, crushing her pod, the metal cross-brace obstructing the pod's release mechanism from firing properly.

The hull howled like a wild beast, the last of the shields failing. From the ship's bowels, the engines rumbled like a volcano about to erupt. Before she could issue an order, Kali picked her up, slipped her into his pod, and closed the canopy with a click of finality. Hit the eject button.

Her last sight of him floored her. He seemed at peace. Eyes closed, his lips moved, and if she hadn't known better, he'd appeared to be praying. At peace with his death.

She shot into space, a rush of emotions flooding her. Relief. Hope. Astonishment.

Holy *Vigo*. Kali had given up his chance to live. For her.

And she hadn't even used her *Quait*. She closed her fingers into fists. Kali had meant nothing to her. His saving her had been the right thing to do, of course. There were millions of slaves. Only a few thousand Firsts. Slaves were easily replaceable. Unworthy. Yet, she'd spent enough time with her second-in-command to know Kali's life had meant everything to him. He'd planned to begin a new life on Zor. Marry. Have children. His dreams would never have happened because of her mission . . . but Kali hadn't known that.

Turning, she watched the ship implode and vanish into the portal. Kali was dead, his body relegated to atomic dust.

She shouldn't have cared. Cold from the sleep capsule spread over her skin like guilt. She told herself slaves died every day. So what?

But if Kali's selfless sacrifice didn't matter, then why was her vision blurred? Why were tears freezing on her cheeks?